Praise for James Van Pelt's *The Radio Magician*

"Musicians and magicians, terraforming and trans-dimensional inns, ice cream as a means to defuse interspecies warfare—James Van Pelt has a wide-ranging imagination, but that's only the first of these stories' many pleasures. Van Pelt has an unerring eye for the perfect detail, the understated emotion, and the character that unexpectedly splits your heart along its seam. Read these stories. You will remember them for a long, long time."
— Nancy Kress, author of *Steal Across the Sky*

"There may not be a better science fiction or fantasy writer today, working in the short form, than James Van Pelt. From the story of a boy stricken with polio who learns magic from a radio magician to the sacrificial figure of a musical genius abducted by aliens, these tales will amaze and move you, all written in Van Pelt's smooth, lyrical style, with convincing and memorable characters. This collection is a jewel, polished to the high sheen of the literary short story, but with the heart and muscle of great science fiction."
— Louise Marley, author of *Singers in the Snow*

"James Van Pelt brings a polished, literary style to some of my favorite SF themes. I thoroughly enjoyed every one of the stories in this collection. Jim's characters and the places he takes them are real and delightfully detailed. Each story has its own unique feel."
— Brenda Cooper, author of *The Silver Ship and the Sea*

"Humane, fascinating, original—Van Pelt's best stories excite the reader in a manner reminiscent of great past masters like Jack Finney and Charles Beaumont. Reading the title story, I yearned toward the page, believing an important truth was about to be revealed or confirmed. It was: James Van Pelt is one of the best short story writers at work today."
— Jack Skillingstead, author of *Harbinger*

**Also by James Van Pelt**

*Strangers and Beggars*
*The Last of the O-Forms*
*Summer of the Apocalypse*
*Plot is a Metaphor (forthcoming)*

# THE RADIO MAGICIAN
## AND OTHER STORIES

# THE RADIO MAGICIAN
## AND OTHER STORIES

## JAMES VAN PELT

FAIRWOOD PRESS
Bonney Lake • Seattle

The Radio Magician & Other Stories
A Fairwood Press Book
September 2009
Copyright © 2009 by James Van Pelt

*Fairwood Press*
21528 104th Street Court East
Bonney Lake, WA   98391
**www.fairwoodpress.com**

**Front cover illustration & design by Paul Swenson**
Book Design by Patrick Swenson

ISBN13: 978-0-9820730-2-5
First Fairwood Press Edition: September 2009
Printed in the United States of America

# ACKNOWLEDGEMENTS

"The Radio Magician"                         *Realms of Fantasy, Feb 2009*
"Where Did You Come From, Where Did You Go?" *Alembical* teaser 2009
"The Light of a Thousand Suns"               *Realms of Fantasy, Nov 2008*
"Of Late I've Dreamt of Venus"               *Visual Journeys, 2007*
"Different Worlds"                           *New Faces in SF, 2003*
"The Small Astral Object Genius"             *Asimov's, Oct/Nov 2006*
"Tiny Voices"                                *Talebones #33, Summer 2006*
"Lashawnda at the End"                       *Imagination Fully Dilated: SF, Aug 2003*
"Where and When"                             *All Star Zeppelin Stories, 2004*
"One Day, in the Middle of the Night"        *Talebones #30, Summer 2005*
"Echoing"                                    *Asimov's, Dec 2004*
"The Inn at Mount Either"                     *Analog, May 2005*
"The Ice Cream Man"                          *Asimov's, June 2005*
"Sacrifice"                                  *Paradox, 2003*
"The Boy Behind the Gate"                    *Dark Terrors #6, 2002*
"The Last Age Should Show Your Heart"        *Bones of the World, 2001*
"Origin of the Species"                      *Weird Tales, Summer 2002*
"The Saturn Ring Blues"                      *On Spec, Spring 2001*
"How Music Begins"                           *Asimov's, Oct/Nov 2007*

# CONTENTS

# INTRODUCTION
## Carrie Vaughn

I thought I was going to start by talking about my favorite James Van Pelt story in this collection. But looking over the table of contents, I realized I couldn't do it. I couldn't pick just one. I have lots of favorites—a favorite science fiction story, a favorite fantasy, a favorite time travel, a favorite historical, a favorite story about students and teachers (a high school English teacher, Jim tackles the high school experience better than just about any fiction author ever), and a favorite one about families. This is why a James Van Pelt collection is such a lovely thing to have. I don't *have* to pick a favorite, they're all here.

This is Jim's third collection since 2002, which tells you something about how prolific he is. Jim's been writing a long time. But the last few years—the stretch of time covered in this current book—have seen Jim's career entering a new phase, taking off, maturing, if I can be so bold as to throw out some of those clichés. He's risen through the ranks of "hot new writer" to become, dare I say, established. (He'll probably be shocked to hear this. I know how hard he's worked to get where he is, and he's still working that hard.) These days, he's one of those writers who frequently shows up in the table of contents of top magazines like *Asimov's Science Fiction*. His stories get reprinted in various Year's Best anthologies. More than all that, though, he's one of those writers who you're happy to see in any table of contents. As in, "Oh, excellent, a new James Van Pelt story!" You can count on him to deliver a good story well told, with characters you care about and powerful insights. These are not easy things to accomplish.

Jim's stories cover a lot of ground. On one hand, you never know what you're going to get: the past, the future, time travel, distant space, a quiet story at home, present day in a school. On the other hand, you know exactly what you're going to get, and it's the reason you read a James Van Pelt story in the first place: humanity. In his stories, Jim is in conversation with his culture, with history, ideas, literature, people. Different kinds of people, groups of people, individuals. Students, family, fellow writers, fellow teachers, the world. Across time and space, what's come before us and what lies ahead. He's comfortable writing about the distant past and the end of the universe. His settings, as carefully researched and created as they are ("The Radio Magician" puts us right in the middle of the almost-forgotten polio epidemic), are tools for telling the bigger stories, the *real* stories. Whatever else they're about, they're primarily about people.

That should seem obvious. Every fiction how-to book and writing workshop discusses character development and motivation, how the story grows out of character, and so on. While most stories have characters, I'd argue that not all of them have *people*. Jim's stories are about people. The point of "The Inn at Mount Either" isn't the amazing hotel with interdimensional capabilities. It's about confronting a nightmare: what if you lost the person you love most in the world— but only slightly? I suppose I could also go on about metaphor, since a lot of commentary about science fiction discusses metaphor and how the fantastic elements of the genre symbolize other themes that anchor the story to the real world. In that regard, I could talk about how the Inn is a metaphor for what happens when a couple grows apart, recognizing that the person you married isn't quite the person you're now with, the terrible fear that comes from realizing the comfortable life you thought you had no longer exists. But to say the Inn is "just a metaphor" belittles the story. Because the "what if" of the fantastic taps into our subconscious better than glib metaphor ever could. It's what made the classic *Twilight Zone* episodes so powerful, and what makes the Inn so memorable. Dorian really has lost his wife, without losing her. Glib metaphor is safe and easily glossed over. But that sick feeling in the pit of my stomach I get while reading the story? That's real.

Okay, I changed my mind, I am going to pick a favorite. At least, a favorite at this moment in time, and a favorite when I got to read an earlier draft of it: "Where Did You Come From, Where Did You Go?" is a thought experiment. It's also about two smart high school girls sitting in class, when something completely bizarre and unbelievable happens. The story itself is a lovely, squicky, nerve-wracking mini-thriller that gets under the skin in the best tradition of *The Twilight Zone*. But on a more personal level, Olivia is me. I was an intense, engaged, starry-eyed high school kid who thought she was going to change the world but wasn't sure how she was going to do it. That character is so recognizable, and I'm sure Jim's been seeing her every day his whole teaching career. But the amazing thing is how well he captured her on the page in Olivia. I felt like I was looking in a mirror. What happens to Olivia and Latasha—I take it personally. Talk about getting under my skin.

There's a line from William Faulkner's Nobel Prize acceptance speech that gets quoted, perhaps overquoted, about how the only thing worth writing about is the human heart in conflict with itself. (The speech, delivered in 1950, is available to read and hear on the Nobel Prize website, www.nobelprize.org.)

I looked up that quote, intending to talk about it blithely, like most people do, because Jim is one of those writers who "gets it." His stories, even the ones about mutants and robots, are about people duking it out and struggling to survive and make sense of the world, and themselves. In reading the speech that the quote came from, I discovered what prompted Faulkner to make the speech in the first place and how amazingly out of context everyone's been taking it all this time. He wasn't just tossing off a pithy statement about the function of literature. He was warning us about the death of art.

> "Our tragedy today is a general and universal physical fear so long sustained by now that we can even bear it. There are no longer problems of the spirit. There is only the question: When will I be blown up? Because of this, the young man or woman writing today has forgotten the problems of the human heart in conflict with itself which alone can make good writing because only that is worth writing about, worth the agony and the sweat."

So. Global war and the atom bomb are distracting us from the true worth of art. Maybe even destroying art. People are too afraid of annihilation to acknowledge such a small thing as the internal struggles of the human spirit. The thing is, putting that quote back in context? Jim still gets it. He writes about that very fear, and how to overcome it. (Literally, in "The Light of a Thousand Suns," and in every one of his stories that starts with Armageddon and ends with hope. Jim's written a whole novel about that, *Summer of the Apocalypse*.) He's been able to make that fear concrete, to humanize it— to discover the human heart in it rather than being overwhelmed by the abstract. Here's the end of Faulkner's speech:

> "It is his [the writer's] privilege to help man endure by lifting his heart, by reminding him of the courage and honor and hope and pride and compassion and pity and sacrifice which have been the glory of his past. The poet's voice need not merely be the record of man, it can be one of the props, the pillars to help him endure and prevail."

Yeah. Jim gets it. I think Faulkner would be pleased to know that these stories exist, answering his call to arms, or rather pen.

# THE RADIO MAGICIAN
## AND OTHER STORIES

# THE RADIO MAGICIAN

In the evening Clarence sprawled on the ragged hook rug, facing the cathedral front of the burnished wood Edison, a pillow tucked beneath his chin, a blanket wrapped around his shoulders, and his useless legs encased in casts, sticking behind him. Eyes shut, he listened to KLZ, the Reynolds Radio Company, and then slowly rotated the dial through the other Denver stations. Sometimes late at night he'd pick up WDAF out of Kansas City or WAAF in Chicago. Everywhere he turned he found wavering voices, scratchy baseball games, foreign speech and strange music. News from overseas. Poland invaded. President Roosevelt. Big bands. The slightest twist of the wooden knob brought new sounds, all so far, far away from his tiny bedroom and the ragged hook rug. He wished he could crawl in among the glowing tubes with their tiny suns suspended in glass cages. They warmed his chilled hands. He'd listen as hard as he could so that he wouldn't hear his own breathing, so he wouldn't even *think* about his breathing. Did that breath hurt? What about the next one? Did the muscles in his chest tighten up just a little that time?

Mom had said, "You're luckier than some, son. It's only your legs."

So far, thought Clarence. So far. No, he didn't want to think about breathing.

So, he listened to *The Shadow, Bobby Benson and the B-Bar-B Riders, The Tom Mix Ralston Straight Shooters,* and he loved Charlie Chan stories from *Five Star Theater*, but mostly he listened for *Professor Gilded's Glorious Magical Extravaganza.* On the table by the window, the clock ticked to the hour, just as the announcer said, "Now, for your listening pleasure, Denver's very own radio magician." Clarence shivered in delight, and waited impatiently through a Pepsodent commercial.

"We return today to disappearance and transference," said Professor Gilded. "Last session, we talked of coins that moved from one hand to the next, from your hand to a pocket, from a pocket to a purse, or coins that vanished all together."

Clarence scooted closer to the radio, holding his own coin tight, a gold quarter eagle that felt warm and smooth. Tonight he barely had a headache, so the show was more enjoyable.

"You see, I put a coin in my left hand. I show it to the audience. The coin is there, I assure you. Its edges press against my skin. Everyone has seen it go into my left hand. That is the secret. Everyone must see."

Clarence pictured Professor Gilded on his tiny radio stage. Once *The Denver Post* had printed a picture of the professor's broadcast. Beside him, his top hat rested on a spindly legged table. The audience of ten who were there by the luck of having their names drawn from letters they'd sent the show, leaned forward. Every week Clarence wrote Professor Gilded a letter, but his name had never been drawn.

Last week, Father had patted Clarence's head. "How would we get you there, Clarence boy? You won't be going on that journey while you are sick. But write your letters. It's good your mind is so active." Then Father drew a long breath through his pipe, and held it in his lungs before releasing a steady gray stream.

Professor Gilded continued, "The coin does not know the trick. That is the trick. The coin does not know. So when the magic happens, the coin has jumped from my left hand to wherever I want it to go." He paused. A quiet drum rolled in the background as it did before the magic occurred. "Where do you think the coin has appeared this time? It is not in my left hand as you can see." The audience oohed and then clapped. Clarence squirmed in contentment. He *could* see Professor Gilded's empty hand. "Young lady with the fancy hat sitting in the back row. Yes, you. Would you check inside that beautiful red ribbon on the hat?"

A surprised squeal burst from the background. The audience buzzed with startled conversation.

The announcer said, "Ma'am could you describe what happened for our listeners?"

"The coin was inside my hat! Professor Gilded never moved from the stage!" She giggled suddenly. "I'm going to keep this forever."

Clarence squeezed the quarter eagle, a birthday present. "A ten-year-old deserves real money," Mother had said as she gave it to him. "It's a lucky coin, minted the year your father and I were born." She put her finger on the date, 1910. "You can't spend it. It's not legal money anymore." She leaned close, like a conspirator. "We were supposed to turn all the gold over to the government in 1933, but I held this one for you." The secret made the coin worth even more. Sometimes he thought of what the two and a half dollars could buy, and it made him feel rich.

Clarence pressed the small coin's bumpy edges against his skin, clenched it in his fist, turned the hand over, willed the coin to vanish. He scrunched his forehead, focused, tried to believe the quarter eagle was no longer in his grasp. But it was no good, just like wishing he could move his legs was no good. Even getting around on crutches would be better than his plaster jail. New crutches rested against the closet door. Beneath them in a box waited leg braces with long metal bars, heavy leather straps and black buckles. Someday, his mother promised, he would walk in them. The casts, though, were too heavy, and he couldn't swing his legs to keep himself moving forward. A week ago he'd tried, only to fall face first onto the hardwood floor.

Professor Gilded's voice broke in. "We do not dabble in the supernatural here. Charlatans claim their magic is real. The coin's disappearance is an illusion, a trick of perception only, but our perceptions make reality for us all. If you perceive you are cowardly, then illusion becomes the world. If you perceive you are ill, then illness becomes you."

Clarence's eyes popped open. He turned the sound up, his own attempts at the trick forgotten. Beneath his casts, his legs ached. He remembered running home down the long muddy lane beside the field, its corn already harvested, the broken stalks lying across each other. He'd run on the weeds beside the lane to keep his shoes dry. Then he stumbled. For a second, he thought he'd stepped in the mud, but he could see the shoe was clean. His right leg dragged again. He slowed to a heavy limp, massaging his thigh through his jeans. What was wrong with his leg? The house had never looked so far away. Too far to call for help. He leaned on the fence and felt his strength fading.

Just as he reached the gate an hour later, Mom came out on the porch to look for him. She ran to him as he fell, her face wet with fear. By morning, the left leg had gone weak too. How far would it stretch? As the doctor poked at him later that day, Clarence made a fist, then unmade it, over and over. Would the paralysis spread? Fist. No fist. Fist. No fist.

Professor Gilded said, "The world's illusions cloud perceptions. Most fail to recognize reality before them. They believe they are poor, or ugly, or life's horizons are short. If my assistant will allow me to demonstrate, observe the reality of my four-legged friend."

The sound of clopping came from the speakers before the announcer said, "Professor Gilded's beautiful assistant, Sonia, is leading a horse into the studio, a strawberry roan, courtesy of the Phipps Ranch. I have to tell you folks, livestock in a radio studio is not what you see every day." Chairs scraped across a wooden floor. Someone said, "Give him a bit of room."

The announcer whispered, "The studio is not large, my friends. Our audience has moved to the back wall. The horse, a gentle one, chosen especially for this demonstration, stands no more than five feet from them. Professor Gilded's stage gives him a height advantage. He's removing a large, blue blanket from the chest behind him."

Clarence turned the sound up again. The big trick always ended the show. First, the small demonstrations. Cards that reordered themselves. Balls that multiplied. Flowers that changed colors. Handkerchiefs that metamorphed into birds. All the while Professor Gilded lectured on magic, on the magic he was doing and the magic in the world, as he built to the finale, something so impressive that his audience clapped and clapped and clapped until the sound faded and the show ended. But he'd never worked with a horse! He couldn't possibly make a horse vanish from a small studio in front of an attentive audience. Not even Houdini could accomplish such a feat. For a moment, Clarence didn't think about his legs.

"A beautiful animal, the horse. Much more intelligent than humanity imagines. Please, people, run your hands along the horse's side. Don't be shy. Feel his beating heart. Ahh, a true horse fancier, are you? Yes, check his hooves. This is a hale and healthy representative of his breed. Assure yourselves of his reality, for, I promise you, in a moment you will doubt your memories and senses, and, perhaps, you will wonder what other illusions you harbor about the world."

Outside Clarence's window, a trolley car rattled by. Every fifteen minutes the trolley clattered, reminding him that his parents had moved from the farm so they were close to Broadway and Denver General Hospital. "We can't risk him, Thomas," Mom said. "The doctors warned about the disease migrating into his lungs. We might need Dr. Drinker's respirator until Clarence becomes strong again." Father had only nodded, and soon he completed negotiations with their neighbor to lease the land. Within weeks, both parents had found part-time work, which was remarkable. Jobs were hard to come by. Mom cleaned houses while Dad sorted mail. Clarence envisioned the virus like a horrible mold. Its name sounded like a mold, poliomyelitis. The doctors put his legs in casts. Itching during the day was intolerable, but Clarence could force a pencil, or a ruler, or a straightened coat hanger only so far under the plaster. Maybe the virus really reassembled a mold, growing out of sight in the cast's moist darkness. If the casts came off now, would his legs look human anymore? And that wasn't the worst. In his blood, he pictured the virus marching toward his lungs, filling them with cauliflower-like lumps of gray and green mold until he couldn't inhale. Mom called the machine they would put him in "Dr. Drinker's respirator," an iron lung, and Porter's hospital only had one. Iron lung. Iron lung. Nothing sounded more frightening. It made him think of iron crosses and invasions, a German army charging up his arteries' roads, a blitzkrieg to the heart. But that wasn't the worst. Close as they lived now, the iron lung would do no good if someone else filled the machine. Clarence was not the only sick child in Denver. An eleven-year-old from Broomfield lay in the machine now. The *Post* put his picture in the paper yesterday. The caption read, "Young Sean Garrison, completely paralyzed from the neck down, battles for his life against all odds." But he didn't look like he was battling in the picture. He looked like he'd lost, and all the weight of that loss, and all the grief, were written in his face.

Professor Gilded said, "Could you hold the edge of the blanket, Sonia? There, stand on the stool so you may reach high enough. Ah, it is a good horse, longing for its stable perhaps, for a fresh pile of hay and a rub down for the evening."

The announcer's lowered voice barely leaked from the speakers. "I and the audience cannot see the roan, but we see the blanket's ends. There is no place to lead the horse. I can hardly describe the tension as we wait for Professor Gilded's wonder. I'm afraid he has set himself too daunting a task tonight."

A drum rumbled in the background.

Professor Gilded asked, "Do you believe the horse is still be-hind the blanket? If I have planted doubt thoroughly enough, then the horse may both be there and not be there. You have no way of telling, unless, of course, you walk around my blanket." He paused. The drum rolled louder. "Or, I can pull the blanket away."

A clatter, a scream, then voices in tumult. Another scream.

"I cannot believe what I am witnessing," gasped the announcer. "Too much. Too much." A hard click, as if the microphone hit some-thing. "Oh, be glad you cannot see."

Someone sobbed.

"Professor Gilded holds his blanket over his arm, like a cape. Sonia stands beside him. The horse, the beautiful roan that walked into the studio is gone, but . . . the bones . . . a pile of bones sits on the floor. Horse bones, dry and clean, piled as if flesh and fur disap-peared. No muscle. Oh, please, can we have a commercial now?" Another click.

Professor Gilded's soothing voice said, "An illusion, I assure you. A trick of light and distraction, as all the best magic is."

"Sonia takes the blanket," said the announcer's shaky voice. "He picks up the skull."

"Alas, Horatio, I knew him well." Professor Gilded laughed, a long satisfying chuckle. "The magic show is theater in the best tradi-tion. Shakespeare wove illusions too. The bard said, 'I'll cross it, though it blast me. Stay, illusion! If thou hast any sound, or use of voice, speak to me, if there be any good thing to be done.' As you leave the studio you will find the lovely roan on the street, awaiting your inspection."

The show's closing musical notes played. Clarence realized he had pressed himself off the floor with his hands so his head was closer to the speaker. His arms trembled with the effort.

The announcer appeared to have recovered composure. "Tonight's show was brought to you by the kind attention of our sponsors. Be sure to shop for products that support the continued broadcast of *Professor Gilded's Glorious Magical Extrava-ganza.*" The music rose, but Clarence heard the announcer say to someone in the background, so muffled that Clarence wondered if he heard it at all, "What the hell was that?"

Clarence's bedroom door opened. He twisted to his side to see his mother holding a basin, several towels, and a filled bucket heavy enough to make her lean.

"Show over, son?" She put the towels, bucket and basin next to him on the rug.

"Yes, it was a good one." He shivered with the thought of bones. Professor Gilded *said* the horse was outside the studio and that the show was a trick, but how could he fool that many people who stood so close? A horse is not a coin to be hidden in a sleeve or to be gripped by the back of the hand while the audience sees an empty palm. Clarence knew coin tricks and the names of tricks: the gangster spin, the backspin bounce, the knuckle roll, the horizontal waterfall. He could flick a coin into a hidden pocket, make a coin between two cards vanish, pull a coin out of someone's hair, but they were practiced techniques, not magic. Making a coin disappear just involved making the audience's eye go to the wrong place. When he did the tricks for his friends, he watched their eyes, and when they looked away from the coin, he had them.

Clarence turned his hand over. Where was his quarter eagle? A red circle showed where he'd held it so tight for so long, but where was it?

"I'm going to need you on your back, Clarence. Help me here."

She knelt beside him and lifted his right leg over his left as he rolled. Still, despite her care, his casted foot thumped when it hit the floor. "I'm tired of waiting this disease out," she said. She sat back on her heels. "Are you tired of just waiting?"

Clarence nodded. On his back, he looked for the coin. Perhaps it rolled under the radio. She'd tied her hair into a bun behind her ears, but strays escaped from all sides, touching her cheeks with black threads and sticking to the sweat of her forehead. He rested on his elbows so he could see the casts, smudged now with weeks of dragging around. "What are you thinking?"

Mom took a heavy pair of scissors from the basin, then filled the basin from the bucket. Steam eddied off the surface. "There's a nurse in Australia who claims that putting children in casts is exactly the wrong thing to do." She snipped the scissors open and shut a few times. "Your muscles are paralyzed, but they're not dead, so we're going to remind them what it feels like to be active." As she talked, she worked her way down the cast, using both hands to clip through the plaster-stiffened cloth. Clarence wanted to shrink away from the blade as Mom cut past the knee and down the shin. "President Roosevelt himself recovered from polio, and look how far he's gotten. There." She pulled the cast apart like a long clam. Clarence's leg, marked with grime at the thigh and ankle, lay as pale as a fish in the middle. No mold! But it smelled like the root cellar. Clarence wrinkled his nose.

Mom moved to the next one. When she finished, she dipped a towel in the basin, then cupped her hand under his knee and gently lifted. A ripple of pain flashed from his knee to the back of his thigh. Clarence gasped.

"Sorry," said Mom. She draped the hot towel over his leg. Water pooled in the cast. "The Aussie nurse says that the muscles will respond to stimulation. I'm going to rub the muscles, but I also have to move your leg, son. It might be uncomfortable." She put one hand under his knee again and the other on the foot. Her serious eyes stared into his. Clarence nodded. Mom pressed the foot toward him while pulling the knee up.

Clarence had read that polio is the cruelest of diseases: it paralyzes but feeling remains. Liquid fire poured down his leg, like the skin would turn inside out. He scrunched his eyes tight. Thigh muscles stretched, moved, tore apart, melted, screamed a thousand tiny voices of death and torment, remade themselves into agony battalions, fought bloody battles, crushed each other with stones, ground salt into their wounds, flailed their backs with rose stems, broke their bones, pulled their fingernails off, stuck each other with rusty pitchforks, then twisted them deeper and deeper.

"There," said Mom. "That's one. Four more on this leg before we go to the next."

In the middle of the night, Clarence lay on his back in bed, his legs' memory a throbbing reminder of the session Mom said they would go through again in the morning. The clock ticked loudly in the hallway, forever holding tonight's pain and the inescapable progress to tomorrow's session.

From the bedroom next door, Mom and Dad argued. "How could an Australian nurse know more than our own doctor?" Dad talked calmly, his voice a steady rumble. "If her system was good, don't you think doctors here, American doctors, would prescribe it?"

"Sister Kenny has shown results. I don't have faith in that 'convalescent serum.' It doesn't make sense to pump blood in him from people who have recovered from the disease. That doesn't work for other diseases."

Like all of their arguments, they were reasonable with each

other, but Clarence still rolled over carefully, helping his left leg to go over his right, biting his lower lip until it stopped moving, then buried his head under the pillow. The sheets smelled of the menthol and petroleum jelly Mom had rubbed into his skin.

A little while later, their voices quieted, then their bedroom door clicked open. Steps creaked in the hallway before his own door opened. Mom padded into the room. Peeking under the pillow, Clarence saw her bare legs beneath her short robe and the thick wool socks she wore as slippers. She rubbed his back gently.

"I'm awake," Clarence said, sliding the pillow aside.

Mom's hand stopped. "You should be asleep. Sleep heals." She kneaded the muscles under his shoulder blade. The motion felt comforting. Clarence sighed. He remembered today's broadcast. He had wanted to tell Mom about it earlier, but hadn't had a chance. "Do you think Professor Gilded can really make a horse disappear?"

Mom laughed. "I saw a magic show once. The magician sawed a woman in half, and then he put her back together. He made a table float, so I suppose, but, Clarence, it's a *radio* show. He could tell you he was making the state capitol vanish and you wouldn't know any different."

"There were people there, ten of them. They saw Professor Gilded turn a real horse into a pile of bones, and then the horse was whole again, outside the studio."

Mom moved to the other shoulder blade. "They *said* ten people were there. They could be actors." She scooted farther up on the bed so she could rub his shoulders. "But maybe it is true, son. Marvelous things happen all the time, miracles, even."

"Do you think Professor Gilded makes miracles?"

She stopped rubbing again. "You have to believe in miracles. Miracles and hard work. That's a powerful combination."

"Does Dad believe in miracles?"

"Well, that's a good question. He told me once that he believes in Jesus, but he doesn't believe someone who says he's talked to him lately."

Clarence giggled.

She patted his head. "Now, you go to sleep. In the morning we'll try a little of the hard work and see if we can't help our miracle along. How do your legs feel?"

"They hurt. They didn't hurt as much in the casts."

"I think they'll feel better soon. Remember, they haven't moved in a month." She pushed herself up from the bed. "Oh, I found your birthday quarter eagle in my sock when I put it on." The coin clicked when she placed it on his nightstand. "I have no idea how it got there, but you better hold onto it. Remember, it's for luck." She tucked the covers in so they pulled snug against his chest. "Don't forget, tomorrow your dad and I will both be at work. Mrs. Bentley from next door will come by to see if you need anything."

Clarence nodded. In all the times Mom and Dad had been gone together, Mrs. Bentley never dropped in, which was okay because Clarence could listen to the radio as long as he wanted.

After she left, Clarence pulled himself close enough to the nightstand to reach the coin. New aches broke out as his legs shifted, but he gritted his teeth until his fingers found its mellow, round shape. From the light coming in off the street, he examined its soft gold. It fitted neatly into his palm, then vanished into his fist. "Now you see it," he said in the empty room. "Now you don't." He opened the hand where the quarter eagle still sat, but he imagined what it would be like to make it go away. When his hand hid it, the coin was both there and not there. He only had to choose the reality where it wasn't, and the hand would be empty. How did the coin get into Mom's sock? What had he been thinking about the coin during Professor Gilded's show?

He fell asleep thinking about coins appearing out of a lady's hat, and long red velvet lined black robes, and then, finally, as he slid into the deep darkness, he dreamed of a horse galloping across a field of spring hay, a divine roan with a long tail whipping behind, until it staggered on suddenly weakened legs, trying so hard to stay upright and running. It buckled, whinnying in terror as only a horse can, its eyes wide, its nostrils snorting, before the fur and flesh disappeared. Pathetically, it took one skeletal step, then clattered into a pile of crisp white bones. Green hay poked up between its ribs as the skull rolled a few feet more, the last of its momentum used up. In the dream, Clarence cried until he saw a gold glimmer reflected in the horse's jaw. It was his quarter eagle clenched between the teeth, catching the sun.

Then, he slept.

In the morning, the massage hurt even worse. Mom bit her lips in as she pushed her thumbs deep into Clarence's thigh muscles, and she rubbed and bent and twisted and grinded and pinched for weeks until Clarence couldn't hold his breath any longer. He released his pain in short gasps, concentrating on the radio as she dug her thumbs deep into the back of his thighs. The news reported Britain, France, Australia and New Zealand declared war on Germany. Then a commentator argued America should stay out of the conflict.

"There. Not so bad, was it. Just ten minutes this time," said Mom. She used the back of her wrists to wipe her eyes. "We'll have you walking before Christmas."

When she left, Clarence lay on his back, staring at the ceiling. Polio, he realized, had made him a little kid again. He couldn't see the tops of tables without someone lifting him. He couldn't reach the upper drawers on the dresser. All he saw when looking up at the window were clouds and the leafy branches. With the casts, he could at least slide himself around the room and even get to the bathroom without help, although it took a gymnastic maneuver that left his arms quivering to get himself onto the toilet.

From the higher vantage point of the bed, he could see most of the tree. Someone yelled to someone else, and their feet pounded on the sidewalk as they ran by. Maybe they were playing tag. Maybe they were throwing a ball back and forth. Clarence couldn't see enough to tell. Then the trolley rattled down the middle of the street. The trolley stopped at the end of the block and ran all the way to downtown Denver, passing the radio station with its soundstage. Even now, Professor Gilded could be preparing for today's show.

Clarence rolled onto his side. The crutches and leg braces rested in the shadow next to the window. Professor Gilded's show began in two hours. By trolley, he could be there in fifteen minutes, if only he could get to the trolley's stop at the corner.

It took most of an hour to get into his pants. The pant legs folded over and kept twisting, so he had to inch them up his legs. He looked up every time the house creaked, afraid Mrs. Bentley would choose this moment to check on him, sitting on the floor in his underwear. His feet wouldn't cooperate, and when his toes caught the cloth, sharp pains raced up the back of his legs. By the time he buttoned the top button, perspiration ran into his eyes and dripped from his chin. Getting into the braces took less time, but the leather was stiff and fastening the heavy buckles hurt his fingers. When he finished, he rested on his back. Placing the crutches under his arms while maintaining his balance seemed an impossible task, but there was only fifty minutes until the show started, and his legs felt so much lighter and flexible without the casts that he was sure he could get to the trolley on time.

He clumped through the hallway to the front door. In his left pocket nestled the quarter eagle; in the right, five dimes. He had no idea what the trolley cost. At the door, he rested his hands on the doorknob. For a month he'd been lying or sitting. His head hadn't been this much higher than his feet for weeks. Every muscle from the hips down tingled and ached. Clarence bit the inside of his mouth and opened the door, clenching the crutches tight under his arms. When he stepped outside, he realized he hadn't felt the sun on his face since he'd gotten sick.

The trolley man took a dime for the ride after lifting Clarence to a seat. "You hurt your legs, son? Where you going?" He smelled of garlic and cigarettes.

"The KLZ radio studio." Clarence tried to keep the tremor out of his voice. The half block walk to the trolley stop had been the longest sustained effort of his life. Every crack in the sidewalk, every pebble, every movement threatened to pitch him over. In the house, he'd used a footstool and chair to get himself upright enough for the crutches. There was no way to help himself in the open. He would just have to lay there until someone saved him.

The woman on the seat next to him, holding a basket full of knitting, nodded and smiled. "You'll need to get off at 15th street. I listen to KLZ all the time." She glanced at his leg braces. "Must be hard getting around in school. I hope your schoolmates are kind."

Clarence leaned the crutches against the trolley's wall, careful to keep them from falling. The trolley lurched into motion, clacking over the tracks toward downtown Denver. Even the jiggling hurt. He focused on the shops passing by the windows and smiled through the pain. The radio station was only fifteen minutes away, now. He fingered the quarter eagle. It's here and it's not here, he thought. Only thinking makes it so.

A few minutes later, the trolley passed the hospital. A pair of marble lions, their jaws open, flanked the double door entrance at the top of a flight of stairs. To the left, a wheelchair ramp rose along the side of the building for the crippled. The building's severe white face rose six stories into the sky punctuated by rows of dark windows. Clarence's breathing tightened just looking at it. Somewhere inside, Sean Garrison stared at the ceiling, the iron lung squeezing his chest to expel the air, then reversing the pressure so he could inhale. Clarence could almost hear the wheezing sounds. He wondered, how does he itch his nose? He couldn't move a muscle below his neck. What does he think about? Clarence was glad when they left the hospital behind.

KLZ wasn't directly on Broadway, it turned out. The conductor lowered Clarence to the sidewalk, clamping his arms to his crutches so he hit the cement ready to go. "The station's a block that way, son," he said, pointing. "Watch your step."

Clarence's legs quivered beneath him as the trolley rumbled away. The radio station's sign looked awfully far. He gritted his teeth and leaned forward.

Ten minutes later his arms ached with the effort to keep him upright, but he stood before KLZ's front door, a heavy metal and glass barrier. In the shadow of the room behind the door, he saw a secretary looking at him, a prim blonde with dark-framed glasses, like a librarian. Before he could brace himself to pull the door open, she was holding it for him.

"My word, child, what are doing here by yourself? Where are your parents?"

"They're at work. Do you mind if I sit down?" Clarence lowered himself gingerly onto one of the two worn leather chairs in the lobby. He sighed, his eyes closed, as the weight fell from his arms and legs. A ceiling fan creaked through slow revolutions and stirred the smell of furniture polish and old magazines. Across the small receiving area, in the other chair, a balding man wearing a blue bow tie and a white shirt studied a newspaper. He glanced at Clarence, briefly meeting his eyes, then turned a page and returned to his reading. Behind the secretary's desk, three doors, marked STUDIO 1, STUDIO 2 and SOUND ENGINEER, were closed. Drooping wires high on the wall connected to a bare speaker, playing KLZ's afternoon news softly, a litany of political reaction to the events in Europe. Polish soldiers were in retreat. British bombers attacked German war ships.

"You look like you could use a glass of water." The secretary disappeared through the sound stage door.

Sweat soaked the sides of Clarence's shirt. His legs throbbed from the arch of his feet, where the braces' metal bar clamped against his shoes, to the grinding spots where the leather upper straps dug into his hips. Even his fingers hurt from squeezing the crutches, and he doubted he could make the one block trip back to the trolley stop, but he was here. He had arrived! He couldn't keep a smile off his face.

The secretary returned with the water. Clarence rolled the cool glass against his forehead before drinking half of it in one long swallow.

"Is Professor Gilded here?" he asked. "I'd like to meet him."

"That old fraud?" said the man in the bow tie, putting his newspaper down. He winked at the secretary. "He's a bore."

Clarence's jaw tightened up until he realized the man was teasing. At least he was pretty sure he wasn't serious.

"Do you know him?" Clarence pulled the quarter eagle out of his pocket. "I've been practicing magic." He did a quick knuckle roll back and forth with the coin.

The bow-tied man put his paper aside. "Can you do a pass under and around?"

Clarence rolled the coin between his fourth and little finger, tucked it under, caught it on his thumb, then brought it around from underneath. "Sure. I learned that one first."

The man produced a half dollar from a vest pocket, then walked it from finger to finger on his right hand. "Okay, we'll race. First one to get the coin around their hand ten times wins. It's a little unfair. My hands are bigger and the coin has farther to go."

They counted out loud. Clarence was at eight when the man reached ten, flipped the coin into the air, and then watched solemnly as the white feather it had turned into drifted to the floor.

"You're pretty good for a kid. Can you do a sleeve flick? How about a coin cascade?"

Clarence nodded.

The secretary, who had returned to her desk, laughed. "Don't get him going. He'll talk your ear off about magic." She looked at the clock. "Bob will be here in a couple minutes. You'd better get into the studio."

The bow-tied man dismissed her comment with a wave. He leaned toward Clarence, his elbows on his knees. "So, why do you want to see Professor Gilded?"

Clarence tried to recall the picture of Gilded from *The Denver Post*. His hair had been thick and black, almost touching his shoulders, and a moustache hid most of his mouth. Was it possible that the bald, bow-tied man *was* Professor Gilded? But where was the accent? Clarence imagined Gilded as tall, like a black-cloaked Abraham Lincoln. Who was this guy?

As if reading his mind, the bow-tied man said, "I'm John Albenice, his understudy. You can tell me."

A couple dressed in their Sunday best pushed through the door. The woman in a floral print dress with her hair pinned up, whose pinched cheeks and pointed chin made her look a little like Clarence's fourth grade teacher, walked straight to the secretary and said, "We're here for Professor Gilded's afternoon performance. We have an invitation." She put an envelope on the desk. Her husband stood behind her, his hands pushed into his pockets, as if he really didn't want to be there.

"Of course, studio two, please." The secretary opened the door for them. Clarence glimpsed a short hallway.

"Will Professor Gilded be here soon?" He raised himself out of the chair to get a last look before the door closed. "He said perception is reality. He said if I perceive that I'm sick, that I am. I wanted to ask him what he meant by that."

John leaned back in his chair. He idly pulled his bow tie. "Professor Gilded says a lot of things on the air you probably shouldn't listen to, kid. He's paid to talk, you know. He's an entertainer."

The secretary cleared her throat and looked purposefully at the clock.

"Look, I've got to get ready for the show. He just meant that magic happens in your head." He stood up and started for the studio. "Are you as proficient with cards as you are with coins?"

"I can do a pretty good fan and a table spread, but my hands are too small for a one-hand shuffle. I'll have to grow into lots of tricks." He held up his hand like a starfish.

"Huh," John said. "Have you tried cutting down a deck? Smaller cards might do it." He tapped his chin thoughtfully. "I hadn't considered that before. I'll bet small cards might get a lot of kids interested in sleight of hand."

"Oh, no," said the secretary.

The door opened. A gray-headed man carrying a briefcase walked partway into the foyer, and then froze when he saw John.

"I told you to stay the gawd damned hell away from me, freak," said the man, bringing the briefcase to his chest like a shield.

The secretary stiffened. "Bob, there's a child in the room."

Clarence recognized the man's voice. He introduced and narrated *Professor Gilded's Glorious Magical Extravaganza.* He said "hell" on the air at the end of the last show.

John straightened. His voice deepened. "I'm not responsible for your irrational fears. If you can't separate a trick from reality, then you have the problem, not me." It was Professor Gilded's voice, without the accent. He stood in between the two chairs, only a yard from Clarence, and he didn't look like he was going to move.

Keeping his briefcase between them, the other man scooted along the front windows until he reached the sound engineer's door. He found the knob without looking away from John. "I'll announce the show, but I don't want to have anything to do with you. Keep your distance. There's nothing natural about you." The door slammed behind him.

John shrugged. He looked at Clarence. "Sorry you had to see that. He had difficulty with the horse trick. It . . . disturbed him."

"Did you . . . I mean, did the professor really make a horse turn into bones?" Clarence's heart thumped in his throat.

"If you think so, then he did. That's the perception trick. An audience thought he did. And Bob there . . . well," he moved toward the studio door. "He believes."

He stopped at the secretary's desk. "The only thing I really know about magic, kid, is that if there isn't some of it in the world, then we live in a dark, dark place. If you've got any, you have to share it."

The secretary reached into her hair. "Hey, what's this?"

John plucked the object off her palm. He looked at it, genuinely puzzled. "1910 quarter eagle. Isn't this yours?" He walked back to Clarence, the coin between his fingers. "Nice trick."

The coin dropped into Clarence's hand. He hadn't even realized that John had taken it.

"Nice trick yourself."

John paused. "I didn't do anything. How'd you pull it off? Pass it when she gave you the water? No, don't tell me. A magician never tells. But I like it. Effective illusion. Okay, gotta go. There will be a whole audience here soon, and the stage isn't ready." He shook Clarence's hand. "Somebody's got to amaze them all." He laughed, and Clarence thought he'd heard a hint of a European accent in it.

Then, he was gone. Clarence tossed the gold piece from one hand to the other.

The secretary looked at him pityingly. "If there were room in the studio, kid, he'd let you in, but we're booked for weeks."

When Clarence stood on the sidewalk outside the radio station, his arms felt completely without strength. Had he used up everything he had to get to the station? He stepped forward, letting most of his weight rest on the crutches, his breath ripping in short gasps against his aching legs. No hike could have ever been longer. He thought about soldiers marching to far off fronts, their courage flitting about them, not knowing if they would make it back, but he kept pushing forward, his braces clicking against the cement. The metal creaked at the knees, and he went steps at a time with his eyes closed.

By the time he reached the trolley stop, he could hardly inhale, and his heart flurried like a trapped bird. Was this the beginning of a new paralysis? He whimpered. Cars passed on Broadway in the afternoon sun, and only after agonizing minutes the trolley trundled into sight.

"Please," gasped Clarence as the same driver from his ride downtown lifted him into the car, "can you take me to the hospital?"

Every bump jarred his legs. He held the back of his thighs to try to keep them from bouncing, but he couldn't anticipate the next jolt. His cheek rested against the wooden sill under the window, and tears leaked between his closed eyelids. Finally the trolley stopped.

"Hospital, young man," said the driver, concern in his voice.

Clarence struggled to get his crutches under his arms.

"No need. I've sent someone in to get you a wheelchair." He placed his hand on Clarence's shoulder. "You don't look good."

A nurse appeared at the trolley door and helped Clarence into the wheelchair.

"I'll take him to emergency," said the nurse. "We can evaluate him there."

"No," said Clarence. The trolley driver wrung his hands. Passengers crowded at the windows. A little girl holding a book waved at him through the glass. Clarence waved back weakly. "I need to go to the polio ward. I need to get to the iron lung."

The nurse started pushing him up the sidewalk toward the ramp. "You have polio? Are you experiencing breathing difficulty?" She sounded businesslike.

Clarence relaxed his head against the back of the wheelchair.

He rested his hand on the quarter eagle in his pants pocket, its shape a solid comfort. "I'm not sick. I'm visiting. I want to see it."

"You look sick." The nurse walked beside him as they rose up the ramp and into the hospital's entrance way.

"Honest, I'm okay. I think I probably tried to do too much today. My legs hurt a little," he lied, "but I really want to see the polio ward."

He rolled into an elevator.

"There's someone in the iron lung already," she said.

Lights flicked beside each floor as the elevator went up. Clarence had never been in an elevator before. "I know. Sean Garrison. He was in the paper. How is he doing?"

"You're really not sick?" She looked down at him doubtfully. "If you're not, you're the sorriest looking healthy boy I've ever seen."

"I walked to the trolley all by myself."

"Hmmm." The elevator stopped and the doors opened. "I hope you don't mind if I have a doctor check you anyway, and we need to talk to your parents."

Forty beds separated by light green curtains filled the polio ward. At some, family members sat by the wan children. Antiseptic smells filled the air.

She wheeled him into a broad hallway, and then into a room where a large steel canister dominated the middle. A compressor whirred under the device, stopped, shifted, then whirred again with a lighter tone. Clarence knew the machine was switching back and forth between exhaling and inhaling. A dark-haired boy lay face up, only his head outside of the iron lung, looking at him blankly through a mirror positioned above his face. Grief lines marked his face. His eyes were bloodshot and red-rimmed. Clarence had never seen anyone so sad. A long window in the metal showed his arms and chest, while another showed his legs. Two rubber-lined holes permitted doctors to reach in to rearrange the patient if necessary, but the only way to actually touch him would be to undo the heavy clasps that locked the head end to the rest of the machine.

Clarence pushed the top of the wheels to move closer. "Hi, I'm Clarence."

In the background, the motor clicked. "I'm sick," whispered the boy, and Clarence knew that he could only whisper because the power to speak came from the machine compression. He could talk when the iron lung made him exhale. Putting his hand on his own chest, Clarence tried to imagine being inside the canister.

The motor cycled several times. Clarence looked at Sean's reflection in the mirror. Sean looked back.

"Would you like to see a magic trick?" said Clarence.

The motor whirred.

Sean's voice was a falling leaf. "No."

"I'll show you anyway." The 1910 quarter eagle came out of Clarence's pocket. In the sterile hospital light, its gold glowed. He did knuckle rolls for Sean. He did false drops and sleight of hand passes, showing the coin and then vanishing it. He stacked the gold coin with the three dimes he had left, hid them under a tissue, then asked Sean where the coin was, top, bottom or middle. Wherever Sean said it was, when Clarence uncovered the coins, there it was.

Two more nurses came into the room, watching Clarence go through his repertoire. They clapped when the coins reappeared in unexpected places.

"Magic is about perception," said Clarence, leaning close to Sean. Sitting in his wheelchair, his head was on the same level. "What we perceive is our reality. If you think you are hungry, then you find food. If you think you are cold, you shiver." Clarence paused. He thought about Professor Gilded on his stage talking to an audience. What happened that night when the horse turned into bones? How did Gilded perceive it? Did the animal shimmer before the flesh dissolved? Clarence flourished the quarter eagle. Sean watched, his eyes dark and intent.

"Now I'll show you a trick that will amaze you. I don't even know if I can do it, but I'll try. Are you ready?"

Sean nodded, mostly with his eyes.

The nurses leaned in.

Clarence clasped the coin in his right hand hard enough that he could feel the ribbed edge marking his palm. He let his thoughts drift from it, so that he was both holding the coin and not holding it. Forced distraction, but to himself, not his audience. He thought about war news and Pepsodent and *Bobby Benson and the B-Bar-B Riders.* Instead of the coin, he imagined the Edison's polished wood tuning knob in his fingers as he slowly turned from station to station, of how delicious the sound tasted late at night when his parents had gone to bed and the search for voices made the time flee. Clarence thought about magic. He thought about "take a card, any card" and "abracadabra" and "there's nothing up my sleeve." There were illusions and tricks, and then there was magic. There was a horse that was there and not there. Perception made it real. Perception ruled.

When he opened his hand, the coin was gone.

One of the nurses sighed, disappointed. After all the other tricks Clarence had done, this one must have seemed anticlimactic.

Clarence smiled. He said to Sean, "The coin is gone. Do you know where it is?"

Sean waited until the machine reversed so he could speak. "Is it . . ." The motor clicked. He inhaled. It flipped into the exhalation cycle. " . . . in my hand?"

"What?" said a nurse. She stepped to the side of the iron lung to look through the window. "Oh, my gosh." The other two nurses crowded around her. "He's got it in his hand! How did the coin get in there?"

Clarence touched Sean's forehead. "A friend of mine told me the world is a dark, dark place, if we see it that way, and if we've got any magic, we should share it."

Sean waited for the machine to give him the air. "Okay."

"You need to get better. Someone else might need that iron lung."

"I will."

Clarence shifted in his wheelchair. One of the braces clanked against the chair's metal frame, and he realized his legs didn't hurt as badly as they had on the trolley. He'd barely thought of them while he did the magic. The thought made him happy.

The nurses were still marveling about the coin. Clarence could see it through the window in the paralyzed boy's hand.

Slowly, Sean's fingers closed over it.

# WHERE DID YOU COME FROM? WHERE DID YOU GO?

onday started bizarre. At the bus stop, the sun rose like a diseased orange, dark and ruddy at the bottom and a sick yellow at the top. "It's the fires in California," said someone as we shivered in the October cold, but it looked like an omen to me. I shouldn't have worn a skirt.

The bus arrived late. A little girl who'd missed her ride to the elementary school sat in my seat. I asked her to move. She said, "Who do you think you are?" I had to sit on the other side and watch houses slide by I'd never watched before. At the high school, scraps of paper and an empty milk carton littered the hallway by my locker. The janitors must have taken the weekend off. My locker combination didn't work the first three times, and then it did. In the meantime, kids walked back and forth behind me, headed to their rooms. I didn't catch what anyone said, and what I did hear sounded foreign.

My stomach hurt.

And to top it off, Ms Benda didn't show up for English. A stranger stood at the door, wearing a substitute teacher badge, checking off names as we entered the room. There was a line. He looked up when I stepped behind Carmen Tripp, and then did a double take, before looking away. He didn't meet my eyes when he asked, "Do you know who you are?"

I said, "Olivia Langdon."

"Of course." He studied the clipboard and made a mark.

He wrote his name on the board before the bell, Mr. Herbert. Thirtyish. Bad complexion. Black tie. Shirt untucked in back. One gray sock and one blue one peeking out from pants an inch too short. He carefully put his briefcase on the desk, patted it twice, like it was a pet dog, then stepped behind the podium. The school district scrapes the bottom of the barrel for subs. Latasha texted me before the bell rang. "wrdo." I sent back, "no kdng."

To open class, he said, "You're all dead." He glanced at his briefcase. "But two of you will be famous. Hey, nonny, nonny."

This is going to be interesting, I thought. Ms Benda had spent the last week discussing symbolism in Steinbeck's *The Pearl*, a book that had taken me all of a half hour to finish. Her idea of an entertaining class was to move onto a grammar lesson after fifteen minutes of spirited defense of Steinbeck's contribution to American literature. The week before she'd done the same routine, except the author was Sherwood Anderson. She practically collapsed with joy while reading "I'm a Fool" out loud.

Mr. Herbert said, "In the future, I mean, you're dead. A hundred years from now, high school students will be reading the classics, maybe some of the same books you are studying today, but you will be long gone, so how are you going to spend your days now?"

Latasha, sitting near the front, said, "Doing college applications." A couple of kids laughed.

"Thank you, Latasha." He didn't consult the seating chart, but stared at her intensely. I wondered if he'd memorized everyone's name at the door. My phone buzzed. Latasha texted, "& drnkng beer."

"Of course, maybe they will be reading what one of you has written. Mark Twain was your age once, you know, and so was Sylvia Plath and Ernest Hemingway. I wonder if they knew they would be literary legends when they were seventeen. If they could feel it." He paced slowly from the podium to the desk, looking out at us. "I wonder what the rest of the class would think if they had known they were in the presence of greatness."

Latasha texted, "17 yr old Hmngwy on a date—yum."

I sent back, "perv."

Tyler what's-his-name, from the golf team, raised his hand, and then said before Mr. Herbert could call on him, "We're studying *The Pearl*. Are we going to have a quiz on yesterday's reading?"

Somebody groaned. Depend on Tyler to bring up the quiz. I texted to Latasha, "a-hole."

She snickered. Like me, she palmed her phone in her lap, out of sight. She typed with her thumb without looking. Beneath the desks where the teacher couldn't see, a whole other conversation was taking place. I'll bet half the kids were texting at any time. I once had an argument with my boyfriend, broke up with him, made up and broke up again before the end of a lesson on Emily Dickinson's "Twas Just This Time, Last Year, When I Died."

Mr. Herbert touched a pile of papers on Ms Benda's desk. Undoubtedly the quizzes. "Nobody reads Steinbeck anymore." He looked mournful. When I think back on the incident, this is where I started creeping out. I thought for a moment he was going to cry in that way a street person will just start crying for no reason, or have an argument with himself.

"What do you mean?" said Tyler. "We started on Monday. It was *The Pearl* or *The Red Pony*. We got to vote."

Mr. Herbert gathered himself and shrugged. "Literary reputations wax and wane. How many of you read Rudyard Kipling now?"

Nobody raised their hand. I looked around. The class was sitting up, watching Herbert warily. They caught the same vibe I did.

He moved up and down the rows, then stopped at my desk. "How about you, Olivia? Have you read 'The Man Who Would be King'? How about *The Story of the Gadsbys*?"

"You mean *The Great Gatsby*?"

He leaned too close too me, and his hands were on my desk. The little hairs on his knuckles caught the light. Definite boundary issues. Hospital breath. "No, that was Fitzgerald, another fading star."

I wanted to bolt.

Somebody whispered to someone else on the other side of the room. Their heads bent together in my peripheral vision, but I couldn't look away. Mr. Herbert's face moved a half foot from my own. "Even you might be famous in the future." His shoulders scrunched up, and his tongue clicked against the back of his teeth twice. Then he straightened. My heart pounded in relief as he moved away.

"Wouldn't that be something, to teach in the class where a young William Shakespeare listened to your words, where you could observe the child on his way to becoming . . . a shaper of culture?"

Latasha texted, "bghs ntfk," which translated as "bughouse nutfuck."

What Latasha said out loud was, "If I had a time machine, I wouldn't want to teach Sylvia Plath. I'd go back and kill Hitler when he was in high school."

Mr. Herbert jumped like he'd been shocked. "Interesting example, Latasha. Almost prescient. But how would you know him? Hitler, I mean. When he was seventeen, he wanted to be an artist."

He sidled to the front of the class. I'd never actually seen anyone "sidle" before. Peculiar looking.

The class watched, all of them. Something wasn't right with his voice; it quivered, and when he reached the desk and actually stroked his briefcase, I could almost hear the goosebumps rising on the other kids' skin.

Latasha seemed unperturbed, but that's the way she has always been, utterly confident. She called it detachment. She'd told me once that you had to be able to step back from what was going on or you couldn't judge it. When she burned her leg so badly on a motorcycle exhaust pipe last summer (who hops on a motorcyle with a guy she just met while wearing a short skirt anyway?), she said that she smelled the burning skin before she felt it, and it was like it was happening to someone else.

"I'd have a picture of him, of course. Even Hitler didn't know he was Hitler at seventeen."

"Yes." Mr. Herbert laughed, and by then everyone had to have been convinced he was not right. "Hitler didn't know. Mark Twain didn't know. Twain thought he would be a riverboat captain."

He toyed with his briefcase's latch. Suddenly, I pictured a gun in it, or a bomb.

"Now here's an interesting thought." His finger popped the latch, then he pressed it closed with a click. "What if Adolf Hitler and Sylvia Plath were in the *same* high school class? Wouldn't that be an incredible coincidence? Don't you think a historian would love to see their interactions, if he could?" The latch popped open again. He snapped it shut.

Mr. Herbert looked out at us, waiting for an answer. Finally, Taylor said in a shaky voice, "They couldn't be classmates, could they? He was in Germany, and she was American?"

I texted Latasha, "911?"

"Did you know that Plath's epitaph on her tombstone reads, 'Even amidst fierce flames the golden lotus can be planted.' If she and Hitler had been classmates, wouldn't that have been an appropriate message? He would have destroyed and she would have created. But Plath isn't influential enough. No, imagine William Shakespeare and Adolf Hitler in the same class. The bright and dark, side by side, maybe drinking buddies when they were young."

He glanced at his watch. "I don't have much time. Hey, nonny."

No one said anything to that. I wondered if I could text the main office to send help. Maybe I was crazy, and Mr. Herbert was just an eccentric, or he was setting us up for an amazing lesson on John Steinbeck. I was in a classroom once where the teacher staged an argument with a principal. The principal came in and began yelling at her, but it was nonsense, like, "We don't flatter pancakes when they are stuffed with raisins." Then Ms Benda took an umbrella from her desk, put it in the corner of the room, while he pulled an apple, a bouquet of flowers and a flashlight out of a red backpack he carried, dropping them one by one into the trashcan. She walked to the black board and started writing, all the time they were still yelling. This went on for a minute, before she said, "Thank you," and he left. She told us to write down everything that happened in detail in our notebooks. It turned out the whole façade was an exercise in observation and description.

What if Mr. Herbert were doing something like that to us?

Mr. Herbert opened the briefcase. I took a deep breath.

He said, "The real question is what would you do if you met Shakespeare *and* Hitler in the same room. Would it be better to save the literature at the cost of the lives, or should the lives be spent? What if that was your only choice because you couldn't come back in time with a weapon, not even a knife—your companions would know—but you could make a bomb?" When his hand came out of the briefcase, it held a switch. His thumb rested on the button.

My fingers quivered above my phone. It wasn't his words, so much, but the posture of his back, how his head jutted forward to scan us, like a vulture. And, of course, the button.

He said, "The first row is dismissed. Take your books." They filed out, sweat on their brows. One girl whimpered. I knew I didn't need to text anyone. They'd get help. Mr. Herbert dismissed the fourth and fifth row. That left my row and Latasha's. I sat in the back seat. She sat in a front seat, near the door. He walked toward me. "Everyone from here forward can leave."

In a minute it was just Latasha, Mr. Herbert and me. I said, "Why would you kill Shakespeare too?" Under my desk I thumbed a message, "I wll dstract & u run." I hit send. The way Mr. Herbert was turned, he couldn't see her. She shook her head.

He sat on a student desk, his feet on the chair. His pants pulled above his socks, revealing a strip of pale skin. "What if a writer was only great because she wrote out of great suffering? What if she wrote about war and loss so well that she destroyed war forever after that? She'd have no destiny without Hitler. Better she write nothing at all than less than her best."

My phone hummed with a new text, but I couldn't look down. Latasha said, "You can get help."

When he turned to look at her, I checked the message. "Rscue in t/hall."

"I don't need help. I'm saving the world."

A sharp buzzing filled the room. Mr. Herbert's button hand glowed blue and sprayed a shower of sparks. He howled as two men ran in. One tackled him, knocking over seats and desks. The other bent over the briefcase. I found myself standing, backed into a corner. I don't remember getting out of my chair or stepping back.

Latasha hadn't moved. "You boys from the future too?"

They looked at her. For a moment the scene seemed ludicrous. Mr. Herbert wasn't moving. Maybe he was unconscious. The man who had tackled him put a device in his pocket that looked a bit like a toy gun, while the other man held up a box that he'd yanked from the briefcase. It dangled a couple of wires.

"Uh . . . no. We're . . . um . . . the police."

The one at the briefcase had two buttons in the middle of his shirt that were undone, and I'd never seen a police uniform that looked like his. Kind of cheesy, like one that you'd get at a costume shop. But I didn't have much time to look because they both picked up Mr. Herbert and hustled him and the briefcase out the door.

Latasha and I faced each other, then dashed into the hallway. At the end toward the main office, a crowd of kids and the assistant principal stood. Mr. Herbert and the two policemen were gone.

Much later, after we'd been interviewed and debriefed, after our parents came to pick us up, after we stayed up to watch the evening news, I lay in bed staring at the ceiling. My heart had long since settled into a calm rhythm, and my hands had quit shaking, but every time I closed my eyes I could see Mr. Herbert's face six inches from my own, breathing his antiseptic breath in my face.

My phone buzzed beside my head on the nightstand. I picked it up, opened to the screen. The text message from Latasha glowed in the dark. "Whch 1 R U?"

I closed the phone. My counselor at school told me once that most kids change their minds four times about what they are going to be while in college, and very few students end up as they imagined themselves. I pictured a young Adolf Hitler lying in his bed at night, his future stretching out before him like a canvas. Did he know, deep down? Could he sense his destiny?

I thought about how I would text it. How would I send the message? It would be a question I'd send to myself, "Whch 1 M I?"

But I didn't know the answer.

# LIGHT OF A THOUSAND SUNS

*Without beginning, middle or end, of infinite power,*
*of infinite arms, whose eyes are the moon and sun,*
*I see thee, whose face is flaming fire,*
*Burning this whole universe with Thy radiance.*
                                    *-from the Bhagavad Gita*

Trellis noticed the trailer parked at the edge of the Lynwood Mall's parking lot, but he didn't think much about it. He hadn't been sleeping well. Troublesome dreams he couldn't recall. In fact, the idea that maybe the trailer had been there for a couple of days tickled the back of his mind until he dismissed it in the morning's hassles. Penney's had started their big ½ off sale, making traffic in the lot heavy and crowd control a nightmare, so Trellis didn't spend much time watching the monitors. First, a tiny woman who must have been at least ninety-five tried to muscle a thirty-two inch Radio Shack plasma screen television into her minivan and sprained her neck. Waiting for the paramedics to get there, he held her hand. "I'm not really hurt, dears," she kept insisting as they strapped her to a backboard.

Then he spent a half hour helping two high school boys change a flat. After that, a woman so overweight the backs of her arms shifted from side to side when she walked stuffed four hundred dollars worth of stretch slacks and extra-extra large blouses into a baby carriage before strolling out of Foley's. He knew she was a shoplifter the second she came into view of the south exit camera. The bad ones kept their heads down and tried not to look like they were in a hurry. He sprinted to the exit and confronted her before she left the sidewalk. Of course, she swore she knew nothing about the clothes until he started pulling out one item after another.

"They're for my baby girl," she mumbled over and over when Trellis sat beside her as the policeman processed her for arrest. Trellis felt sad. "This isn't the end of the world. You'll grow from this." Catching shoplifters bothered him. He liked it better when he could give tokens to a forlorn five-year-old wandering in the arcade where his mom put him while she shopped. He liked to jiggle the tokens in his pocket when he walked, knowing he would give them away later. Trellis liked watching people buy gifts, and he liked families smiling as they talked to each other, packages in hand.

Trellis didn't look at the trailer again until night had fallen and the mall closed. An old Airstream, a beat up silver bar of soap on wheels, sat at the parking lot's edge, hitched to an even older red pickup with busted running boards. A lone figure walked into the streetlight's illumination, knocked on the door, then disappeared within.

After finishing his rounds, making sure the gates pulled down in front of the stores were latched and the kiosks covered, he checked the parking lot monitors for the last time. No movement from the trailer and no lights within. He signed out for the evening before handing his keys to the night man, a retired car salesman with an extensive collection of dirty jokes.

"How'd it go today?" A long mustard stain marked the night guy's left sleeve.

"Another day, another dollar."

"Ain't it the truth?" The night guy settled into the office chair in front of the monitors. Dim lights showed empty halls, the central fountain no longer spouting, quiet loading docks, and a half dozen views of the parking lot. A sheet of wind-pushed newspaper slid across one screen. "How long you going to keep working both day shifts?"

Trellis shrugged. "Until they get somebody new. I don't mind. Sleep's overrated anyway. I get bad dreams sometimes." He winked. "I'll check that trailer on the way out," he said, looking toward the image.

The hallways smelled of linoleum polish and warm chocolate. Trellis twirled his car keys on one finger as he left the building and walked to his car.

It wasn't until he was ready to pull out of the mall that he noticed the trailer parked by the exit, and he remembered that he said he would check it. He thought it was funny he'd almost forgotten.

Peeling bumper stickers decorated the trailer's back: FRODO

FAILED! THE GOVERNMENT HAS THE RING, and FIGHT-
ING FOR PEACE IS LIKE F***ING FOR CHASTITY. He chuckled at the last one. It struck him as cute when people substituted
asterisks for a curse word, as if that made one not think of the
word. A decal of a mushroom cloud under a red circle and slash
covered one of the dark rear windows.

As he turned onto the street, still laughing, he realized that he
hadn't actually gotten out of his car to check the trailer. Isn't that
odd? he thought.

At home he watched Fox News for an hour. Tucked between a
story about a celebrity scandal, and another chronicling which starlets were pregnant, was a brief piece about a pair of Middle Eastern countries with atomic ambitions. The commentator pointed out
that forty-four countries operated nuclear power plants, all capable
of producing weapon-grade nuclear material. What did a couple
more or less matter?

That night, the dream Trellis remembered was of F***ING
FOR CHASTITY while a television in the background moaned
out an emergency signal. "Seek shelter now," a voice called out.
SEEK . . . SHELTER . . . NOW. Trellis slid around in his dream
bed, never quite able to hold the starlet, and he couldn't tell if what
he heard close by was his breathing or the shrill call of air raid
sirens, and all the time a light so bright he couldn't close his eyes
against it burned in the room. In the dream, the flare beat into his
head, and his heart flapped like wings against his ribs. How can I
catch her under the light of a thousand suns?

It was a most unsatisfying erotic dream.

Trellis found the night guy filling out his records in the security
room. The dawn's golden gleam caught the top of the silver trailer.
Wonder how long that's been there? Trellis thought before remembering he'd seen the Airstream the night before. He checked his
watch: 6:30. On the interior monitors, the morning cleaning crews
worked the mall floors and buffed the display windows, readying
for the 9:00 start of business. A motorized flatbed dolly loaded with
boxes for restocking moved from store to store, but Trellis, munch-
ing his morning donut, concentrated on the trailer where three people
stood in line at the door. It opened, letting one in, and the two re-
maining stood with their arms crossed against the morning cold.
Another person coming from the bus stop walked the length of the
parking lot, vanishing at the edge of one screen to appear at the

edge of the next. He joined the two. They nodded to each other the way strangers do.

"People can't camp out at the mall. Did you call the cops on that trailer?" Trellis asked the night guy.

"What trailer?"

"West parking lot, next to the highway."

The night guy put his flashlight in his locker. He looked puzzled. "I thought about it. I'm pretty sure I did."

"Call it in?"

"No, think about it. Are you positive it was here earlier?"

"Yeah, all day yesterday."

"If it's still parked at closing, we can report it." Then he told Trellis a ten minute long joke about a skinny blonde, her fat boyfriend and a wheelbarrow filled with wet cement.

Trellis glanced at the monitor before heading on his rounds. "Did you notice that trailer?" A strong sense of déjà vu swept over him.

"What trailer?"

While Trellis tested his walkie-talkie's batteries and read the morning's routine, thoughts about the trailer flitted away.

Later, when Trellis stopped at Pretzel Palace for a mid-morning snack, he found himself thinking about a mushroom cloud under a red circle and slash. He finished the pretzel before rushing back to the video surveillance room. No cars were parked next to the trailer, but four people stood outside the door. He headed for the west exit, keeping the trailer's slippery image in his head, pretty sure that if he stopped thinking about it for a moment, it would squirt off like a minnow.

Acetone smells from the nail salon distracted him, but he ignored them long enough to make it to the doors, and by then he could see the silver shape at the parking lot's edge.

"What are you folks doing out here?" Trellis asked as he approached.

"Waiting our turn," said a house-wifey woman in a tie-dye blouse and fringed jeans first in line. Sleep circles so dark that she might as well have a pair of black eyes marked her complexion.

Without a tinge of irony, the man behind her said, "Saving humanity." He wore an "I Served" Marine Corps patch on a flight jacket. His face too was haggard.

Behind them, beyond the sidewalk, traffic zipped by, thirty minutes short of rush hour.

"Do you mind if I go in?" he asked. The people in line creeped him out. Their postures were odd, a strained mix of nervousness and resignation. He imagined inmates on death row if they had to form a line for executions.

"No rush," said Marine Corps patch.

Trellis knocked on the door. The woman who answered stepped onto the metal stair protruding from the trailer's side. A piece of black yarn tied her gray hair into a ponytail. She blinked against the sunlight. "We're going as fast as we can," she said.

"Um, sorry. I'm not with them. Mall security."

"Oh." She turned to the inside. "Mall security."

"Invite him in."

A powerful wave of incense surrounded Trellis as he mounted the stair, and it took a second for his eyes to adjust. A woman who could have been the twin to the one at the door sat at a short and narrow table on the opposite side of the trailer. Beyond her, a small sink, a spice rack, and a drainer holding three plates and three cups were tucked under the cabinets. A curtain hung from ceiling to floor and wall to wall, hiding the rest. The ceiling pressed close enough to Trellis's head that he had to duck. No one else was in the trailer that he could see.

"Sorry to bother you ladies. It's just that you have been in the parking lot for a while, and it doesn't look like you're shopping." He sat on a chair bolted to the wall next to the door.

The lady who had let him in sat next to the other. If they weren't twins, they had to be sisters. "No, we're not."

"We're not doing anything illegal," said the other. She looked at her sister. "At least nothing immoral."

"I didn't say you were," Trellis said. "But what are you doing?"

A man wearing a hooded sweatshirt, the hood up over his head, pushed aside the curtain. In one hand he held a fat white candle, in the other, a long black-bladed knife. "What's the holdup? We're on a schedule."

"Mall security," said the woman next to the curtain.

The man in the sweatshirt glowered at Trellis. "Send the next one in." He closed the curtain with an impatient tug.

The woman closest to Trellis rose. "Excuse me." She squeezed past him and opened the door. "Next."

The tie-dyed housewife shuddered. "Okay." Trellis caught a glimpse of the man behind her before she climbed the stair. He put his hand on her shoulder. "God bless you," he said.

"He will." She stood just inside as if afraid of fully entering.

"How did you find us?" asked the ponytailed women next to the curtain.

The tie-dyed woman rubbed her eyes. "I Googled 'ban the bomb' and followed the links. It was a lot of links."

"We get many that way. It's not too late to go back. You can still change your mind."

The woman closed her eyes tight before taking a ragged breath. "No, this is the right time. It's a good time in my life."

Trellis looked at the three of them, a strange tableau of women talking without making sense. Also, the hooded figure with a knife unnerved him. Trellis put his hand on his walkie talkie, but wasn't sure that a better strategy would be to bolt for the door. None of them were paying attention to him. He'd never listened to a conversation that felt so charged with subtext.

"You know it works?" said the tie-dyed woman "It absolutely works?"

"Yes," said both of the other women.

"I'm in." She took a deep breath, let it out, and then breathed again before walking to the curtain and through. The ponytailed woman closest to the curtain followed her.

"What in the hell is going on here?" said Trellis, perched on the edge of his seat. His voice raised an octave by the end of the question, and his pulse drummed.

The woman eyed him impassively. Finally, she said, "This isn't a good way to start. We haven't been introduced yet. My name is Jennifer." She put out her hand.

Trellis took her fingers in his own. She had a firm and pleasant handshake. "My sister's name is Chastity."

"Trellis," he said, then flinched, recalling his dream. "Chastity?"

"My parents named the younger children after the virtues. My other sisters are Hope and Patience." She paused as if thinking over the practice of naming children. "How old are you?"

"Fifty-four," he said without thinking. How much space was in the trailer beyond the curtain? By his figuring, there could hardly be room for three people on the other side. Whatever they were doing in there, they weren't making any sounds.

"Do you remember nuclear fire drills?" She rested an elbow on the table and the side of her face in her hand.

"What does this have to do with you and whatever you and those people outside are doing?" His chest constricted, as if his skin had shrunk a couple of sizes, compressing his lungs.

"I do," she said. "I remember 'duck and cover.' I remember radiation shelters in the basements of public buildings. You're old enough. Do you remember too?"

She sounded so reasonable and matter of fact. Trellis concentrated on slowing his breathing. For a second he thought he'd just felt coronary twinges, his fate from eating most of his meals in Café Court for the last fifteen years, rotating from one fast food outlet to the next. He was on his feet all day, but he'd noticed the bulge of belly that hung over his belt more and more lately, and his mantra, "I'm big boned," carried less conviction each time he said it. Yes, maybe it was a coronary.

Not that a heart attack was any more comforting than being in a trailer talking to two strange women and a man with a knife.

Trellis felt as if the mall were a thousand miles away, that the trailer existed in an alien landscape. He returned to a familiar script, but it sounded ridiculous to say it. "Ma'am, you can't sit a trailer in a public parking lot overnight. There's zoning to consider."

"Do you want to know why we're here?"

"Sure." His head swam a little. The incense was strong, even stronger than he'd first thought. He could taste it, an exotic flower coating the back of his throat. "Can I have a glass of water?"

Jennifer filled a cup she took from the strainer. He sipped it gratefully.

"It's about the bombs," she said. "It's about duck and cover, and confronting the sword of Damocles."

"I'm sorry?"

She leaned toward him, her hands clasped now, elbows on her knees. "Don't you remember? Didn't you have nuclear nightmares?"

For a second he relived being ten (or was it last week?), where he looked out his windows at the orange glow climbing in the sky, and the sick, lost feeling of recognizing it, too late. Rushing toward him, like in those Civil Defense films, a death wall filled with long glass teeth ready to shred him in an incinerator of instant motion. And he couldn't move, not in the dream. It was always too late. He remembered hiding beneath his desk in third grade like all the other kids, rumps poking out of one side and hands-covered heads poking out the other. Even at the time he thought that his desk would be poor shelter if the roof came down. He sucked his breath in sharply. He had had that dream last week! The illusive dream he never recalled. "I never knew where my family was, in the dreams. I couldn't help them," Jennifer said sadly.

Trellis leaned against the sun-warmed wall. His head swam with incense and the weirdness of the conversation, but what troubled him more were all the nuclear war images he'd ever stored up trying to leak out, every mushroom-clouded nightmare he'd ever dreamed. Nobody talked about nuclear bombs anymore. Atomic bombs were a part of the '60s. They were yesterday's fears. Weren't the bombs locked up safely or destroyed now? "Really, ma'am, this is . . . interesting . . . but I think you're going to have to move the trailer." He stood, being careful not to thump his head on the ceiling. "Um . . . what was that you said about the sword of Damocles?"

She considered him for a moment, still leaning forward. "You came all the way out here to see us. Most people can't come this far. You should see the rest. Come downstairs. Would you tell the folks outside that we'll be a few minutes?"

Trellis opened the door. Sunlight glinted off windshields, and he could hear automobile traffic again. "The lady asks you to be patient." The Marine Corps guy shrugged. The line looked like it had gained a few more people since he'd come in.

The closing door shut out all noise.

Jennifer opened the curtain. "Watch the step," she said as she started down. "There's no bannister."

A long flight of stairs lit by a light at the bottom fell before him.

"How can you have stairs in a trailer?" After a few steps, he knew he was below the surface of the parking lot. "You'll get in trouble for excavating on mall property." But the roughly-carved rock walls didn't look new, nor did the rock stairs worn to a groove in the middle appear freshly quarried. His fingers trailed down the stone as he descended, and patterns cut into the cool rock passed beneath them, like hieroglyphs or maybe something even older: cave carvings perhaps. When he came back, he decided, he'd look at them more closely with his flashlight.

"The mall's a Johnny-come-lately," said the woman. "Besides, the stairs come with the trailer."

The descent emptied into a round chamber fifty feet across with a domed ceiling lit by a large chandelier dangling from chains in the middle and four muted lamps mounted on wall sconces. Chilly, dry air moved across Trellis's face. The hooded man and Chastity sat on a long stone bench in the middle of the room, facing them. A shadow fell across the man's face, so Trellis couldn't see his expression, but he was breathing hard. Chastity's head hung low, and her hands rested flat on the bench, like a woman so tired she'd never get up again.

"Where's the lady who came down here with you?" Trellis couldn't see a door or any place where someone could hide.

Jennifer said, "She made a blessing for all of us."

The man on the bench swept back his hood to reveal a black border of hair around his mostly bald head. He had a vaguely Arabic cast to his skin. "We're suicide bombers," he said, his hand draped loosely over the knife.

Trellis wondered if his walkie-talkie would work underground or if it wasn't already too late for him to think such thoughts.

"Nobody covers us on the ten-o-clock news, though," said Jennifer. "People don't even see us unless they are already looking." She walked across the room to her sister. "Your turn to work the trailer. Maybe a cup of tea would do you some good."

Chastity sighed and gathered herself. "That woman had kids, she told me. An eight-year-old girl and four-year-old boy. I begged her not to go through with it, but she did. I don't like the ones with kids."

"Where is she?" Trellis asked again.

Chastity said, "Over 2,300 people are reported missing every day. Some never turn up."

The hooded man looked at her, clearly annoyed. He turned to Trellis. "Didn't you ever wonder how suicide bombers could do it? Strap the explosive around their chests. Give up everything they ever will have for what? To kill a handful of people. Even the most successful ones don't get more than a score or two. Doesn't the trade seem inequitable? Everything for a few lives, and they have to know that their single sacrifice won't make the difference. Most of the time they aren't even killing their enemies. They're just killing. They have to have seen the results of the other bombers' work. A line or two in the newspaper. Maybe a poster in their neighborhood celebrating their gesture. That's it. Conditions don't change. So how do they do it?"

"Are you saying that woman blew herself up? I didn't hear an explosion."

"It's for the magic," said the hooded man. "There's magic in the sacrifice, they figure. If they make the sacrifice, then the gods will smile at them to drive their enemies away. They do it to better the world. They think they are saving lives in the long run, making the world a better place."

"But it's evil. What kind of motivation is that, suicide for evil?" asked Jennifer. "And their magic doesn't work. They don't really have magic."

Chastity walked past him toward the stairs. "Over 2,300 people a day. Almost 900,000 a year. Some vanish for sacred reasons. I'll bring the next one down."

The hooded man checked his watch. "Good. We're running late."

"Late for what?" Trellis glanced from one to the other. Nothing made sense.

"The clock's ticking. It's just a few minutes to midnight," said the hooded man. "It's always ticking."

"No, it's the middle of the afternoon." Trellis took a step toward Jennifer and the hooded man, not sure of what to do. This situation certainly wasn't a part of mall security training. Behind them, on the other side of the bench, he saw a pit. He sidled around the bench, keeping his distance from the two of them, and the pit's dimensions became clearer. Eight or nine feet across and deep, so deep that he knew now where the breeze he'd felt when he entered the chamber came from.

"We have real magic," Jennifer said, "and better motivation." She turned on the bench so her feet nearly dangled over the drop. "That is the throat of the world."

"Sort of the ultimate wishing well," said the hooded man. He crossed his arms, still holding his black-bladed knife. "We don't toss in coins."

Trellis felt stupid and so weirdly out of place that he wondered if he wasn't still dreaming last night's dream. The air rising from the well tasted like a museum, a clean and dry library breeze that had traveled across a long desert, brushing the tops of dunes and rows of books for hundreds of miles before funneling to his face.

"Magic's like life," said Jennifer. "It's all a trade."

Trellis stood on the well's edge but he didn't feel vertigo or the normal nervousness he had about heights. At his feet, though, a dark wet stain marked the stone, and he knew before he dipped his finger in that it was blood. "What happened to the lady who came down with you?"

"Do you still have nuclear nightmares, Trellis? Do you know how many nuclear warheads there are in the world?" Jennifer stared at him intently. "Twenty-eight thousand, give or take several thousand."

The hooded man said, "She made a trade. I told you, we're suicide bombers. We're anti-war wizards and witches."

The sound of footsteps came down the stairs. Trellis turned from the pit. Chastity led the Marine Corps patch man toward them. Her hand held his as they walked into the chamber. The man's knuckles were white. His eyes were closed. Trellis imagined how hard he must be gripping.

"You might not want to see this." The man with the knife pulled his hood over his head.

Trellis backed away until his hands met the wall.

Chastity stood on her tiptoes to whisper into the Marine Corps man's ear. He mouthed something back to her, and with evident difficulty, let go of her hand. She directed him to the edge of the pit, then faced him toward Trellis, his eyes still closed.

Without a word, the hooded man drew his knife across the candle, as if he were coating the blade. He stepped around the bench to stand beside the man. Their breathing filled the room along with the thudding rush of Trellis's pulse. The hooded man met Trellis's eyes. "It's a one to one trade. One life. One bomb."

He plunged the blade into the man's chest and then pushed him over the edge in a single move.

Trellis blinked. Except for a runnel of blood creeping down the hooded man's wrist and a single drop that fell to the stone floor with a hollow plink, there was no motion and no sound. The rush of Trellis's beating heart seemed to have stopped. No one breathed.

"What did you do?" asked Trellis, his voice a dry squeak.

Jennifer said, "Made the world safer."

Pushing himself away from the wall, Trellis approached the pit's edge. The hooded man and Jennifer moved aside. From the pit, air continued to push steadily out, just as clean and dry as before.

The hooded man crossed the chamber and knelt at a small chest. He took out a towel and carefully wiped the knife blade. A hand touched Trellis's wrist. Jennifer stood beside him. "Somewhere in a

Kansas silo or a Russian submarine in the Atlantic or an arms depot in India, what used to be a warhead is now an inert hunk of metal, and thousands, maybe hundreds of thousands of people are a little safer. You need the right knife, the right spell, and the throat of the world." She swallowed hard. "And a suicide bomber."

"Did you really kill him?" Nothing about the scene struck him as real. The feeling that he could still be dreaming came to him again. In a moment, he would be back to pursuing starlets, and maybe this time they wouldn't be too slippery to hold. He clenched his fingernails into the palm of his hand, but the pain did nothing to wake him. Was the Marine Corps man still falling? Trellis thought about the line of people waiting outside the trailer, all the people he'd seen gathered at the trailer since yesterday.

"Not killing," said Jennifer. "He allowed it himself. There's a difference."

Blood rushed from Trellis's face. He swayed, and for a second he wondered what would happen if he fainted. "You're monsters."

Jennifer's eyes teared up. "Yes, I suppose we are. It's hard to live with. I won't have to for long. There's a bomb with my name written on it in my future." She still held his wrist. "There may be no forgiveness for us, what we do here, but we're small monsters stopping giant ones, and the victims here are volunteers."

Chastity's voice came down the stairs. "Are you ready for the next?" She sounded profoundly tired.

Trellis twisted his wrist away, covered his nose and mouth as if the air were poisonous, a contagion to be blocked. Half way up the stairs, he nearly knocked over an old man wearing a bathrobe holding Chastity's hand. In a blink Trellis stood inside the mall, gasping for breath. Soft music washed over him. A young mom balancing a toddler on her hip put a dollar in quarters into the rent-a-stroller display. Three teenager girls wearing ear phones talked animatedly as they looked into each others' bags from The Gap. "That color would look so good on me," said one. "Oh, you can borrow it whenever," said her friend.

Trying not to stagger, Trellis found an empty table in Café Court. Shoppers came and went carrying trays filled with pizza or hamburgers or rice bowls. Conversations babbled around him. After he'd sat for over an hour, his breathing settled but his muscles hung without an ounce of strength. The mall music played an instrumental version of Barry McGuire's "The Eve of Destruction." A string and piano rendition of Bob Dylan's "A Hard Rain's a-Gonna Fall" followed.

In the music he could hear the stone chamber breathing before the man with the Marine Corps patch pitched backward, the solid thud the knife made when it connected, like a fist hitting a watermelon. But he also heard air raid sirens and the chant of "duck and cover." And for a long time his thinking locked into a droning mantra, *the light of a thousand suns the light of a thousand suns the light of a thousand suns* (It was murder, wasn't it, what he saw? Surely murder!). He caught himself sobbing. Seek safety now, he longed to shout to the patrons around him. SEEK . . . SAFETY . . . NOW, and he wondered how he could have gone day to day for all his years with such denial, such forgetfulness.

How would he go on from today?

Time passed. He knew it did. It didn't matter. All that mattered was what he should do. All that mattered waited in a silver Airstream sitting on the edge of the parking lot, ten feet from passing traffic, a block from a Starbucks to the north, a block from Barnes and Noble to the south, and directly above the throat of the world, a deep, dry and hungry well.

The night guy sat in the chair opposite Trellis. "Mall's closing in twenty minutes, bud, and you haven't started the evening check list. You all right?"

Trellis leaned back. His vertebrae crackled. How long had he been hunched at the table? He looked around. A couple of the restaurants had pulled their security gates part way from the ceiling, even though they weren't supposed to close up before the end of the day. The dark blue of twilight filled the skylights above.

"I'll be there in a minute." His voice didn't quiver, which surprised him.

The night guy's expression turned concerned.

Trellis forced a smile. "Really, give me a minute."

Soon after the night guy left, Jennifer filled his seat. In the mall's light her hair was more silver than gray and the age rays around her eyes were more pronounced.

"I would have thought you would pull up stakes when I left."

Jennifer shook her head. "You wouldn't call the police. Only people willing to come our way find us."

"I don't know what you mean," he said, but it occurred to him that the night guy wouldn't have known what Trellis was talking about if he had asked him about the trailer.

She wrapped her hands over his. "You didn't answer me earlier. You do have nuclear nightmares, don't you? You wake up at night so sick with fear you can hardly move? That's why you came to us."

Trellis tried to remember. Did he have those dreams often? Were his dreams so horrible that he blocked them from his memory every night? With Jennifer's warm hands covering his own, he was suddenly sure that he did. He'd always had the dreams. They truly were ghastly, and now that he knew, he doubted he would ever fall asleep again with peace in his heart.

He thought Jennifer saw what he was thinking in his eyes. Maybe she'd said this very thing to other souls who quit denying what they'd known all along, who looked up and saw Damocles's dangling sword. She said, "There's magic in the world, Trellis. It's not the magic you think about from fairytales, but it's there just the same trying to protect you. There's magic out there trying to save us all."

She squeezed his hands once. "There will be a place for you in line, Trellis. There will always be a place for you, when you're ready." She stood to leave. "I have to get back. Midnight's coming."

# OF LATE I DREAMT OF VENUS

Like a shiny pie plate, Venus hung high in the observation alcove's window, a full globe afire with sunlight. Elizabeth Audrey contemplated its placid surface. Many would say it was gorgeous. Alexander Pope called the bright light "the torch of Venus," and some ancient astronomer, besotted with the winkless glimmer, named the planet after the goddess of love and beauty. At this distance, clouded bands swirled across the shimmering lamp, illuminating the dark room. She held her hands behind her back, feet apart, watching the flowing weather patterns. Henry Harrison, her young assistant, sat at a console to the window's side.

"Soon," he said.

"Shhh." She sniffed. The air smelled of cold machinery and air scrubbers, a tainted chemical breath with no organic trace about it.

Beyond Venus's wet light, a mantle of stars shown with measured steadiness. One slipped behind the planet's fully lit edge. Elizabeth could measure their orbit's progress by the swallowing and spitting out of stars.

Elizabeth said, "Did you talk to the surgeon about your scar?"

Henry touched the side of his face, tracing a line from the corner of his eye to his ear.

"No. It didn't seem important."

"You don't need to live with it. A little surgery. You heal in deep sleep. Two hundred years from now when we wake, you'll be . . . improved." She lifted her foot from the floor with a magnetic click and then snapped down hard a few inches away. "I hate free fall. How long?"

"Final countdown. We'll be back in the carousel soon and you can have your weight again."

The scene from the window cast a mellow light. Silent. Grand.

A poet would write about it if one were here.

"Ahh," said Elizabeth. A red pustule rose in the planet's swirling atmosphere. She leaned forward, put her palms against the window. Orange light boiled in the clouds, spreading away from the bloody center, disrupting the bands. "It's begun."

Henry read data on his screens. Input numbers. Checked other monitors. Tapped keys quickly. "A clean hit, on target." He didn't look at the actual show beyond, but watched his sensitive devices instead. "Beta should strike . . . now."

A second convulsion colored the disk, this one a brilliant white at its center which settled into a deep red, overlapping the first burst's color. A third flash, duller, erupted on the globe.

"Was that . . .?"

"Perfect as your money could buy."

In the next ten minutes, four more hits. Elizabeth stood at the window while red and orange storms pulsed in Venus's disk. Henry joined her, mirroring her stance. He pursed his lips. "You can see the dust. If this had been Earth, the dinosaurs would have died seven times."

The planet's silver sheen faded somewhat, and lightning flashes flickered in the roiling confusion.

"No dinosaurs ever walked there, Henry."

He sighed. "Venus has its own charms, or it did."

Elizabeth looked at him. The reflected light from the window caught in his dark eyes. They were the best part of him, the way they looked at her when he didn't think she noticed. Sometimes she wished she could just fall in love with his eyes, but then she saw the scar, and he really was too short and so young, ten years shy of her forty, practically a child, although a brilliant and efficient one. She'd ask the surgeon on her own. Henry would hardly object to a few cosmetic changes while he slept. What else was there to do during the down time anyway except to improve? She had been considering thinning her waist a bit, toning her back muscles.

Henry clopped back to his station, then studied figures on a screen she couldn't see. "There are seismic irregularities, as predicted, making the final calculations more difficult, but the planet is spinning slightly faster now, just a bit. We've also pushed it out of its orbit a bit. The next series will bump it back. You're one step closer to your new Earth."

She turned from him, irritated. "If Venus *only* becomes another

Earth, I failed. We can make it better. A planet to be truly proud of. How are things on Earth, anyway?"

His fingers flicked over the controls. "In the twenty-seven years we slept, your corporation in the asteroid belt has tripled in size, improving the ability to redirect asteroids above projections. We're two years ahead of schedule there. The Kuiper Belt initiative is also ahead of schedule." He reread a section. "We're having trouble with the comet deflection plan. Lots of support for redirecting the Earth-crossing asteroids, but opposition to the comets. Some groups contest our aiming them *all* at Venus. There's a lobby defending Halley's Comet for its 'historical and traditional values,' as well as several groups who argue that 'comets possess a lasting mythic and aesthetic relation with the people of Earth.' The political wing of the advertising and public relations departments are working the problem, but they have requested budget increases."

Elizabeth snorted derisively. "Give them Halley's Comet. It doesn't have as much water as it used to anyway."

"Noted." Henry sent the order. "Your investments and companies are sound."

"How is the United Nation's terraforming project on Mars going?"

"Badly. They've lost momentum."

"Too big of a project to run by democracies and committees. Too long." She sighed. "If nothing needs my attention, then I suppose it's time for bed."

Henry shut his monitors off, powered down the equipment. A metal curtain slid across the view window, separating them from Venus's tortured atmosphere. "Two hundred years hardly seems like going to bed. Everyone I know will be dead when we awake."

Elizabeth shrugged. "They're all twenty-seven years older than when you talked with them last. As far as they're concerned, you're the dead one."

A door opened in the center of the floor. Elizabeth looked down the ladder that connected the alcove with the rest of the habitat. The ladder rotated beneath her. She timed her step to land on the top rung, then moved down so she held the ladder, leaving her head and shoulders at floor level. The room turned slowly around her. "No second thoughts, Henry. You knew the cost going in."

He nodded at her. She saw in his eyes the yearning. The dream of a terraformed Venus hadn't brought him onto the project, made him say good-bye to everyone he'd ever known, committed him to a project on a time scale never attempted.

No, he came for her.

The rotation turned her so she didn't have to see his gaze. She continued down the ladder. Mostly she thought about the project and the long line of asteroids on their way to add their inertia to Venus's spin, but below those thoughts ran a thread about Henry. She thought, as long as he remains a reliable assistant, what does it matter why he signed up? Henry Harrison isn't the first man who worked for me because he wanted me.

Two hundred years of suspended life, trembling on death's edge, metabolism so slow that only the most sensitive instruments detected it. Busy nanomechs coursing through the veins, correcting flaws, patching breakdowns, keeping the protein machine whole and ready to function. Automatic devices moving the still limbs through a range of motion every day, maintaining joint flexibility, stretching muscles, reminding the body that it was alive because really, really, Elizabeth Audrey, the richest human being who ever lived, whose wealth purchased and sold nations, whose power now stretched over generations, was mostly dead. A whisper could end it.

Maybe in her dreams she heard that deadly voice caressing her, and she would hear it for sure if she were a weaker woman, but if she did hear, she ignored it. Instead she dreamed of Venus transformed. A vision big enough for her ambition. A Venus fit for her feet. A planet done right, not like old Earth, sputtering in its wastes. A Venus fit for a queen.

Elizabeth walked spinward in the carousel; the silky robe she donned after the doctors revived her flapped against her bare legs. Two hundred years didn't feel bad, and the slimming in her waist gave her a limberness she didn't remember from before. The air smelled fresher too, less metal-washed. It should, she thought. Much of her money was devoted to research and development.

Henry joined her in the dining room for breakfast.

"What's the progress?" she asked. Bacon and egg scents seeped from the kitchen.

He smiled. "How did you sleep? How are you feeling? Good to see you. It's only been two centuries."

Elizabeth waved the questions away. "Are we on schedule?"

Henry shrugged. "As we projected, the plans evolved. There have been breakthroughs that make the job easier. We've shaded the planet with a combination of solar shields, aluminum dust rail-gunned from the moon, and both manned and unmanned reflective aerostat structures in the upper atmosphere, cooling it considerably, although we have a long way to go. An unforeseen benefit has been dry ice harvesting, which we've been selling to the U.N's Mars project. Venus's frozen greenhouse gasses are heating Mars. Of course, the bombardment of asteroids and comets has been continuous."

A young man, carrying a tray of covered plates, walked toward them from the kitchen. He wore his dark hair short, and his loose, pale shirt was buttoned all the way to his neck. He nodded at Henry as he put the tray in front of them, but he seemed to avoid looking at Elizabeth. Without waiting for thanks, he backed away.

"Who was that?" Elizabeth uncovered a steaming omelet.

"Shawcroft. He's a bio-ecopoiesis engineer. Good man. He helped design an algae that grows on the underside of the aerostats for oxygen production. The surface is still too warm for biologicals."

Elizabeth tasted the omelet. The food made her stomach uneasy, and didn't look as appetizing as she hoped. "What's he doing serving me breakfast then?"

Henry laughed. "To see you, of course. You're *the* Elizabeth Audrey, asleep for two hundred years, but still pulling the strings. His career exists because of your investments. He won a lottery among the crew to bring out the tray."

"What about you? He acted like he knew you."

Uncovering his plate, Henry revealed a pancake under a layer of strawberries. "I've been awake for four years. He and I play handball almost every day."

Elizabeth chewed a small bite thoughtfully. Henry's face did look older.

"What did you think of my gift?"

Henry touched the side of his face between his eye and ear. Without smiling he said, "For a couple of years I was mad as hell. I'm sorry you reminded me." His fork separated a strawberry and chunk of pancake from the rest.

Elizabeth tried to meet his eyes. He couldn't be seriously angry. Without the scar, he looked much better.

He put the fork down, the bite uneaten. "Are you ready for a visit to Laputa? You can check the facilities, and they would be honored if you came down."

"Laputa?" She relaxed in the remembering, not realizing until then that she'd been tense. After two hundred years, so much could have changed. When she let the doctor hook her to the complicated devices, she had thought about unstable governments, about unplanned celestial events, about changes in corporate policy. Who could guarantee that she'd wake up in the world she'd designed? This was the great leap of faith she'd made when she started the project. The plan for her to see it to the end would be to outlive everyone around her, and the way to do that was to be the test subject for the long sleep. Henry, for obvious reasons, accompanied her. "You really named the workstation that?"

"A city now. Much more than a station. The name was in your notes. I don't think Jonathan Swift imagined it this way, though." He pushed his plate away. "It's quite a bit bigger than the initial designs. The more functions we built in, the more cubic feet of air we needed to keep from sinking into the hotter regions of the atmosphere. It's the largest completely man-made structure in the solar system. Tourist traffic alone makes it profitable."

The trip from the carousel to Laputa took a little more than an hour under constant acceleration or deceleration except for a stomach lurching moment midway when the craft turned. Out the porthole beside her seat, she could see Venus's changed face. Where the sun hit, it was much darker, but the sun itself was darker too, fuzzy and red, partly blocked by the dust umbrella protecting the planet from the heat, cooling it from its initial 900 degrees Fahrenheit. Henry offered a glass of wine. She sipped it, enjoying its crisp edge. Wine swirled in the bottom of the glass. She sipped again, held the taste in her mouth for a few seconds before swallowing. "I don't recognize this."

He sat across from her. The wine bottle rested in a secure holder in the table's center. "It's an eighty-year-old Chateau Laputa. One of the original bottles of Venusian aperitif. Bit of a gamble. Some of this vintage didn't age well, but it turns out being thirty percent closer to the sun makes for excellent grapes. They grew them in soil from the surface, heavily treated, of course." The ferry shuddered. "Upper edges of the atmosphere. We'll be there soon."

Through the porthole, Laputa appeared first as a bright red glimmer on Venus's broad horizon, and as they grew closer, revealing details. Elizabeth realized the glow was the sun's reflected light. And then she saw Laputa truly was huge; it felt like flying low over the San Gabriels into the Los Angeles basin, when the city opened beneath her. But Laputa dwarfed that. They continued to travel, bumping hard through turbulence until the floating city's boundaries disappeared to the left and right, and then they were over the structure, their shadow racing across the mirrored surface.

Inside she toured the engineering facilities where they built floating atmosphere converters to work on the carbon dioxide gasses that trapped so much heat. She met dozens of project managers and spoke briefly to a room full of chief technicians. They didn't ask questions. They didn't act like the groups of upper management she was used to working with. There was no jockeying for position, none of the push and pull of internal politics that made corporate board rooms so interestingly tense. None of the high stakes adrenaline she was so used to. They listened. They took notes. They answered her questions, but they were quiet, attentive. Worshipful, almost.

Henry drove her in a compact electric cart to the physics labs that controlled the steady rain of Kuiper Belt objects bringing water to the planet, even though it still boiled into vapor on the scalding surface. In a large presentation room, dominated by a map of the solar system alive with lights, each representing a ship or a station, the chief geologist finished his speech. A long line of dots representing asteroids and Kuiper Belt objects in transit traced a curved path through the system ending at Venus. "Fifteen years from now, liquid water will exist at the poles. We should have northern and southern hemisphere lakes by the time you inspect again, perhaps the beginning of an ocean if the weather patterns develop according to the models." He bowed when he finished and kept his eyes lowered.

Everywhere they went, and everyone they talked to treated her with the same deference. Only Henry would meet her gaze. "You are *the* Elizabeth Audrey," he said again when she complained. "Maker of worlds. Come with me. I think you'll enjoy this. We have transport waiting."

They walked out of a physics lab, leaving behind obsequious scientists and engineers. Henry led, and Elizabeth noticed as she had before that he was a short man. If he were only six or seven inches taller, he might earn more respect. Their next sleep was scheduled for four hundred years. If she talked to the doctors, they could do the work and Henry would not need to be bothered with the decision himself. After all, if he was going to be her sole representative in the future where no one knew her except as the ultimate absentee boss, then he should look the part.

"This is it," he said as the car sped from between two buildings. He stopped and sat beside her while she took it in. A wall of structures a mile away loomed over a plain, a part of the huge circle that enclosed the space. High overhead, Laputa's roof arced to the far horizons. The sun glowed sullenly, a red bright spot in the dark sky. Away from the city's artificial light, red tinted her arms, the metal edges on the car, Henry's face. She turned her hands over. Even her palms took on a red shade.

"What is this place?"

"Blister Park. Come on."

As soon as they stepped out of the car, Elizabeth saw. The floor was clear. Beneath their feet swirled the clouds of Venus, almost black in Laputa's shadow, but far away the city stopped and sunlight came down, illuminating a smoky show of reds and oranges and browns. They moved farther from the car, away from the building, and soon the illusion that they were walking on air seemed almost complete.

Below, in the shadow, bright red and yellow lights twinkled.

"Volcanoes," said Henry. "Venus was volcanically active before, but our asteroid and comet bombardment to spin the planet provoked eruptions. The atmospheric technicians tell me this is good, though. They use the new chemicals in the air to catalyze out what they don't want and to create what they do. There will be a breathable atmosphere before they are done."

"Keeping in mind the improvements in technology, how long until I can walk on the ground unprotected?"

"Still another thousand years or so. If we engineer ourselves instead, it would be much quicker. We need heat tolerance, and a system that uses less oxygen."

"For the workers, yes. The ones that prepare the way, but Venus will not be complete until it is the planet that Earth should have been." She could picture it, a surface rich with forests, and an eco-system in balance, humanity appropriately humble in the face of a world done right.

"But this has a beauty of its own." Henry moved beside her. The light from below cast shadows on his face.

"It was ugly when we started, Henry. Almost no rotation. Hundreds of degrees too hot. Too much carbon dioxide. Pressure at the surface equivalent to being a kilometer underwater. No life. Nothing. The least attractive spot in the solar system, and it's still ugly now. It will be beautiful, though, when I'm done. When I've re-shaped it."

Elizabeth walked toward the middle of Blister Park. She held her hands away from her sides, palms down, like a tightrope walker. If she didn't look up, all she saw beyond her feet were clouds and the volcanoes' dim pulsing. Surprisingly, she felt no vertigo. She moved on the invisible surface as if she'd been born to it. "I'm a god," she said.

In a four hundred year long dream, knowing she was dreaming, Elizabeth ran down a long hill with her brother. She hadn't known her brother. He died at childbirth, one of the thousands who didn't make it through the still birth plagues where children were so warped in gestation they couldn't draw breath on their own. It became simpler and more merciful to let them die, death after death. Science took just a few years to find the cause of the plague that killed her brother, the first of the toxic-Earth plagues, but it was too late for him.

In the dream, though, he ran beside her toward the stream that flowed through cool grasses. At the edge, they stopped. No frogs today. No crawdads hiding under rocks. She didn't know why she'd expected frogs and crawdads; they were never in the dream, never, but still the same disappointment washed through her. A boggy flat stretched from both sides, and the reeds that poked up through the smelly muck were brown and broken. A mass of cardboard stuck out of the water, covered with a noxious-looking slime.

Elizabeth held her brother's hand as they walked downstream, careful to keep their feet dry. Around the corner the stream ducked under a fence and into a park. They pushed open a gate. Here, closely clipped lawn painted the hill to a cement curb lining the stream, which now flowed through an open culvert. Signs warned them to stay out of the water, but her brother lay on his chest, reaching down to touch the ripples. In the dream, Elizabeth tried to shout, but her throat constricted. His fingers brushed the water, and then he turned to look at her, his eyes serious and dark (where had she seen those eyes before?). A scar marked the side of his face. She wanted to rub it away, but when she dropped to her knees to touch him, his skin had grown cold, like a statue. And then he was a statue, a bronze of a boy lying on his side by a stream, his clothes a solid metal, a patina of corrosion in the places that were not buffed smooth.

Elizabeth sat beside him, beside the contained stream. In the sky, no clouds, but a dozen contrails crisscrossed each other, like a giant tic tac toe game. The air smelled of city and too many people piled on one another, story on story in high rises beyond the park. A clatter of metal against metal clanged in the distance. More construction. On the stream's other side, flowers in unnaturally neat rows filled a garden held behind a plastic border. She looked back beyond the fence where trash filled the water. Neither was right. She knew neither was right, but it was too late to shout. Her brother was dead, and she had no breath behind her scream. The statue couldn't hold her hand.

Elizabeth couldn't breathe. She choked and then coughed, an unproductive spasm that didn't give her a chance to inhale before she coughed again. Her chest hurt. People bustled around her, but she hadn't opened her eyes yet. She was suffocating. Someone held her hand. A mask went over her face, and pressure built up within it, pushing against her eyeballs.

"Relax, Eliza. Let the machine help you."

She opened her mouth, allowing the pressure's force to open her throat, filling her lungs. The air tasted sweet! She could feel tears pooling where the mask wrapped her cheeks. The pressure relented and she exhaled on her own before it built again, respirating her at its own pace.

She took slow breaths, each one quivering on the trigger of another spasm, but breath by breath the urge to cough subsided until her lungs moved easily. "I don't need this," she tried to say, but the mask muffled her. She tapped the hard surface with her finger. The mask came off. She was in the awakening room. A doctor stood to one side, the mask clasped, ready to put it back if her breathing struggled. Beside him, a technician bent over what looked like a small clipboard. When he turned, she saw information flashing across the surface. Her information, she assumed. Henry sat on the edge of the bed, holding her hand.

For a minute she inhaled and exhaled carefully, testing each movement. Then she looked at him. "Did you call me Eliza?" Her voice cracked and felt dry in her throat.

He let go of her hand. "Sorry. Emotional moment."

"Don't let it happen again." She shut her eyes. "Where are we?"

"Laputa, but we've anchored. The floating city's era has passed. Not enough pressure in the atmosphere."

Later, Elizabeth and Henry walked a hallway in the infirmary. Her steps were unsteady. When they turned a corner, she almost fell. Henry grabbed her arm to hold her upright. They had dressed her in a white robe with stiff, exaggerated collar and cuffs. Change of fashion she guessed.

"It was harder this time."

"We're into new territory in long sleep. Others have been packed, but it's just until cures for their diseases are found or they outlive their enemies or they want a one-way trip to the future. If they've got the money, they can buy the bed. The arc ships heading to the Zeta Reticula system use long sleep too. It's a 4,000 year trip, but they're waking up every one-hundred years for equipment maintenance. Only you and I have slept so long uninterrupted."

Elizabeth shook her head, trying to clear the fuzziness. "Am I damaged?" She took longer steps as if she could force strength upon herself.

"I hope not, or I'm damaged too. They're still testing me, and I've been up for six years. I told them I was okay after a week." They turned another corner in the hall. Henry held her arm again, making Elizabeth feel like an old woman, which she was, now that she thought about it. "We're walking to an auditorium now. There will be a ceremony. The people want to see you."

"Public relations never goes away."

Henry looked diplomatic. The extra years he had been awake gave his face more character than Elizabeth remembered. A map of tiny wrinkles sprung from the corners of his dark eyes. "Well, the situation's a bit more complicated than that. We should have foreseen."

Elizabeth moved steadily forward, already more confident, eager to see how much closer they were to her goal. "Complicated how?"

"Lots of changes. Governments have risen and fallen. Politics went through several evolutions. The business environment metamorphed during the time."

"They didn't nationalize me, did they?" Elizabeth stopped. The idea that she might have lost control frightened her. Her stomach knotted. The companies, the investments, the foreboding weight of her multi-industrial empire might have fled her grasp in the years she slept. Anything could have happened while she slumbered. "They haven't taken my assets?"

Henry gazed down at her solemnly. Elizabeth realized the doctors had done their work. He was now at least two or three inches taller than she. His hair matched his eyes, still black. Some gray there would give him more distinction. She made a note to herself to order the change for him, maybe a deeper timbre to his voice to give him authority.

"We should have known that a corporation couldn't last for hundreds of years, Elizabeth. Even a dozen decades would be asking for a lot, but your CEOs, multiple generations of them, made decisions to preserve your initiative. We're still on schedule."

"I can talk to heads of state. Solidify our position." She pictured the crowded board rooms, the private conversations over expensive dinners at exclusive restaurants, the phone calls and e-mails, all with her at the center, pulling threads, massaging egos, handing down favors with imperial aplomb.

"You won't need to." He led her to a set of double doors. Inside, two lines of exquisitely dressed men and women gave them a hallway to walk through. Many of the people bowed as Elizabeth and Henry passed. Elizabeth still didn't feel completely focused. A surreal air hovered about the scene. "Madam Audrey," one man said as he touched the back of his hand to his forehead and bent at the waist. No one else spoke. At the hallway's end, an ornate set of doors that reached to the high ceiling swung open. Elizabeth slowed. She couldn't see the other side of the dark room beyond, but it seemed huge, and there was movement in the dark. Lights flooded a stage that she and Henry stepped onto. She shaded her eyes, and the roar began, hundreds of thousands of voices, cheering, cheering, cheering, and they were cheering for her.

Henry leaned in, cupped his hand around her ear. "They arranged for you to become a religion. It's the only organization that would last long enough to see it to the end."

The next morning, Elizabeth joined Henry in a vehicle garage where a heavily insulated truck waited for them. "First," said Henry, "I want to point out that we are going to exit through those doors and into a Venus morning. Thirteen hours from now, the sun will set. Your original plan was for a twenty-four hour day/night cycle, but after four-hundred years of asteroid and comet bombardment, the terraformers saw that we were getting diminishing returns. At some point, each collision produced more problems for them to undo than they were solving, so they decided to stop and leave Venus with a longer day."

Elizabeth frowned. "I don't like compromise." She did feel steadier on her feet than she had yesterday, and climbed into the car before Henry could give her assistance. "What's second?"

"Best I show you." He pulled the truck into an airlock. When the outside doors opened, a red, dusty light flooded the bay. Elizabeth slid close to the window. A graded road led into a series of low hills that faded in the hazy red air. The car pulled out of the garage, and for the first time, Elizabeth could see first hand what her efforts had produced. A brisk breeze whipped dust off the road ahead of them.

"Still warm, still too much carbon dioxide, still too much surface pressure, but we're very close, Elizabeth." The truck climbed the first hill, and from the top, as far as the dusty air allowed, similar hills reached all around. "The final changes go the slowest."

In front of them, the morning sun glared red and unbelievably large. The truck lurched through a turn as it ascended a second hill.

"I thought there would be more evidence of the meteor strikes."

Henry laughed. "Oh, heavens, there is, but it's all on the equator. We have created a badlands like nothing this solar system has ever seen. Some of the strikes broke the tectonic plates, bringing up rock from thousands of feet below the surface, liquefying, vaporizing, shattering. Venus' equator regions are already legendary. Anything could get lost there or hide there. It truly is untamable. See this?" He held out his wrist. A shiny black bracelet set with green and yellow stones caught the sun light. "The metal is carbon nanotubes. If you need it made out of carbon, Venus can make it.

Every spaceship hull in the solar system is manufactured here. The jewels were mined in the badlands. Ah, we're here."

He stopped the truck on the hilltop. Before them, a lake rippled in the wind, filling the valleys so that what she had thought were other hills earlier she could see were islands.

Elizabeth gasped. "Liquid water."

"Do you want to go fishing?"

"Really?"

Henry rested his forearms on the steering wheel and looked out onto the lake. "Kind of a joke. No, not this time. There are thermophilic shrimp, though, and adapted corals, engineered crabs, modified algaes, mutated anemones, evolved sponges, and dozens of other heat-happy organisms who like water just short of boiling. About the biggest thing out there that we know of is a heat tolerant eel that grows to a foot or so. I've been boating at night. Almost all the species we introduced bioluminescence. It makes them easier to keep track of. Blues, yellows, greens. The boat's wake is a trail of fire." He sounded meditative. His fingers dangled, nearly touching the dashboard. Elizabeth had never noticed before how strong his hands looked. Calluses marked the fingertips. A line of dark grit was under his fingernails. "On land, we've introduce lichens, soil bacterias, nothing complicated. They do best near the lakes. Rain is undependable."

"How long did you say you were awake before you woke me up?"

He didn't turn his head. "Six years. I wanted to make sure everything was ready for you."

She looked at the lake again. A film of black dust piled at the corner of the window like a soot snow drift. The wind picked up, tearing froth off the tops of waves, and it moaned, passing over the truck. Elizabeth couldn't imagine finding anything attractive in the desolate landscape. Dry, toxic, inhospitable except for the most primitive of life. She pictured its surface in six hundred years, when she awoke. Brush would cover the hills and heather would fill the valleys. Willows would line the bank of this heated lake. What did Henry see in it now?

Henry said, "The doctors are worried about putting you to sleep for so long. Your system didn't respond the way they would like."

Outside a bank of clouds moved across the sun, casting the lake and hills into a weird, maroon twilight. Dust devils twirled off the road before beating themselves into nothingness in the rocks higher on the hills. If the wind uncovered a bizarre version of a cow's skull, dry and leering, by the road, Elizabeth would not have been surprised. Nothing was right about the planet yet. Nothing was done.

"I can't stay here, Henry. I have to see it to the end."

Henry nodded, but before he put the truck in gear to take them back to Laputa, he faced her. "Do not try to change me again as we sleep. Do not, ever, be so impertinent again."

For a second, Elizabeth thought she saw hatred there, just a glimpse that flashed in the back of his dark eyes, and she respected it.

But two weeks later, when it came time to sleep, she met with the doctors. She gave orders. Just a touch, a tweak, a fine tuning. Henry wouldn't mind, she thought, if he loved her like she knew he did, he wouldn't mind at all.


In the six-century dream, Elizabeth, watched the rain from comets covering Venus. The water ice started beyond Neptune's orbit, like ghostly icebergs drifting in space so distant that the sun was merely a bright star among other stars. Gently nudged, they began their long journeys inward, finally, catastrophically for them, exploding into Venus's atmosphere, contributing water to a planet long without.

Rain fell. It fell in spurts, in squalls, in flurries, in long sizzling sheets that worked their way into cracks beneath the surface, nourishing the alien life planted there, until there came a time when the rain didn't just fall on rock. Plants grew, their leaves upturned, catching the water as it fell, spreading it to roots.

The rain eroded. Cut through stone. Carried silt. Formed rivulets, creeks, streams, rivers. Gathered in pools, ponds, lakes, seas. Evaporated, formed clouds, fell again.

And then, finally, in the highest of high places, appeared the first snow.

Elizabeth saw herself standing in Venus's snow, the perfect crystals falling on her bare arms, one by one pausing for a moment as petite sculptures before melting. Snow cleared the dust and smelled crisp as a fresh apple. She ran through the white blanket, splashing her legs as she ran, looking for her brother. Where was he? This was water he could play in. This water wouldn't harm him. She'd made it safe in her dream. At a lake's edge, she stopped, looking both directions as far as she could, but he wasn't there, just the silent snow falling onto the red-tinted water. Each snowflake, when it met the lake, glowed for a second, until the water's surface itself provided the only light in the dream. Plenty of light to see him if he was there, but he wasn't.

She stood at the lake's edge for centuries.


"She's awake."

Soft light fell all around, like snow. Time passed. Darkness. Light again. I'm under the snow, she thought. Darkness.

"She's awake."

Her arms were moved. Light was provided. A question was asked. A tube was pulled from her throat. She was hurt. All very passive. Darkness.

"She's awake."

Elizabeth forced her eyes open. An older man sat on the bed beside her, holding her hand. Beside him stood a medical technician in a lab coat. The man holding her hand had a haggard face. Worry lines across his forehead. A little baggy in the jowls. It wasn't until she blinked her vision clear that she could see his eyes.

"Henry?"

He mouthed a silent, "Yes."

"How long?"

He patted the top of her hand. "Six hundred years."

She tried to sit up. Before she was halfway, though, her calves cramped.

"Probably easier to lay still right now," Henry said. "The doctors here have some wonderful treatments. Since you've made it this far, you should be up soon."

Breathing softly, Elizabeth considered what he said for a moment. "There was a doubt?"

"Big one for a long time."

The ache in her legs dwindled to a dim reminder, no worse than the one she felt in her neck and back and chest. She squeezed his hand. "Henry, I'm glad you're here."

"You can take care of her now," he said to the lab-coated man.

For the next two days, doctors came and went. They wheeled her from one examining room to the next. Most of the time she couldn't tell what they were doing. Strange instruments. Peculiar instructions. Doctors nodding to each other over results that didn't make sense to her. Even their conversation confused her, speaking with a dialect too thick for her to decipher. Although she did have one moment of relief when one asked her to stick out her tongue and say, "Ahh." The tongue depressor even appeared to be made from wood.

They weren't subservient, however. Brisk, efficient and friendly, but not servile. When she saw Henry again, she asked him about it. He met her in a sitting room where other patients sat reading or visiting quietly. The medical techs insisted she stay in a wheelchair, although she walked quite well in a physical therapy session earlier in the day.

"All that I've learned from our strange journey, Elizabeth, is that time changes everything. You're not a religion anymore. Actually, now you're kind of a curiosity. I expect someone from the history guild will want to talk with you. Marvelous opportunity, you know, to actually chat face to face with the Elizabeth Audrey."

Something in the way he said it caught her ear. "What about my holdings? What about the corporations?"

Henry covered her hand with his own. "Gone, I'm afraid. Long, long gone now."

The tears came unbidden. She thought of herself as a strong person. Finally, she shook the tremors off and dried her face. "We need to get to work then to get it back. How close are we to finishing the project?"

Henry smiled. She'd always liked his eyes, but now the years in his expression set them off beautifully. "I'll let you judge for yourself."

When he stood, a medical tech who had been waiting a few seats away, rushed over to help.

"That's okay. I'll take her," Henry said.

"Thank you, sir," said the tech. "I'll be close if you need me."

Elizabeth looked from the tech to Henry and back again. She recognized a power order when she saw one. "How old are you Henry? How long have you been awake this time?"

He turned her chair toward the exit and began rolling her toward the door. "Twenty-two years. I'm sixty-two now."

The door opened into a wide space. A ceiling a hundred feet

above enclosed the multiple levels and balconies she saw on the other side. Pedestrians walked purposefully to and fro.

"What is this, a mall?"

"More like a business park, but you've got the right idea."

A pair of woman dressed in dark, functional leather longcoats walked past them. One laughed at something the other said. Pale clean circles surrounded their eyes in faces that were uniformly filthy.

"Prospectors do a lot of trading here," said Henry, as way of explanation.

He wheeled her to a garage a level lower and helped her into a car. This one didn't appear nearly as heavy as the truck she'd ridden in with him what seemed like a lifetime ago.

"It's time for you to see Venus in its glory," said Henry.

A half hour later he parked the car on what might have been the same hill he'd taken her to before, but now the burgundy sun rested low on the opposite horizon, and where before the landscape was marked by wind, rock and water, plants grew everywhere. Thick-stemmed vines clung to the rocks beside the road. Low bushes dotted the slope to the water's edge. Here and there, short pine-looking trees poked from the soil, their trunks all leaning the same way and their branches pointing away from the lake. And there was color everywhere. Not only were there the gray and black rocks she remembered, but also tans and browns and yellows. Across the face of the hill to their left, a copper sheen caught the sun, and on the hill to their right, the mossy clumps growing between the rough stones were a vibrant blue.

But no heather covered the hills. Where she imagined a world with waterfalls, there was only sharp-edged stone. Where she hoped for soft yellow light on fields of flowers, there was a red sun, bloat as a toad on the horizon. She saw a rough land.

A figure dressed in a leather longcoat, goggles covering the eyes, walked past their car, saw Henry and tipped his leather hat as he continued on toward the lake where a small complex of buildings serviced two long docks and a dozen moored boats.

Elizabeth tried to contain her disappointment. "This is not even close to what I worked so hard for. I wanted a world that was what Earth should have been, what it could have been if we hadn't ruined it. Venus could have been paradise!" The outburst left her short of breath. In the car's confines, her breathing sounded loud and harsh. "I had a brother . . ."

"You were an only child." Henry sounded quizzical.

"No, I . . ." Panic rose in Elizabeth's throat. She *did* have a brother, didn't she? It took a second for her to sort it out for herself. A thousand years of dreaming could feel more convincing than a few decades of reality.

"We have to get out of here. Take me back."

"Wait," said Henry. He reclined his seat a little before folding his hands across his chest. He watched the sun setting on the lake's other side. Elizabeth leaned back in her chair, her heart thudding hard.

The sun slipped deeper into the hills behind the lake. Elizabeth relaxed. Could she get the money back again? She knew no one. The game was surely different now. A wind scurried across the water, rocked the boats, and then rushed up the road to toss sand against the car. Shadows lengthened. She felt so tired, so truly, truly *old*.

"You know," Harry said, "I talked to the doctors before I went to sleep the last time. It took considerable persuasion on my part, but I discovered you'd told them to work on me again. For a while, I thought the best action would be to go to your bed and kick out the plug. It was tempting."

Henry didn't move while he spoke. His hands stayed still as he watched the setting sun.

Elizabeth floundered for a moment, unsure of how to reply. When they'd started this project a month ago ("No, a thousand years ago," she thought), he would have never spoken to her like this, and she would have had no trouble telling him what she thought, but this wasn't the same Henry, not by any measure. "I'm sorry, Henry. I didn't think you would mind, really. They were changes for your own good."

"I loved you once, but you have a mean sense of perfection, Eliza."

The sun's last glimmer dropped out of sight. "Watch now," he said. The horizon glowed like a campfire coal, then, as sudden as a sunset can be sudden, low clouds that had been invisible until now picked up red edges, their middles pulsating cherry gold, and the air from the horizon line all the way to nearly directly overhead turned a deep purple with scarlet streaks, changing shades even as she realized they were there.

A half hour later, still in silence, they watched. Stars appeared in the moonless sky. A boat left the quay, trailing a bioluminescent streak behind it.

Elizabeth found she was crying again. "My, god, it's beautiful, Henry, but it's not what I was trying to make. It's not better than Earth."

"It's Venus," he said. "It doesn't have to be better."

By now, night had completely fallen. There were no board room meetings to attend. No calls to make. No projects to shepherd to success. Elizabeth felt very small sitting in the car with Henry. Her muscles ached. She suspected she would never be physically as capable as she once was. A thousand years of long sleep had taken their toll.

"What about you, Henry. You said you loved me once. Will you stay with me?"

She couldn't tell in the dark if he turned to look at her or not.

"You couldn't shape me into what you wanted either."

He started the car, which turned on the dashboard controls, but made no noise. The light revealed his hands on the wheel.

"My days of shaping are done, Henry."

He drove them the long way home, over hills and around the lake. They didn't speak. Neither knew what to say to the other, yet.

# DIFFERENT WORLDS

Ten-year-old Jenny crossed the street first, staying low until she reached the broken wall and had to clamber over. Robbie cleared the rubble in one clean leap, then looked at her, eyes wide, panting, ready for the next adventure. Then his ears flicked up, and he cocked his head to one side. His tail quit wagging. Jenny watched closely. He was her early warning system.

In a moment, from up the street, came a familiar hum. "Don't bark," she whispered. If they caught her, all would be lost: Robbie, her dad, herself.

Heart in her throat, she stood. Visible above the broken rooftops a block away, the top of one of the alien's vehicles lumbered toward them, its legs moving. Across the street, Dad peeked through the busted door. She waved her hand in a frantic stop sign.

"Don't come, Dad. Don't come," she mouthed.

For a second he paused as if he didn't understand, and Jenny had a vision of him wandering into the street in clear view. Earlier in the day he'd walked off, talking to himself when she found him. "It's a states' rights issue. Just like the old South," he had been saying. She'd held his hand as she led him away from the open where he could be spotted so easily.

This time, though, he nodded, then dropped out of sight.

Jenny knelt, holding Robbie. The dog pressed a wet nose under her chin and licked her once. "You're safe with me. They won't get you," she said.

The house had no roof, and the sun was a light spot, low in the smoke-filled sky. Jenny crawled to the shattered frame where the picture window had once been. Grit and ash permeated the carpet, itching at her palms; the air tasted oily in the back of her throat, and it burned her nose to breathe. From the window, she could see smoke rising from several ruined houses, but no flame.

The humming grew louder.

Jenny pushed back out of sight, then drew herself in tightly. I'm a little stone, she thought. They can't see me if I'm just a little stone.

The alien craft, with glassy-eyed monitors gyrating this way and that, stepped between her and her father. Jenny stared through a crack in the wall. None of their vessels looked right. They were too broad at the top, inverted pyramids slapped together with wrinkled metal, supported by six spindly legs. They should tip over.

"Don't be scared," she murmured. The vessel stopped. It lowered itself until its narrow base almost touched the street, while its mirrored legs reached above its top, as if the machine had been modeled on a cricket. The metal eyes rotated in their sockets. Jenny trembled, holding the dog close.

After a long moment, the machine stood tall and resumed its march down the street.

Jenny peeked both ways, then beckoned Dad across. He stepped gingerly over glass shards on the sidewalk before crossing the asphalt, bent double, holding his book close.

"It almost got us," Dad said. "If you hadn't stopped me, I'd have been in the street." He squeezed the book to his chest.

"No it didn't. We just have to be careful." But she couldn't tell if he had heard. His focus, like it had been more and more over the last few days, was on some middle distance. Hardly ever on her.

Dad cleared rotten sheet rock off the floor before sitting down on the carpet so stained that Jenny had no idea what color it had once been. He leaned against the remains of a couch, its stuffing bursting from a dozen places, oozing a mildewy, fetid smell. Robbie sniffed at it, decided there were no rats, then put his snout on his front paws.

He was a white dog with black patches and a black head. When Mom gave him to Jenny, she'd said he would be "medium sized," but he turned out rather small. She'd brought him home in a shoe box from the small animal clinic she ran. A mix between a spaniel and a terrier. Short haired. Prone to running circuits around Jenny's back yard that wore ruts eventually. When Jenny still had a back yard.

Dad shifted uncomfortably against the couch.

Jenny said, "Does it hurt?"

He moved his shoulder. The bandages under his jacket gave

him a humped look. "It's fine. If we find a doctor, it will be fine. But I need to rest. Can I rest, Delaney?"

Jenny winced. "I'm Jenny, Dad. Sure, take a nap."

Within seconds he was breathing deeply. She put her palm against his forehead and then against her own. He felt warm. She studied his face. Under his eyes were dark smudges, like bruises, and his beard was black and fierce, as if he'd become a Viking. She'd teased him a week earlier for not shaving. Most of the men they saw now needed shaves, and the women needed their hair done. Jenny looked down at her own smudged hands and dusty jeans. I could use a bath myself, she thought before closing her eyes.

Robbie's whining woke her. The sky had grown darker. Whether it was more smoke or the sunset, she couldn't tell. Dad was awake too and thumbing through his book.

"I remember this one," he said. His finger rested on a picture of Jenny standing at the end of a pier, a fishing pole in one hand and an empty net in the other. Robbie sat at her feet, tongue out.

"That was just last summer, Dad. Of course you remember it." But the memory eluded her. So much had happened. She wrinkled her brow. "That was before the fighting started?"

Dad turned the page to the pictures from the anniversary party. Jenny remembered the cake. It had been white with chocolate letters on it: "Happy Twentieth, Dan and Delaney." Mom held a piece to the cameraman in one picture, the cake huge and blurry in the foreground; her face glowing and white behind it. During the party, Jenny had caught her finger in a door. She remembered how she sat on Dad's lap while Mom held ice against her swollen knuckle. She remembered how solid his hands were, wrapped around her, how Mom took the ice away and blew on the hurt. "Is that better, Jennybird?" she said. The memory wasn't fuzzy like the days they spent fishing. Those mostly blended one to the next. In her memory, she could almost touch her mother's cheek. She could smell the little bit of wine Mother had on her breath.

Jenny looked away. The animal clinic had been in the center of the first attack weeks earlier. Mom hadn't come home.

Dad lolled his head back so that if he'd had his eyes open, he would have been looking straight up. Eyes closed, he said, "I had a student from Japan once. He wrote English better than he spoke it, but I never understood a single one of his papers." He brushed his fingers against his beard. "I couldn't grade his work. It wasn't the language. It was his understanding of the concepts behind the words. We were from the same planet but different worlds."

"We have to get out of here, Dad." Jenny stood. The remains of someone's living room were scattered about. Burnt drapes still hanging from a crooked curtain rod. Books splayed across the floor, moldering from the rains. Scorch marks flowed up a table top tilted on its side. She picked her way around the trash. The back half of the house was flat, as if an explosion had pushed it away from the partly standing front walls. Wire twisted out of the shattered woodwork. A broken porcelain base showed where the toilet had been, and on the partial wall beside it a dented medicine cabinet, its mirror a cobweb of cracks, drew Jenny over. There was nothing in it though. She sighed.

From the remnant of the porch, the city reached before her, smoke shrouded, stinking of burnt rubber and other, fouler things. A jet roared overhead, away from the city, but she couldn't see it through the haze.

"We thought we understood them at first, Jennybird." Dad put a hand on her head. "My job was to understand them."

Jenny put her hand on his, their twin weight resting on her head like a heavy hat. "If we hurry, we might be able to get to the hospital before dark."

Dad trembled; she could feel it through his hand. He said, "I should have known. In the end, it was the principle of the thing. Not everyone in the South wanted to keep their slaves, you know, in the Civil War. They just didn't like being told that they couldn't. Different planets, different worlds." Jenny shook her head, nearly ready to cry. Almost everything he said he'd said before, and he jumped from topic to topic. She wanted to shake him, to shake out the old Dad. He'd tell her what to do. He'd hold her and keep her safe.

Dad opened the photo album. "Do you remember this one? I've always liked this one."

He pointed to the same photograph of her on the pier.

"Come on, Dad." She led him onto long, dry grass, past a swing set with bent bars and a swing dangling from a single chain. The fence at the back of the yard had been knocked over. A cedar plank groaned when she stepped on it.

Robbie paused at a dog house partly hidden under some tree branches. He poked his nose in, tail waving madly, then trotted beside Jenny, head high, sniffing everything.

It took an hour to go ten blocks. At each street, Jenny checked for the enemy's patrol cars . . . vessels . . . she wondered what to call a vehicle with legs. They moved into a neighborhood where houses were standing, although most windows were gone and there was no evidence of life. Maybe people are in some of them, she thought. They haven't been caught, but they're afraid to be out. She couldn't remember the last time she'd seen a civilian car driving. Two days ago the streets were filled with military trucks and humvees, frantic with movement, but they'd left before the bombardment.

Then she heard the angry beating of an alien's plane in the distance. They ducked behind a barrier of dried shrubbery. Behind them a half empty pool, its surface black with floating ash, reflected nothing. The throbbing of movable wings filled the air.

"Ornithopter," Dad said. "I bought one for you, Jenny, at Christmas. It didn't fly well." He coughed, covering his mouth with a fist. "What made us build aircraft with fixed wings? How strange we must look to them, ignoring our models in nature."

The enemy's plane dipped from the clouds a block away, its shiny cockpit turned partly away from them. Jenny thought about dragonflies, although it wasn't really dragonfly-shaped. The body was as wide as it was long, except for a tail section connected to the ship with a long, slender tube that was almost invisible at this distance. Its short, blurred wings held it at a hover for a few seconds. Then it darted left, dropped out of sight, the rhythmic, vibrating pulse all around them. Jenny felt it in her chest, like music with a heavy bass turned too loud.

"Do you think it's trying to find us, Dad?" Jenny tugged on his arm. He didn't look at her. With his free hand he pulled a leaf from the bush, crackling it between his fingers.

"They knew English and Chinese. We were so surprised. First contact. But they couldn't make an 'S' sound."

The plane rose suddenly, straight up, vanished into the low haze, until its thrumming voice was lost. Jenny pulled Dad forward. When he stood, he grimaced and leaned his head against his shoulder.

"It was pretty funny when they said 'Sister Sally.' Do you know 'Sister Sally?'"

She wished he would quit talking. It didn't scare her as much when he was quiet.

"Zister Zally Zold Zea Zells by the Zea Zore." Dad laughed,

his voice reverberating in the silence. His cheeks were flushed and his red-rimmed eyes looked gummy.

A man wearing a brown coat, blue jeans, and bright yellow running shoes jumped over the low fence on the other side of the pool and rolled against the wood, trying to look small.

Robbie barked.

The man looked up. Jenny couldn't tell how old he was; his face was so dirty, but when he spoke, she decided he was a teenager. "Christ! Get down. They're all over the place," he hissed.

Jenny listened carefully. Their vehicles made distinctive sounds. She'd never seen one that didn't. Now that the ornithopter had gone, there was no noise in the neighborhood.

"I don't think so," she said.

He got up and brushed his pant legs, but she didn't think they looked any cleaner.

"Do you have an aspirin, mister? My dad has a fever."

The man shook his head as he slid along the house's wall until he reached the corner, then glanced around it. "They're going to get me. There's no place to hide. I saw them herding people toward the stadium this morning. Thousands of people in the streets. None of them saying a word, but I could hear their feet shuffling. What do you think they do to them in the stadium? I don't buy that 'reorientation' garbage."

Dad kicked some gravel into the pool and watched the ripples. For a second, Jenny believed he might fall in, but he didn't make a move. He stared instead.

"I really need to get him to the hospital, the one at the university. Do you know how much farther we have to go?"

The man's attention snapped skyward for a moment, as if he expected something to swoop out of the smoke. "Yeah, sure. I was a student. You're only about a mile away."

Jenny sighed in relief.

He continued, "But I don't know if any of the doctors are still there."

Robbie joined Dad at the pool's edge. The man flinched. "You have a dog! I haven't seen a dog in weeks."

"That's Robbie. Are you sure you don't have aspirin?"

Dad sat on the edge. His feet dangled a few inches above the black water.

"No, none. Can I pet him?"

Jenny nodded.

The man approached Robbie at a crouch, his hand out, gently, as if stalking a rabbit or a small bird. Robbie tilted his head to the side, and when the man stroked his ears, he licked his hand. "Isn't that something? I used to have a dog. A hairy little mutt. I left him at home when I came to school. Don't know what happened to him." He sounded very sad to Jenny, like he needed a hug.

"Did he have a name?"

He ruffled Robbie's fur on his back. Distracted, he said, "Ralph. We got him from the pound when he wasn't bigger than a football. Always thought we were doing him a favor." Suddenly angry, he looked at Jenny. "We were good folks, taking that dog. Mom wanted a purebred, but Dad said we should save a castaway. They kill dogs at a pound. We were good folks. Don't let anyone tell you different."

Jenny retreated a step—he was so intense!—and Robbie growled. The man snatched his hand to his chest.

"They're going to get me if I stay still. They'll get you too." He stood. "You keep that dog close to you. Nobody should have to give up a dog. Fucking aliens." Looking at the sky again, he stepped back. "Hope you find a doctor. Your dad needs something." With three long strides and a jump, the man was over the fence and out of sight.

Dad said, "Somebody should clean this pool. Maybe if there was a skimmer." He looked around.

"We'll fix it after we get to the hospital." She pulled on his arm to help him to his feet, but he was so much heavier than she that she wasn't able to budge him. Dad grunted, then stood unsteadily.

"I used to read stories about alien contact," Dad said to the air as he followed Jenny to the gate. She checked the alley before letting him out. Light was fading rapidly, and a cold breeze stirred papers on the ground. "They were always something like us. I mean, we could communicate with them. We wanted the same things in the stories, and these aliens were like that at first. 'Dawn of a new era in interstellar contact,' the president said." Dad slowed to cough, each explosion wrenching his face into pain. When he finally stopped, he wiped his mouth with his sleeve. "I need to take a nap."

Jenny looked at the darkening sky. "We can't, Dad. Not now. You just took one. Tell me more about the aliens. Keep talking." She wasn't really listening. As long as he talked, he would keep walking. Nothing he said would be as scary as him giving up.

They were at the top of a house-covered hill. At the bottom of the street, several blocks below them, the highway overpass shadowed the road. A hunk of the bridge's middle was gone and a semi-trailer truck hung partly on the overpass, its cab dangling above the broken section. Beyond that, the red stonework of the campus was just visible through the smoke, but the hospital was on the far side, out of sight.

Dad said, "Different planets, different worlds, and states' rights. It's a stupid war. Our negotiating team laughed at the demand. Dogs aren't people. We laughed; they attacked. No counteroffers."

The path was downhill now, although she didn't dare let them take the sidewalk. They stayed close to the houses, crossing lawns, stepping over privet hedges or knee-high fences some people put on their yards to know where to stop mowing. There was still a lot of broken glass, although little sign of burning now. As they passed a white two-story with blue trim, she noticed a sign by the door, "God Bless This Home." She thought a curtain flicked behind one of the windows, but she couldn't be sure.

She watched Robbie. He ran ahead of them, poking his nose into bushes, then running back as if he had important news. Robbie always heard the aliens before she did. If he stopped with his ears up, they needed to hide.

"Lots of people don't own dogs, you know," Dad said. "They just don't like to be told by extra-solar beings that they *can't* own a dog. They didn't understand the relationship, or they understood, but they didn't like it. Called it, 'repressed, emerging sapiency.'" He hummed an off-pitched tune to himself for a few steps. "Good thing horses weren't 'emerging' or, God forbid, pigs. We'd really been in trouble then," he added, then went back to humming.

Jenny could feel the fever in his hand. In the morning, when she'd decided they couldn't hide in their basement any longer, the skin under the bandage had an angry yellow and purple look to it, and the cut, which hadn't seemed that bad when he first got it, had deepened and widened. She'd bathed it the best she could before wrapping his chest clumsily. She was afraid of what she'd find if she looked at it now.

On the other side of the overpass, a light shone in several windows of the nearest university buildings. It was really getting dark now and cold. The going was tough. They traced a zig-zag pattern from the house, out to the sidewalk to get past taller walls or impenetrable bushes, Jenny jumping at every sound or shadow, then back to the hiding places of the homes. Dad's fingers rested limply in her own, and each step seemed a prelude to a fall. He mumbled to himself, his eyes closed. "Even the trees spoke."

"Dad?"

He took several steps before saying, "What?"

"What's that about talking trees?"

"*Wizard of Oz.* How'd you like it if someone picked *your* apples? Everything's in how you look at it. I'll get you, my pretty. You and your little dog." He stumbled, caught himself, then straightened his shoulders. "It's *Old Yeller* and *Where the Red Fern Grows.* Alien horror documentaries."

He squeezed Jenny's fingers, then fell backwards. Jenny dropped to her knees, shook him, called to him, but he didn't stir. Robbie looked on quizzically.

She tried to pull him toward the house, a pleasant looking two-story Victorian, but it was useless. He weighed too much.

In the house, at the bottom of a ransacked closet, she found a tablecloth—all the blankets were gone—and took it outside. He hadn't moved.

"Dad," she said. "Dad? I'm going to get help. The hospital's just a few more blocks. I won't be gone long." She smoothed the tablecloth over him. Above, the clouds roiled in a luminescent gray, nearly touching the rooftops. There was no traffic on the street. No voices. Only Dad's wheezing breaths.

"You stay here, Robbie. Stay with Dad." Robbie lifted an ear, then dropped it. "Do you understand? Stay. Be a good dog." She kissed Dad's forehead before running down the street. Robbie followed.

"Go back! Stay with Dad! You'll be safer." She shooed him away. He sat instead.

They were nearly to the underpass. "Go back," she pleaded.

Without waiting to see what he'd do, she turned toward the campus. Even when she heard his claws clicking against the cement, she didn't look behind.

The dangling truck cab creaked when she ran under it. Broken asphalt and bent lengths of rusty rebar sticking from cement slabs made walking treacherous. A sharp cordite smell lingered. Only a block separated her from the university, but after she negotiated the last obstacle beneath the overpass, she slowed to a walk. Across the road that entered the campus grounds, the same road the hospital was on, stretched a tall fence. Footlights every ten feet along the ground illuminated the shiny chain link structure, and in the exact middle of the road was a small gate, not nearly big enough for a car, a people gate. Two dark figures sat on the other side. As she approached, they stood. One of them shined a flashlight, blinding her.

"It's a little girl," a voice said.

"What do you think she's doing out there?" the other voice asked. "I thought everyone had been detained."

"My dad's hurt," Jenny called. "I need to get him to the hospital, but he's too weak to come. I need help." She tried to see them, but the light was too bright.

"Oh, Jesus!" yipped one of the guards. "Don't come closer, little girl. You stand right there."

They took the light off her, and after a few seconds of blinking, she could see one of them talking on a portable phone. Robbie leaned against her leg. She reached down to scratch him behind the ears. "It'll be all right. They'll get a doctor," she said.

A couple of minutes later, while Jenny stood silently and the guards stared at her, a figure on a bicycle pedaled up the road from the campus. It stopped by the guards, leaning the bike against the fence.

"Let me out," she said. When the woman got close, Jenny saw that her blonde hair was tied into a ponytail, and that she wore a medical smock.

"Are you a doctor?" Jenny asked. "My dad needs a doctor right away. He's only a couple of blocks on the other side of the bridge."

The woman stopped, six feet away. Her voice sounded strained, as if she were trying not to scream. "We can help you, but you need to come inside right now. You can't be outside the fence without permission."

Jenny nodded and took a step forward.

"No, no!" gasped the woman. "The dog has to stay here. You can't bring him inside."

Confused, Jenny stopped. "This is just Robbie. He won't bite or anything."

The woman sidled toward Jenny, keeping away from Robbie. "You don't understand. We can get your dad help, but the dog has to stay outside. We have to get behind the fence now, without the dog, or it might be too late."

She put her hand on Jenny's arm. "The dog will be fine, but we won't be if we stay out here. Obstructionists disappear. They've let us keep the hospital open, but we have to do it by their rules."

In the distance, Jenny heard a humming.

"Oh, God," the woman whispered. "Quick, girl. We've got to go now."

Jenny let herself be led to the fence without thinking. The humming grew louder. One of the aliens' walking vehicles was coming. Suddenly she pulled free. "I can't leave Robbie out here!" But the men at the gate grabbed her, hustled her to the other side of the fence and closed it. One of them picked her up so that she faced backwards, looking at Robbie as they ran from the humming sound.

The last she saw of Robbie, he was still sitting on the street, his head tilted to one side and then to the other as if waiting for her to call him.

"Run away, Robbie! Run away and hide!" But the dog didn't move. The man carried her into a building, closing the door behind them.

Inside, the woman in the medical smock gathered supplies. "We'll get your dad when the machine's gone," she said. "They're automatic. Doesn't matter who you are if you're on the wrong side of the fence. You'll have to take us to him."

"Robbie will run away. He's a smart dog," Jenny said. "They wouldn't hurt a dog, would they?"

The woman paused, her hand partway into her medical bag. "No, darling. They don't hurt dogs. They take them to a better place, far away from us." She looked down, hiding her eyes, and continued stuffing equipment into the bag. "They took my dog. He was a big, friendly Labrador, and I guess I was a monster, because they took him away too."

Thirty minutes later, Jenny led a line of people out of the building. They carried a stretcher, and they all had flashlights. The spot where Robbie had stood was empty. He wasn't under the overpass.

Dad had rolled on his side under the tablecloth, and he was shivering. Jenny put her hand on his back as the woman inserted an I.V.. She felt his shaking, but he was still alive, and she'd found help. As soon as they arrived, she felt the responsibility lifting from her shoulders. Doctors would help. Doctors could cure anything. She picked up the photo album from the dew-slick grass.

As they marched back to the campus, Dad in the stretcher, Jenny shined her light into every shadow, and when they passed houses, she checked behind bushes, expecting at each new spot to see him, snout on his paws, tail wagging, waiting for her to pet his head. She called and called until one of the men asked her, not unkindly, to stop.

He wasn't on one of the lawns, nor was he hiding beside a cement block beneath the broken overpass. He wasn't waiting by the fence.

Jenny stopped at the gate as the line of people went on toward the hospital. She could hear their feet on the cement until they faded away. Fingers hooked in the chain-link, Jenny listened as hard as she could for a long time. Robbie would bark if he couldn't find her. He always barked when he was lonely. Jenny listened, but he never barked. There were no noises at all. Not a single sound in the entire city.

No dog anywhere sending a joyful yelp into the night.

The cold metal of the fence burned against her hand while the smoke-filled breeze pushed against her face, irritating her eyes. Light only reached to the bridge, and the world beyond was all shadows, empty and lifeless.

I'm not a monster, Jenny thought, I don't care what anyone says. She remembered the photo of them on the pier, the dog sitting before her. Suddenly the memory was very clear: the sun warming her shoulders, the water slapping at the wood beneath her feet, a hint of fish and wet sand in the air.

I'm not, she thought, I'm not, I'm not, I'm not a monster.

Robbie loves me.

# THE SMALL ASTRAL OBJECT GENIUS

Dustin set the Peek-a-boo on his desk next to the computer. The softball-sized metal sphere rolled an inch before clicking against the keyboard, the only sound in the silent house. The house was almost always quiet now, noiseless as an empty kitchen with its cabinets neatly shut, the plates and dishes gradually collecting dust. Where to send it? Maybe this time something incredible would happen, if he just kept trying.

His computer listed options, starting with large objects or small ones. After he'd first bought the Peek-a-boo, he spent weeks sending it to the large ones: galaxies, nebulas, the gaseous remains of supernovas, star clusters. He'd double check the batteries, make sure the lens was clean, then choose one of the preprogrammed destinations. Sometimes he'd balance the device on his palm, hoping to feel the microsecond that it vanished in its dash across the light years before returning to his hand, but he never did. Not even a tingle. It sat against his skin, cool and hard and heavy, its absence too brief to sense.

An instant later, his computer pinged and the "picture taken" icon blinked red and green. Immediately would follow a confirmation from the Peek-a-boo Project website. "Thank you for participating," the message would say, or, if he was really lucky, "New object! You have contributed to man's knowledge of the universe," and his face would tingle with joy.

He'd heard rumors among his friends that there were other messages, but he'd never seen them himself.

Lots of times, of course, the monitor showed nothing, just a black screen with maybe a wink of a star here or there, but every once in a while, the Peek-a-boo appeared in the distant space oriented perfectly and captured a spectacular image. He used to like nebulas best. Several DVDs full of pictures rested on the shelf above the computer. He'd devoted an entire disk to the Rosette Nebula, taking pictures from all the angles over the course of two weeks, its vermillion gasses thrown out in parsecs wide petals, but lately he'd turned his attention to small objects: individual stars, planets, and moons.

On the monitor, the computer gave him hundreds of preprogrammed selections. He carefully entered instead the coordinates for a planet circling Bellatrix, a giant star about 240 light years away on Orion's right shoulder, then sent the Peek-a-boo. "Picture taken," winked the message. The image began forming on the screen. Dustin leaned back in his chair, his hands resting one on the other on his chest.

Behind him, the door to his bedroom opened. He knew by the click of the doorknob, the distance the door swung into the room, a hint of lavender in the air, that it was his mother. She stood behind him without speaking for a moment, then sighed.

"Yes?" Dustin said.

She sighed again.

He turned his chair. Her hand cupped the doorknob with fingers so delicate that he wondered how she could pick up anything heavier than a pen or a book.

"Are you coming to dinner?" Her lips were colorless and thin, like her voice, but dark circles marked her eyes. He couldn't remember when Mom looked like she'd had a good night's sleep.

"Now?"

She blinked, as if his question was cruel.

"Unless you want to eat later. Your father is eating later."

"I'm not hungry." Almost half the image had appeared on the screen. Already he could see the planet's curve. This could be a good one, he thought. He forced his eyes away from the picture. If he phrased the question just right, he could make a difference. "I don't think I'll have anything. Could we wait?"

She shook her head, and then slowly backed away, pulling the door with her. "I'll put a plate in the refrigerator for you in case," she said as the door closed.

Dustin shivered for a second in the room's silence. She was like a ghost in her own house, drifting from room to room. He couldn't remember the last time she'd touched him. Maybe she wasn't even capable of it anymore. If he tried to hug her, would his arms pass through?

The planet on the monitor finished forming, a violet sphere with darker bands, like Jupiter, the arc of the terminator hiding a third of the surface. "Thank you for participating" popped over the image. He shook his head as he cleared the message. He hadn't "contributed to man's knowledge of the universe." Other people had taken this picture and added it to the database. No rings on the planet that he could see. No moons. Still, how rare, he thought. Perfect trade material. The smaller the object, the less chance his friends would have it. Space wasn't just mostly empty; it was depressingly, hugely empty. If all space was the size of his bedroom, the total mass of every galaxy and star and planet wouldn't fill a thimble. Getting a picture of an object as small as a planet 240 light years away boggled the mind. He tweaked the coordinates and sent the Peek-a-boo again for a closer look, but the image came back black. The unit might have appeared closer to the planet but with its lens pointed the wrong way, or a number in the coordinates so far down the decimal line that he couldn't imagine it ticked up or down one time too many, and the Peek-a-boo wasn't in the planet's range.

He sent it again. Black screen.

Again. Black screen.

Again.

His door opened. Dad said, "Dustin, I'm eating dinner in forty minutes. The dining room should be free then."

"I'm not hungry, Dad. I'm working on something."

Dustin could almost hear his Dad grimace. "You didn't eat already, did you?" He stepped next to Dustin's chair. Dustin looked at Dad's feet, which were bare. The toenails were trimmed neatly, although they'd grown longer than he was used to seeing. "You didn't eat with her, did you?" Dad said.

"No, really, I'm working on my computer . . ." Dustin drew in a shaky breath, ". . . but I'll go down now, if you want." Dustin tapped in an adjustment before sending the Peek-a-boo again.

Dad leaned in toward the screen, his hand on the chair's back behind Dustin's shoulder. "It's a hoax, you know. That toy doesn't go anywhere. It generates random images. Everyone knows you can't travel faster than light, and certainly not with a half pound of plastic and a couple AA batteries."

The computer indicated that the coordinates were ready. Dustin pressed the send command. "It's aluminum, not plastic, and it's not a hoax. Didn't you read that stuff I gave you about Peek-a-boo theory? Interstellar distance is a mathematical conception or something like that. Wrinkly space, they call it. Just a little push the right way, and the Peek-a-boo bounces across the wrinkle and back."

"It's Crackerjack physics, son. Nobody believes it."

"Scientists do. Every time I take a photograph, it downloads into NASA's database. We're expanding the knowledge of the universe! People all over the world are part of it! Amateurs have always been a big part of astronomy."

Dad humphed. "You know what the scam is? Sporadic reinforcement. Every once in a while you get a pat on the back, and you keep trying. It's why fishermen fish. You wouldn't believe how many Pokemon packs I bought when I was a kid, just hoping for a first edition holographic rare. Hundreds of dollars lost, I'll bet."

"The pictures are real, Dad," he said as a new image formed on the screen. At the very bottom a hint of violet curve filled in. "See, it's the same planet. I've been peppering these coordinates for a couple days." The image looked so authentic. Dustin thought, no way this is fake. No way!

Dad shrugged his shoulders. "I'm heating a pizza later. Come down if you want any."

"Not tonight. Sorry." Dustin punched the send button again. Maybe he could get a full globe shot for trade tomorrow.


Through Dustin's open shades, the stars above the western horizon flickered behind the maple's waving branches. Slowly, the nearly full moon slid through the last of the November leaves, then past each branch, lower and lower. Before it touched the top of his neighbor's house, Mars joined the gradual descent. The planet and the moon appeared close in the sky, but he knew it was an illusion. Even if their edges touched, they were really millions of miles apart. Still, he liked seeing them so close. If only he could send the Peek-a-boo there! What wonders he might see, but wrinkly space didn't wrinkle at that distance. The closest he could send the Peek-a-boo was about one hundred light years.

One by one, Pisces's last stars disappeared, and Aries, its twinkling lights wrapped around the war god, followed the creeping parade.

The clock next to the bed flicked to 4:00 a.m. Dustin listened intently. Not a living sound in the house. His parents' bedroom was directly below his. A year ago, he could hear them talking. No words, but a comforting, conversational rise and fall. Sometimes, even, laughter. Then, six months ago, it had been arguments. Shouting, to weeping, to nothing. Mother slept there still. If her shades were open like his, the moonlight would flood her space, but Dustin hadn't seen her windows open for months. In the middle of the day, she'd be in bed in the darkened room, or she'd vacuum by the tiny vacuum cleaner's light, like a dim-eyed Cyclops rolling along the carpet.

Dad slept in his study by the garage.

Dustin pushed his covers aside, crept down to the kitchen, and ate a piece of cold pizza. The milk tasted sour, and the label said it had passed its expiration by six days, so he washed it down with orange juice.


"I'll trade you a shot from the interior of the Horse Head Nebula looking toward Earth for that planetgraph you have there," said Slade. He'd dyed his Mohawk blue the week before but hadn't touched it up since, so it had turned a coppery green. A spread of pictures covered the desk before him, and his CD carrier, filled with thousands of other images he'd either taken himself or traded for sat in the black case next to the prints. "Come on, it's a good deal. All the UV bands are expressed. You could hang it in a museum." In the hallway beyond the classroom door, voices rose and fell, the busy traffic of the middle school at lunch.

Dustin handled the print, a really lovely image marked by delicate curtains of pink and vermillion. A series of numbers printed at the bottom told him how many pictures Slade had taken, and how rare the current image was. The higher the number at the bottom combined with the rarity of the image and the prestige of the photographer determined its tradability. *Peek-a-boo Monthly* printed profiles of individuals who captured the most spectacular and rare shots. Both Slade and Dustin had been listed in the "honorable mentions" in past issues, which made all their prints more valuable. He put it down. "Nice picture, but it's common. Peek-a-boo defaults to the nebulas. My grandmother could get it."

"Yeah, but not this quality."

Three other boys had gathered at their table in the empty classroom, their lunches in their laps. Each had a folder with their own pictures and their own CDs filled with images. "I'll trade for it," said one. He wore a t-shirt that read, IF I WERE AN ALIEN, I WOULDN'T TALK TO US EITHER.

Slade hardly looked at him. Dustin knew that Slade had already taken every image of interest from the boy already. The only other person in the school with anything that might appeal to Slade was Dustin.

"I've never taken a close up of an object smaller than a star. You're like a small astral object genius. How are you finding them?"

Dustin thought about the hours of punching the send command, the boxes of batteries, the long stretches of useless images that made him wonder if his monitor still worked, the quiet creak of the door behind him that told him either Mom or Dad was checking up. He would hunch closer to the screen and pretend he hadn't heard. Dad had told him once, when he was much younger, "Accept the things you can't change and change the things you can." He couldn't get them to talk, but he could take pictures of the stars, so he pressed the send button again and again.

"I keep trying," he said.

"Where's this one from?" Slade put his finger on the violet planet from last night.

"Bellatrix. I like the named objects. Tonight I thought I'd go for stars in Pisces. Maybe Torcularis Septentrionali."

"Too small. Too far away."

Dustin put the planet's image back into his stack. "I got this one, didn't I? Persistence pays."

A dark-haired girl with hair hanging over her eyes opened the door into the classroom, filling it with hallway sound. Another girl stood behind her, her eyes just as hidden. "Oh," dark-haired said, "I thought this room was empty at lunch." Dustin turned in his chair so he could see her better, his images in hand. She said, "Ewww, it's the star geeks. Weren't you guys doing role-playing games last year?" The two girls laughed as the door shut.

After school Dustin reluctantly put aside the romantically named stars he'd concentrated on for the last months: Dubhe, Alphard, Shedir and others (Their names made him think of an old Sunday school tale about Shadrach, Meshach and Abednego. The idea of their names and stars and fiery furnaces had mixed in his head ever since.), and instead turned to G, F and K class stars, all which possibly could support life if they had planets the proper distance away. Numbers and letters labeled them. Sunlight through the window warmed his desktop, and he thought about drawing the curtain, but the heat felt good on his hands and arms.

The Peek-a-boo database contained over two million celestial objects. He picked a G-class star randomly, set the coordinates and punched the send button. The Peek-a-boo rested on its display base by his keyboard, a bit of dust marking its smooth curve. It didn't twitch, but within seconds a few pinpricks of light showed on the monitor. "Thank you for participating," said the popup message. He sent the Peek-a-boo again. A completely empty image this time. He rested his chin on his forearm, pressed the send button over and over. Eventually the sun slipped below the horizon, and for a while the maple tree stood as a shadow against the sunset sky. But the tree faded away, and only the early evening stars were visible. Vega and Altair shone brightly high on the window.

He thought about the Earth's orbit. If an Earth-like planet circled this star (which he hadn't even seen yet—it was possible the Peek-a-boo was missing it by dozens of light years), then it was like trying to find a dime on a high school track in the dark. He pressed the send again.

Downstairs, the front door opened. Dustin didn't stir. It would be his mother. She came home first. Her keys clattered into the bowl on the table by the coat closet. Her steps creaked on the squeaky third and seventh stair. Without looking, he knew when she stopped in the hallway behind him.

"Hi, Mom. You're home late."

"Did your father call to check on you?"

"No."

"It was his turn."

Dustin turned in his chair. Mom's hand rested on the door's frame. Everything about her, her hair, her make-up, the tidy lines of her blue pantsuit, was realtor neat. Her matching blue purse dangled from the crook of her elbow.

"Did you sell a house?"

"*He's* supposed to check up on you today. That's the agreement."

"It's no big deal." Dustin squeezed the back of his chair. His knuckles ached. "Maybe he did call, and I missed it. I've been on the computer."

The rumble of Dad's engine filled the driveway. Then, the click of his car opening and closing. Mom looked panicked for a moment, before coming into the room. She sat on the edge of Dustin's bed, her purse in her lap.

"What are you working on?" She glanced at the door.

"It's a new star," said Dustin. "I haven't tried to find it before." On the screen, the popup said, "New object! You have contributed to man's knowledge of the universe." Heart thumping, he cleared the message, and behind it, dead center, glowed a white disk the size of a silver dollar. "I got it," he said.

"That's a star?" She sounded doubtful.

"A new one, or at least I've taken a picture that no one else has. That's what the message meant. Look, I can manipulate it." He clicked on the "effects" choice in the toolbar and chose "eclipse." The disk blinked out, but the star's corona remained, a bright ring of light marked by a small flare on the lower right side. "This star is a lot like the sun."

"It probably is the sun," said Dad.

Mom flinched.

"I hope your grades aren't suffering because of this game." He walked past Mom without looking at her, then said to Dustin, "I brought Chinese if you're hungry."

Dustin saved the image, nudged the coordinates and sent the Peek-a-boo out again.

Dad picked up the Peek-a-boo, and flipped it from one hand to the other. "There's a guy in my office who brought one of these to work." Dustin rose partway from the chair, then forced himself back.

"They're a little fragile."

"They caught the guy playing with it during work hours." Dad tossed the sphere to Dustin. He caught it with both hands, cushioning it, before putting it back on its stand. Dad said, "They fired him. Good career shot because of a kid's toy, but I figured he wouldn't last anyways. Talked about *Star Trek* episodes like they were Shakespeare. Idiot."

Mom said, "I'll fix something for myself later, if you want to eat, Dustin." Dad closed his eyes for a second. She stood, then walked stiffly out of the room. Dustin wanted to ask her to stay, but he didn't speak. The two of them together were like split-screen videos: both animate and responding, although not to each other.

"You're not sending these Peek-a-boo people any money, are you?"

"Dad, there's just the connect charge, and I pay for that."

"With allowance money I give you. No one can prove the images you are taking are of anything, son. There's an article in today's *Newsweek* that shows it's a fake. Why don't you just get involved in online games like a normal kid?"

Dustin watched his computer's monitor. Three stars appeared in the upper left corner, but the screen was otherwise dark. He rested his fingertips on the keyboard. "Can I ask Mom to eat with us?"

"You can't take a picture of what's not there." Dad stepped toward the door, loosening his tie. He paused, one finger caught in the silk, the knot half undone. "She hates Chinese."

For the rest of the night, Dustin sent the Peek-a-boo out, over and over. He changed batteries at 2:00, when he realized twenty black screens in a row and no "Thank you for participating" messages meant the device hadn't moved. The challenge was that not only did Dustin not know if the star had planets circling it, but he didn't know what their orbital plane was. He could send the Peek-a-boo the right distance from the star and miss because the planet could be anywhere in the sphere of distance that far away. Plus, the Peek-a-boo could appear pointing in the wrong direction. All he could do was to keep trying.

He did get several more good shots of the star, though. He spent an hour running the best ones through the effects: corona analysis, blue-light shift, red-light shift, x-ray rendered, radio rendered, various luminosity lines emphasized, all the filters. In every way, it came out within a few percentage points of the sun. Twice more he received, "New object! You have contributed to man's knowledge of the universe."

Slade looked glum. "Have you ever lost a Peek-a-boo?" He hadn't opened his portfolio or his lunch. It didn't look like a trading day.

"No," said Dustin. His eyes felt heavy, like they were filled with syrup. When he'd finally fallen asleep, the sun had risen. "Did you leave it somewhere?"

"Not misplaced. I mean *lost* the whole fricking thing? I sent it out, and it didn't come back. One second it's there, and the next it's gone."

Dustin sat up. "Gone? Like gone, gone?"

"Yeah, bang, loud noise-hurt-my-ears gone, and get this: a message from the Peek-a-boo Project pops up and says, 'An unexpected anomaly occurred during transmission. You must replace your unit. Thank you for participating.' It gave me a 10% off coupon for my next purchase. What a ripoff!"

"So, what did you do?"

"I called Peek-a-boo, of course! Twenty-four hour service, my ass. It's a recorded message and a gazillion choices. So, I work my way down the menu, and you know what they said? 'Although very rare, an unexpected anomaly could include your Peek-a-boo unit occupying simultaneous space with a solid object, such as a star.' My aunt told me the whole thing is a con to get kids to buy more Peek-a-boos. That they really aren't taking pictures at all."

Dustin looked at Slade's folder. He did have beautiful images. "Are you going to quit?"

Slade pushed away from his table. He touched his hand to the side of his Mohawk to make sure it was still straight. "Even if they're fake, I like the pictures. I'll talk my step mom out of the money when she's in a good mood." He smirked, "Besides, my grades in science have never been better."

None of the other kids who traded at lunch were in the room. Dustin's own folder, with the new star pictures, unshown inside, rested under his hand. A thought occurred to him. "Did you pick up the pieces?"

"What?" Slade pushed his portfolio under his arm so he could open his lunch bag.

"The pieces from your Peek-a-boo, when it exploded?"

Slade laughed. "There weren't any pieces! There wasn't even any smoke. It exploded into nothing. Total whack job."

When Dustin was alone, and the only sounds were kids yelling to each other in the hallways, he smiled.


Mom sat on the edge of the bed, just as she had the night before, except this pantsuit matched her beige purse. "We may need to make some changes soon, Dustin."

Warily, Dustin watched her. "Like what?"

She toyed with her purse's clasp. "School, maybe. Probably a different house. A condo, perhaps. I know of some nice ones below market price nearer my office." She glanced up, dry-eyed, just for an instant. "At least for part of the time."

Dustin felt his lungs constricting. It took effort for him to say, "This is temporary, right? It's just til things patch together?"

She slumped. "If it makes you feel better to believe that, sure."

In the empty time after she left, Dustin pushed the send button repeatedly, not really looking at the monitor, even when he got a good shot of the new star. He saved the image mechanically. No planet. Send. Send. Send.

A half hour later, Dad delivered almost the same speech, except it was an apartment with a great view of the mountains.


Dustin had lined the AA batteries on his desk like bullets. Every couple hours he popped two used ones out of the Peek-a-boo. Spent casings, he thought. They dropped to the carpet.

His hands trembled on the keyboard. He swallowed dryly. Somewhere around this star, maybe, circled a planet the same distance as Earth. He'd found the system's Jupiter about 11:00. So many systems had a Jupiter, an oversized lump of a planet, always about the same distance from the center. Star system evolution turned out to be remarkably similar, time after time. Many stars formed planets, and they formed them in about the same way, and it was because of their Jupiters that the inner planets were shielded. Jupiters inhaled planet-busting comets and shepherded the loose debris into tidy orbits that would otherwise careen about unchecked. But the inner planets were so much smaller. The giant planets protected, but they also overwhelmed with their size and strength. They distracted.

Where was the tiny glimmer of the inner planets? Dustin fine tuned the coordinates, kicking the Peek-a-boo from one side of the star to the other, always taking a half-dozen pictures from one coordinate before shifting again. Even at the same coordinates, though, the unit might appear millions of miles from the last spot. A three-dimensional graph of the appearances would eventually surround a location, but there was no fine control. He could only keep trying.

At 3:00 in the morning, the Peek-a-boo felt slick and cool under his fingers. A twitch on the keyboard sent it out again. Stars appeared on the monitor. "Thank you for participating." He sent it out again. The Peek-a-boo never failed him. It always came back (but Slade's hadn't!). Graveyard silence filled the house. Out the window, clouds covered the night sky, so all he saw was his own shimmery image, like he was someone else: a small boy's spirit, his elbows planted on his ghost desk in a ghost world looking at his ghost computer. Dustin almost waved, but something stirred behind him in the reflection. He was too tired to be startled. Standing at the door, illuminated by the monitor's faint light, his Dad in pajamas looked in. His face had no color, no life, and two shadowed pits marked where his eyes should have been. Dad leaned against the doorjamb, watching Dustin, or he might have been looking beyond him, or his eyes could have been closed. The pose held for a marble moment.

Dustin blinked, and the apparition was gone. Had he really seen him? A few seconds later, the stairs creaked; Dad going down.

For a hundred heartbeats, Dustin stared at his reflection, and then through the ghost boy to the maple tree he couldn't see, and beyond that to the clouds that covered the stars, and through them to the stars themselves, trying to understand. Dad had appeared and disappeared without a sound except the squeak on the stair. Everything done in silence. No noise that Dustin didn't make himself in the perpetually quiet house. He pressed the send button again, and the key's cricket click seemed big in the muffling stillness.

The image of himself in the glass and the wavery memory of his dad behind him defined Dustin's universe. Nothing else existed. Then a new image began forming on his monitor from the top down. Not black. Yellow from side to side, like candle flame. Not a starscape. Not even a distant planet hovering in the velvet abyss. On the screen's left side, a corner of something red appeared. A straight line built toward the screen's bottom, and then an orange sphere formed on the screen's right side. The computer pinged three times. A new popup message flashed across the image: "DO NOT TOUCH YOUR PEEK-A-BOO OR TURN OFF YOUR COMPUTER!" At the same time, his phone rang. A second later, his cell phone, recharging on the nightstand chimed for attention.

Dustin jerked back. Who could be calling at 3:00 in the morning? They'd wake his parents! He picked up the phone. A recorded announcement said, "This is a Peek-a-boo priority communication. Information from your Peek-a-boo unit indicates a unique contact. Please do not attempt to send your Peek-a-boo device out again or switch programs on your computer. Representatives from Peek-a-boo will communicate with you immediately. . . . This is a Peek-a-boo priority communication. . . ."

Dad's voice interrupted. "What have you done, Dustin? Do you know what time it is?"

Mom said sleepily over the phone, "What is going on? What is going on?"

The image finished forming on the monitor behind the popup message. Dustin hesitated, the phone still to his ear. "Please do not attempt to send your Peek-a-boo device out again or switch programs on your computer," repeated the voice. Dustin closed the popup window; the screen glowed yellow, orange and red in crisp lines and shapes.

"I didn't do anything," he said. "I don't know."

"I'm coming up," said Dad.

The stairs creaked beneath his mom's slippered feet.

Mom arrived first, then Dad. They gathered behind his chair.

Dad said, "Why are they calling you in the middle of the night?"

"I don't know, Dad. Something about this." He gestured toward the monitor.

Mom said, "Is that a screensaver?"

In the distance, a police car siren sounded, coming closer.

Dustin's face flushed, the phone still in his hand, repeating the message over and over. "No, my Peek-a-boo took it."

"What is it?" Dad leaned over Dustin's shoulder. The upper half of the monitor showed colored shapes in sharp geometry. A mottled gray and yellow texture filled the bottom half, but all the angles were skewed so the image seemed to be sliding off the screen's left side.

The siren turned onto Dustin's street, its flashing blue and red lights reflecting off the neighborhood trees until the car parked in his driveway. The siren wailed to silence, and a few seconds later, a heavy knocking came from the front door.

His parents looked at Dustin first, and then toward the pounding downstairs. "Don't touch your computer, son," said Dad.

Another car without a siren or flashing lights pulled into the driveway. Doors opened. Voices jumbled together outside.

Minutes later, his room full of strangers, Dustin sat on his bed's edge and said, "I just kept sending it out." An earnest older man whose shirt was tucked in on only one side wrote Dustin's comment in a notebook.

"Had you seen a planet on that coordinate earlier?" he asked. Dustin shook his head. At Dustin's desk, two women, one in a bathrobe, and the other in a nice pantsuit, whispered vehemently back and forth about the image. "We'll need his hard drive. It could be a fake," Pantsuit said. "I don't see how," replied Bathrobe.

A man in uniform, but definitely not a policeman, carefully rolled Dustin's Peek-a-boo into a plastic bag that zipped closed when the unit plopped to the bottom.

From the hallway, Mom's voice said, "He's always been a determined boy."

Dad said, "So, you think he really found something, do you?" His tone was skeptical.

Someone in the hallway said, "He'll be famous."

"Look at this," said Bathrobe. She moved the cursor to the menu bar at the top of the screen. A few clicks later, the image reoriented itself. Now the gray and yellow texture moved to the top and became sky. Dustin blinked, then blinked again. What had seemed abstract before suddenly made sense. "Is that . . ." he said, and swallowed. "Is that a building?"

Pantsuit pointed to what had been a red blob before, "Yes, and that looks like a tree to me. . ." she bent close to the screen, ". . . with a park bench under it. A yellow one with brown arm rests."

"I don't believe it," said Bathrobe, in a voice that was clear she did.

The older man sitting on the bed with Dustin said to himself, "It's such a big universe. What are the odds a Peek-a-boo would appear close enough to a planet's surface, oriented just the right way, to take a picture of a park bench?"

Bathrobe said, "A park bench 380 million light years from Earth."

Dustin lay in his bed. The clouds had cleared, and early dawn lightened the sky enough through his window to dissolve the stars and show the blank area on his desk where his computer had sat earlier that night. Now, though, only a clean square outlined by a fine dust film showed that anything had been there at all.

"We'll replace this computer," Bathrobe had said as she left with the CPU. Pantsuit added, "And a new Peek-a-boo, even better than your old one. Later today, there will be a news conference."

The older man patted Dustin on the head as he left. "There will be a lot of news conferences, I'd say, now that you showed us where to look."

After all the bustle, after the doors slammed below and the cars departed, Dustin finally climbed into bed, but he couldn't sleep. For the longest time he stared out the window, his sheets pulled to his chin, hands locked behind his head. A few days ago, the moon had preceded Mars to the horizon, but now the red planet set first, while the moon followed, dragging Pleiades like star babies close behind. He thought about the stars passing by his window as if they were friends: Hamal, of course, and Menkar, and the sprinkling of tau stars, omi Tau, xi Tau and f Tau, then Aldebaran and Algol, and Betelgeuse, who faded last in the lightening sky. They all seemed so comforting that he didn't notice at first that the house had changed. For the longest time he tried to place the difference. Not just the missing computer. Not just the strangeness of the night's events. Something else.

He gasped in surprise, then silenced his breathing so he could hear. Below him, in his parent's room, he heard voices: his mom and dad, talking. The conversation rose and fell. It had been going on since they'd left his room. Once, he could swear, he heard laughter. Long after the morning sky had brightened to blue and the maple tree cast its shadow on the fence and their neighbor's house, Dustin listened, and not once, that morning, did his parents quit talking. Not even when they moved into the kitchen. Not even when they began fixing breakfast. Their voices broke the long silence, and Dustin knew he wasn't alone in the house.

He wasn't alone, and it was time to eat.

# TINY VOICES

More than the thirty feet and a wall separated the two women. Stella sipped breaths, her sheet pulled under her chin, eyes closed tight, but she saw the room from a dozen vantage points: from the television's self-focusing eye, the coffee pot's proximity control, the light switch's finger pad, the medical sensor's finely tuned perception field that reached not just to her, tracing each labored heart beat and marking the sluggish progress of her blood through her body, but also picking up a fly's tiny buzz near the ceiling fixture and a beetle crawling along the baseboard under the bed. She saw herself lying beneath the covers, old, old, old, as old as crumbling epitaphs, as old as weathered wood, her face a shrunken fruit barely making a dent in the pillow. I.V. lines dangled from her arm. She pitied herself as if from afar, and it was all she could do to keep from weeping. In fact, when she looked closely, she could tell she was weeping shiny glinting tear tracks from the corners of her eyes to her ears. It didn't seem fair, so close to death that she could sense so much. With an electron's nimbleness, she switched her attention from device to device. I can't be dying, she thought; I don't want to.

Stella saw Corey too, sitting at her desk beyond the door in the receiving room, talking to her pencil.

"It's just a memo," Corey said. "Thirty or forty words, no more. I won't even press hard." If Stella's traveling senses could have reached Corey's inner ear, she would have heard the pencil's tinny voice in reply. "I'm only good for five thousand words, and that's if you write small ones, but you like 'tremulous' and 'serendipity.' Please, write with someone else."

Corey put the pencil on her desk. It was an ordinary yellow pencil with number two lead, but with the addition of a sentient chip. Everything had a sentient chip. Her chair reminded her occasionally that she was gaining weight, and her desk chatted amiably about waxy buildup and the loose paperclips in the bottom drawer, just as her car talked about traffic, and her blouse reported dirt and perspiration. Everything talked, but her pencil was difficult. It talked of death.

"My doctor needs to know what I want to do," Corey said. "If I don't write it down, he won't know." She placed a fingertip on the pencil's pointed end and another on the pink eraser, holding it above the blank paper. "You need to do your job. This is important. You're just a pencil." She thought about the tests she'd already taken, and how her doctor had blanched when he told her, "You're pregnant."

"I haven't ordered a baby," she had said, her hands pressing the sides of the papery robe to the examination table.

"No," the doctor said, "*You* are pregnant. Your body is."

He'd left the room after giving her a handful of brochures with fifty-year-old copyright dates and illustrations of third-world women in front of mud huts.

She had to write him a note, but she didn't know what to say. Nothing on her small and tidy desk helped. A clock. A leather-edged desk pad. A picture of her mom leaning against a tree the year before she'd fallen sick and died. If Corey stretched her arms, she could wrap her hands around both of the desk's edges lengthwise. A hat rack stood near the door next to an uncomfortable chair. The walls were a clean, smooth beige and had a wiped-down shininess to them that made her think of dentist offices.

The pencil moaned. "My life is measured in words."

In the other room, Stella cleared her throat, and Stella heard it in the telephone and the stereo and the sink and every other voice-activated device. She was wired in everywhere, as fast as a thought, dexterous and lively in her mind, not old and declining. With effort, she concentrated on her throat, swallowing hard, controlling the muscles and making sure that it was clear when she was done. The nurse told her that she had to be careful with her swallowing. A careless moment could mean choking to death, not that being careful would prevent the inevitable.

"Corey," she croaked, but it was too soft a sound. She imagined it didn't even reach the end of her bed.

In the other room, Corey said to her pencil, "I'm not talking to you anymore," and she wrote a note furiously.

"Corey," Stella said, louder this time. Her lungs wheezed shut like wet tissues. Stella would have pushed the call button, but she couldn't find it. She couldn't feel her fingers well, and it was possible that she was holding the button without knowing. Disgusted at her faltering body, Stella slid into the television, upped the volume and boomed, "Corey, dear!"

Corey put the pencil down, read her note, then threw it in the trash can, a wadded ball. "Thank you," said the trash can's voice in her ear. "This is a type one recyclable."

"Coming." Corey's chair creaked without comment when she stood. Then, as if on cue, the outer door opened and Harlow walked in, his jacket hanging on one arm, his thick blonde hair tousled across his forehead in a nonchalant fashion that said, "I'm carefree; can't you be too?"

In a blink, Corey pictured him in a different light, his clothes carefully draped over the top of a chair under his neatly folded jacked, his face close to hers, breathing fast but delicious and warm as roast beef. What she noticed most in the memory, though, was his hair with its deliberate indifference, the same as it looked now.

"How's the old Stella-witch today?" he said, with a long, slow, polished smile as he walked by.

Corey started after him, then flinched. Had she thrown away the note? A glance assured her it was in the trash.

Stella saw the flinch from three angles. A quick dip into the trash can's sentience didn't help. No visuals. Paper, the sensor told her. Low rag content.

Reluctantly, Stella pulled herself back into her head. Harlow's hand rested on her arm. He gave it a tiny squeeze, then said too loudly, "Hi, Stella. It's me, Harlow, your nephew."

She tried to clear her throat again. No luck. Phlegm, solid as a hockey puck, clogged it. "I know who you are," she bellowed from the television.

"Jeeze!" Harlow jumped. "I hate it when you do that."

Stella used the mental connection to turn the volume down. "I'm old, not ignorant." She tried to focus on him, but her eyelids hurt to stay open, and she teared easily. He was a tall, dark blur against the ceiling lights. Switching to the television made him easier to see—of all the devices in the room, it had the best optics—but his back was to that point of view. Corey stood on the other side of the bed, though, and her face was clear, not looking at Stella. Her head was down, studying Harlow from beneath her long lashes.

"You're not that old, Stella. The doctor just yesterday told me how well you were doing." He winked at Corey. "We'll have you dancing again in a week."

Corey smiled back, but Harlow had already looked away. She watched his hand on Stella's arm. The night they'd been together had been so vivid. His hand had toyed with the top button on her blouse for the longest time, not unbuttoning it, but not going away either.

Harlow sighed, somewhere between annoyed and bored. Until two months ago, he'd always lingered longer at Corey's desk then he did at Stella's bedside. But that was two months ago. Corey could almost see him checking the time. She searched for something to say. "Stella's improved her connections. A tech was in here this morning. He told me that's he's never hooked up so many devices into one interface, but Stella doesn't move much, so there isn't a problem with range and interference like there would be for you or me."

"Really?" Harlow crossed his arms. "Expensive, I'll bet."

"I don't know. I suppose." The interface relay, a flat box an inch thick and six inches on each side, hung on the wall directly behind Stella's head.

"I like to keep the seat of my consciousness movable," Stella said from the small refrigerator on the counter. "What's really expensive is the internal gear. Sight, sound, touch, taste and smell. The whole shooting match."

Harlow glanced around the room. "What have you got in here with a sense of taste?"

"Not me. That's for sure. Coffee maker. Microwave. I've got a stirring ladle at the house that could probably tell me a bunch. Can't access it from here, though." Stella laughed from the refrigerator's speaker, which normally only said things like, "The milk has gone bad," or "There's a special on broccoli this week."

Corey wanted to move to Harlow's side of the bed. Maybe if she got close enough to him, he would have to acknowledge her. He'd been so distant lately, as if she was someone he'd never met before. Only his hand on Stella's arm seemed vulnerable, and even that gesture looked perfunctory. His jacket hid his other hand, and he held his arms close to his side. He was self-contained. Locked in.

Harlow shrugged. "Everybody has to have a hobby, I suppose.

Whatever makes you happy, Aunt Stella. Don't know if I could stand the extra information. Bad enough that doorknobs and sidewalks talk."

Corey said, "You have a business interface, don't you?"

"Of course, business. Phone calls. That's it. I block the rest." He moved his jacket to his shoulder. "Everybody who wants to stay sane does that. Too much noise otherwise. Silly ads and chatty appliances."

"I suppose," Corey said. "I hadn't thought about it that way before."

He smiled at her again, like he had when he'd passed her desk, all teeth and glittering eyes like a light flicking on, then it was gone. "Your message said there were more papers to sign. I should get to them."

"And more for tomorrow too. Today's are on my desk."

"Don't mind me. I'm just dying here," said Stella from the light switch.

Corey looked down at her guiltily. Stella's arms seemed no more substantial than flower stems, and dark mottles covered the parchment-thin skin.

"Are you comfortable, ma'am? Can I get you some water?" She moved the pillow under Stella's head to give her a better angle.

The old woman's eyes peeked from between the eyelids. A tip of tongue moistened her lips. Corey leaned close. "Yes, dear. That would be nice," Stella whispered. Corey smiled. Stella always called her dear or deary, terms of endearment Corey had never heard from anyone else. They were archaic, like Stella.

Water poured from the faucet before she reached it. "Forty-two degrees and pure as a spring," said the sink's voice in Corey's head. Beside the sink sat the microwave, and beside that the coffee maker. Four white cabinets containing medical supplies filled the rest of the space to the counter's end. She could smell the ointment she rubbed into Stella's elbows and knees. The jar's lid was loose, so she tightened it. When she returned to the bedside, Stella appeared to have gone asleep, her face tilted to the side, her breath raspy and dry. Corey reached to touch Stella's shoulder.

"I'm still with you," said the microwave. "Just wandering around the room. I love the new interface, deary."

Stella turned on the pillow, and when the straw touched her lips, she drank gingerly. "Oh, that's better," she murmured.

The old woman swallowed a couple more times as if it hurt. "Your young man is gone," she said.

"My young man?" Corey's fingers rested on the bed's cool, aluminum side rail. "Oh, Harlow!"

The outer room was empty. On her desk, the papers were signed. In the trash can, next to her wadded note, lay a pen. The trash can, with a hurt tone, said in her ear, "This is a mixed-composition non-recyclable item. It should be disposed of properly."

Corey straightened the papers before bending down to retrieve the pen.

"Thank goodness," the pen said when she picked it up. "I'm properly functioning and three-quarters full."

It glistened in her hand, an ordinary black and gray businessperson's pen. "So, why'd he throw you away?" The pen's button depressed smoothly under her thumb, revealing the ball point with an authoritative click.

"I skip sometimes," it said, sulkily. "It's a manufacturing flaw. Not my fault."

"Did you tell him?" She clicked the pen closed and set it on the desk next to her pencil.

"He never ever listens. He misspells all the time, you know. Will he make a correction? Nope. I might as well be mute."

"I'll bet he's hell on pencils too," said the pencil.

"Oh, yes. He chews them when he's thinking."

"The bastard."

Corey said, "How old are you?"

"My battery expires in six months, but I wanted to go down writing."

"Do you mind if I use you to compose a note? My pencil is reluctant." She opened a desk drawer for a piece of paper.

The pencil barked, "Not reluctant! I'm *solar* powered. No expiration date, if she would just quit using me!"

"Not at all. I'm here to serve. Umm, I do skip occasionally. Is this to be a final draft?"

"Just a note." Corey held the pen next to her ear, clicked it open then closed a few times. The paper's blankness seemed a mile wide. What could she write on it? What could she tell the doctor? He'd seemed as confused as she was at first, and apologetic. "Ovulation has been blocked for you. Technically, I don't know how it could happen." She had closed her eyes on the examination table, ticking off the symptoms that had brought her in: light-headedness, tender breasts, constipation and fatigue.

"Are you sure it isn't a vitamin deficiency?" she had said.

He shuffled through screens on his clipboard. "No, you're eight weeks along, give or take a couple days. There's a heartbeat. I'd have to do field work in back-country Africa for an opportunity like this. It's fascinating."

Then he talked to her about abortion. "If we had caught it earlier," he said, "we could consider a fetal extraction and a normal laboratory gestation. But . . . eight weeks." He shrugged and told her to take a day or two to choose the best date to come in.

Corey twirled the pen from finger to finger. Her other hand rested on her belly. It was hard to imagine a second heartbeat inside her. The idea was so . . . retro. The only picture she could associate with it was of a frontier woman sitting on the seat of a covered wagon, her hands loose on the reins, a belly full of baby resting on her legs. She thought about talking to Harlow. "By the way," she might say, "you know how sometimes the most unlikely things can happen?"

"Is this to be a business correspondence?" said the pen. "I can suggest several good salutations if that is the case."

"How about letters to distant boyfriends?" The pen clicked open and closed again under her thumb. "No, forget it. I'm thinking."

She looked at the clock on her desk that she'd brought from home when she took the job caretaking for Stella. It was an old clock. Pre-sentient. Practically an antique. Thirty minutes until she could go home for the day, the glowing numbers told her. It could talk, though, if she asked for the time. So it could listen. Corey wondered if Stella could access it from the other room. Was it listening to her right now? Could she hear the breathing? The pen clicking? The oddness of her thoughts?

Corey put the pen in the middle of the blank paper, pushed away from the desk. Maybe Stella needed company. Poor woman. On death's bed with no one to sit with her. Harlow was her only relative, and he came by twice a week. What must it be like to be in her place, tied by gravity and age to the bed?

Stella's consciousness hovered in the middle of the room. She upped the sound reception on the coffee pot, and it seemed she moved toward it. When she zoomed in on the television, she moved there. In the bed, she giggled, and the giggle echoed in the microwave and the sink and the telephone, her voice leaking from each.

She peeked at herself from the television. Old woman, still beneath the sheets. Could that bag of infirmity really be her? Straining, she raised her hand off the blanket and wiggled her fingers in a weak imitation of a wave. Her arm struggled to hold the hand even in inch in the air. Her shoulder ached, and the muscles in her back were within an instant of cramping. She dropped the hand back to the bed.

A brush of air touched her. But it wasn't her skin that felt it; it was the much more sensitive light switch. She could feel more than pain again! Stella turned the television on its gimbal so she could see the door. Corey walked in, quietly, but her shoes scraped loud enough for the microphones in the room. Stella listened mightily. Yes, she could hear the young woman's breathing, the rustle of her skirt against her legs.

Stella said from the microwave, "I'm awake, dear."

"I was trying to be quiet."

Corey stopped at the medical readouts displayed at the foot of the bed. Stella felt around in her head until she found the readouts too, clear in her mind, pulse, temperature, blood pressure, chemical balances, respiration. She held her breath to see the breathing stop. Soon, the pulse accelerated.

"Ma'am?" Corey said, a touch of concern in her voice.

Stella released the pent-up air in a whoosh. "Oh, this is fun."

"Fun?"

"I'm mobile again."

"I don't understand."

Stella wished there was a camera on her bed so she could see Corey's expression, but all the eyes in the room were behind her.

"I told you," Stella said. "The seat of my consciousness is on the move."

Corey shook her head.

"The seat of your consciousness is where you picture yourself. It's where you feel the center of who you are emanates. Where is the seat of your consciousness, dear?"

The young woman sat in a chair next to the bed. Now the side of her face was clearly in view. Fine, blonde hair that fell to just above her shoulders. High cheekbones. A mouth that turned down when she wasn't smiling, so she often looked pensive. Stella tried to remember when her own face was so unlined.

"In me?" said Corey.

"Yes, but where within you? Try this. Close your eyes and just listen. Where are *you*, your essence, the seat of your consciousness?"

For a minute, neither woman made a sound.

Corey laughed. "Between my ears, just behind my eyes."

Stella sighed. "Yes, that's where it would be. But what if you couldn't hear or see? What if your only sense was of touch? Would the seat of your consciousness be in your hands then?"

Corey's brow furrowed. "I don't know. Maybe." She stood. "The night nurse and your dinner will be here soon. Is there anything I can do for you before I go?"

"No, dear. I'm enjoying my independence," she said from the medical sensor.

A voice Corey didn't hear often said inside her ear, "This is the mattress speaking. The sheets are soiled and need attention."

After the night nurse came and they changed the sheets—the old woman seemed almost weightless as they transferred her to and from the bed—Corey put on her coat. Her hands smelled of antiseptic. The nurse, a solid-looking woman with sturdy calves, stood in the doorway into Stella's room, her arms crossed. "I don't give her a week at this rate," she said. "Nutrients aren't being absorbed. She dehydrates easily. Next coma will be her last."

Corey felt a sudden itchiness in her eyes, but she resisted the impulse to rub them. "I know."

"I've got another patient signed up in her spot at the end of the month. It'll be a scheduling problem if this one hangs on that long."

It wasn't until Corey reached the park across the street from the building that she let herself cry. The park bench said, "You are upset. Can I contact a counseling service for you?"

Corey blew her nose. The air smelled of elm and warm streets, and the afternoon sun cast long shadows of buildings and trees across the lawn. Traffic hummed quietly on all sides. A few feet in front of her, four small gray birds pecked at the sidewalk. They moved in little hops from one spot to the next, tapping for a moment, then straightening to look for threats. Corey leaned forward, her elbows resting on her knees, a tissue hanging from one hand.

One of the birds hopped toward her, its black eyes like pencil tips glistening in its feather-smooth head. The bird cocked its head to one side, then the other, looking at her. It pecked at a seed on the cement, then looked at her again. Corey half expected the bird's voice to erupt in her ear. "What are you staring at?" it might ask, or "Any bread crumbs?" But the bird was mute. The tiny intelligence functioned on its own. Corey pressed her palm on her belly. Still flat. The doctor had said there was a heartbeat, but she couldn't feel it. The doctor had said, "We'll throw it away. Just a handful of cells. An annoyance, no more." How big was it growing inside her now? Was it as big as a wren? Where was its voice?

When Corey went to bed, she stayed awake for hours watching the shadows from the tree outside her window play across her ceiling. As she finally grew drowsy, the shadows took the shape of small gray birds, hopping from tile to tile.


Stella didn't feel tired in the least. If she concentrated, she realized she could identify a sound's location. All she needed was to triangulate from the microphones. A minuscule scritching sound behind the closed doors under the counter told her a mouse was hard at work. The night nurse's steady tapping of the pencil on the table while she contemplated a crossword puzzle seemed as distinct as a bell. She heard the pencil's beat echo from the walls, and without accessing video, she could see the room like a bat, each tap clarifying the dimensions.

Stella chuckled. Maybe what she could do would be to order a remote control sensing device. Something she could direct through the interface. She could walk the streets again, or at least her senses could go.

The medical sensor clicked. A valve opened inside to release a dose of something from Stella's I.V. line. She moved her consciousness into the sensitive machine. Of all the devices in the room, the medical sensor provided the most information. Her own pulse was a sound, a feeling and a color, throbbing like a dull red sun. Her breathing rasped in rainbow hues, dazzling in the medical sensor's perception. Her body's temperature registered in numbers and grid lines, the coolness of her fingers and feet, the warmth of her chest and stomach.

She watched herself on the bed, probed her organs, listened to the crackle of air through her nose, the snap of her lips as they separated for another breath, the gurgle of her intestines.

After a couple hundred steady beats of her tired heart, Stella realized the sound of her breathing had changed. The snore vibrated in the room, stopped for a moment, resumed.

The mouse paused in its investigations in the cabinet. The night nurse kept tapping.

I'm sleeping, Stella thought. I'm wide awake and sleeping. How interesting.

The tram from Corey's apartment to work was only half full. Across the aisle, a man, a woman and a five-year-old girl hunched over a coloring book. The girl said, "I'm making the sky purple because purple is Mommy's favorite." The woman smiled. She wore a yellow blouse and pants that left most of her midriff bare. No lines on her slender belly. She's never been pregnant, Corey thought. Pregnant. The word itself felt alien in Corey's head. No queasiness for the yellow-blouse lady. Of course not. Corey couldn't picture what it would be like to sit on the tram, her belly gravid and alive with motion. She'd read that a pregnant mother could feel the baby kicking inside. What was that like? Little fleshy earthquakes. People would stare. She shuddered.

"I like purple too," said the child.

The man tousled the girl's hair. He was Harlow's age. How had the man and woman got together? Had his wife said I love you first? Did she know then that she loved him?

Corey closed her eyes and rested the side of her head against the window until she reached her stop.

The family exited first. Corey gripped the handrail near the door, waiting for them to leave. The little girl turned and held up a broken crayon to her dad. He took it, shrugged, and dropped it in a waste bin on the sidewalk.

Was it alive? Corey thought. Did it have a voice, and what was it thinking now, laying in the dark among thrown away paper and empty soft drink containers? Did they talk among themselves, the tiny voices, the thrown away, knowing the recycler would pick them up soon?

"Good day, ma'am," the waste bin announced in her inner ear when Corey touched it.

She snatched her hand back.

A voice mail awaited her in the office. "I've had a cancellation, so we can schedule your procedure for tomorrow if that would be convenient," said her doctor. "If you don't mind, a couple of interns have expressed interest in observing. Your condition really is quite fascinating."

The night nurse came in from Stella's room. "She's gone under for the last time. Another coma," she declared as she put on her coat. "I'd give her twenty-four hours, tops."

Corey felt her shoulders drop, a physical unleashing, as if the muscles had died. "No."

The nurse buttoned her coat, her face a closed door. "We knew it was on the way. She was used up."

When the nurse left, Corey sat in her chair, her hands resting limply on her legs. She realized she'd been staring at them for some time, when a thin keening voice echoed in her ear. Not words, just a long howl of grief and loss, but so quiet she thought at first it might be a subconscious sound, a part of her imagination.

She found the pencil in the bottom drawer, but instead of the length she'd left it the day before, it had been sharpened down to its last inch. There was almost more eraser than pencil. From end to end, it didn't reach to both sides of her palm.

"What happened?" she said.

The sobbing continued. It would be so easy for her to block it out. A simple adjustment and the pencil would no longer be able to talk to her. Harlow could do it. He walked through a world of tiny voices screened to silence. But she didn't. She waited until the cries settled down.

Finally the pencil gasped, "Crossword puzzles."

"Huh?"

"All night, crossword puzzles. The nurse writes and writes and writes, then resharpens. Always, always resharpening. I'm a splinter away from annihilation."

"Toss him in here," said the trashcan.

"No, don't," said the pen from the desktop. "The pencil's a good egg. Do you know there's a couple thousand jokes stored on his chip? And he makes up new ones all the time."

"My pencil makes up jokes?" Corey rolled the wood between her palms.

"I have skills," said the pencil. "I have other interests."

"Well, let's hear one."

The pencil hesitated. "Okay. How about this? Did you hear the joke about the pencil?"

Corey shook her head and then said, "No."

"Never mind. It's pointless."

The pen snickered.

Corey looked at the pencil incredulously. "That's terrible. I can't believe I listened to that." She put it on the desk and stood.

"Maybe this one will be better," said the pencil. "Where do pencil vampires come from?"

Corey picked up the pen and put in her blouse pocket, then moved to the doorway between her office and Stella's room.

"Pencil-vania," the pencil said across the distance.

If anything, Stella appeared even smaller than she had yesterday. Her mouth hung open; her chest was still. Corey stepped toward her, then Stella gasped and sucked in a raspy breath.

Red lights flashed on the medical sensor. Electrolytes dangerously low, read one display. Blood oxygen dangerously low, read another. Brain patterns indicate serious distress, reported a third. Corey tapped the communication interface. Hospital contacted and no heroic measure order confirmed said the note. Stella's heartbeat pinged forlornly from the medical sensor.

Corey's hand quivered when she touched Stella's forehead. "Where are you, Stella? Where's the seat of your consciousness now?"

But Stella couldn't process the question. She heard the words without sorting them into meaning. Colors pressed in on her, and sounds, and the shape of smells, all confused and muddled. This is death, she thought. I can fight it, if I can just find myself. So she moved as best she could through the forms and notes and blustery textures that batted against her. I'm dying! My mind is collapsing upon itself. She could see an abyss around her. A sucking blackness just beyond the chaos on every side. Maybe I'm already dead! She tried moving her hands, but she couldn't feel them. She felt nothing at all. A tumbling. A falling down. An endless repetition of glassy ringing like crystal wind chimes behind cotton walls.

Stella would have wept if she could, but she fought instead. If I can grab something. If I can center myself, all will not be lost. And the ringing continued. Was it a voice echoed and transformed? Was it the sluggish firing of her last brain cells like a Fourth of July sparkler nearly gone dead?

Corey sat beside the old woman's bed for an hour. Each life sign's graph slid slowly down. The pulse barely twitched every couple of seconds, sounding its tiny tone. The pause between them was excruciating. Even Stella's smell seemed stale, as if she'd already passed on and had gone bad.

Finally, after Stella's dying sounds became a background noise, the door to the outer office opened, startling Corey out of her chair, but Stella didn't move when Harlow came into the room, his hands jammed into his pockets, and his always careless hair waving across his forehead.

"Last call, isn't it?" he said. "I'd better get those papers signed or we'll be postmortem, and what a mess that would be."

"I have to talk to you," Corey said. "It's important."

He smiled. "I know you liked Stella, but she's gone now. You'll get a severance package and a good recommendation. Don't worry."

Corey blinked. For a second what he said didn't make sense to her. The blood rose to her face, and for an instant it was if he was breathing on her again, warm and tense, a half beat from the end.

"No, it's not that. I'm pregnant."

Harlow moved to the other side of the bed. "I suppose we'll have to return all this equipment. Do you know if it's rented, or did Stella buy it?"

Corey's hands rested on the back of the chair by the bed. She could feel the sweat on her neck. Harlow was looking at Stella's interface box on the wall behind her head.

"I'm pregnant," she said again.

"Bad timing, that," said Harlow. "But you'll come up with another job in no time. You could delay delivery if you want. All the better companies give you a few months either way. A buddy of mine and his wife didn't take delivery for sixteen months because he got cold feet."

"No, Harlow, you don't understand. I'm pregnant. Me. I'm physically with child." She pressed her hand against her stomach. "There's a baby in here. Your baby."

He blinked back at her, then his brow furrowed. "I didn't order a baby. I haven't even deposited anywhere."

"In me, you did, the old-fashioned way. It's not supposed to happen, but we're going to be parents."

Harlow didn't speak.

"I thought you should know," said Corey.

"You're pregnant?"

The pen piped up in Corey's ear. "I told you he was an idiot."

"And he chews pencils," said the pencil from the other room.

"It's in you? Like a parasite?" Harlow's nose wrinkled as if he'd smelled something distasteful. "What a bother."

"My doctor wants me to make an appointment." Corey's hands covered her stomach that still felt flat and familiar. "Soon." She felt as if she were playacting. A *real* pregnant woman wouldn't feel so . . . so normal. Maybe she could just shake her head to wake up. Stella wouldn't be dying. Harlow would wait for her at her desk for long talks, his lovely eyes locked on her own. She'd still know the long anticipation of his fingers on her top blouse button, toying, toying, toying, and always a second away from committing.

"It's just a toss-away," said Harlow. "Get a reset at the doctor's office and start from scratch. Plus, you probably have a good malpractice lawsuit. Nobody gets pregnant nowadays." He pushed away from Stella's bed. "How about our lease? Are we committed to paying for the room until the end of the month, or do they prorate it?"

A muscle in the corner of Corey's mouth twitched. Suddenly, she wanted to take a handful of his wavy hair and jerk it out by the roots. "I don't know." She moved next to the medical sensor. The device's cool, smooth surface slid beneath her fingers. Stella's heart beat quietly in the background.

"Lend me your pen," he said. "I'll sign these papers now." He took it, then wrote on the documents, awkwardly across his knee. "There, she's still alive, and I've taken care of this." The pen clicked open and closed twice under his thumb. "The pen skips," he said, flicking it into the trashcan as he left, where it clattered loudly.

The peace in the room after the door snapped shut lasted for only a second before the trashcan said to the pen, "Ahh, I knew you'd come back. They always come back."

"The bastard," said the pencil.

"Save me!" cried the pen.

Corey covered her face with her hands, "Oh, just shut up, all of you." She leaned her backside against the medical sensor to keep from collapsing to the floor.

Several long sobs later, she shook her head as if she were trying to wake up, then wiped her hands hard on her pants legs. "I knew that would happen," she said. "I knew he wouldn't care, Stella."

Stella, or course, didn't answer. Her lips were parted, her head, turned to one side; her eyelids, thin as parchment, didn't move. She looked like the photograph of a woman rather than the woman herself. Corey sat in the chair next to the bed and touched the old woman's fingers that dangled over the guard rail. No response, but

Corey didn't expect any. A few minutes later she realized Stella's heartbeat wasn't pinging from the medical sensor.

Silence consumed the room.

"Where'd you go?" said Corey, feeling so much like a ten-year-old that her adult voice surprised her.

Somewhere else, in a clattering chaos of shapes and sounds and rough currents, the question echoed. Stella heard it from a dozen directions, repeating and looping on itself until it became a refrain boiled down to "Go, go, go." She reached out as best she could, but she had no hands to grab with. She could only follow, so she did. Drifting after the strongest sound, driving her forward, urging, "Go, go, go." Stella didn't know: was she lost or found? Was she still herself, or was she fragmenting, breaking into pieces in the sloppy overload of textures and odors? Still, she moved, because there was nothing else to do, and as she did, she thought she saw a place she recognized. Is this the afterlife? she thought. Is that my angel?

She tried so hard to see.

Corey let Stella's cold fingers rest against her own. The room looked surreal to her in its stillness. The white cabinets. The refrigerator. The clean walls exactly the same as they'd been yesterday and the day before, but now as different as sleep from waking. She hesitated to move. It would break the spell. Stella would become just a dead and fading memory. For now, though, Stella's touch was real. Corey stayed motionless, almost afraid to breathe, not really thinking. Then, she saw a tiny speck creeping along the baseboard beneath the bed, a beetle making its way across the room, and, soon, she heard a gentle scratching within the wall behind the cabinets, and she realized there must be a mouse there, fending for itself. She almost smiled at the thought when another movement caught her eye: the television mounted in the room's corner had rotated slightly toward her.

Corey froze.

The television turned another half inch.

"Stella?" Corey said, almost choking on the sound. "Stella?"

The television's speaker hissed.

Without willing herself to rise, Corey found herself under the television, straining to make out the breathy whisper. A voice murmured behind it. Corey said, "I can't understand you, Stella." Finally, a ghost of speech resolved itself into something almost audible. What it sounded like was, "I'm here, deary." Then the hiss faded away.

"I'm still here," said a louder voice.

Corey jumped. It was the pen.

"Leave him," said the trashcan. "Mixed recyclable or not, when you're done, you're done."

"No," Corey said. She retrieved the pen from the trashcan's bottom. "I need it to write a note."

"Oh, thank goodness," said the pencil. "I don't have another word in me, I'm afraid."

Corey took a sheet of paper out of the desk and clicked the pen open. "Do you know a fancier phrase than 'I am sorry?'"

The pen said, "I regret."

"Or, 'with regrets,'" suggested the pencil.

Corey wrote her note, thinking about frontier women riding west, their bellies full of babies, of little flesh quakes shaking within her. She thought of the pencil's pathetic quest to stay alive. One, tiny, sentient voice among a million voices, like Stella's voice somehow preserved in all the connections. The seat of her consciousness cut loose and free.

She thought of the tiny voice she hadn't heard yet, like the speechless gray bird on the sidewalk, hopping from seed to seed.

# LASHAWNDA AT THE END

We landed in steam. It billowed from where we touched down, then vanished into the dry, frigid air. From that first moment, the planet fascinated Lashawnda. She watched the landing tape over and over.

Lashawnda liked Papaver better than any of the rest us. She liked the gopher-rats that stood on their hind legs to look curiously until we got too close. She liked the smaller sun wavering in the not-quite-right blue sky, the lighter gravity, the blonde sand and gray rocks that reached to the horizon, but most of all, she liked the way the plants in the gullies leaned toward her when she walked through them, how the flat-leaved bushes turned toward her and stuck to her legs if she brushed against them. Wearing a full contamination suit despite the planet's thin but perfectly breathable atmosphere didn't bother her. Neither did the cold. By midday here on the equator the temperature might peak a few degrees above freezing, but the nights were incredibly chilly. Even Marvin and Beatitude's ugly deaths the first days here didn't affect her like it did everyone else. No, she was in heaven, cataloging the flora, wandering among the misshaped trees in the crooked ravines, coming up with names for each new species.

When we lost our water supply, and it looked like we might not last until the resupply ship came round, she was still happy.

Lashawnda was a research botanist; what else should I have expected? For me, a commercial applications biologist, Papaver represented a lifetime of work for *teams* of scientists, and I was only one guy. After less than two weeks on planet, I knew the best I got to do was to file a report that said, "Great possibilities for medicinal, scientific and industrial exploitation." Every plant Lashawnda sent my way revealed a whole catalog of potential pharmaceuticals. The *second* wave of explorers would make all the money.

Lashawnda was dying, but was such a positive person that even in what she knew were her final days, she worked as if no deadly date was flapping its leaden wings toward her. That's the problem in living with a technology that's extended human life so well: death is harder. It must have been easier when humans didn't make it through their first century. People dropped dead left and right, so they couldn't have feared it as much. It couldn't have made them as mad as it made me. Her mortality clung to me like a pall, making everything dark and slow motion and sad.

Of course, the plants stole our water. We should have seen it coming. Every living creature we'd found spent most of its time finding, extracting and storing water.

Second Chair pounded on my door.

"Get into a suit, Spencer," she yelled when I poked my head into the hallway. "Everyone outside!" A couple of engineers rushed by, faces flushed, half into their suits. "I'm systems control," said one as he passed. "There's no way I should risk a lung full of Papaver rot."

When I made it out the airlock, the crisis was beyond help. Our water tanks stood twenty meters from the ship, their landing struts crunched beneath them just as they were designed to do. They'd landed on the planet months before we got here, both resting between deep, lichen-filled depressions in the rock. Then the machinery gathered the minuscule water from the air, drop by drop, until when we arrived the tanks were full. A year on Papaver was enough. Everyone surrounded the tanks, heads down. Even in the bulky suits I could see how glum they were, except Lashawnda, who was under the main tank. "It's a fungus," she said, breaking off a chip of metal from what should have been the smooth underside. Her hand rested in dark mud, but even as I watched, the color leached away. The ground sucked water like a sponge, and underneath the normally arid surface, a dozen plant species waited to store the rare substance. Even now the water would be spreading beneath my feet, pumped from one cell to the next. Ten years worth of moisture for this little valley delivered all at once.

She looked at me, smiling through the face shield. "I never checked the water tanks, but I'll bet there was trace condensation on them in the mornings, enough for fungus to live on, and whatever

they secreted as waste *ate* right through. Look at this, Spencer."
She yanked hard at the tank's underside, snapping off another hunk
of metal, then handed it to me. "It's honeycombed."

The metal covered my hand but didn't weigh any more than a
piece of balsa wood. Bits crumbled from the edge when I ran my
gloved fingers over it.

"Isn't that marvelous?" she said.

First Chair said, "It's not all gone, is it? Not the other tank too?"
He moved beside the next tank, rapped his knuckles on it, producing a resonant note. He was fifty, practically a child, and this was
only his second expedition in command. "Damn." He looked into
the dry, bathtub-shaped pit in the rock beside the tank where the
water undoubtedly drained when the bottom broke out.

Lashawnda checked the pipes connecting the tanks to the ship.
"There's more here, after only ten days. How remarkable."

First Chair rapped the tank again thoughtfully. "What are our
options?"

The environmental engineer said, "We recycle, a *lot*. No more
baths."

"Yuck," said someone.

He continued, "We can build dew traps, but there isn't much
water in the atmosphere. We're not going to get a lot that way."

"Can we make it?" said First Chair.

The engineer shrugged. "If nothing breaks down."

"Check the ship. If this stuff eats at the engines, we won't be
going anywhere."

They shuffled away, stirring dust with their feet. I stayed with
Lashawnda. "A daily bleach wash would probably keep things clean,"
she said. She crouched next to the pipes, her knees grinding into the
dirt. I flinched, thinking about microscopic spores caught in her suit's
fabric. The spores had killed Marvin and Beatitude. On the third
day they'd come in from setting a weather station atop a near hill,
and they rushed the decontamination. Why would they worry? After all, the air tested breathable. We all knew that the chances of a
bacteria from an alien planet being dangerous to our Earth-grown
systems were remote, but we didn't plan on water-hungry spores
that didn't care at all what kind of proteins we were made of. The
spores only liked the water, and once they'd settled into the warm,
moist ports of the two scientist's lungs, they sprouted like crazy,
sending tendrils through their systems, breaking down human cells

to build their own structures. In an hour the two developed a cough. Six hours later, they were dead. Working remote arms through the quarantine area, I helped zip Beatitude into a body bag after the autopsy. Delicate looking orange leaves covered her cheeks, and her neck was bumpy with sprouts ready to break through.

At least they didn't suffer. The spore's toxins operated as a powerful opiate. Marvin spent the last hour babbling and laughing, weaker and weaker, until the last thing he said was, "It's God at the end."

A quick analysis of the spores revealed an enzyme they needed to sprout, and we were inoculated with an enzyme blocker, but everyone was more rigorous decontaminating now.

Lashawnda said, "Come on, Spencer. I want to show you something."

We walked downhill toward the closest gully and its forest. She limped, the result of a deteriorating hip replacement. Like most people her vintage, she'd gone through numerous reconstructive procedures, but you wouldn't know it to look at her. She'd stabilized her looks as a forty-year-old, almost a tenth her real age. Pixie-like features with character lines radiating from the mouth. Just below the ears blonde hair with hints of gray. Light blue eyes. Slender in the waist. Dancer's legs. Economical in her movements whether she was sorting plant samples or washing her face. Four hundred years! I studied her when she wasn't looking.

I picked thirty for myself. Physically it was a good place to be. I didn't tire easily. My stockiness contrasted well to her slight build.

Lashawnda suffered from cascading cancers, each treatable eruption triggering the next until the body gives up. She'd told me she had a couple laps around the sun left at best. "Papaver will be my last stop," she'd said during the long trip here. Of course, every expedition member says that in the claustrophobic confines of the ship. Once we've slept with everyone else (and all the possible combinations of three or four at the same time), and the novelty of inter-ship politicing has worn thin, we all say we're done with planet hopping forever.

I suppose it was inevitable Lashawnda and I ended up together on the ship. I was the second oldest by a century, and she had one hundred and fifty years on me, plus she laughed often and liked to talk. We'd go to bed and converse for a couple hours before sleeping. I'd grown tired of energetic couplings with partners I had nothing to say to afterwards. My own two hundred fifty years hung like a heavy coat. What did I have to say to someone who'd only been kicking around for only sixty or ninety years?

I cared for her more than anyone in my memory, and she was dying.

When we reached the gully she said, "What's amazing is that there are so many plants. Papaver should be like Mars. Same age. Lighter gravity and solar wind should have stripped its atmosphere. Unlike Mars, however, Papaver held onto its water, and the plants take care of the air."

Except for the warped orange and brown and yellow "trees" in front of us, which looked more like twisted pipes than plants, we could have been in an arctic desert.

"Darn little water," I said, thinking about our empty tanks.

"Darn little *free* water, but quite a bit locked into the biomass. Did you see the survey results I sent you yesterday?"

We pushed through the first branches. Despite their brittle looks, the stems were as supple as rubber rods. They waved back into place after we passed. Broad, waxy leaves that covered the sun side of each branch bent to face us as we came close. I found their mobility unnerving. They were like blank eyes following our movements. In the shadow of the trees I found more green than orange and yellow.

"Yeah, I looked at it." Except in a narrow band around the equator, Papaver appeared lifeless. But in the planet's most temperate region, in every sheltering hole and crevice, small plants grew. And peculiar forests, like the one we were in now, filled the gullies. The remote survey, taking samples at even the coldest and deadest-looking areas, found life there too. Despite the punishing changes in temperature and the lack of rain, porous rock served as a fertile home for endolithic fungi and algae. Beneath them lived cyanobacterias.

"If the results are uniform over the rest of the surface, there's enough water for a small ocean or two." She wiggled between two large trunks, streaking her suit with greenish-orange residue. "Do you know why the leaves stick to our suits?"

"Transference of seeds?" I hadn't had time to study the trees' life cycle. Classifying the types had filled up most of my time, and I did that from within the ship. Lashawnda sent samples so fast, I'd had little chance to investigate much myself.

"Nope. Airborne spores and their root systems do that. What they're really trying to do is to eat you."

Obviously she knew where she was going. We'd worked our way far enough into the plants that I wasn't sure what direction the ship lay. "Excuse me?" I said.

"You were wondering what preyed on the gopher-rats. They're herbivores. You said they couldn't be the top of the food chain, and they aren't. They eat lichens, fungus and leaves, and the trees eat them." She stopped at a clump of stems, like warped bamboo, and gently pushed the branches apart. "See," she said.

Half a meter off the ground, a yellow and orange cocoon hung between the branches, like a football-sized hammock. I'd seen the lumps before. "So?"

She dropped to her knees and poked it with her finger. Something inside the shape quivered and wiggled, pushing aside several leaves. A gopher-rat stared out at me for a second, a net of tendrils over its eye.

I stepped back. For a second I thought of Beatitude, her face marked with the tiny, waxy leaves. "How long . . . when did it get caught?"

She laughed. "Yesterday. I startled him, and he jumped into the trees here. When he didn't come out, I went looking."

I knelt beside her. Up close I saw how the plant had grown *into* the gopher-rat. In the few uncovered spots, tufts of fur poked out. The biologist in me was fascinated, but for the rest, I found the image repugnant. "How come he didn't escape? The leaves are a little sticky, but not *that* sticky."

"Drugs. Tiny spines on the leaves inject some type of opiate. I ran the analysis this morning. Same stuff that kept Marvin and Beatitude from feeling pain."

"A new data point to add to the ecology." I rested my hands on my knees. The poor gopher-rat didn't even get to live out its short life span. For a second I thought about burning down the entire forest for Marvin and Beatitude and the gopher-rat, who were dead and never coming back, except the gopher-rat wasn't dead yet. I wondered if it knew what was happening.

"Don't you see what's interesting?" She pushed the plants back even farther. "This is important."

"What am I missing?"

She smiled. Even through her faceplate I could tell that she found this exciting. "The gopher-rat should be dead. If the plants grabbed him just for his water, he'd be nothing but bones now, but he's still living. Obviously something else is going on. There's lumps like this one all through the forest. I dissected one. Without a thorough analysis, I can't tell for sure, but it looks like the plant absorbs everything except the gopher-rat's nervous system. It's symbiotic."

The leaves seemed to tighten a little around the gopher-rat. We stood in the middle of the forest. I couldn't see anything but the trees' tall stems and the sticky leaves that covered most of the ground. The sun had dropped lower in the sky so I couldn't find it through the trees, although their tops glowed orange and yellow in the slanting light. Even through the suit, I could feel that it was growing cold. "It doesn't look like an equal relationship to me."

"Maybe not, but it's an interesting direction for the ecology to take, don't you think?"

"Why would a plant want a nervous system?" I said. We'd turned the lights out an hour earlier. My arm was draped over Lashawnda's shoulder, and her bare back pressed warmly against my chest. I didn't want to let her go. Even though my side ached to change position, I wanted to savor every second. I wondered if she sensed my grief.

"No reason that I can think of," she said. Her fingers were wrapped around my wrist, and her heart beat steadily against my own. "But it must have something to do with its survival. There's an evolutionary advantage."

For a long time, I didn't speak. She was so solid and real and *living*. How could her life be threatened? How could it be that she could be here today and not forever? She breathed deeply. I thought she might have gone to sleep, but she suddenly twisted from my embrace, cursing under her breath.

"What's the matter?" I said.

She sat up. In the dark I couldn't see, but I could feel her beside me. Her muscles tensed.

"A little discomfort," she said.

"What did the medic prescribe?"

"Nothing that's doing any good."

She coughed heavily for a few seconds, and I could tell she was stretching, like she was trying to rid herself of a cramp. "I'm going down to the lab. I'm not sleeping well anyway." She rested her hand against my face for an instant before climbing out of bed.

After an hour of tossing and turning, I got up and did what I'd never done before: accessed Lashawnda's medical reports. After reading for a bit I could see she'd been optimistic. There were a lot less than a couple trips around the sun left in her, and her prescription list was a pharmacopoeia of pain killers.

She hadn't returned by morning.

"It's standard operating procedure," said the environmental engineer. She held her report forms to her chest defensively. "If the atmosphere isn't toxic, we're supposed to vent it in to cool the equipment. We've been circulating outside air since the first day. There *are* bioscreens."

First Chair looked at her dubiously. The four of us were crowded into the systems control room. Lashawnda broke the seals of her contamination suit. She'd rushed from decontamination without taking it off. "I should have thought of it," Lashawnda said. The helmet muffled her voice. "The fungi are opportunistic, and they're adept at finding hard to get water. You reverse airflow periodically, don't you?"

The environmental engineer nodded. "Sure, it blows dust out of the screens."

"The spores are activated by the moisture you vented, and . . ."

"*I* didn't vent *anything*," snapped the engineer. "It is standard operating procedure."

"Right," said Lashawnda, pulling the helmet off her head. She brushed her hair back with a quick gesture. "The fungus grew through the screen, spored, and that's what's in the machinery."

"The *entire* water recycling system? The backup system too?" asked First Chair, a tinge of desperation in his voice.

"Absolutely. There are holes in the valves. All the joints are pitted. The holding tanks would have more fungus in it than water, if there was any water left. Pretty happy fungus at that, I'd guess." She pulled the top half of the suit over her head, then stepped out of the pants. "Here's the unusual part: The water that was in the tank isn't in the room anymore. There are skinny stems leading to the vent that go down the ship's side and into the ground. The fungus pumped the water out. These plants are geniuses at moving water, which they have to be to survive."

First Chair asked, "Why weren't the external tanks already ruined when we got here? They were exposed to this environment much longer than our recycling equipment."

"They landed in the winter. That's the same reason the initial probes didn't find the spores," said Lashawnda. "It's spring now. The plants must only be active when its warmer. Bad timing on our part."

I looked through the service window into the machinery bay. Even through the thick glass the fungus was evident, a thick fur around the pipes. "You're sure the growth started inside the ship and went out, not the other way around?"

Lashawnda smiled. "Absolutely."

"So what?" said First Chair. I could see the wheels spinning in his head: how much water did we have stored elsewhere? How well were the dew-catchers working? Then he was dividing that amount of water by the minimum amount each crew member needed until the resupply ship arrived. By his expression, he didn't like the math.

Lashawnda said, "That means the plants cooperate. They share the wealth. It's counter-Darwinian. I compared the fly-by photos of this area from the first day until now. Since we've landed, plant growth has thickened and extended, which makes sense. When we lost the external tanks we introduced more free water into the system than it's seen in a years, but the forests in the neighboring gulches also are thicker. We thought they were separate ecosystems. They aren't. Water we lost here is ending up as much as five kilometers away. The plants move moisture to where it's needed."

"Will knowing that help us now?" asked First Chair. "I don't care if the plants are setting up volleyball leagues, we've got to figure a way to find enough water to last us five months." He glared at the environmental engineer on his way out. She turned to me.

"I know," I said. "Standard operating procedure."

"Let's go outside," said Lashawnda. "We've got the afternoon left."


"Could we harvest the trees and press water out of them?" I asked.

Lashawnda attached another sensor to a tree stem, moved a few feet along, then fastened the next one. She straightened slowly, her eyes closed against the discomfort. I wondered how she really felt. She never talked about it.

"You did the reports. How many plants would we have to squeeze dry to get a single cup?"

I didn't answer. She was right. Although the plants tied up most of the planet's water, it was spread thinly. I dug into a bare patch of dirt between two stands of trees. Only a dozen centimeters below the surface, a matted network of plant tendrils resisted my efforts to go deeper. I picked one about a finger in width and fastened a sensor to it.

We were deep into the tree-filled gulch. With no sun on us, I had to keep moving to stay warm, and my faceplate defogger wasn't working well.

I looked into a bundle of tree stalks. An old gopher-rat lump hung between the branches. Now that I knew where to look, I found them often. "Have you gone this deep into the gulch before?"

Lashawnda consulted her wrist display. "No, but by the map we are nearly at the end. We'll save time if we go back along the ridge."

Fifteen minutes later Lashawnda pushed through a particularly heavy patch of trees, and she disappeared.

"Oh!"

"What?"

Pulling my way through the vegetation, I found what stopped her. The gully pinched to a close twenty meters farther, and there were no more trees, but the same kind of sticky leaves that captured the gopher-rats covered the ground in a bed of orange and yellow, like broad-surfaced clover. The setting sun poured a crimson light over the scene, and for the first time since I'd landed on Papaver, I thought something was beautiful. As I watched, the leaves turned their faces toward us and seemed to lean the least bit, as if they yearned for us to lay down.

Lashawnda said, "Let's not walk through that. We'd crush too many of them." She fastened the last of the sensors to the delicate leaves at the end of the little clearing. Her movements were spare, exact. The final sensor fastened, she paused on her knees, facing the bed of plants. She reached out, hand flat, and brushed the leaves gently. They strained to meet her, leaves wrapping around her fingers; a longer stemmed leaf encircled her wrist. Within a few seconds, her hand, wrist and arm to her elbow were encased.

I stepped toward her. The expanse of leaves had changed color!

Then I realized the color was the same, but the plants had shifted even further to face her. Sunlight hit them differently. All lines pointed toward Lashawnda. My voice felt choked and tight. "What are you doing?"

"If I move, I must contain water. They're just trying to get it. They work together; isn't that superb? If they got my water, they'd send it to where it was needed." Gradually she pulled her arm free. The leaves slipped their hold without resistance.

Careful not to step on the plants, we made our way to the edge of the gully and clambered out. The startlingly pink sun brushed the horizon, and yellow and gold glowing streamers layered themselves a third of the way up the sky.

"That's amazing." I held Lashawnda's hand through the clumsy gloves, the same hand the leaves had covered.

"You haven't seen one before?" She squeezed my hand back. "Every sunset is like this. It's the dust in the atmosphere."

The streamers twisted under the influence of upper air disturbances that didn't touch us.

"I saw your medical reports," I said.

She sighed. The sky darkened as more and more of the sun vanished until only a pink diamond winked between two distant hills, and the final golden layer dulled into a yellow haze. "You're the last one. Are you going to wish me well too? You'd think everyone turned into death and dying counselors. If I hear, 'You've had a good four-hundred years' again, I'll scream."

"No, I wasn't going to say that." But I don't know what I was going to say. I couldn't tell her that I wanted to do some screaming of my own.

By the time we returned to the ship, it had grown incredibly cold, and the decontamination chamber wasn't any warmer. I longed for a hot spiced tea, but First Chair was waiting for us on the other side.

"I need you to drop your other projects and concentrate on the water problem." His eyes had that haunted I-wish-I-didn't-have-a-leadership-position look to them. "The geology team is looking for aquifers; the engineers are making more dew traps, and the chemists are working on what can be extracted from the rock, but none of them are hopeful we can find or make enough water fast enough. Is there anything you've learned about the plants that might help?"

Lashawnda said, "They've spent millions of years learning how to conserve water. I don't think they'll give it up easily. Spencer and I are working on an experiment right now that ought to tell us more."

"Good. Let me know if you get results." He rushed from the room, and a few seconds later I heard him say to someone in another room, "Have you made any progress?"

"We'll need to sedate him if we want to work uninterrupted," she said.

"What *is* the experiment we're doing?"

"Electroencephalograph."

"An EEG on a plant?" I laughed.

She shrugged. "You wondered why a plant would need a nervous system. Let's find out if it's using it."

In her lab, Lashawnda bent over her equipment. "What do you make of that?" She pointed to the readouts on the screen. "Especially when I display it like this." She tapped a couple keys.

The monitor showed a series of moving graphs, like separate seismographs. "It could be anything. Sound waves maybe. Are those from the sensors we placed?"

"Yep. Now, watch this." She reached across her table and pressed a switch. Within a couple seconds, all the graphs showed activity so violent that the screen almost turned white. Gradually the graphs settled into the same patterns I'd seen at first.

I leaned closer and saw the readouts were numbered. The ones near the top of the screen corresponded to the sensors we'd placed at the far end of the gully. The bottom ones were nearest to the ship. "What did you do?"

"I shut the exterior vents into the equipment room. The change in the graphs happened when the hatches cut through the fungus stems connecting the growth in the ship to the ground."

"The plants felt that? They're thinking about it?"

"Not plants. A single organism. Maybe a planet-wide organism. I'll have to place more sensors. And yes, it's thinking."

The lines on the monitor continued vibrating. It *looked* like brain activity. "That's ridiculous. Why would a plant need a brain? There's no precedent."

"Maybe they didn't start out as plants. As the weather grew colder and it became harder and harder for animals to live high on the food chain, they became what we see now, a thinking, cooperative intelligence."

Lashawnda put her hands into the small of her back and pushed hard, her eyes closed. "A sentience wouldn't operate the same way non-thinking plants would. We just need to discover the difference." She opened a floor cabinet and took out a clear sample bag stuffed with waxy orange shapes.

I barely recognized it before she opened the bag, broke off a Papaver leaf, and pressed it against her inner arm.

After a moment, she opened her eyes and smiled. "Marvin said, 'It's God at the end,' so I thought I'd give it a try. He wasn't too far off." She enunciated the words carefully, as if her hearing were abruptly acute. "The toxins are an outstanding opiate. Much more effective on pain than the rest of the stuff I've been taking. I don't think the gopher-rats suffer."

No recrimination would have been appropriate. Although it was most likely the leaves wouldn't affect her at all, the first time she did it she might have just as easily killed herself. "How long?" I took the bag from her hand. It wasn't dated. She'd smuggled it in.

"A couple of days."

"Is it addictive?"

She giggled, and I looked at her sharply. She seemed lucid and happy, not drugged.

"I don't know. I haven't tried quitting." She held her hand out. I gave her the bag. She said, "I wonder what an entity as big as a planet thinks about? How *old* would you guess it is?" The bag vanished into the cabinet. "Not very often I run into something older than me."

"Did you tell the medic about that?" I nodded toward the cabinet.

She levered herself up so she could sit on the counter. "I'm taking notes she can see afterwards. No need to bother her with it now. Besides, we have bigger problems. If First Chair is right, in a month we'll have died of thirst. How are we going to convince a plant to give us back the water it took?"

Sitting where she was, her heels against the cabinet doors, she looked like a young girl, but shadows under her eyes marked her face, and her skin appeared more drawn, as if she were thinning, becoming more fragile, and she was.

"How do you feel?" I asked. I had tried to maintain within myself her concentration, her ability to ignore the obvious fact, but I couldn't do it. I worried about the crew and the water they needed. But for me? I didn't care. Death would find Lashawnda before it took me.

She slid off the counter and tapped in a code into her work station. The recording of our landing came up again. Clouds of steam surged from the ground. She said, without meeting my eyes, "Look, Spencer. I can't avoid it. It's not going away. So all I can do is work and think and act like it's not there at all. You're behaving as if I should be paralyzed in fear or something, but I'm not going to do that. There's still a quest or two for me in the last days, some effort of note."

I had no answer for that. We went to bed hours later, and when she held me, her arms trembled.


A nightmare woke me. In the dream I wandered through the twisted forest, but I wasn't scared. I was happy. I belonged. The crooked stems gave way before my ungloved hands. My chest was bare. No contamination suit or helmet or shirt. The air smelled sharp and frigid, like winter on a lake's edge where the wind sweeps across the ice, but I wasn't cold. I came upon a thick stand of trees, their narrow trunks forming a wall in front of me. I pushed and tugged at the unmoving branches. I'd never seen a clump of Papaver trees so large. Nothing seemed more important than penetrating that branched fortress. Finally I found a narrow gap where I could squeeze through. At first I wandered in the dark. Gradually shapes became visible: the towering stems forming a shadowy roof overhead, other branches reaching from side to side, and the room felt close.

"Spencer?" said Lashawnda.

"Yes?" I said, turning slowly in the vegetable room. Waxy-leafed plants humped from the ground, but I couldn't see her.

"I'm here, Spencer," she said, and one of the humps sat up.

I squinted. "It's too dark."

A dim light sparked to life, a pink diamond, like the last glimpse of the sunset we'd seen the day before, growing until the room became bright, revealing a skeleton-thin Lashawnda.

"I'm glad you came," she said.

I stepped closer, all the details clear in the ruddy light. Her eyes sparkled above sharp cheekbones. She smiled at me, the skin pulled tight across her face, her shoulders boney and narrow, barely human anymore. She wore no clothes, but she didn't need them. The plants hid her legs, and leaves covered her stomach and breasts. Like the gopher-rat, she'd been absorbed.

"The plant is old, old, old," she said. "We think deep thoughts, all the way to Papaver's core."

I put my arm around her, the bone's hardness pressing against my hand.

In the dream, I was happy. In the dream, the plants sucking every drop of water from her was right.

"And, Spencer, this way I live forever."

I woke stifling a scream.

She wasn't in bed.

In the decontamination unit, her suit was gone.

I don't remember how I got my suit on or how I got outside. Running, I passed the empty water tanks, avoided the lichen-filled depressions, and plunged into the forest. The sun had barely cleared the horizon, pouring pink light through the skinny trees. I tripped. Knocked my face hard against the inside of my helmet. Staggering, I pushed on. The dream image hovered before me. Had the pain become too much for Lashawnda, and the promise of an opiate loaded bed of leaves, eager to embrace her become too tempting? I imagined her nervous system, like a gopher-rat's, joining the plant consciousness. But who knew what the gopher-rats experienced, if they experienced anything at all? Maybe their lives were filled with nightmares of cold and immobility.

Trees slapped at my arms. Leaves slashed across my face-plate.

When I burst through the last line of trees at the clearing's edge, she was crouched, her back to me shoulders and head down in the plants. I pictured her faceplate open, her eyes gone already, home for stabbing tendrils seeking the moist tissue behind.

"Don't do it!" I yelled.

Startled, she fell back, holding a sensor; her faceplate was closed. For a second she looked frightened. Then she laughed. I gasped for breath while my air supply whined in my ear.

"What are you doing, Spencer?" A bag filled with the sensors we'd put on the plants sat on the ground beside her. She'd been retrieving them.

"You weren't . . . I mean, you're not . . . hurting yourself . . . you're okay?" I finally blurted.

She held me until I quit shaking and my respiration settled into a parody of regularity.

The sun had risen another handful of degrees. We stayed still so long that the plants turned away to face the light. She hugged me hard, then said, "I know how to find water."

I hugged her back.

"Can you carry the bag?" she said as she pushed herself to her feet. "It's getting darned heavy."

The crew stood around the one meter deep depression beside an empty water tank. Like every sheltered spot, lichens covered the rock. Lashawnda supervised the engineers as they arranged the structure she'd sketched out for them, which was two long bars crossing the hole, holding an electric torch suspended above the pit's bottom.

First Chair stood with his arms crossed. "What do you mean, we should have figured out how to get water from the first day?"

Lashawnda sat in a chair someone had brought for her. "The plants here are cooperative. They're not just out for themselves like we're used to seeing. I watched the records of our landing. The ground *steamed*, but, as Spencer will tell you," she nodded to me, "you couldn't get an ounce of water out of a ton of the lichen no matter how hard you tried."

First Chair looked puzzled.

Lashawnda pressed a button, and the electric torch began to glow. I could feel the heat on my face from ten meters away. Lashawnda said, "The plants were protecting each other, or, more accurately, protecting itself. They're geniuses at moving moisture."

In the pit, some of the yellow lichens began to turn brown, and then to smoke. Suddenly the bottom of the pit glistened, rivulets opened from cracks in the rock. Water quickly filled the bathtub-sized depression.

The crew cheered.

"The plant is trying to protect itself," Lashawnda said. "You better pump it out now," "because as soon as the heat's off, it will be gone."

First Chair barked out orders, and soon pipes led from the hole into temporary tanks in the ship.

That night I held Lashawnda close, her backbone pressed against me; my lips brushed the back of her neck.

"Did you really think that I'd kill myself by throwing myself into the plants?"

She held my wrist, her fingers so delicate and light that I half feared they'd break.

"I didn't want to lose even a single day with you," I said.

Lashawnda didn't speak for a long time, but I knew she hadn't drifted into sleep. The room was so quiet I could hear her eyelashes flutter as she blinked. "I don't want to lose a day with you either." She pulled my arm around her tighter. "Four hundred years is a good, long time to live. I don't suppose when I do go that you could arrange for me to be buried in that clearing at the gully's end?"

I remembered how the plants had grasped her hand and arm, how attentive they were when she passed.

"Sure," I said.

It occurred to me that I wanted to be buried there too, where the beings work together to save each other and share what they have to help the least of them.

"But we're not there yet," I said.

# WHERE AND WHEN

The two scientists surveyed the cabin's interior from their positions behind the crowd at the windows. Jake flicked the command that turned his recorders on, his eyes and ears sending the signal to the computer buried in his jawbone, while Martin stepped to a table and retrieved what turned out to be a menu. He held the pages like they were holy script.

"After all these years," Jake exulted while turning slowly for the recorder's sake. A silk wallpaper imprinted with a map of the world covered the wall beside him. Rich contrasting carpet. Recessed ceiling lights. The transition had been without effect. No sound or dizziness. No flash of light or sensation of falling. Just a blink. "What did we do differently?"

"The math never came out even, but it should have always worked. Maybe there are more opportune moments." Martin carefully opened the thin document. "A thousand failed attempts. Wouldn't Brownson be proud."

Jake grimaced. "If he had survived." For an instant, he thought he saw Brownson among the people at the window. Broad shoulders. One arm. Gray hair. But the light shifted, and Jake could see he was wrong. Two arms. Blonde hair. A stranger. The project had been Brownson's from the beginning. All the theoretical work, most of the construction, only letting them help when he needed two hands. Spending long nights bouncing his ideas off them. Arguing with them about paradoxes. His faith buoyed them when they were ready to quit. His determination to succeed drove them on. His obsession. He should be here, Jake thought. This day belongs to him.

A soft thrumming filled the air, and both men compensated slightly as the floor moved beneath their feet.

Jake's breathing came hard. It *had* been a thousand attempts.

They'd poured over Brownson's papers until their vision had blurred. Constructed and reconstructed the device dozens of times. Was it a math problem? Was there a flaw in the underlying theories? Were the old saws about paradox and the impossibilities true, the ones that worried Brownson incessantly? "We must be able to get around it," he'd said. If only the old man had confided in them more before he'd died in the explosion, alone in the lab. "I'm going to try something," he'd said. The investigators concluded later that a bomb destroyed the building. They found chemical traces and a melted timing mechanism. Rival government? Terrorists? Jake and Martin had labored from then on in paranoid secrecy.

"Where and when are we?" Jake said to himself. We're here! he thought, wherever here is. And we're now, whenever that is. He panned around the long room, across the backs of the people at the windows, and over metal-framed chairs pushed up to the tables. He lingered his focus on a yellow piano in the room's center. A wine glass and crystal carafe poised above the keyboard tossed bright glisters from the ceiling lights. The room smelled of cologne and perfume and roast beef. His fingers glided coolly on the silk wall. Jake smiled. What style were the clothes the people wore? 1920s? 1930s? If he queried the computer, it might tell him, but it was more fun to guess. None turned to look at them.

At the window, a middle-aged woman with a cane hooked over her arm said, "Finally. The family has been waiting for hours." Reading glasses hung from a silver cord around her neck.

Ahh, English, thought Jake. He spoke French, German, Italian, Spanish and a smattering of Mandarin. Martin knew Portugese, Swiss and Russian. If needed, their computer implanted in his jaw could translate, but that was an awkward way to talk. Jake hoped the recorder caught what the people said. Voices from the past. Real ones. The linguists would salivate over the subtleties of vowel shifts, the nuances and shading of pronunciations from hundreds of years in the past. Not radio recordings or movie voices, but real people talking among themselves. The social historians would write treatises on the ways of the era based on his recordings. Whole new areas of study would be opened up. They'd succeeded! They'd jumped the unjumpable chasm.

"The Germans build a marvelous ship, but they can't control the rain and wind," an older man with dark muttonchops and a gray smoking jacket replied. "Not yet, anyway." From the way the woman with the cane and the muttonchopped man stood together, their arms almost touching, their chins at the same angle as they looked out the window, Jake guessed they were husband and wife.

Jake moved to an unoccupied length of window. By putting his face next to the glass that leaned out from the top, he could see that three hundred feet below a grassy airfield waited. He strained to see what was to the right and left beyond the cabin: long stretches of silver-gray fabric, and above them a bulging gray fabric shelf that blocked part of the sky. No wings, he thought. We're in a blimp.

Cars the size of matchboxes covered the ground on one side of a long wooden building. People ran beneath them. He hoped the glass wouldn't mess up the recorder's images.

The muttonchopped man said, "We're tail heavy. If those folks don't watch out below, they'll get a good soaking."

"How so, dear?" asked his wife. She smiled at him, a brief look, then she gazed out again.

"Water ballast."

A nearly subsonic, mechanical thump bumped the room, then the people who'd been running scattered, their hands covering their heads as water streamed down from somewhere aft of the cabin.

The muttonchopped man laughed.

Martin sidled up beside Jake. "Look at this," Martin whispered, holding the menu he'd retrieved from the table.

Jake scanned the German text. "Nice wine list. Do you want the beef broth with marrow dumplings or the cold Rhine salmon with spiced sauce and potato salad?" He could barely keep from giggling. They had done it!

"No, not the food. Look at the name." He stabbed a finger at the top of the page.

Trying to settle his heart, trying to keep the grin off his face, Jake read the heading.

"We're going to Hindenburg? Is that where this airfield is?" Were the people he'd listened to American or English tourists on holiday in Germany?

Martin shook his head. "No, no. We're *on* the *Hindenburg*. The zeppelin. *The Hindenburg*."

Jake's computer squeaked for attention with a bone-induction message only he could hear: *The* Hindenburg, *first commercial flights in 1936. Final flight, May 6, 1937. Gas volume of*

*7,062,000 cubic feet. Gross lift of 242.2 tons. Originally designed for helium, the ship . . ."* Jake flicked the voice off.

Ahead and to the left of the ship, a solid-looking tower of crossbeams and heavy struts awaited them. The zeppelin turned ponderously toward it.

The tower slid slowly toward the front of the ship. The grass below had given way to cement and tarmac, dark with long puddles of standing water. Fragments of the ship's reflection shown back at them.

"*When* are we on the *Hindenburg?*" said Jake. A crew member opened one of the windows so the passengers could see better. A refreshing, rain-scented breeze filled the cabin.

Martin tapped his finger against the top of the menu impatiently. "What does it matter? We're on the *Hindenburg*. The go-down-in-flames-oh-the-humanity *Hindenburg*."

"It *does* matter. The *Hindenburg* flew for a year before it blew up. If it's 1936, we're in great shape. Can you imagine? 1936! Franklin Roosevelt is president. The Berlin Olympics. The Spanish Civil War. Picasso is alive, and so is Errol Flynn and Ginger Rogers. We can go to Hollywood! What are the odds of all the places and times in the world that we'd end up on the *Hindenburg* in 1937 when it goes down?"

"Why are we in an airship at all?" Martin looked out the window at the ground. "Brownson said temporal and physical destinations were random. No guessing where we'd end up, but this seems precise. If we'd arrived ten feet that way," he waved beyond the cabin, "our visit here would have been short."

Long cables dropped from the front of the ship. Men on the ground ran to catch them. The hum that pervaded the background shifted, and the cabin shuddered. Jake braced a hand against the slick metal window sill to compensate for the change in speed.

Martin shook his head. He stepped around Jake. "Excuse me, sir," he said to the man with muttonchops. "My friend here is a little confused. Would you tell him what year it is?"

Before the man could answer, Jake heard a soft pop from outside the window, like a gas burner being turned on. The woman with the cane over her arm leaned out the open window, looking up. "What is that, dear?" She reached behind her without turning her head and grabbed the muttonchopped man's wrist. "It's like a sunrise."

A pink and yellow glow brightened the zeppelin's fabric toward the tail. Jake leaned out too to record the image, but the soft glimmer turned into flames racing toward them, furiously fast.

Jake pushed away from the window.

"It's on fire!" someone screamed. The floor began to sink beneath their feet.

Martin faced Jake, his expression serious. "1937."

They reached for their panic switches under their shirts at the same time. Before the world blinked away, the muttonchopped man and the woman with the cane threw themselves out the window. We're still 300 feet above the ground, Jake thought before it all flickered and they were back in the laboratory.

Collapsed in a chair, Jake still breathed in interrupted hitches, his heart pounding in his throat. His hand fluttered as he reached for the coffee cup. Martin, though, bustled from his workbook full of figures, to the computer, and back again.

"*Nothing* in Brownson's notes said we could end up in a zeppelin."

Jake closed his hand on the cup. Gripped hard to stop the shaking. "Not *any* zeppelin. The *Hindenburg*." He shut his eyes for a second, but he could see the mooring mast looming in front of him, beams and struts reflecting a hard, blazing light. In his vision, the woman, her cane still carefully tucked over her arm, tumbled out the window after her husband.

Martin ran his finger down a line of notes, turned the page, kept reading. "A hundred to four hundred years in the past, Brownson said. Location variable. But the math kept us on the ground I thought. Of course, the damn math never made any sense in the first place. Equations never balanced equally. Nothing reduced perfectly. Nothing was absolute."

Jake shivered as he pushed away from the chair, glad for the coffee's heat. From their lab's single window, he could see the tar paper and gravel roof running to a low, brick border. Beyond that, a few clouds rested on the horizon. Their lab perched on the roof of the industrial park's highest building. If he opened the door and walked to the edge, a handful of equally nondescript structures with equally bland roofs would lay out before him, like a bleak checkerboard. They were far from Brownson's destroyed lab and whoever bombed it. He remembered the last time they'd seen Brownson, his only hand protectively over the top of the device, the place for the sleeve for his other arm sewn shut at the shoulder. No sleeve dangled. "Don't want it catching in the equipment," he'd said. Brownson, now, was gone, in explosion and fire, like the passengers on the *Hindenburg*.

"Those people are all dead."

Martin looked up from the notebook. "You're being sentimental. They've been dead for two hundred and fifty years. Their children are dead too, and their children. But if you're talking about the people on the *Hindenburg* we saw, that's not true. Only thirty-three died because of the crash. Sixty-two lived."

The flames had come down so fast. "Only thirty-three?" Jake's mouth was dry. Every swallow hurt.

After a moment, Martin, his voice distracted and preoccupied, said, "Yes, and two dogs. The rest got out when the ship was low enough. Didn't your computer tell you all this?"

"I turned it off."

Jake could still feel the radiant heat. The people screaming, all of them at once. The floor slipping away toward the ship's tail. Glassware tumbling from the tables, and chairs falling toward the back wall. He had kept pressing the panic switch. How long would the device take to snatch them back? What if it wouldn't?

"I behaved badly," said Jake. "I . . ." His gaze roamed the room. Electronic equipment piled on the work table. Security video displayed on four monitors. No one would plant a bomb in their lab! The table, the monitors, the lab on a building's roof were so far away from the collapsing ship, from old people jumping from windows. "I didn't help anyone."

Martin turned the computer off. He shut the notebook. "Jake, those people were dead before we got there. They'd been dead for a quarter of a millennium. You couldn't help them. You couldn't harm them. You couldn't change their fate." He sat on the table's edge and smiled. "I know it's a shock. I'm still quivering myself." He held his hand out, but if it was trembling, Jake couldn't see it. "We traveled in time, Jake, and we returned. All that nonsense about causality loops and killing your grandfather so you won't be born, and a dead butterfly changing human history, it's wrong. Brownson's fears were wrong. We can travel in time. Think about how wonderful you felt when you realized what we'd done."

Surprisingly, the coffee tasted good. Jake took another sip.

"That's true. When we arrived. Yes, it was great." He brightened. "We've made history."

Martin laughed. "That's the spirit." He checked the clock on the wall. "It's early, still. You know what we need to do, don't you?" Jake sat up, put the coffee cup on the table, straightened his shoulders, ran a quick diagnostic on his implanted computer. "Yes, I do."

"That's right," said Martin. "We have to go again."

He pressed the button that activated their synchronized devices.


"See, we're on the ground," said Martin.

They stood on a narrow brick-paved road between a line of two-story shops, neatly-swept concrete stairways leading to their doors, arched stone lintels over the windows. The signs were in French. *Tobacco and Supplies. Fresh bread every morning at 10:00.* Overhead, low, dark clouds grayed the sky, but the sun on the horizon cut under them, casting shadows on the buildings across the street.

A newspaper hung inside the bakery's window. "*Les Colonies*, 'Voice of the French Peoples Everywhere,'" said Jake. His computer said, *There are 785 unique matches to newspapers entitled Les Colonies.* Then it pinged off. Jake needed more information for it to give him a useful analysis. He wiped a thin layer of dust from the glass, then read from the top story. "It says the governor and his wife are in town and not to worry." He struggled with the translation. "The commission, it says, declares that the crisis is past. It doesn't say what the crisis is. Lots of news about an upcoming election."

"So, where and when in the French speaking countries are we?" Martin walked part way down the street, peering into the windows. "Everything seems closed."

Jake scanned the rest of the paper he could see. "Religious holiday. Ascension day. Early morning services at *Notre-Dame de l'Assomption.*" The computer chirped to define Ascension Day.

Martin looked back at him, eyebrows raised.

"Catholic holy day in May. Everyone goes to mass. No date on the paper, though. No city name."

Ladies' hats rested on red velvet stands at the next shop. Martin sniffed. "Do you smell that? It's the ocean."

Jake joined Martin walking up the street which curved slowly to the left. Their shoes kicked up puffs of dust, and when Jake turned, he saw their footprints buffed the bricks clean as if they had just missed a momentary snow storm, but the air was warm. A pile of wooden baskets were turned upside down beside one shop door, shreds of lettuce clinging to the slats.

"Ah, there you go," said Martin. A gap between two buildings revealed a bay to their left only a couple blocks away. A handful of single and double-masted boats, their sails furled, rested quietly on the smooth water, where sea gulls perched on the docks' pilings or skimmed the surface between the ships.

Appearing from around the street's curve, a family walked toward them. The man wore a jacket with wide lapels, and he carried a walking stick. Beside him, the woman held the front of her long dress up to keep the hem from trailing in the dust. A pair of ten-year-old boys walked primly behind them, both hugging a book to their chests. When they passed, Jake offered a "Bonjour."

The man stopped, tipped his hat, revealing dark hair slicked to his skull and parted in the middle. "Bonjour. You are scientists?" the man said in a French Jake barely understood. Some kind of creole? The woman stood beside him, and the children hid behind, but they peeked around her skirt.

"We are visitors," Jake said, confused. Why would the man call them scientists? It would only be more startling if he'd called them time travelers. "Yes, scientists, I suppose. Why do you ask?"

"Your clothes, monsieur. The fashion on the continent, I suppose. We don't get important visitors on the island often."

"We are safe?" said the woman. Her voice was surprisingly deep. "There is noise at night, and the dust. The children worry." She waved her hand at the air.

One of the children shook his head. Jake put his hand to his mouth to hide a smile.

"Of course we're safe," said the man. "The governor's family, after all. Would they be within a hundred miles of here if we were not? Come, we will be late. Au voir."

The man set off at a brisk pace. The woman gathered a child's hand in each hand, and followed.

"What did you find out?" said Martin. "Did you get a date?"

"No. We're on an island, though. Not France. And he said something about the continent. A French colony then. And they're worried about something. He thought we were scientists."

Martin looked at the road. "There's no room for an automobile here. No radio or television antennas. Sailing ships in the harbor. We could be in the 1800s." He laughed. "It worked again, Jake. We've slipped time's surly bonds."

Unease kept Jake from joining Martin's joy. The memory lingered too strongly of the growing roar, the flames reaching around the zeppelin's side. How could they have arrived then and there? A change in the light caught Jake's attention. Where the sun cut a sharp shadow on the buildings now all was a uniform shade, as if dusk was falling. Rolling like a slow ocean at storm, the clouds squirmed overhead. The two-story buildings standing so close together under a ceiling of black clouds suddenly seemed imprisoning. Jake ran ahead. What hid on the other side? Why were the clouds so strange? He passed an old man in his Sunday best, walking with a heavy limp. A young girl, leading a dog on leash, watched wide-eyed as Jake dashed by.

"What are you doing?" yelled Martin.

Jake reached a junction. Across the street, a small park held cast-iron benches with brightly painted red seats. In a small white gazebo, surrounded by yellow flower beds, a man in military uniform leaned on the railing, smoking a pipe. He tipped his hat at Jake, but Jake's attention was beyond the gazebo, up and up. Martin joined him. "We should stay together. This is an unfamiliar time, and . . ."

Beyond the park, beyond and above the rows of houses that made the rest of the city, a mountain rose against the sky, pouring black clouds from its peak. No gentle oozing of clouds either. They catapulted from the shrouded mountain, ascended, caught in a high wind that didn't reach the ground, and flattened over the town.

Jake strode across the street, into the park, his gaze trapped by the silent display. The mountain was close, no more than five miles. Houses in rows lapped against the sloping flank of it. How quiet the town was. None of the seabirds called out. Water in the bay made no sound under the docks. Only his muffled footfalls in the dusty grass. His own breathing.

On the gazebo, the soldier watched Jake's approach.

"Where are we?" Jake demanded. He gripped the gazebo's railing as if to vault himself beside the soldier, a teenager, by his unlined face, so new to his uniform that he looked uncomfortable in it.

"Martinique," said the man with a rise in his voice, like he had asked a question.

Nervelessly, Jake's hand fell away from the painted wood. All the horizon held was the mountain and its billowing performance. "What town is this?" he nearly whispered. Martin walked to the gazebo's side, staring at the volcano.

Puzzled, the young man said, "It is St. Pierre. My company is here to proctor the election."

"Oh, no," said Jake. "We've done it again."

Martin turned back to him. "What?"

"I know the mountain."

From somewhere in the town behind them, a church bell rang out, breaking the silence with its somber tolling.

The soldier laughed nervously. "The Angelus bells. I must be going, monsieur."

"That's Mount Pelee, isn't it?" said Jake in English. "C'est Mont Pelee?" He grabbed the soldier's arm as he went down the steps. Under the heavy flannel uniform, the man's arm felt slender. He's just a boy, thought Jake.

"Yes, Pelee. I must go to the cathedral," said the young man. "I'm already late."

Jake's computer said, *Mt. Pelee exploded in . . .* A thunderous clap of sound overwhelmed the rest of the message.

On the mountain, a cloud wall boiled down the slope, its folds and wrinkles glowing like veins on fire. Trees vanished behind it. Within seconds, the upper half of the prominence became all cloud, rolling down, swallowing land, obscuring what before had been clear. Martin said, "Should we be worried about that? What is it?"

The soldier wrenched free from Jake's grasp, glanced over his shoulder at the mountain, then ran down the street, away from the engulfing cloud. In its squeaky voice, the computer recited a litany of facts.

Jake didn't move. Didn't even twitch. His thoughts slowed down and felt cold to him. Emotionless. "Pyroclastic flow." Another explosion ripped the hidden mountain top.

Martin took a step back. "Will it reach us?"

"In about two minutes." Near the peak, the smoke radiated an incandescent orange, and a series of smaller detonations like cannon fire rattled the park. Jake's insides had emptied. Had the family with the two little boys reached the church yet? If they were lucky, they had time for a short prayer. The computer talked to him. Twenty-nine thousand people would die in the next few minutes: the governor and his wife, in town to calm the population, the scientists who pronounced the volcano safe, the farmers who had fled fields where crops had died in the weeks of ash fall, the people who'd abandoned villages close to the mountain for the safety of St. Pierre, all of them would be gone. Only a prisoner in a basement cell would survive. Rescuers would find him days later, horribly burned, crying weakly from beneath the jail's rubble. "Geologists call it *nuee ardente*, the glowing cloud. Super-heated air and volcanic ash traveling a hundred miles an hour. Strong enough to knock down buildings. So hot that breathing it boils the lungs."

"How did we get here?" shouted Martin above the growing roar. Furious, he glared at the cloud that reached the town's edge, hiding homes and shops and factories. "This is not random at all!" He touched the button inside his shirt, vanished.

Jake could feel the fear around him. If he turned, citizens would be on the street, drawn by the noise. The cathedral would empty. Hymn books in hand, they'd be waiting. Children, grandparents, craftsmen, soldiers, wives. Trash in the street beyond the park stirred. Now, all was dark. As if it contained a thousand freight trains rumbling headlong down their doomed tracks, the mountain bellowed. Before the heat. Before the flesh-stripping wind. Jake pressed the button within his shirt.


Without taking his hand off the monitor input, Jake flicked from one image to the next, grainy black and white photographs of buildings without roofs, all the windows gone, bricks scattered in the street, and everywhere, bodies burned black. "They had plenty of warning, you know," he said. "The mountain had been misbehaving for weeks. People had already died. There were mud avalanches and a tidal wave and ash falls, but they didn't leave. How can you keep your children with you when there are . . . signs . . . portents?" He sighed and turned off the monitor. "When there are evil omens in the sky?"

"Damn it, Jake. What's important here is the impossibility of us showing up at two disasters. History is mostly boring, repetitious, day after day existence where people go about their ordinary lives. Historic events are rare. How could we possibly be present for two of them in a row?"

"I don't know what the science is, here. Brownson's math looks more like chants and incantations to me than physics anyway. We built a machine that we don't understand. I wonder if Brownson even knew. If only we could ask him."

Martin swore and slapped his notebook closed. "The one-armed bastard. Maybe if he hadn't been so cryptic with us, we'd have a better chance of figuring it out." He paced around the lab, head down. "We've been time travelers for all of what, ten minutes total? Both times we've been scared. We're not thinking straight." He paused, looked at Jake. "We need rationality. *We* were never in danger. We could come back to the lab anytime." He paced again, circling their work table, passing behind Jake at the monitor. "Here's the problem: we only have two points on the graph. We can't reach a conclusion without more information. I say we try again."

The blank screen looked back at Jake, but he could still picture the old images from centuries past. He'd never thought of the people who'd lived before as people, really. Those lives were abstractions. Nothing to do with him. But he could see them now, the living, beating, desperately intense faces from the past, trying to avoid their fates, staring down the rushing pyroclastic cloud burning toward them at a hundred miles an hour, or on the *Hindenburg*, waiting for the ground to come close enough so they could jump, not knowing if the raging hydrogen and diesel-fueled fire would reach them first.

"I don't want to visit the dead anymore," he said.

Martin put his hands on the back of Jake's chair. He could see Martin's reflection in the monitor overlaying the ghost images of a destroyed town. "I told you already, they were dead before we started. *We're* dead, Jake, to someone in our future, but you're thinking about it all wrong. They're alive too. Everything they've ever done is still being done. Nothing is in the past now. It's all redoable. Replayable."

He checked the equipment strapped across his chest under his shirt. "We have to go again, and we need to do it now. I can't tell from Brownson's figures why it's working. So much of his calculations are about the paradoxes, and they're a waste. 'Solve the paradox!' he said. 'Solve the paradox!' There's no paradox. We've traveled, but we can't guarantee we can keep doing it. Maybe the Earth has to be in the right place in its orbit. Maybe the atmospheric conditions have to be just perfect. If we don't go now, we might not be able to go again."

For a moment, Jake didn't stir. It was like the weight of Mount Pelee coming toward him and nothing mattered. He pushed away from the monitor and faced Martin. Finally, he nodded. Martin was right, he was dead any way he figured it.


At first Jake thought he'd gone blind until he saw the nearly full moon through thin clouds. A cold wind pushed against his face. He took a step, kicked something yielding, and a sleepy voice said, "Watch it, goll darn ya. Can't a soldier get a decent sleep anywhere on this boat?"

Standing still, Jake listened until his eyes adapted to the pale light. Water sloshed heavily to both sides. A substantial pounding vibrated the floor beneath his feet, and before the first faint lights grew visible on the shore a couple hundred yards away, he'd already decided they were on a steamboat near the bow. He turned his back to the wind. Moonlight revealed twin gray smokestacks belching smoke and sparks above a pilot's cabin, and dark forms that covered the deck like a lumpy landscape. He looked down. The man he'd kicked had rolled onto his side, pulling a thin blanket over him. The bundles were men sleeping on nearly every inch of exposed surface. Walking without stepping on someone would be hard. "When and where are we?" said Martin.

"Someplace that's going to sink soon, or catch fire, or be attacked," Jake said.

Martin grunted. "I should have brought a coat."

"Go back and get one." On the shore, ghostly trees touched their branches to the water. A lone cabin, a dim light flickering in its window, peeked out from the woods. On the boat's other side, the river reflected the moon like a long, undulating silver plate until it vanished in a low fog that hovered just off the surface. The air smelled cool, wet and muddy.

"Big river. Steamboat. English spoken here. The Mississippi." Martin strode over a silent shape, careful not to step on it. Jake followed. Gingerly they moved toward the shore-side railing. Men sat up there, some leaning their heads on the shoulders of others. Some talked among themselves.

"He's dead, the bastards," said one. No one replied. "A coward's shot, I tell ya. A yella deed, it was."

Jake took a place at the rail. Below, the river flowed past slowly.

The ship's headway was gradual. The cabin on shore crept astern. "You'll feel better when we hit Cairo and head home," said another voice.

"Vicksburg, Memphis, Cairo, Evansville. What's it matter? Dead is dead."

Farther down the boat, the paddle wheel churned, digging into the water with quick, ponderous movement.

"You didn't even vote for him."

"I would've."

Dampness on the rail chilled Jake's arms. The only warmth was Martin standing beside him, blocking the wind.

"Who is dead?" said Martin.

A log with one crooked branch sticking out like a bony, broken bone drifted by only thirty feet away. At the end opposite the branch, a pair of birds, their beaks tucked under wing, huddled side by side. "The president, ya cracker. Ain't ya talked to anyone? Some southern dog of an actor they say done it."

Jake leaned back, but the men were swathed in shadow. He couldn't see who spoke.

"Lincoln?" said Martin. "Are you talking about the assassination of Lincoln?"

Someone snorted in disbelief. "Twarn't Jefferson Davis."

Jake's computer squeaked to life. Before he muted the citation, it said, *Abraham Lincoln died on April 14, 1865. John Wilkes Booth fired on the president during a performance . . ..*

"How long ago?" said Jake. He couldn't remember much about the Civil War beyond the obvious. If Lincoln was already dead, then the war was over. Antietam and Gettysburg and Chancellorsville were in the past. Certainly nothing to fear, like the destruction of the *Hindenburg* or Mt. Pelee erupting. The shooting had ended.

"Don't know what today is," said the voice. "Ten days, maybe. Two weeks."

Jake activated a search for the dates with attention on disasters. A second later, the computer said, *At approximately 2:00 a.m., April 27, 1865, the massively overloaded steamboat,* Sultana*, exploded. At the time it carried approximately 2,100 repatriated Yankee soldiers, most from the Andersonville prison camp. Between 1,700 and 1,900 men died.* The voice carried on. Facts, figures.

Jake swallowed hard. "This is the *Sultana*, isn't it?"

"Yep."

"Would you know what time it is?"

"Don't know that neither."

Jake whispered to Martin. "The boat is going to blow up."

Martin's head dropped to his arms. "That doesn't make sense. The figures . . . the math . . . random times, Brownson said."

Closer to the pilot's cabin, another man slouched on the rail. Jake's gaze lingered on him. The moon's light burnished him like a bleached shadow. Was this also a soldier who would never make it home? His posture seemed familiar and out of place.

"We should leave, Jake. An explosion won't give us time to escape. I need to get to the lab and redo the calculations. I've missed something."

Jake straightened, moved toward the pilot house. A rift in the cloud cover brightened the light for a moment, showing the man's shirt sewed shut at the shoulder. No arm. Jake thought, these are Civil War veterans; many of them have lost a limb. As he looked at the landscape of sleeping men, he saw a half dozen crutches resting across blankets. Still, Jake's neck tingled. No empty sleeve dangled from the one-armed man. It was gone, sewn up, as if there had never been an arm for that space.

Martin sounded panicked. "I'm going."

Jake's back grew cold. Wind brushed against him, and the air felt empty. Without looking, Jake knew that Martin had gone. He approached the man at the rail, stepping over outstretched legs, until he stood next to him.

"You were fools to come. It's not worth it," said Brownson. The old man stared into the water, the side of his face a chalky reflection of moon and river air. "How much time did you give yourself?"

"I don't know, but it can't be long." Jake imagined the boilers deep in the ship's bowels, leaking steam, overpressured, fighting the current and the crowded deck, maybe seconds from ripping at the seams. He put his hand next to Brownson's, and behind his eyes he felt a sudden pressure. His voice caught in his throat. "Your lab . . . they've bombed it. You can't go back."

"They?" Brownson sounded tired. His voice was flat.

"Yes. Someone. Maybe another government. They might have found out what we were doing and became scared. Maybe they thought you could solve the paradox. But there was a bomb. You sent us away that day, or we would have gone up too."

"So, how did you get here? How did you arrange it?" said Brownson.

Jake could feel his brow wrinkling. "What do you mean? Your machine, of course. Your design worked. There's no paradox."

Brownson turned to face him. Moon shadows under his eyes made him look a hundred years old. "I didn't solve the paradox—I worked around it, and so did you, or you wouldn't be here."

No answer worked. What did he mean? "We just activated the device. We didn't solve anything."

Closing his eyes, the old man sighed as if he never wanted to breathe again. "The information paradox stops time travel, as I argued. Information that would change people's actions can't go forward or back. The timeline is immutable."

If it wasn't for the beating of the paddle wheel and the soaking Mississippi breeze, Jake could almost feel back home in the lab. This was the direction of a hundred arguments. It was where the math piled up, making no sense. "But we're here."

"Yes, we are, and we can go anywhere the information we carry doesn't matter. We go to time's dead ends, like this sad ship." Jake's thinking felt sluggish. So much had happened in the last hour. Too much to comprehend. "I don't understand."

How close were the boilers to letting go? Jake's hand crept up to the panic button under his shirt.

Brownson said, "We can't bring information from the future to the past, but we can't bring it forward either. Not if we could tell other people what we found. I planted the bomb."

Overhead, the moon vanished within the clouds, and darkness covered the steamboat. Brownson's voice came out of the black. "It was sealed. Undefusable. When I set it, when I couldn't get away, I made the first trip. I've proven that you can travel in time, but no one will ever know."

"How much time?" Jake's hand caressed the switch.

"How much time did you give yourself?"

"We didn't do anything."

"You didn't? Then it must be something else. Something unexpected." Brownson faced away from the river, looking over the sleeping forms. The two soldiers Jake had talked to earlier were still conversing. "Lincoln's dead, the cowards. Lincoln's dead," spoke one, his voice without feeling. Brownson said, "You poor boy. These men didn't do anything either, but their stories are over. The unexpected is on its way for them, the inevitable, as it is for me, here or in my lab or somewhere else." He paused for a raspy breath. "Just as it is for you. Your lab won't be there long."

Before he could hear another word, before the boilers could let loose to fling hundreds of men into the frigid Mississippi, before the bitter soldier talking in the cloud-veiled night could say again that Lincoln was dead, Jake pressed the button and disappeared.

Martin sat at the worktable, his hands wrapped around the back of his head, his forehead pressed against the scarred work surface. He didn't look at Jake when he appeared in the room, but he talked anyway. Perhaps he'd been talking the whole time. "Our destinations weren't random. The physics of the paradox tossed us where we couldn't matter."

"I know."

"The math says that Pelee is here, right here in the room with us, and so is the *Sultana* and the *Hindenburg* and everything else. The end is on its way." He began weeping.

"What did you say about Brownson's math?" said Jake.

"Tornado. Earthquake. Meteor strike. Nuclear bomb. Fire. Flood. Famine . . . quick famine. It's on the way. That's how the equations balance."

Jake ripped open his shirt. Double checked the equipment. Power was good. "You told me something about the math once, about the equations." He looked out the window. Was the sky turning dark? Was there a rumble in the building's basement. The unexpected was surely on its way. "Brownson told us that information couldn't travel in time. That's the paradox at work, but you said the math never solved perfectly. The numbers were always a little unbalanced."

"I don't get you," said Martin. "The numbers don't matter now."

"Only thirty-three people died on the *Hindenburg*. One man survived Mount Pelee. Five hundred or so lived through the *Sultana*." Jake spoke fast. What had happened began to make sense, if he had enough time. If he could get to where he needed to go before the time ran out. "If information is prevented from traveling backwards and forwards *perfectly*, if the equations add up *perfectly*, then we should only have been able to travel where there were no survivors. There could be no chance for escape, but if I get to the right place I might have a chance."

He pressed the button and found himself on a steel deck, slick with ice. The ship's name, *Halifax*, was printed across a lifeboat.

He pressed the button. Martin flinched when he reappeared.

Jake pressed again. Another mountain rose up before him. Its top too was smoke-covered.

He pressed the button. Martin said, "Where are you going?"

The button gave way. A cityscape. People streamed by, many on bicycles. Street signs were in Japanese. Without looking, he knew a lone bomber flew over the city.

"Tell me where and when," shouted Martin.

Jake paused, ready to go again. How much time did he have? None to be wasted, for sure, but the numbers didn't lie. Their imperfections held all the hope he needed. Maybe *most* of information could not go from the future to the past. All he could believe was that in the fractions that didn't add up, he could slip away.

"The *Hindenburg*," he said. "If I wait long enough. If I jump from the widow not so high that I'll die, not so low that the ship will crush me, then I'll survive. Sixty-two people lived. I can be the uncounted sixty-third."

There's no point in not trying, he thought, and he pressed the button.

# ONE DAY IN THE MIDDLE OF THE NIGHT

*Two Dead Boys Got up to Fight*

R edmond came out of coldsleep fast, an amphetamine and neurostimulator crashload whacking about his head and limbs like fire alarms. Even before his pod opened he ran security on Grant and found his sleep-pod was warm, bios off. A quick check confirmed what Redmond feared: they were thirty-seven years too soon; everyone else slumbered on, teetering so close to death's edge that their bodies forgot to age. Just the two of them were awake on the *Atonement*, a half million ton starship slowly accelerating toward Zeta Reticuli with enough colonial equipment and frozen, fertilized ova to seed a new world, and Grant meant to kill him.

Pulling sensors off his chest and arms, Redmond cursed under his breath. He'd programmed the system to alert him much sooner, when there was any change in Grant's readout. Grant must have figured a way to fool part of Redmond's security, or he'd weaseled a gimmick into the meds to wake him quicker. Either way, his plan wasn't good enough, or Redmond would be dead now.

The computer told him every door between the north and south sleepbays was locked. So, unless Grant was already in the south sleepbay with him, he had time to prepare a defense, and if he didn't get him that way, to hunt him down.

Maybe Grant *was* in the chamber with him. Maybe he was standing beside the pod, waiting, rage in his eyes and something deadly in his hands. Redmond watched the countdown before the pod opened. One minute to go. He drummed his fingers on the luminescent, slick inner surface, glowing a thin crimson around him. He imagined Grant poised outside. Redmond reached beneath his thigh and wrapped his fingers around the zoology supply tranquilizer gun he'd smuggled into the pod. Cool metal felt ominous against his palm.

He couldn't picture shooting his brother, but it was time to end this.


## Back to Back, They Faced Each Other

The sleeproom was empty. Redmond sat, his gun in hand, and surveyed. Half the crew slept in this end of the ship; the other slept nearly a mile away. That way a catastrophe might not take them all. They'd be able to continue. A movement in the corner of his eye startled him. He tracked the gun toward it. It was a maintenance robot rolling toward a bot tunnel, an aperture barely large enough to accommodate the eighteen inch tall and two foot wide machine. Redmond shuddered. The round-shelled mechs reminded him of cockroaches, really big ones, scuttling behind the walls. The bot scooted through the hatch that opened with a distinct, pneumatic wheeze. Even that sounded insect-like and horribly organic.

He moved to a workstation, keeping his gun raised, and woke the rest of the system. Vid monitors flickered into life.

"Where's Grant?" he said.

"There is no one named Grant aboard the ship," said the computer.

He nodded. That made sense. With the doors locked and under Redmond's command, Grant would have to go outside. He could be in transit now, incredibly vulnerable. Redmond accessed the meteor defense system. It wouldn't take but a few commands to control the cannons manually and threaten him as he made his way along the hull. But the computer couldn't find him. "No external activity detected," it said. Redmond checked the vids and other sensors. Nothing.

Suspicious, he called up the exterior suit inventory. They were all there.

"Where's Grant?" he said again.

"There is no one named Grant aboard the ship."

"Grant Mayer, when did he wake up?"

"Redmond Mayer is the only member on board with that last name. Would you like to see a crew roster?"

Redmond thought the computer sounded mocking, and he

squeezed his eyes shut in frustration. "Damn." Generally he liked the computer; it was Grant who hated it, although he was just as genius in programming as Redmond. Grant once said darkly, "What does it think about the hundred years we're asleep?"

Redmond glanced at the north sleeproom's vid. A pod gaped open, a mirror image of his own.

"Computer, where is the crew member who exited pod N49?"

"N49 has never been occupied."

"Double damn." It took him several minutes of going through the records, but he discovered it quickly enough. Every mention of his brother had vanished, neatly erased. As far as the computer was concerned, Grant didn't exist, and if he didn't exist, then the computer wouldn't track him. All Grant had to do was stay away from the vids. He had free reign and was effectively invisible, which is just the way he'd want it. Redmond keyed in a find and repair routine. Now that he knew the computer had been tinkered with, he could search out the changes and neutralize them. A progress counter winked into existence, but it couldn't tell him when the routine would finish. It was possible the changes were too deep or too well hidden.

Redmond rubbed sweat from his forehead and glanced up. Everything was perfectly still: the pods with their comatose cargo, the conduits running overhead, the shadows on the wall, but Redmond felt an expectancy, as if the ship were holding its breath, waiting for him to move. This was the stillness of the stalk, of the patient wait.

## Drew Their Swords and Shot Each Other

Four long corridors, interrupted every fifty feet with doubled airlock doors, stretched between the north and south ends of the *Atonement*. As far as Redmond could tell, all the doors were secured, and only he could open them. Before preparing himself for the long sleep, he'd spent hours and hours programming subroutines into the computer for just such an eventuality as this. Theoretically Grant would be marooned in the north end or trapped between two doors in one of the corridors.

Of course, according to theory, Grant couldn't exit his sleep-pod before Redmond did, and according to theory, he couldn't erase himself from the computer. Redmond stared at the monitors thoughtfully. Were they accurate? Were they showing real time, or had

Grant figured a way to have them display empty rooms as he walked in front of them? For that matter, were all the doors truly closed? He toggled a key; the doors showed locked and airtight. Could he trust the computer? After all, he had hidden his work from everyone else, yet Grant had subverted at least part of it. He wished he could ask it if it were trustworthy so he could listen to its tone of voice. Maybe he could hear a lie if it existed, but that was Grant kind of thinking. Grant talked to the computer like it lived. He called it the Blind Man. "All vids and no eyes," he said. It was his eccentricity. Every crew member developed one.

The back of his neck prickled, and he twirled, gun up, so close to squeezing off a shot that he couldn't believe the dart didn't slip away. The sleepbay was empty. One hundred pods in four rows filled the room's middle. Air whispered out of the vents, the sole sound other than his breathing. Normally when he was awake, so were the forty-nine other members of his shift. He hadn't been alone in the ship from the time the trip started a thousand years earlier. Since he was awake two weeks of every hundred years, he'd experienced about five months of travel time, but it still felt as if he'd been on board his entire life. He could barely recall another time where the gray walls didn't bind his existence. They cradled him and comforted him. They held him close, focused him, concentrated him. His imagination coalesced into a ship-shaped, palpable entity a mile long, no wider than the largest room, just as it molded his creativity and hopes, his knowledge and his fear, but mostly his fear.

No one can understand you more and hate you for it than a brother, Redmond thought. It's a mile long ship, and there's no place to go. Once the hatred exists, hiding it is hard. Ignoring it is impossible. After a while, there doesn't need to be a reason. But he remembered it in the top bunk twenty-two years ago—if he didn't count the thousand years they'd dozed—in the top bunk and who would sleep closest to the wall. Redmond slept on the edge when he was seven, forced there by his brother, facing the room's empty middle, Grant behind him, whispering, "The monsters will eat your face, Redmond. They'll eat it, and I'll have time to run." Redmond believed only the knowledge that their parents were in the next room kept Grant from throttling Redmond in his sleep.

By breakfast they were the wonder twins again, competitive, cooperative, and grades ahead of the pack.

The computer told him all of his routines were in place. The complex was geared to Redmond's voice. Grant wouldn't even be able to get basic information, and certainly not control. Or, at least from here it appeared Grant didn't have control. It was impossible to know. The *Atonement*'s computers were so huge, decentralized and redundant that no one really understood the system. Redmond had never felt so paranoid.

Where was Grant, and what was he doing?

Two doors led from the sleeproom. One opened into living quarters, workstations, the power plant and engines behind him; the other would take him to workshops, the ova repositories, the cafeteria, hydroponics and gym. Beyond them waited the corridors with their locked airlocks. If Grant had passed through, he could go around the sleeproom and get him from behind. Redmond dogged the back door so it couldn't be opened. Wearing a visor with a computer interface and heads-up display, he toggled the other door open. A vid showed the room beyond was empty, but he didn't completely trust the information. The door sighed on its hinges. He waited for a minute before moving; his ears ached from listening.

Staying next to the wall, Redmond peeked around the door. The vid was right.

After the workshops, he stalked between the cafeteria's empty tables. He paused to cycle through the vid views again. Two hundred and thirty-seven cameras in total. Three had failed since the last crew had done maintenance thirteen years earlier. The next crew wouldn't be up for twelve years. They'd have two weeks to fix or replace the broken equipment, check their course, and nurse the ship into another twenty-five years of automated competence before the third of the four crews woke. The ship had already lasted a thousand years, and it had three thousand to go. By the time they arrived at Zeta Reticuli, every part of her would have been remade. Only the crews and cargo would be original equipment. Camera failures were common, but he'd have to check each one for Grant. Redmond glanced around. No dust on the tables—the bots took care of that—but the ship felt utterly abandoned, like a museum after hours, or a morgue. It made him feel like a child again, like he did when he was fourteen, separated from his tour, hiding from Grant with half a Roman brick pried from an ancient wall along the Appian Way for protection, ready to smash Grant's teeth to the back of his throat if he had to, but a teacher came by first. For as long as they had fought, there was always a third party in the way, as if an intelligent fate kept them from tearing each other apart and goaded them into excellence.

As he passed the tanks in hydroponics, he checked fluid levels, pumps and chemical balance from habit. The computer cared for it, of course, but the plants were vital to their existence. Besides handling the air, they manufactured pharmaceuticals, cleaned the water, provided fresh food, and anchored the *Atonement's* tiny ecosystem.

He tapped his fingers against a vat of brine shrimp swirling about under their own lights. When Grant erased himself from the computer, he made himself a nonentity. It wouldn't track him. It ignored his med signals. There was no way for the computer to directly recognize him, but maybe there was an indirect way.

Redmond sat on the floor between the shelter of two tanks so that he could see the doors. He called up the ventilation readouts. If Grant breathed in one room long enough, Redmond might be able to find him.

It took him a while to get the computer to display the readouts the way he wanted. He looked for oxygen demand. Air circulated in all the rooms, but the computer adjusted for need. Finally, a tiny difference in one segment of the C corridor showed up. Something produced carbon dioxide there. Redmond checked the vid for that segment. Nothing visible, but Grant could be in the blind spot beneath it. Still, the computer showed secured airlocks, so Redmond's plan must have surprised Grant as he rushed from the north end to the south. The doors would have flashed a stay-clear, then closed. Grant wouldn't have been able to stop them.

Maybe the thing to do would be to go back to the sleeproom, climb into his pod, and resume the long sleep. When the next crew woke, they'd find Grant's remains. Redmond could manipulate the computers to show anything he wanted. He scratched his chin. That was Grant kind of thinking.

He shook his head. No, he had to end it now. Leave the computer records intact. They'd show that Grant had started it. Redmond had acted in self defense. When they reviewed the records, they would know.

How long had Grant been trapped? He was clever, and he knew the ship intimately. Was there a way out of the passage other than the airlocks? Was there anything in it that could be used as a weapon?

The computer showed that segment's emergency locker's manifest: food, water, some tools. No obvious deadly weapons. But Redmond would have to be careful. He would take all precautions. Grant was malicious in his intellect. He was three minutes older, but it was three minutes of planning, three minutes to get a head start on his brother emerging a shade later.

Leaving hydoponics behind, Redmond moved into the corridor.

At each airlock, he rechecked the vids and oxygen uptakes; Grant wasn't moving. The next segment looked empty, and the tiny warning light above the airlock glowed yellow, meaning there was pressure beyond, then flashed to green when he activated the door. After the ten second cycling sequence, the twinned, massive, metal doors swung open to reveal another long section of empty corridor. A second maintenance bot scuttled out of sight in front of him, disappearing with a creepy squeak. Redmond squatted at the bot's tunnel entrance. It wasn't very big, but a determined man might squeeze into it, and once in he could feasibly bypass the blocked corridors. Of course, he'd have to get through the safety features in the tunnels too—they had their own airlocks—but he could do that without tripping the alarms Redmond had set up.

A few minutes search revealed no tampering within the maintenance tunnels. There weren't vids in them though. Still crouched by the entrance, Redmond chewed his lip. The closer he got to the segment with the elevated carbon dioxide, the more nervous he became. Catching Grant in between doors was too easy. In fact, this was Grant's style, to let Redmond think he was winning until the end.

Something rattled beneath his hand. He threw himself backwards, slamming a shoulder into the wall in the process. Flat on the floor. Gun ready. Breathing in gasps through his mouth. He laughed in relief when the bot reemerged from the tunnel. It rolled on its hidden wheels to the corridor's middle, twirled until it faced him, its tiny vid eyes unblinkingly aimed. Redmond's laugh died in his throat. When the crew was awake and they all busied themselves with their two week regimen, the bots almost never came out. He could ignore them, but now he realized he was awake during bot time.

The machine pirouetted, then rolled down the corridor back the way Redmond had come. He laid his head on the deck, weak with relief.

He pushed himself off the floor. Another few minutes, and he would have him. Redmond licked his lips. The long feud would be over. Dimly he considered again how he'd explain this to the rest of the crew. He didn't worry about punishment. Grant was the dangerous one, the diabolical one. *Grant* had broken protocol by emerging from the pod too soon. *Grant* had reprogrammed the computer to hide himself; that would show his intent. Surely the crew would understand. Now that he was this close, Redmond almost felt sorry for him. A great career wrecked by unchecked passion.

He reached the second to last airlock. Trembling, he rechecked his gun. Tranquilizer dart ready. Safety off.

As he pressed the button, he glanced up. The status light above the door was out. Time slowed. *Not* out. A piece of tape covered it, one edge curling. He didn't have to pull it off to know the light glowed red. There was no air in the chamber beyond. Time nearly stopped; he turned, ran, each stride taking minutes to finish, the door at the other end impossibly far away. He thought, how long do I have to cover fifty feet? Did I take two seconds to start running, or five? How thoroughly did Grant subvert the computer? Enough to lure him down the corridor. Enough to hide the vacuum in that segment. Enough to create a subtle bait in an elevated carbon dioxide count in the chamber.

A klaxon screamed an alert. Two steps from the airlock, one step. He was through. Hit the button to close the door, which started its lumberous trip. Grabbed an access panel handle. How many seconds?

Wind, then a roar, tearing at him, *sucking* him back. Feet off the floor. Mouth open to equalize the pressure.

Very slow time. Hours in his head until the door closed behind him. Blood flowing from one ear, trickling into the corner of his mouth. Air cascading through the vents to replace the loss. Emergency lights pulsing in the ceiling. More klaxons, a virtual chorus shouting around him.

Then time caught up. Redmond let go of the handle, slid to the floor. Told the computer to shut down the alarms. He couldn't move his left arm. Carefully he felt his shoulder; it wasn't shaped right, a dislocation.

Grant hadn't been in the segment at all. It was a trap.

On Redmond's visor, numbers and reports scrolled past, the ship reacting to the segment's emergency. Attitude jets fired, nudging the *Atonement* back on course. External repair bots activated and rushed to seal whatever hole Grant had created. How Grant had fooled the computer into ignoring the damage at first was a puzzle. Redmond flicked from system to system. Nearly every part of the ship responded to the damage. Medcentral kicked into high alert, poised to warm a crew if needed. Every bot on board looked to be on the move. He couldn't track the commands being issued, and through the blizzard of numbers, he searched for Grant. It all came down to Grant who hated Redmond so much he'd risked the integrity of the entire ship to get him. How could he know that blowing that segment wouldn't have collapsed the entire corridor? Every door behind Redmond had been open. If he hadn't closed the airlock that saved his life, half the *Atonement* could have explosively decompressed. This was beyond any feud.

Redmond dragged himself upright. As soon as the computer ferreted out Grant's meddling, he'd find him and deal with him. Briefly he considered waking the crew himself. With forty-eight extra helpers, they'd neutralize Grant in a hurry.

No. That wouldn't be good. In their lifetime of battle, the only rule that couldn't be broken was that it remained private. Only Redmond could hurt Grant, and only Grant could hurt Redmond. When they were eighteen and playing football, Grant took on a linebacker who was going to blindside Redmond. Strained all the ligaments in Grant's left knee. Redmond had watched the video later, seen how Grant had broke his pattern to save him. Grant took an injury rather than letting someone else hurt Redmond. On the next play, Redmond went purposely low on a block and snapped the linebacker's ankle.

No, he wanted to see Grant himself, to look him in the face before he pulled the trigger. There would be no outside help. Redmond's arm hung awkwardly at his side as he walked toward the sleepbay. The gun he carried loosely in the other hand.

*Two Deaf Policemen Heard the Noise*

At first Redmond didn't hear the whispering voice. He had turned his earplug down low to tune out the computer's constant yammering.

"The doors are locked, you bastard."

Redmond paused. It was Grant, his raspy breathing filling Redmond's ear.

"You almost killed everyone with that stunt," said Redmond, forcing himself to speak calmly.

"If you wouldn't have screwed with the computers, the doors behind you would have closed. Nobody was at risk."

The computer beeped. "Program done," it announced. A report popped up, showing the changes Grant had made to the system. Redmond reactivated Grant as a crew member, and the computer showed his location in the living quarters lounge, directly behind the south sleepbay. Another adjustment, and the vid showed the true image. Grant stood in the middle of the lounge, his hands on his hips. So he'd only been one door away when Redmond had awakened. He swallowed. Had Grant got there just before Redmond had dogged the door, or had he been in the sleepbay before Redmond revived?

"What the hell did you do to the bots?" said Grant.

Redmond ran a dozen scenarios through his head. With the decompression as evidence, immobilizing Grant would look like an act of good will. The crew would give him a medal. Redmond could leave a record of the events and wake with the rest of the crew, a hero.

In the vid, Grant moved sideways through the room, his eyes intent on one wall. He didn't look seventy-three years older than when Redmond had seen him last. His hair was dark, still messy from the long sleep, and his face still baby-like, which belied his biological age of twenty-nine. He carried himself gracefully, like a spider, Redmond thought. One of those garden spiders with long legs that moved from thread to thread with perfect certainty.

"What's wrong with the bots?" Grant said again.

"What do you mean?" said Redmond. Grant's ghostly image floated in the air before him. Redmond cut through the gymnasium's bare space—all the equipment was stored—and into the hallway that would bring him to the lounge's back door. If he jammed it like he'd done the one into the sleeproom, Grant wouldn't be able to get out, even if he talked the ship into cooperating.

"Damn it! A bot's hunting me!" yelled Grant, an unusual tenor in his voice. He was frightened.

Something moved at the bottom of the display. In the middle of the empty gym, Redmond stopped walking so he could concentrate

on the image. Grant maneuvered himself behind a couch, his posture wary. A bot slid through one corner of the picture, almost out of
view. Redmond sent a command, and the vid went wide angle.

"What's it holding?" said Redmond. A multi-limbed extension
had unfolded from the bot's round shell, and it gripped an odd tool.
Grant held himself taut, ready to spring away, and his normally
graceful movements became panicked. The bot rolled a couple
feet to its left, then rotated so the tool pointed at Grant, but the vid
resolution wasn't good enough for Redmond to see what it was.
Hands on the couch's top, Grant sidled away, apprehension on his
face. Redmond flicked through ship data until he ran into a block.
Puzzled, he tried another query. Blank. All information on the bots
was locked up. It wouldn't access. This wasn't his work; it wasn't
Grant's either. Redmond tried a data runaround. Nothing. A
backdoor he'd built into the programming was closed too. Tension
rose in his throat. The bot skittered around a chair, keeping the tool
aimed.

Redmond said, "Stay low. Stay away from it." He pressed the
earplug hard against his head so he could hear better. Grant's quick
breathing rasped.

A pop.

"Damn it!" Grant clutched his chest. "It shot me." He took a
shaky step toward the door, then fell. The bot withdrew the extension before heading for a tunnel.

"Grant! Grant!" Redmond ran toward the lounge, Grant's vital
signs displayed in the air in front of him. Breathing and pulse slowed.
Only his hands and the top of his head were visible; the couch hid the
rest. One hand clenched. Then he spasmed for a couple seconds.

### And Came and Killed the Two Dead Boys

The airlock swung ponderously closed before Redmond could
get to it. He pounded on it, his hardest blows failing to elicit more
than dull slaps. Even as he punched the button to open it, he knew it
was useless. The heads-up display revealed more and more of the
ship's control locking out. None of them responded.

Across the gym, the door he'd come in was closed too.

Almost weeping, he watched Grant's vitals retreating to straight
lines. How had this happened? Who else had tinkered with the com-

puters? He could have sworn that only he and Grant were capable of this kind of work.

When the bot tunnel door squeaked open, though, he knew. It was the ship. Grant alerted a deep self-preservation program when he blew open the corridor segment. The Blind Man was awake; the ship was protecting itself. As the bot rolled toward him, tool arm extended, grasping the same weapon that shot Grant, Redmond looked at Grant's vital signs one more time. Were they flat, or was there the tiniest twitch in all of them? Would the ship kill them, or was it only putting them to sleep for the rest of the crew to deal with?

He didn't try to dodge, but even as he surrendered he couldn't help shuddering. The beetle-backed bot, its tiny vid eyes shining, seemed nearly alive. And it paused. Why did it pause if it wasn't to savor the moment?

Redmond stared at it, and it stared back. Only the sentient gloat. The bot fired.

*And if you don't believe this lie is true,*
*Ask the blind man, he saw it, too.*

# ECHOING

The semi's engine roared steadily while the heater poured warmth on Laird's ankles. His headlights cut into the snowstorm, flakes coming hard. He rubbed his eyes and stifled a yawn. There hadn't been another truck or car for the last hour on the long stretch of I-25 between Trinidad and Albuquerque, but he wasn't surprised. Christmas Eve in a snowstorm, who would be moving then?

The road unfolded. No tracks. Every twenty seconds or so he passed a highway reflector on his right. He moved the truck closer to the middle, or at least what he hoped was the middle. Snow dove from the darkness, slashing straight toward him, blindingly white. His knuckles ached from gripping the steering wheel. It had started snowing when he pulled out of Denver after dinner, soft at first, and glowing in the late afternoon light. The radio had played an instrumental medley of carols. Laird hummed along, thinking about his family waiting in Albuquerque. After he checked the shipment in at the warehouse, he would climb into his car and drive home in plenty of time to be awakened by the kids. Denver to Albuquerque: eight hours on a good night.

Laird downshifted, but the snow swept in just as hard, erasing distance. Sometimes it didn't look like snow coming toward him; it looked more like streaks of darkness exploding from a black center, wiping out the white. He blinked and shook his head. If this were a normal storm on any other night, he could find a pullout, park the truck and sleep until dawn, but the last weather report he'd heard said highways were closing behind him. They'd stopped traffic between Denver and Colorado Springs twenty minutes after he'd traveled that route. "Looks like our first big winter storm, folks," the DJ said.

Laird twiddled the radio dial. Nothing but static now. Most times he picked up stations the whole way.

Last year a trucker froze to death in a pullout thirty miles from Taos. No CB, just like him. No cell phone. The storm closed the road, and two days later when the plows broke through, they found him wrapped in a sleeping bag in his truck's cabin. Laird hunched over the steering wheel. They weren't going to find him like that because he wasn't going to stop. Nothing would prevent him from getting home to his kids.

Still, the snow shot from the darkness. When he switched on his brights, it was worse. He thought about being alone, about the long distance. What if, he thought, the snow wasn't snow at all, but stars? What if I were flying through the galaxy, passing stars . . .

. . . passing stars? Watch Commander Tremaine shook his head. For a moment the flying stars in the viewvid made him think of snow, but he hadn't seen snow for the last third of his life. What he'd seen instead, between long sleeps, were representations of stars scooting through the wall-covering viewvid during the long journey from one edge of the galaxy to the other, 100,000 light years, past one hundred billion stars at 2,000 times the speed of light.

He checked the [M]-space figures again. This couldn't be right! He refigured them. The ship didn't know where it was. Through the mental interface the computer wailed, scared into incoherence. Sometime while he'd been sleeping, they'd been thrown off course. Stars zipped by. Some swelled, became perceptibly larger. How close were the stars coming? The ship was off course! Tremaine shuddered. Even in [M]-space, they could not go *through* a star. The collision would create a spectacular display, destroying not only the star, but swallowing up its neighbors. The ship was supposed to slip *between* the stars. Their course had been designed for that. The passengers slumbering in the long-sleep cots in the holds depended on that, and so did he. After the long trip was done, he would find a place in the cots himself for the return voyage home where his family waited.

He broke open the emergency console, concentrating on the scores of steps necessary to slow the ship, to bring it below light speed where it could recalibrate itself. Be calm, he thought to the computer, and its keening voice silenced for the moment. Tremaine didn't look up. He watched his hands instead. Anything so he wouldn't see the cascading stars. He could almost hear them: deep gravitational wells and surging gases compressed to unimaginable density at their cores. They hissed in his imagination as they went by. As he worked, he wondered if the star that would kill them all would be visible. Might he have a chance to see it, appearing as small as the others at first, then growing out and out in the vidview's display as the computer scrambled to keep up with the data it was representing? Would he have time to flinch?

He'd quit working. His gaze locked on the viewvid. Stars appeared from nowhere, still at first, picking up speed as they moved from the center. His eye caught on one, followed it until it vanished to his left. Picked up another, followed it too, until it missed. A beautiful representation, if it weren't so dangerous. Of course, if he really could look out a window, he wouldn't see anything. Light in [M]-space wasn't light anymore. Nothing his senses could respond to existed in [M]-space, and what he thought of as the ship's movement was only a metaphor for what was happening. His understanding of [M]-space itself was metaphoric. It changed reality and the perception of reality. Still, the computer showed him a starfield, the ship rushing forward, a thousand near misses a minute.

Tremaine breathed hard. What would it be like to see one appear and never move, only grow? He felt like a child for an instant, staring forward, mesmerized. The sense that he was someone else, someone younger, a girl, gripped him. He shook his head. What if just for once, the screen changed . . .

. . . the screen changed. Brianna flinched. For a second the pixels spreading to the edge of the screen didn't look like pixels to her anymore: not plain white specks on a flat black background (her dad's 17-inch flat screen monitor), but glowing, moving, 3-dimensional diamonds, and the black wasn't screen-black; it was palpable black. She let go of the monitor, then fell back into Dad's leather office chair. For a second, she'd been someone else: a man, panicked at a console, afraid, so afraid. Afraid of what? Brianna breathed hard in the dark room. Through the closed door she could hear the Christmas party. Aunt Agnes sang something off tune. Her brother, Ray, played the piano in accompaniment. He was so much better than Agnes that he made her almost sound good.

Brianna rubbed her eyes. She played the screensaver game often. Once after smoking some of Ray's stash. Once when she'd snuck home from school to miss a sophomore English test on *Julius Caesar*. Mostly when she wanted to get away. Her therapist had asked her once what her personal motto was. "Everyone has a motto. It's what guides them in how they behave in the world. Mine is 'Make everything right.' I struggle with that," said the therapist, a perky woman who rubbed her cheek when she paused between words. Brianna wondered if the cheek ever became chapped. "So what's *your* motto, Brianna?"

Without thinking, Brianna said, "Ignore them, and they'll go away." And what she thought was, it's about isolation. It's about not connecting to anyone or anything, like Sylvia Plath who wrote a poem describing her stay in a hospital after a suicide attempt. Plath liked the sterility of the room. She despaired when friends brought her flowers because they broke up the porcelain and steel solace of white walls and shiny, tiled floors. Brianna loved that poem. "I'm an eyeball on a pillow," said Brianna to the silent screen, "just observing." Plath tried an overdose to kill herself. Brianna rested her hand on the drawer in her dad's desk where she'd put the baggie full of barbiturates. Light blue capsules with pink logos. Ten times more than the job required.

The door to the study opened behind her. Brianna pulled her arms close, hiding in the office chair. The door closed. She'd already taken a dozen pills. If they found her now, it would be too soon. The pill's acrid bite lingered in the back of her throat.

"I don't know where she is," said her father. "She's going to miss the eggnog."

Brianna sighed in relief. If it wasn't the eggnog, it would be the popcorn balls, and if it wasn't that, it would be the Christmas video. Probably *It's a Wonderful Life* again or *White Christmas*, which wasn't nearly as good as *A Muppet's Christmas Carol* that they never watched, even though she asked for it every year.

On the screen, the stars seemed different again, sweeping away from the vanishing point in the monitor's center. Brianna leaned forward. The room felt cold, her chair rigid, and the stars came too fast, too fast by half. She gasped for breath. It couldn't be the pills working already. She'd just taken them. The screen game was about going somewhere else, leaving her life, but it had never *worked* so well. These weren't pixels. They weren't even stars anymore. She cocked her head to the side. What were they? Snow? Her breath came out in a visible plume. Was a window open? That couldn't be it, or she would be freezing. For a second she could feel a winter's coat on her arms, her hands gripped a steering wheel, her foot reached forward to find a brake pedal. There was too much speed. It was dangerous. She had to slow down. Where was the brake . . .

. . . where was the brake? Laird pressed so slowly. The wheel squirmed under his hands. It must be pure ice beneath the snow, and his headlights didn't show what waited on either side. Ditch or cliff, it didn't matter; the shoulder that would grip his tires and send him into a deadly jackknife threatened more. Gently he pumped the brake. A reflector appeared on his right, so he was on the highway—for a second he hadn't been sure—and he still could be home for Christmas morning, but he'd have to be oh so careful. The speedometer needle crept downwards: thirty miles per hour, twenty-five, twenty. He downshifted, letting the clutch creep out so as not to break the tires' traction with the road. Now the snow swirled, no longer diving toward his windshield, but twisting in the headlights. The snow wasn't that deep. No more than a few inches. If he could make his way from reflector to reflector, he could find his way home.

His watch said 3:30. Five hours until dawn. At this speed he'd make Albuquerque by . . . he checked his watch again. How long ago had he gone through Trinidad? He remembered the lights at the edge of town, blurred by the whirling storm, and Raton Pass, he was pretty sure . . . yes, Raton Pass for sure, but had he made Maxwell yet? It was only another twenty-five miles or so. Had he gone through? He shook his head. Surely he had. But what was the last exit he'd seen? So many little towns off the highway: Springer and Colmor, Levy and Wagon Mound. He knew he hadn't reached Wagon Mound yet.

Laird leaned forward, pressing his chest against the wheel, close to the windshield. I-25 was a broad road, clearly marked. There was no way he could be lost, but he thought about the way exit lanes curved off so gradually, and they were lined with reflectors too. Could he be heading away from Albuquerque? He tried to picture the map. What if he'd taken the Springer exit without realizing it, and he was headed east now instead of south? No way to tell, and nobody would know where he'd gone. If only he'd pass a sign, a lighted building, a marker of any kind.

He thought, should I stop? At least now I'm still on the road. The engine will idle for twelve or thirteen hours. Plenty of heat. Surely someone will come along before then (but what if this isn't I-

25? What if I've lost the interstate and this is state highway 56? Eighty miles of empty back road that never gets plowed).

He stretched away from the wheel. The backs of his arms hurt, and he realized his jaw was clenched. What can you do if you're lost except to press on and look for a landmark? Through the steering wheel, he could feel the road, still slicker than slick . . .

. . . Watch Commander Tremaine wiped the sweat off his forehead, slicker than slick. The ship was slowing. He imagined the eddy of [M]-space behind them, like a boat's wake, spreading evenly from their passage, washing up against the stars. The psychic disruption wouldn't matter. Life was so rare that a million systems wouldn't feel the ripple, but he'd never heard of a ship slowing as fast as he was slowing his. Tortured reality could be catching up to them now. He watched his hands. Were they blurring at the edges? He glanced up. The stars weren't coming toward him anymore; they gyrated in their paths, curving randomly. [M]-space was catching them. How could he trust anything he saw or did? Even his thoughts could become scattered, the neurons flowing unpredictably. The confusion was already there: for an instant he thought he was a young girl; for a blink he was driving down a long, snowy road. Or was it confusion? Could he be close to a world with sentient life, connecting to them through the no-space of faster-than-light travel? Causality stripped away. Trembling [M]-space turning distance into concepts no farther apart that two thoughts.

He pictured the passengers, helpless in their cots. What dreams could [M]-space's backwash cause them? Would they sense his fear? Would that be the last thing they knew, his fear quivering on disaster's edge? How could he find their way home?

Tremaine held a sob close in his throat. He didn't have to see the controls to slow the ship. He'd trained through the procedure a thousand times. He let his reflexes take over. Fear didn't matter if he kept moving. But the ship would know that he was scared. It would respond.

Now the starfield slowed, or maybe his perceptions speeded up? No, no, they had to be going slower now; he'd completed so many steps. He closed his eyes. Just feel my hands, he thought. Fingers on controls. Push this one. Slide this one over. Listen to the calibrations reset. I want to go home. Everything must be done right so I can go home. Where am I?

Through the mental interface, Tremaine felt the computer struggle. A trillion stars! It needed an orientation, a landmark, a point of view to start a search. How long would it cast about in its memory trying to find a match? Laird could grow old and die while it sorted through the images, the old star charts.

Tremaine imagined his wife, a tall woman waiting at the edge of the woods where they'd met. At night they looked at the stars, and in the day everything was green. He could smell trees, so pungent, green on green, he could smell it, and there was music . . .

. . . playing behind the closed office door. Brianna opened her eyes. The feeling she was someone else possessed her so strongly, she nearly threw up. Ray had switched to "Angels We Have Heard on High." Strong bass line countering the melody. He held the high notes before dramatically entering the chorus. The room smelled of pine. Dad had bought a real tree this year, and no matter where she went she couldn't escape the resiny odor.

"I'm not lost," whispered Brianna. "If I open the door, I'll be home. That's all I have to do. I'm home now."

But that wasn't the lost that she felt. With her eyes closed she'd broken contact with Earth, for a second, as if she'd been cut loose and was spinning. "Where is the galactic center?" she'd thought. She clenched her fists. On her fingertips she could still feel the dials and levers and touch pads of what . . . a ship . . . a slippery road without a landmark . . . and there was something about [M]-space (she almost giggled at the sound of the term), but where am I? This is *way* out of control. What would my therapist think of this?

There is an answer, she thought. Her hand crept toward the desk drawer. There's no confusion in the baggie. But her motion stopped when she touched the handle. In the room beyond, they sang, *Angels we have heard on high, sweetly singing o'er the plains, And the mountains in reply, echoing their joyous strains.* She leaned toward the monitor. The stars had stopped moving, or at least they were moving very slowly now. What did the screensaver represent? All the time she'd looked at it, she'd only thought about where she was going, never about where she'd come from. What star had she started from? Where was she? (A tiny voice said, "Yes, where are you?" and she felt again the panic of the man at the console. "I need to know where you are.")

Brianna shook off the sleepiness growing in her. The room

seemed so dreamlike. It was the drug spilling into her like ink in water, spreading away, darkening the center. Languidly, she touched the enter button, and the screensaver blinked off. She chose her encyclopedia program. Typed in "Milky Way." A schematic flickered into focus on her monitor, spiral arms spinning away from the thickened blob of a middle, a little arrow pointing to a place halfway out on one of arms, closer to the edge than the middle. "You are here," it said, and Brianna took a deep breath. "I am here," she said. She switched to a picture of the night sky, the Milky Way, like light leaking around the edge of a closed door . . .

. . . Where am I? thought Laird. The truck barely moved now. His heater worked better at seventy miles an hour. At this speed he had to wipe frost off the windshield with his coat's sleeve. It would be so easy to stop, but he had another vision: his truck parked not at the side of the highway, but in the middle. What if another truck, later in the night when things had cleared a little, came barreling down the road? It wouldn't have time to swerve when the bulk of his truck loomed up through the snow. But I want to stop. He was so tired that he didn't trust what he saw in the headlights. Fantastic shapes forming in the drifting flakes. Faces. He tried to think of his family, his wife, his son, his daughter, but they seemed so far away. They were the dream. Endless snow, a cold that bit through his coat, that numbed the backs of his legs, that was reality. He thought about hypothermia, dementia, the end of reason. There's rest, he thought, in a bag full of blue pills with pink logos.

Laird punched his leg hard with a closed fist. The pain, for an instant, felt good. Cleared his head. What was that thought about pills? He could see them, resting in a desk drawer, Christmas piano playing in the background. I'm in trouble, he thought. She's in trouble too. She's *stopped*, parked in the middle, waiting to freeze.

He punched his leg hard, twice, twisting his fist when he did to sharpen the sting. It's just a road, and I'm a few miles from *somewhere*, if I can keep going, but within minutes the snow ceased to be snow again: it fashioned itself into hands reaching to get him, into the backs of monsters blocking the road. Vertigo gripped him, and an impression that he was falling straight down instead of driving forward surprised a scream out of him. The storm was a mouth; he saw it open, teeth at the edges, swallowing him and the truck whole, but he couldn't stop. He drove on. I saw it! He wept in fear. Hallucination or not, I saw it . . .

. . . Tremaine closed his eyes and opened them again. What had he seen? For an instant, it was there, a schematic of the galaxy, an arrow pointed on one spiral arm. The girl had thought, "You are here," and then he'd seen a photograph of the stars. If he could align what he'd seen, just an approximation, the computer might be able to do the rest. He concentrated on the memory, the gauzy middle of the galaxy, the arrow, the long strands circling away, and the computer watched what he watched. The diagram was such a rough location, but the computer hummed contentedly while it worked, because even a rough guess eliminated the near infinite number of wrong choices.

For the first time since Tremaine had realized the ship was off course, he relaxed. The stars in the viewvid weren't moving now, and he wondered which star held the girl with the diagram. In answer to his question, without breaking its rhythm, the computer brightened one dot on the display. Tremaine enhanced the image. A plain star, unremarkable to look at. On further magnification he noticed an unusual ringed planet in the system. That wasn't where she was. Third planet from the sun, almost a double planet, its moon was so large. Maybe if he concentrated, he could send her a thank you, although she'd never know for what. When he tried to see what she saw again, he only saw stars moving, and beneath the stars, a bag full of blue pills with pink logos. No galaxy. No arrow saying, "You are here." On the viewvid he studied the planet's blue face until the computer whistled happily. It had located them. Reluctantly, Tremaine clicked off the display while the computer recalibrated their course. I'm going home, he thought. They would be on their way soon, and he had duties . . .

. . . What duties? thought Laird. Where did that thought come from? All that kept him going was habit, now. Nothing he saw could be trusted. The reflectors, when they came seemed too far or too near (or too high or the wrong color). Was this hypothermia? He imagined his brain settling into a solidifying jelly, growing colder by the minute. For a second he thought the snow was stars, and he thought he could set a course by them, but now it was just snow again, flying through his headlights.

I could pull off, let the snow pile up. It would be so easy. His hands barely held the wheel, and his eyelids slid closed on their own accord. It's dark in here. So comfortable to fade away into sleep, into dreams where a piano played "Angels We Have Heard on High" and a Christmas tree beyond a closed door smelled of pine resin and popcorn strings and people laughed at a joke he didn't hear.

The truck can recalibrate itself, he thought. But if I keep moving, it will find my way home. . .

. . . I'm already home, thought Brianna, aren't I? The sense of *home* formed within her, a longing for it. A vision of a forest with a woman someone loved; a Christmas morning so far away, and so wished for. *Home*, like she'd never thought of it before. She reached around her. There were the office chair arms; there was the desk, although they seemed vague, and she was so cold. She wrapped her hands around her arms, the skin stiff as marble.

How could this be? She gasped. The pills were working. She could barely move. After a long struggle, she put her feet on the floor. If she could get out of the office, maybe, and into the other room where it was warm, they could save her.

I'm alone, she thought, and I'm lost. The highway will never end. I'm in snowy hell. Her hands rested on the steering wheel. There was no place to go, only the truck cab stuck in front of clouds of dancing snow. (I'm *not* in a truck—I'm in my dad's office) The steering wheel's solidity seemed more real than the computer monitor. Frost on the window. The low rumble of the geared-down diesel engine. The accelerator and the clutch, more real than the office carpet beneath her feet. I'm going to sleep, she thought, but I have to get to my family . . .

. . . my family. Laird forced his eyes open. If he slept, he'd never get home. He imagined opening the front door on Christmas morning. "I'm home," he'd say into the empty room, and there would be a giggle: his son behind the couch, his daughter behind the chair, waiting to surprise him. His wife smiling in the hall, just out of sight.

I've got to get home, he thought . . .

Yes, said Brianna in the darkness of her dad's office. I've got to wake up . . .

They both hunched forward. Stay focused, they thought. Keep moving . . .

Brianna staggered out of the chair. Braced herself on the desk's edge. She wept with fatigue . . .

Laird waited for the next reflector. There it was. The speedometer hardly twitched, but he was still going forward. The road ended somewhere, as long as he didn't stop. . .

How far away was the office door? Brianna couldn't see it. She couldn't see anything now. Why not? The headlights were on. The reflectors marked the road, if she just kept them to her right. (Don't stop now, came the thought through the diesel noise—there's a light ahead).

There's a light ahead; it came from under the door, where the piano played . . .

There's a light ahead, beyond the headlights and the crashing snowflakes; it's a gas station next to the highway . . .

Brianna grabbed the doorknob. It twisted beneath her hand. The door was opening. The light poured in, and the piano played "Angels We Have Heard on High." Before she entered the room, she thought, how many times has he played that song? Maybe he's played it all night.

She stepped into the light . . .

. . . light in the darkness. The sign said WAGON MOUND GAS AND CONVENIENCE. Laird edged the truck onto the exit ramp. People sat in the café. He could see them, drinking coffee. Beside the window, under the wreath they'd painted on the glass, waited a phone booth topped by six inches of snow.

He could call his wife.

When he stepped out of the truck, the wind picked up. For a second, the snow came straight at him, unswerving lines, glittering in the parking lot's light, like stars sweeping past a starship. He was a Watch Commander. He was a young girl hoping to escape. In the last tremor of [M]-space, he was the three of them, trying to get home.

Laird beat his hands together against the cold.

# THE INN AT MOUNT EITHER

After a minute spent weighing a fear of appearing foolish against his anxiety, Dorian approached the concierge. Behind the glassy mahogany of the concierge's booth, through the floor to ceiling windows, the afternoon clouds swept toward them across the neighboring peaks. As always, the view was spectacular. The sun cast long shadows through the valleys while the racing clouds caressed the mountain tops before swallowing them in gray, whale-like immensity, and when the clouds parted, the mountains would be the same but different, just a little, changed by their time in the clouds. That's why people always looked. Are the mountains the same, they seemed to say, or have they changed?

If Dorian stood at the window, he could peer down the mountain at the long, railed walkways that connected one section of the inn to the next. Curved glass covered some of the walkways so the guests could pass in comfort from the casinos to the restaurants, or from the workout facilities to the spas, or from the tennis courts to the pools, but others were open and guests could walk in the unencumbered mountain air, their hands sliding along guard rails with nothing but the thought of distance between them and the rocks in the sightless haze below.

Dorian cleared his throat. "I can't find my wife, Stephanie Wallace." His fingers rested on the polished wood.

Without raising his head from the clipboard he'd been studying, the concierge looked at him. "It's a big inn, sir. When did you see her last?" The man's eyebrows had a distinctively rakish look to them, turning up at the ends like a handlebar moustache, and his hair was silvery-gray.

"We were supposed to meet for lunch, but she didn't show up." Dorian glanced into the lobby, hoping that she might appear. Behind him, the room towered fifty feet to skylights. Opposite the window, the mountain's rocky side made another wall. Exotic plants that would never grow outside of the inn's protection filled every nook, spilling vegetation over the deep-toned stone.

The concierge put the clipboard on the booth. "Perhaps her plans changed, sir. There's much to do here at Mount Either."

Dorian gritted his teeth. "*Yesterday*'s lunch! I've been looking for her since last night. Stephanie's not *late*. She's *gone*."

"It won't help for you to be short with me, sir. What is your room number?"

"4128."

The concierge tapped at a personal digital assistant that nestled in his palm. "This is your wife, sir?" A picture of a smiling blonde woman, glasses slid part way down her nose, peered back at Dorian from the screen.

"Yes." She'd worn her glasses on the airplane. Once they checked in, she switched to contacts.

"I show that she's still a guest."

Resisting an urge to throttle the man, Dorian said, "I know that. What I want is some help in finding her. Can't you ask the other employees to keep an eye out?"

"Of course, sir. But, as I said before, this is a big inn. Maybe she wants some privacy. Perhaps she's admiring one of our many gardens. She wouldn't be the first guest to spend a few uncounted hours sitting on a meditation vista. In fact, getting lost at the inn is a selling point. We advertise it. 'Lose yourself in the experience.'"

"It's not supposed to be literal!" snapped Dorian.

The concierge picked up the clipboard again. "I will alert the staff. You don't suppose she went through a transitionway unaccompanied, do you?"

Dorian felt himself blanching. "No, of course not." But he remembered how she'd lingered yesterday morning in the Polynesian hallway.

"Guests are to be escorted through the shift zones."

"I'm sure she wouldn't do that."

The concierge sniffed. "We're very specific in our agreement when you signed in. The management will respond strongly to guests who ignore the rules."

Dorian turned away from the concierge. A new tramload of tourists had arrived, pulling their suitcases behind them. Most were couples. Newlyweds, by the look, or retired folk. A pack of bellboys scurried to meet them, while a mellow-voiced recording intoned, "Welcome to the Inn at Mount Either. You are standing in the new lobby, two-hundred and fifty feet above the historical first lobby built on the site of where Mount Either's special properties were discovered. If you are interested in a guided visit to the old lobby, dial 19 on your room phone."

"If she did go . . ." said Dorian. A hand seemed to be grasping his throat. It was all he could do to croak out, ". . . unescorted?"

The concierge said, "It's a *big* inn, sir. We will do all we can to help, but we don't really count a guest as missing until forty-eight hours have passed."

Dorian didn't know what to say. He drummed his fingers on the counter. Some of the new arrivals were at the window, looking down. The glass leaned away from the mountain, and the lobby itself protruded like a shelf, so they had an unimpeded view of the two-thousand foot drop and the rest of the inn on this side of the peak, clinging to the sheer face.

"I can't wait that long. I'm going to look for her myself."

"That is your privilege, sir," said the concierge. "I'm sure she's just around the corner. Nothing stays lost here forever."

The elevator to the Polynesian transition they had visited yesterday was out of order. Dorian looked both ways down the long, curving hall, but there wasn't another elevator. The inn's maps were almost impossible to read since the inn itself was aggressively three-dimensional, riddled with elevators, stairs, ramps, sloping halls, ladders, bridges and multilevel rooms. They'd followed a guide to the Polynesian transition, but none were in sight now. Dorian went left, around the curved hall.

Finally, he reached a stairwell that spiraled down for fifty steps. He didn't recognize the hall it emptied into, but a distinctive arrow in blue and yellow pointed toward a transition. Yesterday, as they approached the zone, the wallpaper had changed from the art deco they'd grown used to, to a palm and beach motif. Following the guide, he'd held Stephanie's hand until they stepped through the transition's door and into a Polynesian mountainscape.

"You're lucky, today, folks," said the guide. "I don't think I've ever seen it looking this good."

The sun pouring through the open veranda spread heat like a warm flush on their skin. Stephanie's hand drifted from his own, and she walked to the platform's edge as if in a dream.

"Oh, Dorian," she'd said. Instead of the snow-capped mountains of the Inn at Mount Either, a series of rounded hills rose in front of them, covered with forest so thick that it was hard to imagine ground beneath it. A flock of long-necked birds wheeled below, skimming the treetops and crying out to one another. She'd stared into the distance, entranced, her blonde hair just brushing her shoulders, and for a moment he saw the young woman he'd married twenty years earlier, the jaunty athleticism in her posture, the grace in her wrists and hands.

A waiter in a flowered shirt offered them drinks off a platter.

"Can you smell it?" Stephanie said, delighted. "It's the ocean."

And Dorian could smell salt and sand under the rich vegetable forest. Stephanie loved the ocean and all that was associated with it, the seals and birds and spiny creatures crawling in tidal pools, and the way the waves slid underneath her bare toes. Her passions were intense. She'd spend hours studying art or collecting children's literature or working with other people's kids. Once she'd gotten hypothermia in a mountain stream while sorting through rocks on her hands and knees. "I thought there might be quartz crystals," she'd said through the shivers. She laughed often.

Stephanie hadn't wanted to leave the overlook. The hotel guide finally had to insist. "My shift ended twenty minutes ago, ma'am. Perhaps you can come back another day if it's still here." Then he took them back through the hallway and into the inn they had left. "This was one of the original shift zones," he'd said as they walked back to the main lobby. "They found it third."

"How marvelous it must have been," Stephanie said. "I can imagine them climbing the mountain. Squeezing through a crevice, and there they were." She looked behind them.

Dorian rushed down the corridor. He remembered fewer doors in the hallway yesterday, and the carpet had been a different color. Closing his eyes for a second, he tried to picture the inn's structure. The elevator had only gone down a couple of floors, which was about the same distance the spiral stairs had taken him, but nothing looked the same. Maybe he was in a parallel passage. He passed another blue and yellow arrow. The decor changed from dark-polished woods and brass fixtures to natural pine siding. A long mural of a desert canyon rimmed with cactus covered one wall. Then the hall ended at a door, a rough-hewn, heavy-planked structure marked by a solid iron handle to open it instead of a door-knob.

It was a transition way, but not the one from yesterday. Still, it was close. Maybe Stephanie had come down this path. The elevator might have been out of order for her too. Dorian took a deep breath and opened the door.

On the other side, a wooden bridge reached an open platform. Drooping ropes hung from thick posts that lined the bridge's side, serving as protection from the drop into the depths below. Dorian leaned on the rope at the platform's edge. The general shape of the mountains was the same, but no snow covered the peaks. The sun glared, radiating off slick-rock, dark with streaks of desert varnish. He shaded his eyes to look up the mountain. Wood structures covered most of the slope, all light-colored pine. For a moment nothing looked familiar, then he spotted the main lobby buttressed by tree-thick pylons jutting from the mountain.

A man wearing a cowboy hat and a leather fringed shirt joined him at the edge. "First time to Mount Either?" he said.

"Yes," said Dorian, confused. "How could you tell?"

"Your duds. Not quite in the motif, pard." He smiled, a gold tooth flashing in the sun, then glanced at his watch, a large-faced instrument ringed with turquoise. "You going to the barbeque? I'm going to find my wife and head that way. Gosh, I love the grub you get here." His leather boots clacked against the wood flooring as he headed to the stairs.

Dorian was alone on the platform again. "I'm looking for my wife too," he said. Overhead a lone bird circled. He thought, is that a buzzard?

A tram like a large ore cart glided past the platform, heading down. Cowboy-hatted tourists sat at one end, while a pile of saddles and bridles filled the other. At the bottom of the ravine where the tram's cable ended at a tiny building, a dozen horses no larger than grains of rice milled about in a corral.

The set of stairs that gold-tooth had ascended looked like they led to the main lobby. Dorian took the steps two at a time. If Stephanie had come this way, she hadn't returned. Would she have realized right away that she was lost? Would she have gone to the lobby for directions? She could be there even now, maybe sipping a cool drink at one of the many, nearby cafes.

But at the top of the stairs were three passages, and none of them looked like they headed up. Dorian paused. If he chose the wrong way, he could become lost himself. A bellboy in flannel shirt tucked into jeans, carrying a tray of dirty dishes on one hand above his shoulder, came out of one hallway.

"How do I get to the lobby?" said Dorian.

The bellboy transferred the heavy tray with practiced ease. His suntanned face crinkled into a weathered smile. "Right hallway until you come to the elevator. The button is marked."

Dorian nodded, then started forward.

"My right," said the bellboy as he descended the stairs.

In the lobby, Dorian took a moment to orient himself. It wasn't that this sage-scented lobby was completely different; it was the similarities that threw him off. The same tall window gazing out on the deserty-looking mountains, the same exposed rock making one wall, a familiar reception desk dominating the room's center, but all the materials were different: hand-hewed timbers replaced the slick chrome support beams, big-looped throw rugs covered the plank floor where before he'd walked on expensive carpet, but what was most disorienting was the concierge, whose distinctive upward-flaring eyebrows and silver-gray hair waited for him at the reception desk as Dorian crossed the room.

"Thank goodness," said Dorian. "I wanted to find the Polynesian transition, but I ended up here instead."

"Excuse me, sir?" said the concierge. His expression was completely bland. No recognition at all.

"It's me, Dorian Wallace. I told you ten minutes ago that I was looking for my wife, Stephanie."

"I'm sorry, sir. You have me at a disadvantage."

"We talked. You said nothing stays lost forever."

The concierge shook his head. "Maybe I was thinking about something else when we chatted. What room did you say you were in?"

The situation was ludicrous. In the window behind the concierge, the sun blasted the peaks. No snow. No smoothly curved walkways stretching from wing to wing. Just heavy rope and solid wood and thick iron cable strapping the structures to the mountain. It was like an 1860 version of Dodge City turned vertical. "I'm from the real Inn at Mount Either. I'm in one of its rooms."

The concierge's forehead wrinkled. "*This* is the real Inn at Mount Either, sir."

Dorian stepped back. The man looked similar, but the business suit Dorian remembered had been replaced with a leather jacket, and where the silk tie had hung before, a silver clasp held a black bolo. Something about his face was different too. More wrinkles maybe? More silver in the hair? Suddenly Dorian was sure that they would have no record of his registration, and he realized he'd gone through a transition without a guide. What had the first concierge told him about management "responding strongly" to guests who ignored the rules?

Keeping the panic out of his voice, Dorian said, "My fault. I mistook you for someone else." He forced a smile. "There's so many employees here."

Nodding, the concierge turned his attention to a stack of papers on the desk. "This is a big inn, sir. Perfectly understandable."

On the way out of the lobby, Dorian paused. Had he come up a short flight of stairs to enter, or had the hallway been on the same level? At the foot of the stairs a mineral gift shop offered its wares on wooden trays inside its door. He vaguely remembered passing something like that, but he'd been in a hurry. Had he?

On an impulse, he entered the shop. Rocks and crystals of all kinds filled the shelves. "I'm looking for my wife," he said to the man behind the counter. "She might have been in here yesterday." Dorian showed him a photo from his wallet.

The man hooked his thumbs in the top of his overalls and leaned to look at the picture. "Yep, Stephanie, I know her. She liked the amethyst. I figure she spent an hour hunting for a good specimen."

Dorian caught the edge of the counter to keep from falling. His legs had no strength. He looked at the crate overflowing with purple crystals.

"Didn't buy anything, though. I offered her iron pyrite, fool's gold. She said if she couldn't have the real thing, she couldn't be happy." The man smiled. "Besides, she said her husband sometimes buys her gifts, and she didn't want to spoil his fun."

"Which way did she go?"

"Didn't really notice. Down the hallway, I reckon."

Dorian dashed to the door, then looked the way the man had indicated, as if there might be a chance to see her still. But the hall was empty. He glanced up the stairs into the lobby. The concierge was talking to a couple of men wearing six-shooters and badges. Security? The concierge pointed toward Dorian.

"Thanks," he called to the mineral shop man.

"Nice lady. I hope you find her."

The elevator at the end of the hall was not the same one he'd ridden up, but he didn't want to talk to security, so he rode it down to the transition level he'd come from. When he stepped out, the doors closed, and the elevator returned to the lobby.

Were they really after him?

After a couple confusing turns down hallways that didn't look the least bit familiar, Dorian stepped onto an open-air bridge that ended at a platform overlooking the canyon. He breathed easier. A quick dash down the transitionway, and he'd be home, but the long cables that carried the tram he'd seen earlier to the ravine's bottom were next to a platform a hundred yards farther away. An updraft ruffled his hair and dried the sweat on his face instantly. Wrong platform. The problem was how to get from the platform he was on to the one that he'd come from without retracing his steps?

He crossed the bridge back to the mountain where three choices waited: the hallway he'd exited from, a short ramp to another hallway, and a set of stairs that at least headed toward the other platform. At the top of the stairs, a blue and yellow arrow pointed in the right direction.

But the hallway's transition theme was heavy stone work, like castle fortifications, and on the door's other side, towering spires and crenelated restraining walls lined the paths. He'd missed the transition back to where he'd started. A dozen flights of stairs, two ramps and an elevator ride took him to another transition, clearly not the right one, but he needed to get back to the Inn at Mount Either he'd come from. Passing through transitions without a guide, he thought ruefully. I'm probably racking up room charges of astronomical proportions.

The next transition felt vaguely Arabic. He ran into a fellow in a rush going through the door in the opposite direction.

"Sorry, my fault," said Dorian at the same time the other man said the same thing. He only had a moment to notice the fellow was wearing the same kind of pants and shirt he wore before they dashed their separate ways.

The next had a rainforest look, but he recognized none of the birds that flew past the walkways. A blue and yellow arrow pointed down a hallway lined with jungle plants and short vines that dangled from the ceiling. He hurried past the closed doors until the hallway curved and the decor on the wall changed from matted vegetation to slick aluminum and recessed light fixtures. He pulled the door at the end of the transition zone open with relief.

The door closed behind him.

The lights were out.

He took a few steps into the darkness, then waited for his eyes to adjust. Slowly, the scene became clear. He choked back a gasp. Nothing separated him from the two-thousand foot drop to the bottom of the canyon. For a heart-stopping moment, he felt suspended, as if at any second he would drop to the rocks in an unstoppable plunge, but he didn't fall. His hands out, he shuffled forward. The floor wasn't perfectly invisible. He could see now that a walkway leapt to an opaque platform before him, and to each side, no more than an arm reach away, nearly transparent walls and ceiling enclosed him. It reminded him of an aquarium he'd visited once, where the visitors could walk in a glass tunnel right through the water. Sharks and rays swam above and below, and the illusion of being underwater was nearly perfect. Except the illusion here was that he floated in space. Dorian looked up. Stars glinted back at him with unblinking brilliance. He'd never seen a night sky so clean-edged. On the horizon, a quarter moon cast a clear, cold light on the mountain peaks in the distance, and its silver hue glinted off the Inn at Mount Either's structures that wrapped tight around the mountain above him, but it wasn't the Mount Either he'd left. Glass and metal flowed smoothly around the contours, seamlessly leading from wall to window to walkway to elevator, and the dim light of the glass told him of the inn's life behind.

Afraid for his balance, Dorian moved back to the door like a man on ice. He tugged, but the handle didn't stir. A lighted sign in red appeared above: SORRY, TEMPORARILY OUT OF SERVICE.

After tight-roping his way across the glass walkway, Dorian found himself in a vista room. A line of comfortably padded couches faced the window and the star-studded night outside. Illuminated by the partial moon, people sat in most of the couches, staring silently at the view. He looked out. Moonlight bathed the nearest mountain in grays and blues. Shadows, like black swaths of velvet, outlined ridges and rocks and filled crevices. Dorian took an empty couch and settled in its deep embrace. Yesterday, when Stephanie missed lunch, he'd sat in the restaurant for an extra hour, and he knew something was wrong. He told himself that she must have forgotten, but that wasn't like her. Using the inn's maps as best he could—the inn's structure was complicated—he'd searched the gyms and shops, the salons and museums, hour by hour, panic building.

He realized that this was the first time he'd rested in the last twenty-four hours. Dorian closed his eyes, just for a minute, he thought.

He dreamed of Stephanie. They were in a boat crossing a broad lake. Behind them he could make out a line of trees and a distant dock, but the other shore was lost in mist. Water slapped at the bow, and the air smelled of fish and wet wood. "You're so far away," she said. Dorian wanted to weep. "I know," he said. "I know, but I'm trying to find you." He was dreaming, and he could feel the couch he was sitting in, and he could imagine the people sitting around him, staring at the night-lit mountain, but he also felt the hard wooden bench and the boat's gentle motion. "Where are you, Stephanie?" In the dream, she laughed the way she always laughed, an honest burst of humor that animated her face and eyes. She said, "No, I mean you're so far away in the boat." Dorian braced himself, lifted his feet over the seat in between them, then slid forward. Their knees touched. Stephanie placed her hands palms up on her knees. Leaning, Dorian covered them with his own.

"Your hands are so warm," she said.

Dorian kept still, his fingers resting on her wrists, her pulse beating beneath them.

Stephanie looked upon the water, the long line of ripples moving past them, breathing quietly. She said, "I could float here forever. I don't have to be going anywhere." The boat rocked, and it was like the lake stroking them. She met his gaze. "If you are with me."

A voice said, "It's beginning."

Dorian opened his eyes, and Stephanie disappeared. For a moment, he imagined the couch moved, as if the floor was the surface of a black lake, but that feeling faded, leaving him with the memory so vivid of her pulse in his fingertips and the way her lips parted when she laughed that he wondered for a second if she'd actually been there before him.

"It's beginning," an elderly woman in the couch next to him said again. Her arms looked frail, but her voice was firm.

"What?" said Dorian.

"Shhh!" she said, and hunched forward, all her attention directed out the window.

At first Dorian thought the mountain was catching fire. A flicker of red glinted from the middle of a cliff. Then it spread over the length of the rock, a brilliant, deep red like an electric ruby.

"My God," someone said. Someone else sighed.

The red spread to neighboring cliffs, but now the center glimmered with yellow, and a few seconds later almost all the red had been replaced by the yellow glow.

Leaning toward the woman next to him, Dorian said, "What is that?"

"Just spectacular," she said.

"No, what is it?"

She didn't look at him. "Refracted moonlight on the crystals. It's only this good a couple times a year, and only from this spot. No other mountain in the world does this, and if this room were any other place, we wouldn't see it. The moon has to be in the right phase."

Now the yellow light enveloped the entire mountain, except at the bottom, which had acquired a purple tint that crawled up the cliffs until the yellow vanished. Purple was Stephanie's color, the color of amethyst.

"There were clouds in the spring. We missed it," the old woman said, then she started crying.

Dorian sat with his hands in his lap, unsure of what to do.

"My husband was with me then. We'd never been here before." She wiped her tears before looking at him for the first time. Her eyes reflected the purple from the mountain. "It's just a superstition, I know, but they say if you see the lights with someone you love, they will be with you forever."

Gradually the purple vanished. The edges of a few of the larger rock faces glinted green for a moment. Finally, the mountain looked like it had when he entered the room. People rose from the couches and headed for the exits. Many were couples holding hands. The old woman didn't move. She'd wrapped her arms across her chest, as if she were hugging herself. Her knuckles were large and arthritic. She said, "I hope you come back when it isn't cloudy. I hope you come back with someone you love."

A chill swept the back of Dorian's head. "I'm looking for her."

She shrank a little deeper into her chair. "Not me. I'm waiting."

At the other end of the room, a bellboy bent to talk to a young couple still sitting. They smiled back at him, then each showed him a small piece of plastic. In the room, lit only by reflected moonlight, Dorian couldn't tell what the plastic was. The bellboy moved to the next lodger, who also showed him a plastic card. There were only a few people between Dorian and the bellboy when Dorian recognized that they were displaying their room keys. His own key didn't look like the ones they showed.

"What's the problem?" said a woman as she put her key back in her pocket.

"Nothing of concern, ma'am. A security issue, misplaced guest."

Dorian slipped out of the room and into a passageway. Half of the wall was transparent, like the entrance bridge near the transition, except the ceiling glowed to provide dim light. He followed the gentle curve and had walked for several minutes when an acetylene-bright brilliance flushed the hall into overexposed surfaces and shadows. He blinked against the glare before shading his eyes. From the mountain's base, the light grew more intense, until, soundlessly, a rocket, balanced on a flaming pillar, rose past him and streaked into the night.

He heard the people in the hall before he saw them, but short of turning back the way he came, there was no way to avoid them. They laughed and joked loudly. At first Dorian thought they must be going to a masquerade. All wore bulky suits and carried helmets under their arms.

"I've never been outside," said a young man with glasses and a moustache.

"Just don't sit on something sharp," said his motherly-looking companion. "And be sure to listen to the safety procedures. Depressurization is nothing to fool around with."

They were too preoccupied to acknowledge Dorian as they clumped past.

When they vanished around the curve, Dorian stopped, put his hand on the glass wall, and looked out again. The stars never had seemed so sharp and unblinking, and, he noticed, there was no vegetation he could see. None at all. The landscape was as desolate and bare as the—he paused as he made the comparison—as the moon, but there was the moon, nearly resting on the horizon. He shivered. Every transition at Mount Either took the guests to an exotic location, but it had never occurred to him to wonder *how* exotic. This is Earth, he thought, isn't it? Clearly Earth! But what happened to it?

The mountains weren't just dead. They were swept clean and bare, like a planet's skeleton, solid, smooth, dry and with no ability to shrug themselves into life. He pressed his forehead against the glass and shut his eyes. Where was Stephanie? She'd be taking pictures. She'd be stopping at every new view, her head cocked a little to the side, as if she were measuring the world for a painting. She'd tell him about what she'd found, and if he was quiet for too long, she'd say, "What are you thinking?" and genuinely want to know.

Dorian pushed away from the glass and continued walking, slowly at first, but soon with a purposeful stride. At a junction he chose the hallway whose stairs led toward the lobby. An elevator took him up, and when the doors opened, a bellboy stood on the other side. The bellboy, wearing a silk vest that sported a shiny name tag that read, NED, CAN I HELP?, held a personal digital assistant in one hand with Dorian's face on the screen.

"I'm Dorian Wallace."

The bellboy checked the image in his hand. "Heavens, you *are* Dorian Wallace! Thank goodness, sir. Your wife has been worried sick. Everyone has been looking for you."

Dorian's hand flew to his heart, and he clenched his shirt in a fist. "You know where Stephanie is?"

Two short hallways later, they were in the lobby; the same long window that seemed so familiar looked out on the moonlit mountains. Dorian's pulse pounded and his face felt hot. The same cliff face covered with plants made the back wall, and, Dorian thought, the same concierge, his handlebar eyebrows pointing upwards, waited at the reception desk. But he wasn't the same. Similar, but not the same. Shorter, perhaps? A little broader in the shoulders?

Stephanie stepped out from behind the concierge.

Wordlessly they embraced. Dorian held her tightly, his cheek pressing against the side of her head. She trembled in his arms. For a moment, all centered on her, on the feel of her breathing against him, of her fingers on his back. The smell of her skin. The texture of her blouse.

For a moment, all was perfect.

But she stiffened——he could feel it in her muscles——and she pushed away.

Stephanie looked at him, her hands still holding his. Dorian studied her. Where Stephanie's hair had been curled, it now hung straight. Where her eyes had been blue with tiny white spokes, they were now blue with tinges of green.

"Who are you?" the woman asked.

"I'm Dorian. Who are you?" He released her hands, and they hung in place where he'd left them. She took a single step back.

"Oh, no," said the concierge. "This is distressing."

"Where's my husband?" the woman said. "Where's my Dorian?"

The concierge took a position between them. "The inn is not at fault here. It doesn't happen this way. If you'll come with me, sir." He took Dorian by the elbow and walked away from the reception desk. "How many transitions did you go through?" he whispered harshly.

"I . . . maybe . . ."

"You went through at least two, didn't you?"

Dorian stopped, pulled his arm away from the concierge. "The damn inn is so confusing that anybody can get lost. Give me a guide, and I'll be happy to go back to where I belong."

"It's a *big* inn. How many?" The concierge wasn't smiling, and he didn't look friendly in the least.

"What does it matter? Five or six, I think."

The concierge blanched. "You don't understand, sir. There are nine transition zones."

"So?"

"When you go through one, you come out at different Inns at Mount Either. Each inn has nine transition zones too. Nine different ones. When you go through two transitions, there are eighty-one different inns you might have come from. If you went through five. . ." He paused, closing his eyes for a second. They popped open. "You could have come from any one of 59,049 realities. If you went through six, we'd have over a half million possibilities." He grabbed Dorian's elbow again with urgency. "Where did you come from to get here?"

Dorian winced and found himself half walking and half trotting. "A jungle, I think. Ouch! What's the hurry?"

They reached an elevator. The concierge punched the button. Then he punched it again. "Zone drift. When you go through a zone, the door you came from is the way back for two or three hours, but if you wait too long, the place you came from isn't there anymore.

It'll be another version of the inn. It might even be a really, really close version of the one you came from, but it won't be the same one. If you didn't dawdle in any of the zones, though, you should be okay."

Dorian glanced at his watch. When had he gone through the first transition?

The elevator door opened. "Jungle?" asked the concierge.

Dorian nodded. "Another version? Like a parallel world?"

The concierge grunted as the elevator started down. "Um, sort of. We prefer to call them non-convergent. There's a lot of variation."

"But the door to the jungle is out of order. I would have gone back through it on my own."

"We locked all the doors when we realized a guest was making unguided transitions."

Dorian followed the concierge, who made turns down hallways and chose stairwells with practiced confidence. They crossed the transparent bridge, but now the door was lit and they passed into the rainforest transition Dorian remembered.

"Okay, how did you get here?" The concierge reached behind a curtain of vines hanging next to the wall, and pulled a phone from a hatch behind.

"From a kind of a desert world, I think."

The concierge's forehead furrowed in frustration.

"I'm sure it was desert, like the Arabian Nights."

He said something into the phone, then listened to the reply.

They hurried around a hallway's long curve. Dorian hadn't looked at the scenery the first time through, but now he noticed solid vegetable weaves that made the walls, and the sweaty smell of wet wood and dripping leaves.

"How come you are here? I mean, you're just like the concierge from the inn that I came from."

They trotted up a flight of stairs, crossed a dizzying walkway over a ravine and entered a small court circled with open booths. Guests sat on stools drinking from tall bamboo cups or coconuts with straws stuck in them. An elevator rendition of jungle music played softly in the background.

"I'm everywhere," said the concierge. "So's your wife. So are you. That's the problem. You are lost, and so are about a zillion non-convergent versions of you wandering about the inn where they don't belong. Of course, there are a lot of you who didn't get lost either. The worlds aren't parallel. At least your wife had the wit to come back through the same doors she exited."

"She has a pretty good sense of direction." Dorian shook his head. "I didn't come this way. I don't remember this."

"Short cuts. Your clock is ticking. With any luck, another version of me is hustling another version of you, the right one, back to my lobby where that woman you met is waiting. How long has it been since you went through the first transition?"

"I'm sure it hasn't been two hours yet." When had he started looking?

"Good. We should make it without any trouble."

Finally they entered a transition with a western theme, rough textured pine walls and the smell of cactus.

"This is the first zone I entered."

The concierge sighed and smiled for the first time since Dorian talked to him in the lobby. "Fifteen minutes back for me. Piece of cake. From here, all I need is your room key."

Looking at the key, the concierge plucked another phone from a hidden niche. He read a string of numbers into the mouthpiece.

Minutes later, they stood at the transition back to the inn Dorian had come from. The concierge put out his hand. "I'm glad that I could help you, sir. A bellboy on the other side will escort you to the lobby, where I'm sure your wife will be glad to see you." He paused. "We've always said that a guest should lose himself in the experience."

Dorian grimaced. "I didn't think that was funny the first time I heard it."

When he entered the lobby, he spotted Stephanie right away. Her back was to him, but her blonde hair, lightly curled at the end, barely touching her shoulders, caught a ray of sun through the window and practically glowed. He remembered that once he'd told her that he liked looking for her in crowded places. "I just tell myself that I'm looking for the prettiest woman in the building, and when I find you, I'm done."

She turned, but her smile was tentative.

"Dorian? The real Dorian?"

He tried to speak. Nothing came out, and his eyes blurred.

She was in his arms. Dorian held her tightly, afraid to let go. She buried her face in his neck, and he could feel her tears on his skin.

He thought about the first time he'd held her, a night when they'd parked on a cliff's edge with the city's lights spread out in the valley below, when he knew that they would be together forever. Her breathing had synchronized with his. Her shoulder fit under his arm as if the two of them had been sculpted at the same time to go together. Dorian shook with sobs, and she held him. Her crying matched his own.

A long time later, it seemed, when they'd dried their faces, made their apologies to the concierge, who just seemed happy that they were where they belonged again, and all thoughts of further repercussions for going through transitions were forgotten, they walked toward their room. Stephanie's arm wrapped around Dorian's waist, and he kept a hand on her shoulder, as if afraid that she might slip away again.

"Where were you at lunch?" Dorian asked. "I waited for an hour."

Stephanie's inhalation still sounded shaky. "I was in the wrong restaurant. When you didn't show up, I went back to the room. But you didn't come, so I started looking for you. That's when I went through the transitions. Dorian, it was all so beautiful. I lost track of time." She frowned. "They brought a man who looked like you, but he wasn't you. I've never been so frightened before."

"I know."

Dorian pulled her even tighter. It didn't matter why they'd been apart, as long as they were no longer lost. He loved the feel of her walking beside him. He loved that he could match strides with her so they wouldn't jar each other. Twenty years of marriage, and he loved that she still surprised him with her laugh.

They reached the room. Dorian slid his plastic key into the lock, but it didn't work.

"Let me," Stephanie said. The door recognized her key and let them in. "I'm so tired, I could sleep for a week." She leaned against the wall, looking at him.

"Me too. I haven't slept since yesterday."

She headed for the bed, and Dorian was glad because she couldn't see the change in expression on his face. He hadn't slept since yesterday, he'd said, but that wasn't true. He'd slept in the moon room, where he'd dreamed of Stephanie. "You're so far away," she'd said in the dream.

How long had he slept?

Stephanie pulled back the sheets. Dorian watched. Was that *exactly* the way Stephanie unmade the bed? Didn't she always wash her face first?

She walked past him into the bathroom. Her fingers touched his as she rounded the corner. "You look like you swallowed something gross."

The sink turned on. Water splashed. Dorian backed up to the edge of the bed, but he didn't sit down. Stephanie had left the door open. She always closed the bathroom door, even to brush her teeth, even to blow her nose. Her shadow moved on the carpet in the light of the open door.

How long had he slept?

Much, much later that night, long after the woman had fallen asleep, Dorian lay with his eyes wide open, listening. Straining. What did his wife sound like when she breathed? Could this possibly be her beside him, and what if it wasn't? How long would it be before she noticed? A year? Ten years? Never?

Or could she wake up right now and know? Would she lever herself up on one elbow and look at him in the dark? "You're not Dorian," she'd say. Her breath wouldn't smell like Stephanie's. Her voice wouldn't be Stephanie's. Not quite. Not exact. Not real.

She stirred slightly. Every muscle in Dorian's body tensed, but she didn't wake up.

Not then.

# THE ICE CREAM MAN

K eegan chose a song from the truck's jukebox after he crossed 6th Street going south on University Blvd.: "You are My Sunshine." It was his Thursday route. The music boomed through the loudspeakers, echoing from the late 19th Century houses. Within a minute, doors opened, people wandered down their sidewalks and waited for him on the street. He muted the song as the truck slowed to a stop. Even through his dark sunglasses, the sun was too bright. Every reflective surface bounced the light in painful intensity. He squinted against the intrusions.

An old lady in a broad-rimmed hat that shadowed her face and a lacy blouse that covered her neck to her chin looked up at him. "Do you have strawberry today?"

He handed her a cone with a single scoop.

The tip of her tongue touched the treat. She closed her eyes and sighed. "Best strawberry ice cream in the world."

He snapped his fingers. "Overripe strawberries are the secret. They're sweeter. You're lucky they're in season."

The lady put a pint of bourbon on the counter. "Will this do?"

Keegan held it to the sunlight, where it glowed like golden honey. "That's a couple weeks worth, darling."

She blushed. "I need a box of .22 longs if you have them. Something's been in my back yard the last few nights."

Keegan searched below the counter. "Short rounds, short rounds, short rounds." He moved the small boxes aside. "Ah, here we go, .22 longs. That would make us even."

Behind her frowned a middle-aged man with a tiny black mustache like a charcoaled thumbprint below his nose. "Where do you get the ammo, hairlip?"

Keegan resisted the urge to cover his mouth. He smiled instead. "It's all in trade. I have something someone wants. Somebody else has something I want. What do you want?"

"Nobody trades bullets. They horde them." He looked suspiciously at the truck. "And how do I know your ice cream is any good?"

Another man a couple folks back in the line said, "Are you going to order, Rich, or are you going to be a pain in the ass? Doesn't matter if it's good or not. You can't get ice cream anywhere else." The man scowled. "Vanilla."

Keegan turned his back to get another cone from behind him. He rubbed his nostril with his thumb, and as he scooped the ice cream he pressed the thumb firmly into the frozen ball before plopping it into place. "There you go, mister," he said. "Since it's your first time, it's on the house."

The next customer wanted a double scoop of chocolate, which Keegan let him have for a nearly full bottle of powdered cinnamon. "Can't get enough good spices," said Keegan to the man who'd defended him. "How are you doing, Laird?"

Laird leaned on the counter, his tanned arm a sharp contrast to the polished aluminum, liver spots sprinkled across the top of his hand like the map of an island chain. "Pretty good, Keegan. You put a booger in his ice cream, didn't you?"

Keegan grinned. "I didn't charge him."

"Maple-walnut for me, if you have it."

The ice cream rolled smoothly into the scoop. Keegan liked the cold air caressing his wrists. It felt better than the waves of heat rising from the asphalt outside the truck, and it was only 11:00. Good for business. Hard to work in.

Laird licked a drip off the cone before it reached his hand. "Can't really blame the guy for his bad temper. He moved in a month ago. No territory. No prospects. Some muta-bastard broke into his house and tore up most of his stores, so he's feeling pinched."

"Is he thinking of scavenging north of Colfax Avenue?" Keegan closed the freezer lid. No need to let the product melt, and the truck used less fuel if the refrigerator unit wasn't working the whole time. "I wouldn't recommend going alone."

"You don't seem to have trouble."

Keegan swept a damp rag the length of the counter, keeping his eyes down. "I know the area."

"Speaking of that, did you find the item I asked for?"

"It's rare. Really rare." The rag swung loosely in Keegan's hand as he leaned against the cabinets, squinting through his sunglasses at the sunlight outside the truck's dark interior. The last two people in line, a middle-aged couple he'd served several times before, wiped their foreheads in unison. Like most folks, they didn't look at his face. He wanted to cover his mouth again.

Laird sighed. "All right. I can double the sugar for next month." He leaned forward to whisper, "I found a cache you wouldn't believe. Geezer who'd filled a double-car garage with goodies before kicking off."

"Great." Keegan pulled two boxes of 12-gauge shotgun shells from under the counter. He rattled them before putting them down. "Got a project?"

Laird pocketed the boxes. "Nope. The boys on the Colfax fence say they're having breakthroughs every night. I want more punch for my dollar. Whatever tore into Rich's house went through the bars on his window. Something new south of the fence, evidently. One of these days I'm afraid I'm going to stumble on a mutoid that's all teeth, scales, tentacles and bad attitude, and I don't want to face it with a popgun."

"You could move to the country like everyone else."

Laird turned to look down the street. Many of the houses were boarded up, their windows staring into the street like blind eyes. On other houses, bars covered the windows and doors. Barbed wire separated them from their neighbors. "What, and leave all this? There's still a lot of scavenging to do before I start scratching dirt for a living. Besides, farms have mutoid problems too." He licked the last of the ice cream out of the cone. "Could you sweeten this up?"

Keegan dropped another scoop on the cone.

Laird said, "The ammo question was dumb. You know the one I want answered?"

Keegan looked at him through his sunglasses.

"Where do you get the cream? The last true cow died twenty years ago."

"I have good freezers."

Laird laughed. "See you next Thursday." He walked away, waving as he went.

The last couple both wanted raspberry, but Keegan didn't have any. They settled for a scoop each of chocolate macadamia nut.

He placed the set of four sundae glasses they'd brought on the floor. The woman looked suspiciously at her cone.

"Just ice cream in that one, ma'am," he said.

When he drove away, he flicked the music back on, "Little Brown Jug." A couple blocks later, a new crowd gathered. By 1:00 he was sold out.

Driving the ice cream truck had been Keegan's first job out of high school. In the dispatch office, Old Josh Granger had handed him the route and an inventory sheet along with the keys to the truck. "Drive slow in the neighborhoods," he said. "Nothing sadder than a little kid who can't catch the ice cream truck."

Keegan nodded.

"Not that there's kids anymore." Granger sat heavily on a stool, cupping his hands over his knees. "God, I remember when the five-year-olds would chase me down. Scads of them. Couldn't even get their change up to the counter. Little hands holding money. Do you remember kids?" Granger looked out the window onto the lot where the trucks were parked. Canvas covered six of them. "You're what, eighteen? No, you wouldn't. You're one of the last batch."

Keegan ground the toe of his sneaker into the cement. "They'll find out what's causing it. I heard the news the other night. They're making headway."

Granger sighed. "Do you have a girl?"

Keegan blushed. "They don't seem to take to me." He scratched his nose, covering his mouth.

"Humph! Sorry, son. Maybe it's for the better. Save you the heartache. No ultrasound horror show. No little bundled buried in the back yard for you . . ." He trailed off. A muscle in his arm twitched, but he didn't seem to notice. "Nobody gives you guff about it, do they?"

"No, sir. They're all real nice." Keegan thought about the whispers in the school hallway. Once he'd heard an entire conversation. "Do you think he's a mutation?" someone had said. "Nah," said someone else. "Cleft palate. It's just a birth defect."

Granger said, "Don't they have operations to fix that?"

"I had it. You should have seen it before."

For the rest of the summer, Keegan drove the truck. Kids his own age and older waited for him. In the shadows, they hardly noticed his face. "I want a bomb pop," one would say. "Ice cream sandwich," said another. For a summer he drove the town, music filling his ears: "Home on the Range" and "London Bridge" and "The Yellow Rose of Texas," calling, calling, and the folks came out, remembering in the music what it must have been like to be five. He imagined them as children, running after him, their eyes on fire, laughter in their throats. It was the best summer of his life. Then, in August, the company went under, and he had to turn in his keys.

When he left his last inventory in the dispatch office, Old Man Granger sat unmoving on his stool, staring off into an unfocused middle distance.

"Here's my paperwork, sir. I filled everything out."

Granger didn't speak.

"I rinsed out the freezer wells too. The truck's clean." Keegan resisted an urge to pass his hand in front of the old man's eyes. "Well, I got to go."

When Keegan turned back to close the door, Granger finally spoke. "Don't ever drive too fast." He could have been talking to himself. "You don't want to leave the kids behind."

It was thirty years before Keegan would drive an ice cream truck again.


The University Blvd. and Colfax Avenue enclave ended south of Cherry Creek, about fifteen blocks from Colfax. Keegan drove through the empty neighborhoods, his music turned off, the ice cream gone, and the boxes of traded goods packed securely behind him. He rested his wrists loosely over the top of the wheel, avoiding road debris with long, sweeping curves. Here the remains of homes sat back from the sidewalk on top of short, weeded slopes. The frame houses that weren't burned to the ground sagged forlornly, holes gaping in their roofs, an occasional glass shard still clinging to a window, catching the sun. The brick homes fared better, though their roofs swooped to black holes too. Nothing worth scavenging in them now, unless there were secrets buried in their basements. Too close to University. Inside, all the drawers would be pulled out, the sheet rock rotted, wallpaper hanging in ragged folds, their owners either dead or moved to the country to raise crops.

Keegan sighed, checked the fuel gauge, and turned north. A

slinky, black form, ten feet long, flowed across the road on short, powerful legs, before vanishing behind some bushes. The sun was still high in the sky. Keegan whistled. Most of the mutoids were nocturnal. He hadn't got a good look at it, but it moved like a predator. Either it had broken through the Colfax fence, or it came out of the Platte River wastes a couple miles west. Keegan slowed the truck.

It appeared again, beside a house, placed a foot high on the worn wood, then pulled itself up. When its front paws reached the gutter, its hind feet were still on the ground. Then, without a break in rhythm, it poured onto the roof, defying gravity in its sinuous path. Before it disappeared over the peak, it looked at Keegan, small eyes buried in a broad, black skull, like a bear's. That high, poised in the sun, it no longer appeared black, but a deep, regal purple.

Back on University, two fence men pushed the barrier aside to let him through.

"Saw something big on the road back there," said Keegan.

"Like a low-riding black panther?" asked the fellow hoisting a scoped rifle.

Keegan nodded.

The man shaded his eyes to look up into the truck. "I got a shot at him yesterday, walking bold as brass in front of those shops on 6th Street. Nothing to eat in the enclave except us, so we've organized a hunting party for tomorrow. Find him and then go north for a bit. Clean out the worst of them."

"About time we went north," said the man's partner, wearing thick glasses and a cowboy hat. "The leave-them-alone and they'll-leave-us-alone policy sucks." He hefted his rifle, a military issue weapon with a curved magazine. "We need as much replacement ammo as you can get us when you come next week. If we're going to clean the area out, we'll be jacking quite a few rounds."

"Tomorrow, you're hunting?" Keegan wondered if they heard the quiver in his voice.

"Couple hours before sunrise. We've got forty rifles. Figure we can make a sweep as far north as 30th Avenue. Some hotheads on the committee wanted to burn everything in that direction, but we figure a lot of the best stuff is up there."

Keegan tapped his fingers on the steering wheel. University Blvd. stretched in front of him. The tops of trees in City Park a couple blocks ahead waved in a breeze that didn't touch them on the street. "No need to go *beyond* the fence, is there? The majority aren't dangerous."

Rifle-scope man looked at him curiously. "Us or them, buddy."

Keegan nodded. "I'll see what I can do."


The afternoon routine was the same as always. First he unloaded the truck in the converted bank building's garage, putting the consumables in the steel-doored storage room, then placing the rest on the shelves except for the glasses he took into his living quarters to add to his display, two rooms of ice cream art under the lights. His favorites were ruby glass banana-split plates, casting red shadows beneath them. Then there were the tall sundae glasses, fluted sides and pouty lipped tops. Fine ice cream bowls of delicate china. Scoops by the dozens, some mechanical (one with a heating element for ease in carving hard-frozen treats), another of ivory, another with knuckle protectors, another with mother of pearl inlay in the handle. In the next room he had the pictures: ice cream trucks from all over the world. Psychedelic ones, and plain ones, and ones that looked like motorized tricycles, and ones shaped like cones or ice cream men or hot dogs or popsicles. Today, though, he didn't pause to admire the collection. The men were coming!

But what could he do? He spent a couple hours in the ice cream room, beating eggs, adding sugar, stirring in cocoa powder and cream and vanilla. All the variations: chocolate almond, blueberry, mango sorbet, cinnamon, and a triple batch of plain vanilla. Pouring the mixture into the ice cream makers. Turning them on. His hands smelled of chocolate. The air smelled of sweet cream.

He checked the diesel generator and the diesel tanks. Finally, he made a round of the building. All doors bolted. All windows barred. The last shred of afternoon light cast lines across the bank's lobby, dust an inch thick on the counters where the tellers used to sit. His heels clicked loudly as he walked from window to window.

By the time night had fully fallen, Keegan had restocked the truck, opened the garage, and pulled onto the street. Lights off, he headed north.

He liked the city better at night. The shadows grew velvety, and reflections were soft moonlight or starlight. At 24th Street, ten blocks north of Colfax, he turned the music on. Not nearly as loud as he did during the day. In the dark the sound seemed to carry farther. "Popeye the Sailor" he played, then "Rock-a-bye Baby."

From out of the empty houses, they came, slowly at first, and then eagerly. Some shambled. Some wobbled on uneven legs. Some trotted, their stony hoofs clicking the cement. Keegan pulled over, went to the back, opened the door above the counter, his scoops tucked into his apron.

"What'll it be?" he said to the first one.

"Chocolate," the creature croaked, its horny bill clacking together.

"What have you got for me?"

The three-fingered creature put a box of .45 caliber shells on the counter.

"Where'd you find them?" said Keegan as he swept them out of sight.

"Chocolate," it said again.

Keegan shrugged, then filled a cone. "Whatever suits you."

When the creature reached for the cone, Keegan pulled it back. "Listen," he said. "Go north tonight. It won't be safe this close to Colfax."

"Chocolate!" it snapped.

"I'm not kidding. You've got to get out of the neighborhood." Keegan pictured the scene before sunrise. The men would carry torches above their heads, watching for eye-shine in the dark. Guns would explode. The mutoids wouldn't run. Most of them didn't know better. Most of them were harmless, the warped children of warped children. Some time a couple generations back, their parents might even have been human. Or maybe their ancestors were dogs or sheep or the zoo animals. Nothing bigger than a rat had bred true since Keegan had been born. There was no way to tell, and why could some of the mutoids speak? Was language passed from the ones who'd been born in human houses and then hidden? Not everyone could give up their twisted offspring so easily. Not every parent could smother a child in its sleep. "Will you go?"

Behind the creature a line had formed. An ape-like animal with an alligator's face, its loose muscles hanging from the back of hairless arms, held a small keg Keegan knew was full of cream. Behind it a three foot tall crab with a shiny blue shell dangled a basket full of eggs from a stubby-fingered claw. Reluctantly, Keegan gave up the cone. The beast popped it into its mouth in one bite, hummed contentedly for a few seconds, then moaned as it put its hands over its forehead, eyes squeezed shut.

"I've told you that you get headaches that way," said Keegan. The thing nodded as it staggered off.

"Don't stay home tonight," Keegan yelled.

"Cinnamon-maple," said the ape, its voice a hissing lisp, when it put the keg on the counter. The heavy cream sloshed inside. Keegan didn't want to think what kind of mutoid produced it.

"The men are coming with guns," said Keegan. The ape's long fingers wrapped the bottom of the keg. He tilted his head to the side as if thinking about Keegan's news.

The ape said, "More cream tomorrow?"

"No, not more cream. You are in danger." A thin cloud slid across the surface of the moon, darkening the street. Keegan glanced up. Dozens of mutoids crept through the houses' shadows. They were stalking him, he figured. The tyranny of the sweets. They heard the music. Most of them were small, youngsters. Were they the sentient ones, waiting for a chance to go for the ice cream? And how sentient were they? North of Colfax the boundary between the self-aware and the purely animal blurred.

"I'll bring cream," said the ape.

Keegan bent down in frustration, resting his head on the counter.

The crab said, "They're simple people." It spoke with a slight English accent and a whir behind its voice as if a tiny windmill nested in its throat. By standing on the tips of its delicate claws, and with a stretch of the clawed arm, it rested the basket of eggs on the counter. Once Keegan had asked it where it got the eggs. "Really old chickens," it had said.

"You'll be hunted," said Keegan. "We've got to get everyone out of here, north of 30th."

"Some might go." The crab clicked its claws together. "The smarter ones. Not many. Are you sure the men are coming? They've never come before."

Keegan nodded.

The crab's eye stalks quivered. Was that nervousness, Keegan wondered. Or was the crab laughing?

Turning north, the crab waved a claw. "It's dangerous out of our neighborhood. There are territories to consider. Borders to be crossed. Not everyone is so friendly as they are here."

"The men won't be friendly either."

"Some of us have talked about burning them out, but we figured if we waited long enough they'd die on their own," said the crab. It sounded meditative.

Keegan nearly dropped his scoop. "What . . . what would you do to me?" He couldn't read an expression in the crab's eyes or immobile mouth. Overhead, the cloud cleared, and for a moment the moon shone strongly, driving the shyest of the young mutoids back to shadows' shelter.

"You're not one of them." It clicked its claws again. "Do you have any sherbert?"

Numbly Keegan scraped a bowl full for the crab. "Don't eat it too fast," he said out of habit.

The crab sidled away.

"You'll get them to go north?" Keegan called. "You'll warn them?"

"Those that listen."

The next mutoid plopped a box of thirty-ought-sixes on the counter. "Vanilla," it grunted. "With sprinkles."

"You have to leave," said Keegan. He shouted to the rest of them in line, to the hidden mutoids across the street. "They're coming to kill you! You have to run."

But none of them seemed to understand. Only the crab, and he was gone. By the time Keegan scraped the last of the ice cream out of the last bin and trade goods covered the truck's floor, he was nearly weeping. It was after midnight. Within a few hours, the Colfax fence would open and the men would march through, their guns cradled, the safeties off.

Exhausted, Keegan leaned on the counter. The street was empty now, and the only movement was the subtle moon-cast edge of shadows crossing the asphalt. Somewhere in the distance a thing howled, a long yodeling uluation that ended like a baby crying.

After a long while, he pulled himself into the driver's seat, started the engine and headed home. Fifteen minutes later, the garage door lowered automatically behind him. For a moment he considered not turning off the truck. It would be easy to leave the motor running in the closed space, to sit with his eyes shut. He could turn on the music and mix the carbon-monoxide sleepiness with "When the Saints Go Marching," or "Greensleeves."

"Us or them," the man at the gate had said. "Us or them."

Keegan turned the ignition off. Mechanically he unloaded the truck, putting the cream and eggs in the refrigerator, sorting through the ammunition, putting the other odds and ends in boxes. When he finished, he looked at the clock. 2:30.

The safe thing to do would be to go to bed. He would need to move his business north. No matter how thorough the men were, they were few and the mutants were many. They wouldn't all be wiped out. He could build a new route in the downtown area, maybe, where the broken skyscrapers crawled with life.

Or maybe he could stop the men.

Keegan opened one of the storage rooms off the garage, turned on the light, scanned the walls filled with equipment: rifles, shotguns, pistols, M-16s, bandoliers, sniper scopes, night vision goggles, gas masks, trip mines, hand grenades, Kevlar jackets, bazookas and mortars. All trade goods that had come in the last year. Boxes of ammo reached to the ceiling. Some shells had spilled. Their brass casings caught the ceiling light. He couldn't walk without kicking them.

He picked up an M-16, turned the heavy and unwieldy thing over in his hands, and realized he'd never fired it. Wasn't even sure if he had clips to load it.

And what good would it do? He wasn't a soldier. He couldn't kill. "Us or them," the voice said. "Us or them." Keegan could hear it in the room quiet as a whisper.

"Who am I?" he said out loud. He smoothed his hands over his apron, sticky with the day's work. They still smelled of chocolate.


An hour's labor refilled the truck. All the ice cream he could fit. Boxes of sugar cones. Keegan checked the clock again. Almost 4:00. They'd be at the gate by now.

Steering by moonlight, he pulled onto the street, heading north. "Row, Row, Row Your Boat" pumped out of the loudspeakers, turned loud. The first mutoid stepped from the door of a house in front of him. Keegan nodded his head, but kept rolling. Soon, another joined him, then a third. The music switched to "Song of Joy." Keegan turned left onto 19th Street, cruising at walking speed. Doors opened. Mutoids crawled from under cars, out of manholes, from behind walls, big ones, little ones, ones that were so misshapen they were hard to look at, and still Keegan drove on, cutting back and forth through the blocks. He beat time on the steering wheel. How far could the music reach?

Old man Granger had said, "Don't ever drive too fast. You don't want to leave the kids behind." Keegan watched through the mirror. Would they keep following? By now the street was crowded. When he reached University again, he turned north. Behind the music, did he hear a gunshot? How far back were the men?

Twelve blocks to go. Fourteen or fifteen if he wanted a cushion. At this speed he could feel broken glass crunching under the wheels. Slowly he passed moonlit cars' rusted-out shells, drooping road signs. A three foot tall mutoid with a body and head like a frog supported on a pair of slender legs, trotted alongside the truck, waving a box of rifle shells.

"Keep coming," Keegan called. They rolled through the 24th Street intersection. "Song of Joy," finished. In the pause between tunes, the patter of feet sounded like rain. "It's a Small World" covered the noise. Another sharp crack from behind, then, two more over the music. Definitely gunshots.

Ahead of him, a bus that had been turned on its side years ago nearly blocked the road. He steered the truck to the left to go around, over the sidewalk. A shadow stirred on top. Keegan leaned forward to look through the window.

The black creature he'd seen the day before arched its head high, its stubby front claws clasped across its chest, like a giant otter. Slowly, the truck passed the bus, within a few feet of the creature. It cocked its head to one side, as if listening to the music, and Keegan was struck again by its graceful posture, an almost regal pose with the moon-filled clouds behind it. The mutoid parade moved to the side of the houses, as far away from the beast as they could, but they kept following.

A dim reminder of gunshots rang out again. The creature looked south, then dropped to all fours before flowing off the bus, onto the street, toward Colfax Avenue, toward the men. "Don't go," Keegan whispered, but the long, black mutoid vanished into shadows.

Keegan didn't pull over until he was past 33rd Street. By the time he'd opened the counter, the crowd had gathered around. Their bodies bumped against the truck. Over their heads, Keegan saw more coming.

He wiped the counter clean. A dog-like face peered up at him, the creature's tiny, pink hands holding a screwdriver for trade. Keegan slung the rag over his shoulder. He grabbed a scoop. "What'll it be?" he said.

When the ice cream ran out, the sun was two hours into the sky and Keegan's wrists burned. He blinked against the daylight. The last mutoids wandered off, cones in hand or paw or claw or tentacle. But he hadn't heard a gunshot for some time. He closed the counter. As he drove home, he turned on the music to the inside. "The More We Get Together."

Five days straight labor replaced most of the ice cream, but Keegan was low on ingredients. It was time to head south again. He'd hadn't unloaded the truck since his all-nighter, and it took an hour to sort the ammunition and knick-knacks. He opened an unused storage closet to stow the overflow, mostly .22 short and longs, but also an assortment of larger calibers, several boxes of shotgun shells, and four clips of what he guessed were M-16 rounds. The mutoids were *good* at scavenging, digging deep into basements and warehouses and abandoned homes.

A dozen men including Laird stood at the Colfax fence as he pulled up. They slid the barrier aside to let him in.

"What's going on?" Keegan asked.

Laird rested his hand on the door. "The boys were eager to see you." He frowned. "Seems they were pretty successful on their trip last week, and they're raring to try it again. Acquired a bit of a blood lust, I figure. Rich there is leading the posse."

Keegan stiffened as he recognized the man with the short mustache from the week before. "How successful?"

Rich joined Laird at the truck. "Not bad, hairlip. Didn't get as many of the bastards as we might have liked, but we got a trophy out of it." He gestured to a tarp on the sidewalk ten feet away. A man next to the shape pulled the tarp back, revealing a broad black head and sleek neck. A chaos of flies descended on the corpse.

"Getting ripe too," Rich added.

Keegan opened the door, stepped onto the street. The sun leaked around his sunglasses, and his eyes teared instantly. He wiped his cheeks with the side of his hand. Up close the fur really was more purple than black. Even a week dead, the creature's muscles stood out, as if with a flex of will, it could rise, throw off death's shroud and rip them apart.

Rich said, "We need to trade for more bullets, though. Our supply is low."

Keegan touched the creature's head. Its eye was gone. Just a raw socket remained. He remembered it standing on the bus. Why had it gone toward the men? What drove it south? He smiled. There had been young mutoids then, or at least small ones. Ones he'd never seen before, like children. The truck played "Love is Blue," and "Music Box Dancer," and "Fly Me to the Moon" while he handed them ice cream. All of them gave him something. He flicked the trade goods behind him, not even looking to see what he was getting. There were so many. He'd scooped and scooped and scooped.

Rich said, "I'll bet there's a lot more of them out there, maybe more big sons of bitches like this one. Took all of us to drag him back this far."

Laird touched Keegan's shoulder. "It's an impressive specimen, isn't it? The men said it didn't even try to run. Stood in the middle of the street as if daring them to go past."

"Impressive, hell," said Rich. "It's us or them."

Keegan said, "Yeah, he's something."

Rich kicked the body. "You got more ammo, ice cream man? We've hunting to do."

The ice cream man's back cracked when he stood. I'm getting old, he thought. The rest of the men faced him, none of them under fifty. The last of their kind. We're all getting old.

"So, what about it? How many bullets can you get for us?"

Keegan thought about the little ones running after the truck. Some of them could speak. Some just pointed at a picture of a flavor. They held their hands open, ready for their treats. He thought about the rooms full of trade goods at the bank, the shiny shells on the floor.

"Scavenging's been tough," said Keegan. "I don't think there's any ammo to be had."

As he left he played "Who's Afraid of the Big Bad Wolf," and within a block the people came out for their ice cream.

# SACRIFICE

Waves lapped against the ceremonial canoe, and Jermone let them lick his fingers while Cynda rowed. When they fished together, they both took a paddle, but today was special, the Whale's run first day, and she rowed him, the king. People pampered the king. They said, "As goes the king, so goes the island." Ever since last year when blonde-haired Glinn handed him the crown, it was true. They pampered him. They served him roasted bananas and flavored goat's milk. He picked the best fish from the day's catch, and Cynda's mother, the Queen's mother, spitted it on a stick to cook separately from the community's meals. He was key to the Whale's run ceremony.

When Cynda once winked conspiratorially across the fire to remind him they were friends the silliness came to him, and he laughed. The Queen's mother laughed too, and so did the others close enough to hear. After all, he was king.

"I like the music the boat makes." His voice sounded oddly deep to him, as it had since the last Whale's run. The ocean's emptiness swallowed it. It was something to say, at least. Something to lighten her mood. "Have you ever listened to it?"

Cynda said nothing for a while, and Jermone let the surge of her paddling lull him. He offered a small prayer to the ocean gods to keep the waves calm and to speed their journey.

Ahead, the waves rippled to the mist that hid the Land. He turned on his shoulder to look at Cynda. Beneath him the damp wood cooled his skin, and the sun burnished his face. Cynda knelt in the stern. She bent forward on each stroke, and her breastcloth flapped; the intricately painted, beaded strings clicked together as they swung against her firm belly. It fitted loosely because it had been tailored for her sister, and no one had changed it. Making the clothes required all year, and the fit mattered less than the ritual. Jermone hid his grin, thinking warm thoughts. He'd dreamed today often, the ritual day.

Cynda's strong and dark arms, much darker than his, tensed with the effort; her face serious; black hair tied back and braided. Her legs, too, below the short, brightly feathered skirt, rippled with muscle. She and Jermone had run races along the beach from Shark Point to the old wreck, and he barely beat her. He'd slap the rust encrusted spaceship an instant before her, and they'd collapse into the shadows, laughing until they could breathe again. The wreck stretched into the sea where the broken and sagging corroded metal slabs merged with orange and red corals. He couldn't tell where the ship's remains stopped and where the sea creatures began.

"Do you believe in the gods?" she said, leaning into the next stroke. "I mean, do you *really* believe in them?" She always asked questions. Jermone recognized Bundi's influence, and he scowled. Trust Bundi to ruin the day. An old, stupid, bitter man from an insignificant family with no daughters, so his name would die with him.

Jermone closed his eyes, sighing. "The gods are in everything, of course." He tried to imagine the sea gods, but instead her ghost image floated, pale and featureless. The sun floated behind, a dark ball in a dark sky. "Gods in the tuna and the clams, in typhoons and in us." He squinted. The sun glared behind her. A few loose hairs caught the light in a silvery halo. "Gods in my hands, Cynda, in my body, just like yours."

"That's not what Bundi says. He told me there are no gods— we didn't believe in gods in the old days. There was no need for ritual."

Jermone's drew a sharp breath and held it for a second. He asked, "You're not thinking . . . you wouldn't . . ."

"No, of course not. I'll go through with it. I'm just talking. That's all. Remember, you've been training for this for a season. I've just had a few weeks."

He relaxed and rested his back again against the boat's moist wood. "We have a responsibility, you know. Glinn did his duty, and so did your sister." Jermone remembered Glinn, tall and startlingly blonde—few islanders were blonde—stepping into the canoe before the last Whale's run. He wore dignity like a robe. All season since the people spoke with admiration of Glinn's departure.

Cynda continued rowing, her expression dark. "She should have never bathed in the river. She was foolish."

"Proud, you mean, don't you? The river gods know a proud person when they see one. Would you rather I was here with her instead of you?" He waited for an answer. He'd envisioned a different version of the trip. The Whale's run first day was supposed to be special, and he'd been waiting for a year. And she was Cynda, his friend.

Her voice softened. "I didn't mean that. What I mean is I don't want to be here at all." Cynda laughed. It wasn't a happy laugh. "Do you know why we are doing the ceremony today and not a few days ago or days from now?"

"The whales, naturally. They spoke to the Queen's mother and told her today is the first day of their run."

"No, I don't think so. Whale's run in the spring, but no one knows the first day. No, mother watched me, not the sea. She watched me to decide when we should go."

He didn't understand. But Cynda's beauty fascinated him, and the sky glowed above like a glad expression, so he remained silent.

She rested the paddle across her legs and let the boat drift. "Jaimie and Clurk declared for each other yesterday."

Jermone rolled to dangle his fingers into the ocean again. "It's a good time to declare. Good omens come with the Whale's run."

"They're a season younger than us."

Water splashed into his hand. He closed his fist, but the water ran out, and he held nothing. A few evenings weeks ago, before the river monster rose up and killed Cynda's sister, Jermone and Cynda had gone into the forest to gather firewood. After a while, they rested in soft grass in a stand of palm trees, and she had tickled him. He tickled her back, but instead of squirming away, she'd pushed herself against him, and her fingers against his ribs had become a caress. Her dusty and smooth skin slid beneath his hand. Her breath filled him, sweet and deep. For a moment, he forgot his kingship, and reached his hand down over her hip bone.

"We can't," she had gasped, "you are promised," but she held him still, and nothing remained in his head but her feel, her back's curve, the pulse pounding in her breast, and they moved. She murmured something throaty; it could have been a plea. But a plea for what? He couldn't tell.

In the distance of the trees, the Queen's mother called for them, and, breathing hard, they had pushed away.

Since then, replaying that evening consumed Jermone's thoughts. Until then, the Whale's run seemed spiritual but unreal. He didn't think about it. Since then, the ritual swamped his imagination. He'd wake in a sweat from dreams. A part of him (he blushed to think) was pleased Cynda's sister had died. He prayed and made sacrifice to the forest gods to ask forgiveness, but the omens were ambiguous and hard to read.

Cynda said, "Bundi told me it's not gods in control but a strange force, genetics. Mutagens. There didn't use to be monsters in the river. He says, unchecked, animals change fast. Whatever took her, he says, might have had a carp for a parent or a salamander."

"You mean like a bad cow or chicken? A blasphemy we'd kill at birth?"

Jermone had a hard time imagining the creature's parent the villagers had netted from the river the next day after Cynda's sister's death having been an innocent salamander. Larger than a pig, the animal had come from the water raging, all teeth and spines and ferocious velocity. It had torn two good nets to tatters before they'd killed it.

"Do you want me to row for a while? No one will know."

"No. We'll do this right. We're there."

The palm trees' dark line peeked through the mist ahead. Waves slipped onto the shore, and their escape down the narrow beach hissed gently. Beyond the sand's long stretch, old stained metal and glass buildings reflected bright bites of sun through the trees and vines that covered them.

"Can you see any of them . . . the clothes-apes?" Jermone asked.

"They hide. They're afraid."

"Do they . . . you know . . . wear clothes?"

Cynda grunted. Jermone couldn't tell if she was mad at him or thought it a silly question. He wanted to make conversation. Anything to not talk about the ceremony. He forced himself to sit still.

Jermone continued, "They hide because you're the queen. You're a special person. The gods protect you, and the clothes-apes know it."

She sighed. "Being special didn't help my sister, but Bundi says it has a lot more to do with hunting parties. Many seasons ago, he says, before you or I were born, a queen's daughter was taken while gathering medicine root. She vanished. A hunting party came and killed clothes-apes by the dozens, and now they stay back in the woods. We're safe on the beach as long as there are two of us. At least during the day."

Jermone wanted to ask about the night, but he bit his tongue. She sounded unsure already, and he didn't want her talking about it again, so he studied the beach instead. A black ribbon moved along the water line, and for a while he thought it was a long snake, undulating back and forth with the waves. As they drew closer, he could tell it wasn't a continuous line at all, but hundreds of separate parts. Finally, as the waves turned from swells to breaking water, he saw crabs no bigger than the palm of his hand made the line. They skittered down the beach, followed the retreating wave, and moved inland when the water returned. When the canoe plowed slushily to rest, and Jermone jumped out to pull it onto the beach, the crabs scurried off or dug themselves out of sight. He could see them a spear's throw away, but they wouldn't come closer.

He crouched at the water's edge and placed the flats of his hands on the wet sand to thank the sea gods for safe delivery and ask the earth gods to welcome them. Cynda stepped from the canoe and didn't pause as she strode up the beach. He prayed for her too.

Long seaweed strands, turned brown in the sun, lay above the water line, and when the wind off the ocean paused, their mossy, damp smell floated down to him. The trees, too, smelled: dark and huge and vegetable. Then the breeze picked up, carrying away land odors and replacing them with salt spray and fish.

"Should we start now?" asked Jermone. He tried to calm his voice, but he couldn't. It quavered.

"No, the tide's not fully out."

"What should we do?" He scuffed his feet through the sand. The texture differed from the island, grittier, as if broken shells filled it, but it was also warm and soft. He sat. In the trees, something screeched.

They both started. "Was that . . .?" Jermone said.

"I don't know. Didn't sound like a bird."

Jermone moved closer to her, keeping an eye on the woods.

Cynda said, "I've never seen a clothes-ape. There's lots of things on land I haven't seen. Bundi says changes happen fast here too. There's no one to check, no Queen mother to pass judgments on births. Other animals might be here beside the clothes-apes."

"Maybe they are the gods."

"I doubt it."

Cynda sat beside him, facing the woods just paces away. Under the dark canopy, the sand vanished and everything became shadow. Great vines wrapped themselves around trunks and swooped from tree to tree. Above the forest, tiny birds darted in and out of the palms, feeding on insects; and more birds, long-legged ones with gray bodies and long beaks trotted along the tree's roots, poking their bills into crevices. The trunks creaked in the sea-breeze; bees or wasps hummed, and behind them the waves whispered their secrets in steady rhythm. Jermone scrunched his fingers deeper into the warm sand until they were under Cynda's hand. She didn't move other than to tilt her head back to look at the ruined buildings that rose from the forest. "Do you believe people used to live here?"

Jermone glanced at her. A grain of sand clung to her thigh, and he wanted to brush it away, but he feared to touch her now with the ceremony so close. He thought about Jaimie and Clurk.

"I don't know," he said. "They're sad to look at. Not like the gods' homes at all."

She turned to study him, propping herself on one arm. "Do you have doubts?"

He shook his head. "Oh, no. None at all. I just thought they seemed broken down, like . . . I don't know . . . deserted. But, of course, they're not. The gods are there, just as they are in the sea and land." He looked for evidence of the gods in the ruins, but rust-streaked metal and broken glass in shiny bits clinging to gaping windows' edges consuming sunlight revealed nothing within.

"You're nervous, aren't you?" she said.

Jermone tried to swallow, but he couldn't. She sat too close, and all he wanted was to hold her. He remembered the run on the beach. She had quivered then. Mystery filled her, and he felt lost within it. But he knew he had to discover it; to find it out, and yearning's ache stirred inexorably, irresistibly. The memory tormented him. Her closeness dominated, not the ceremony's importance. He feared if his mind were not pure, the gods would be displeased. The ritual had to be perfect, but she was so close. He remembered her breath's taste beneath the palms.

She dropped her hand behind her again so she didn't face him.

"I don't believe in gods anymore. There are none, and Bundi is right. My sister wasn't killed because she made a river god mad or because of pride or anything else. She died because a hungry animal needed to eat, and she was there."

"But the ceremony?" he offered.

"It doesn't work. The Whale's run whether we try to please the gods or not. The whaling will be successful whether we do this or not. Some men will die. Some will live. Some cows and chickens and goats and babies will be born who are not what they should be, and the Queen mother will take them behind the hill and smother them. The world is as it is."

"But everyone believes in the ceremonies. If we don't sacrifice to the gods, why would they care for us?"

In the vegetation, Jermone thought he sensed movement. Something watched back there; something that did not want to be seen.

"Bundi says we don't belong here. We're from someplace else. He says we've become magicians, and our magic is associational." She stumbled over the word. "A goat sheared and left in the forest for the goat god. A painted fish for the river god. A handful of blessed grain for the grain god. In the spring . . . well, for the spring, a fertility rite. The whales must run, and there must be ritual and offering. There's cruelty in it, he says. Logic and cruelty."

Jermone crushed his hands into fists under the sand. If anyone else said this . . . but no one else would. Only Cynda, the accidental Queen who had always been the second daughter would be so irreverent, and only because she was his friend could he listen.

But he feared for the ceremony. He thought she was trying to back out.

"Everyone says Bundi is mad. He's old, mad, and no one listens to him."

Cynda went on as if she didn't hear him. Sunlight glistened on her shoulders. She closed her eyes as if shutting out him and the forest and the light.

"The old wreck on the beach shows we're from some other place. Bundi says from another star. It carried us to the island, but the trip or the landing damaged it. People tried to live here, though. They tried, and there must have been a lot of them. Look at their buildings."

"Those are the gods' homes."

A branch snapped in the woods. Strain as he might, Jermone heard no more sounds.

Cynda said, "They built them tall and shiny, but the forest fought back. Maybe their babies all had to be killed, and they couldn't live with the sorrow. Maybe the animals were too much. They lost. They retreated to the island where they could kill any threat."

"The people have lived on the island forever."

"And what about the clothes-apes? What do you think they are?" Cynda turned again toward him, reached across herself and held his wrist next to the sand.

"Devils?" Jermone offered. His thoughts tumbled. There were no elders to answer her arguments. He had to stand for the island and the ceremony's success. He could see it slipping away. What would he tell them if he failed? The hunts would go bad. The whales would run deep and too fast. Fish would flee the nets and fruit would rot in the orchards.

A low frond on a tree near the edge moved, and for a second Jermone thought eyes looked out at him. He blinked, and they vanished.

"Are they apes becoming men, or are they men becoming apes?" said Cynda.

Jermone rubbed his free hand across his mouth, profoundly aware she still held his wrist. "Cynda, if I had not been king, and if you had not become queen, would you have declared for me?"

She didn't answer, but her grip tightened.

"The tide is almost out," she said. "It's time for the ceremony."

"You'll do it?" he gasped. "You'll do the ceremony?"

She stood and straightened clothing, knocking the sand from the feathers in the skirt and untangling the bead strings that dangled from the breastcloth.

"Not for the gods. I'll do it for you, and because you believe in them. It's ritual and offering just like goats and fish and grain. Don't make me talk, afterwards, though. I have to end it then."

She walked toward the water line, then waited till a wave came in and made a mark in the sand where it stopped. She knelt and pushed sand aside, hollowing a place in the beach. Water flowed into the bottom, but she continued digging a long, shallow depression. "It has to happen where the sea gods and the land gods meet. Bundi says we believe in symbolism."

"We believe in gods." Now, so close to the ceremony, Jermone struggled to breathe. They were doing the gods' business, making life good for the island, and they should be joyful. But Cynda moved as if she wore a thousand stones tied round her. Her movements slowed and seemed painful.

He didn't know all the details of the ceremony. These were the Queen's secrets, and the Queen's mother. They knew the ritual's procedures, the hidden words to be spoken and the mystic gestures. Jermone knew just his part, and what he had to do. "I don't want you to be sad." He held his own hands together helplessly. "The gods will reward us all for a good ceremony." But he didn't believe his own words. The gods seemed imaginary, and only Cynda existed.

She stopped and observed the shape she'd dug, a human shape with a place for arms and legs to lay flat, half buried and half revealed. "Next year there will be another king for the Whale's run. I'll be here with a different king. In fifteen seasons, mother had eleven children." Her voice sounded old and distant. A wave slipped over the edge and carried some sand into the depression.

She faced him, eyes so brown and profound he thought he could fall into them. "I am to remind you the ritual is not about you and me as people. You are, today, on the Whale's run first day, a representative of the male force in the universe." She chanted now, not looking at him anymore. "The male force hunts and protects, feeds and builds, fathers and dies."

Moving her feet into the matching shape, she sat. The water covered the back of her legs. "I am a representative of the female force in the universe." Laying half in the earth and half out, she said, "The female force nurtures and instructs, creates and maintains, mothers and dies. If the sea gods and the land gods are with us today, we will make a Queen's daughter to lead the people when I am gone as my mother did before me. We will assure the Whale's run success and the hunters will come home sated and unharmed. Many children will be born live and whole."

Jermone looked at her. Water soaked the feather skirt. Her eyes closed, and the line of her jaw was grim.

"Think of me," she said, "as earth and sea. You are sky and trees. Cynda and Jermone are not here now."

Still, Jermone did not move. From the jungle he could feel eyes upon him, judging him, and nowhere did he feel the gods. For many nights he had envisioned sky and tree gods filling him at this moment; he had imagined Cynda as she was now, willing to be with him and everything would be correct, but he hadn't guessed at this emptiness. He hadn't foreseen reluctance or misery.

Cynda opened her eyes. "Come on," she whispered, reaching her hand up. "We have no choice."

And she drew him down into the sand, into forgetfulness, where the sun warmed him and the sea became a salty caress. And at the explosive, powerful moment, he thought she said, "I want just you, Jermone." But he couldn't tell because he called her name over and over again in his mind. In the sand and the sea, in her and in him, he sensed no gods—or he touched them all. The world was different and new. Nothing mattered.

Afterwards they both cried. He didn't feel adult. He didn't feel like a king. The ritual ended, and he had done his part. Cynda lay beneath him in the sand, and every wave swept around them in warm baptism.

Now, only the sacrifice, the offering, remained.

He didn't talk, and Cynda kept silent as she had promised. Like some earth elemental, she rose from the bed she had dug, the sand and water falling from her. Before she stepped into the canoe, she touched his face once, not like a good-bye, but as if she wanted to be sure he was real. Then she paddled into the ocean, leaving him sitting on the beach, watching her form grow smaller and smaller until he lost her on the horizon.

For a long time, he sat thus.

He thought of her on this beach a season from now, digging a bed for herself with some other king, and the picture left him empty. He could see no gods in it.

Then, something screeched in the jungle behind him. Jermone didn't turn at first. He searched for Cynda on the sea, one last glimpse. Dried leaves crackled; something grunted, and stealthy footsteps crunched in the sand.

When Jermone turned, twenty had come from the forest. Some monstrous, some human, male and female. Others, he didn't know. He wished he could tell Cynda—he wished he could talk to her again—they did wear clothes. Cloth scraps hung from their shoulders or around their waists. One wore a hat, a battered blue cap with leaves stuck in it.

As they drew close, one caught his eye: tall, and blonde and familiar. Jermone only saw him for a second before the others crowded around. Their harsh breath rattled, and they hardly seemed like gods or devils.

# THE BOY BEHIND THE GATE

*As you are now,*
*So once was I.*
*As I am now,*
*So you shall be.*
*Prepare for death and follow me.*
　　　　　　—from a tombstone
　　　　　　　　in the Central City Cemetery

## CENTRAL CITY: TODAY

Pine tree tops creaked overhead, but the air didn't move in the granite-strewn gully as Ron hiked up the steep gulch. He consulted his compass, then rechecked the map. Another hundred yards above him should be The Golden Ingot #9, and if the rusted mining equipment he'd been climbing over and around for the last ten minutes were any indication, the map was right. He scanned the ground, his eyes aching from sun and dust. The backpack, heavy with a powerful flashlight, rope and bolt cutters thumped against his kidneys. Was anything out of the ordinary? Was there any sign? A patch of cloth? A child's shoe? Could Levi have walked this far? Ron imagined the eight-year-old being towed up the mountain, hand-in-hand with the stranger who'd taken him. Would Levi have been crying, aware in his little boy way of the danger he was in?

Ron closed his eyes. He wanted to imagine Levi scared. He hoped he was scared to death because the alternative . . . Maybe he'd been wrapped in a blanket or a plastic sheet slung over the man's shoulder. They knew who the man was, Jared Sims, but Levi wouldn't have known. Ron shivered and continued climbing.

A jumble of cable, thick as his wrist and so rusted that wherever the metal crossed itself it had corroded into one piece, blocked his path. Ron scrambled partly up the gully's slope around it. Piles of yellow and white mine tailings humped up above him, and soon he topped out to the relative flatness of the claim. The old map he'd photocopied in Central City had shown him where the mine was; it wasn't marked on the USGS maps. Most of the abandoned mines and shafts had been filled in. Too much chance of some tourist wandering around old mining property, snapping pictures of busted down mills and what was left of miners' cabins, and then stepping on some rotten boards covering a shaft a hundred feet deep. So over the last twenty years, the state and park service had been closing the properties. Still, the Gilpin County mining district had been huge, and thousands of claims had been made. There were hundreds of openings even now for someone to find if he knew where to look. Perfect, mysterious holes blasted into the mountain, timeless monuments to long-dead miners' hopes. Perfect places to hide a little boy you didn't want found. Here, at the Golden Ingot #9, except for the rust, it could be 1880 again. He half expected to surprise a dozen miners waiting for their turn in the bucket and the long ride down the shaft.

Ron kept his eyes down. Little chance that there'd be a footprint in the yellow gravel, but it didn't hurt. Maybe Levi would have dropped something for him to find. It seemed years ago, but it was only last winter that Ron had read him *The Lord of the Rings*. The hobbit, Pippin, had broken from the orcs and dropped a sign that he was still alive, a beautiful beech-tree leaf brooch. Levi had said, in his little man's voice, "That was very clever of him, Daddy, wasn't it?" Ron remembered Levi's head resting on his arm while he read. He could almost feel the weight of his little boy leaning against him until they got to the end of the chapter. "Read some more, Daddy. Read some more," he'd said sleepily.

A pile of boards laying almost flat looked hopeful. Ron lifted the end of one. It creaked as it rose slowly, pulling a dozen nails from the rotted plank beside it. Dust slapped into the air after Ron moved it aside and dropped it. The next one showed a shaft's edge. A minute later, he'd cleared most of the boards. The pile looked like it hadn't stirred since Grover Cleveland held office, but since he was here, he was going to check.

The afternoon sun showed only six feet of shaft wall, while the rest was black. Was the bottom only a dozen feet away, or was this one of those deep, deep holes reaching hundreds of yards down?

As always, as he had scores of times since the police gave up looking ten days before, he crouched at the shaft's edge, cupped his hands around his mouth and called into the darkness, "Levi! Levi! Are you there, son?"

Wind stirred sand behind him, blowing a little over the edge where it glittered in the sunlight, then disappeared. Only the breeze's sibilant hiss answered him.


## CENTRAL CITY: 1879

Images flitted in Charles' mind as he stayed motionless in his bed, listening to the boy's even breathing on the floor beside him. It was the small hours of the morning, when time came unanchored, and memories piled willy nilly atop one another. Charles could see them all: his wife dying, the Laughlins, the McGarity's, the bloody hands in the mine. The fireplace coals had long since died, and the moon's thin line outside the window cast almost no light through the muslin drape. He'd light a candle if he dared, but if he did, the boy's eyes might be open; he might look at him through the flickering light and know that he knew.

He couldn't sleep. No, not that. Charles would dream, and in his dreams he'd see the Laughlin children burning up, their red skin baking from within. "Scarlet fever," the nurse from Idaho Springs had said. "Poor things."

Charles had stood at the Laughlin's door that morning, a basket of bread and clean sheets hanging from one hand, blinking at the darkness in the room. Only the sun behind him provided light. They'd covered the one window, and the cabin smelled close and moist and sweaty sick. The nurse sat by three-year-old Lisa to his left. Against the back wall lay Evelyn with her mother sitting beside her. The baby's crib rested in the opposite corner. William Laughlin sat at the rough-hewn table in the room's middle, resting his forehead in his hand.

The boy crept around Charles, even though he'd told him to stay with the mule. His arm wrapped around the back of Charles' leg, and he leaned into the room. Charles put his hand down to push him back, but he didn't. He didn't like touching his son, the stranger who lived with him every day. Lisa panted under the blankets, blonde hair plastered to the side of her face. Four-year-old Evelyn turned to the wall, her chest still for a moment before she drew her next wheezing breath. Her mom, a hint of the scarlet flush across her own cheeks visible in the sunlight, pressed a wet cloth to Evelyn's forehead.

"The little one?" Charles said.

William Laughlin shook his head without moving his hand. "She went during the night." He coughed. It sounded wet and pathetic.

"I brung some things," Charles said. He stepped deeper into the room, and the atmosphere pushed back. Outside, the sun shone bright and men filled the valley, moving surely from mine to mill, loading ore wagons or carrying supplies. Blasting echoed off cliff walls above, and Clear Creek murmured like watery wind. But here, the air felt dead with fever.

William draped a hand over the basket's edge. "You're a right Christian, Charles."

"You going to your shift?" Charles moved back. The heat in the room oppressed, and he didn't want to breathe so close to the sick girls.

"I'll be along."

Charles retreated to the porch. The boy leaned over Lisa, his legs bright in the sun pouring through the door, while his upper torso faded in the room's shadows. He drew a finger across the little girl's forehead, through her fevered sweat. He stood, facing his father, his finger up as if he'd erased chalk off a blackboard. For a moment he looked at Charles as if surprised to see him still waiting for him, then he put his finger in his mouth.

When they crossed the footbridge over the creek, Charles said, "Why'd you do that, boy? I told you to stay out."

The boy held onto the mule's bridle, his head not even coming up to the mule's chin. "They'll burn, Papa."

Charles nearly stumbled, then glanced at the boy. He wore an old, flannel shirt too big for him with the sleeves rolled up. Pale, skinny arms. Dark hair cut above his eyebrows. Dark eyes. He was given to long, unblinking looks. A serious mouth, like his mother who died bringing him into the world eight years before.

"I'm glad he's out of me," she'd said in the moment before she died screaming.

"What do you mean, boy?"

"I put the death in them." He held up his finger that had touched the girl as if in proof. "Just like the other lambs."

"Don't talk like that." Charles pulled the bridle from the boy's hand, his own hand shaking. "You go on home, and I don't want to see a mess in the cabin when I get back. Sweep the floor."

"I can smell the fire," the boy said before turning toward their cabin.

Charles thought about his son all day, deep in the mine, as he worked the single jack, bent low in the tunnel only three quarters of his height, placing the steel bit against the stone, pounding it a bit deeper with each blow, rotating it each time to clear the bit. Pausing just before he drove the hammer home. The angle had to be perfect. The placement, perfect. He had to judge before he struck. Striking without looking could shatter the drill. There was always the pause before the hammer came down to be sure he was doing the right thing. So there could be no mistake. It was a feeling of good or bad in the way the drill stood. Charles considered his judgement with the hammer to be his only genius. He never struck wrongly. *Clang!* The hammer would fall against the rod. Rock dust crumbled from the hole. *Clang!* He'd hit it again, his strong right arm driving the blow home. Numbing work to create a hole for the charge. He could raise the hammer all day with that arm; the work had made it larger than the other one, a giant's arm, but he couldn't shape the boy with it. He couldn't even hold him.

The boy had been bad from the beginning. His wet nurse took sick and died. After that, no one would help Charles, so he fed the child himself with goat's milk, certain that the first winter would kill him, having no mother to care for him, but as winter filled the mountains with snow and cutting wind, even as influenza swept through the camp taking many babies, the boy thrived. He was walking by the next summer, and Charles would leave him locked in the cabin when he worked his shift, half expecting to find the toddler dead on his return. But every day the boy met him, a little taller, a little stronger, and never smiling.

Setting the powder took a half hour. Each hole had to be filled with the proper amount. Then the fuse cord had to be measured. Charles worked methodically. This deep in the mine, the stale air hurt his lungs and gritty rock coated his eyes and tongue. He checked the candle burning brightly in its shadowgee stuck in the wall. When he set the last charge, he retreated to the bucket lift, covering his nose and mouth with a soaked bandana to protect against the dust. After the blast, he stood with head bowed, breathing through the wet cloth.

Charles wanted to love him. He tried. The weather in the boy's heart was cold, though, and hugs meant nothing to him. He never played. He never cried. And always, around him, children died. Diphtheria. The grippe. Typhoid. The croup. Pneumonia. Whooping cough. Small pox. Lingering diseases. Wasting illnesses. The cemetery filled with tiny corpses.

The ore cart rattled on the rails as Charles pushed it toward the broken ore. For the rest of his shift he'd fill the cart, take it back to the lift, empty it and return for another load. No candles lit the path, but that didn't matter. Charles didn't mind the dark most days, but today he couldn't stop thinking about the boy. What does the boy do while I'm at work? What does he daydream about? Charles imagined him wandering through the camp, looking for children.

In the spring he'd taken the boy to a funeral. Seamus McGarity had lost both his boys and his wife to dysentery three days apart. McGarity, his kin and friends circled the coffins, two tiny wood boxes and a long one. During the prayer, Charles looked down at his boy dressed in mourning black. The corners of the boy's mouth turned up and his eyes were shining. At the ceremony's end, the boy dropped dirt in each grave. Surreptitiously, he also put a handful of grave soil in his pocket.

"Lucky your kid's doing good," McGarity said to him the next day as they waited for the bucket to take them down the shaft. His lunch pail dangled from his hand, and the miner looked exhausted, as if he hadn't slept for a month. "He came by a week ago. Found him sitting by the door."

"What did he want?" Charles wished he could pat McGarity on the shoulder. How would it be to lose your whole family? There'd been other men whose children died who drank themselves to death. The other miners stood away from them. People died in the camps all the time, but it wasn't easy to be next to the bereft, not at first.

McGarity didn't answer for a while. He stared out over the valley, but he didn't appear to be looking at anything. Finally he said, "Caleb used to sing his little brother to sleep. I don't think he knew I was listening. 'Amazing Grace' it was. Learned it from his mom. He had a nice voice for a ten-year-old."

They found McGarity at the bottom of a shaft a week later. Was he drunk and fell in, or did he jump?

At the blasting site the dust still hung in the air, surrounding the candle in a pale globe. Charles hefted ore into the cart. My boy's not human, he thought as each rock crashed against the metal. Methodically he bent and lifted, bent and lifted. Not human. Not human. Charles pictured the boy with his finger in his mouth, salty-bitter from the Laughlin girl's scarlet fever sweat.

After a while Charles stopped loading. His hands stung. He stepped next to the candle's feeble light and held them up. Blood ran down his wrists from his ragged fingertips. Dully he realized he'd not worn his gloves. And a certainty came to him, a gravestone solid conviction: my boy's a monster!

Charles lay in his bed, motionless. The boy breathed evenly on the floor below him. Only the sliver-moon lit window floated in the dark. Charles kept his eyes wide open. If he shut them, even for a second, the boy might stand. He might lean his unsmiling face close. The boy might run his finger across Charles' forehead.

"I see you burning, Papa," the boy would say. He always called him Papa, like it was a curse.

And dawn was hours away.

Ron sat in his van on the abandoned mining road near the boulders the park service had used to block the path, his map spread out on the seat beside him marked with X's for mining claims. From Central City there were so many. The historical marker at the town limits proclaimed THE RICHEST SQUARE MILE ON EARTH. He shook his head. If only it were that small.

Starting at Black Hawk at one end of the valley to the other end of Central City was a couple of miles. Mine tailings spotted the slopes on both sides. Then there were the gulches: Chase, Eureka, Russell, Lake, Pecks, Fourmile and others the map didn't name with mines of their own, and the road went on to the ghost towns of Yankee Hill, Ninety Four, Alice and Kingston. Nevadaville was only a stone's throw to the west. He could almost see the honeycomb of tunnels.

Ron smoothed the map, but his attention shifted. On the floor, barely visible in the blue dusk of sunset, a red plastic building brick lay canted on its side. He stretched around the steering wheel, crinkling the map with his elbow, and picked it up. The brick had almost no weight sitting on his palm. He straightened, put the brick on the dashboard.

They didn't have building bricks when he was a boy. His dad

had given him Lincoln logs, and over the years, Ron's dad had added to the set until they filled a box almost too big to fit under his bed. Ron made forts and villages and fences and barns. Two short logs crossed over each other served as cannon. His dad came into his room one night and they built a tower together, half as tall as Ron.

Years later, when Levi was six, Ron had said to his dad, "You never told me how much fun being a father would be."

"I didn't think of it at the time," his dad said.

Ron fingered the building brick. He'd never made a tower with Levi.

The sky grew dark, and Ron didn't move. He thought about putting Levi to bed. "Have good dreams," he'd say. For forty nights now, Levi had not had Ron to wish him a bedtime without nightmares. He thought about throwing a baseball back and forth. He remembered reading to him, book after book, Levi's head resting against Ron's arm as they sat on the couch.

Ten days ago the Denver detective in charge of the investigation said, "We're giving up the search, Ron. You're going to have to face the possibility your son is dead. Sims killed his victims. We know that." They sat in the detective's temporary office in the Gilpin County Courthouse. Ron struggled to remain calm. The detective didn't look over twenty, and it was clear Ron made him uncomfortable.

"He didn't kill them right away," Ron insisted. "The Perez girl he kept in his basement for a week. In Colorado Springs he kept that baby in a storage garage for four days. His house was in Central City. My boy is in a mine somewhere. It's logical." Ron held a crumpled flyer. HAVE YOU SEEN THIS CHILD? Levi smiled from the page, a strand of his black hair across his forehead, his dark eyes turned toward his cake before he blew out the candles.

With the detective, Ron had walked through Sims' house, a restored turn-of-the-century Victorian gingerbread with no closets. Posters covered the living room walls, all children. Except for the kitchen, blocked with yellow crime-scene tape and the outline of Sims' body on the floor, the rooms were meticulously tidy. Magazines on the coffee table were fanned out perfectly, the same half-inch overlap on each. On Sims' dresser in the bedroom, a line of brass padlocks stood like sentinels in a military row. They were the only decoration. Ron wondered what could make a man like Sims. Couldn't love have saved him? Love, pure love, might have kept

Sims from hating, just as pure love would find his son. The police didn't love Levi enough to find him.

The detective shook his head. "If he hadn't shot himself, we could ask him. But he did. We've had crews up and down the area. If your son were there, we would have found him. He might have lasted a week without food. Only a couple days without water. It's been a month. Sims buried his victims. I'm sorry to have to say it this way, but I'd guess your boy is in a shallow grave."

Ron gripped the arms of the chair to keep from leaping at the man. "There's bonds between a father and his son. I'd know if he had died."

"The department can arrange counseling, if you request it," the detective said.

"You're not a father, are you?" Ron looked past the detective. Black and white photographs hung on the wall behind him: men standing before a wagon, holding shovels and lunch boxes; a long shot of Central City down main street when it was still dirt; the front of a school, forty or fifty children sitting on the steps, their severe looking teacher standing behind them with her arms crossed.

Ron touched the hard edge of the plastic building brick sitting on the dashboard and thought about the kids in the school a hundred years ago no different than his own boy, all dead by now for sure, and Levi who might not be. Razor-edged stars filled the sky through his windshield. The air had cooled, caressing his face through the open windows. This far up the rutted road he couldn't hear traffic from the highway or crowd noise from the casinos that filled Central City. He canted his head to hear better. Something clicked repetitively in the distance, maybe a night bird or a locust. He wondered if locusts lived this high. For a long time he rested his finger on the brick and listened. The night vibrated with its own muttering. Unidentifiable sounds that he guessed might be the breeze sliding over rocks and through the scrubby grasses. A high squeak that might be a bat. He couldn't tell. The mountain was perfectly black and the cloudless sky danced with stars that provided no illumination.

He turned on the ceiling light to read the map. If someone saw him from a distance, he thought, he'd look like a time traveler in his craft, light glowing through the windows, unattached to the Earth.

Eventually he turned the light out and fell asleep sitting up, his head pillowed on a jacket against the door, windows still open so he could hear if Levi should call.


Charles slipped out of the cabin before dawn, the eastern sky just barely lighter than the west. The wind came up the valley, and in it he could hear the stamp mills thrumming as they crushed ore.

He trudged up the switch-back trail toward the mine, his hands heavy, his head heavy. Had any child the boy met lived? There weren't that many children in the camps. The school in Nevadaville had 150 students last year, he'd heard, but there were 10,000 miners in the district. Central City had a small school and so did Blackhawk. Charles had never sent the boy, but he was supposed to go in the fall. The town was growing. More families came in every day. They were building churches.

At the top of the hill, he paused. From here in the pre-sunrise grimness, most of the town was visible in purples and blues. He couldn't find his own cabin though. Then, he gasped. A black aura like a cloud hid it from him, and for a moment it seemed as if it grew tentacles that flowed down the dirt roads, over the wooden side-walks, sniffing at each door. The wind rippled the cloud's top, then blew in his face, carrying the smell of a crypt and the fevered damp-ness from the Laughlin cabin.

Charles shook his head. There was his cabin! There was no black cloud. He held his hands over his pounding heart. Am I going mad? A hallucination! But the question echoed hollowly. This was not madness. He'd seen the cloud as a vision, a sign. He backed up the trail, afraid to take his gaze away from the cabin.

When a man's dog goes wild, he shoots him. It's his responsibil-ity. What was his responsibility as a father of a monster?

When Charles worked the mine that day, he stuffed his pockets with candles, and he kept one lit no matter where he was. The shadows beyond the weak candlelight were like the shadow creep-ing from his own house.


If Sims had locked Levi in a mine, it would have to have several qualities, Ron thought as he shouldered his pack. Pine lining the mountain top glowed in the morning light, but the sun wouldn't touch the valley's bottom for another hour. Ron checked his map and began the long hike up the old road. It had to be both close enough for him to get to, but far enough off the beaten track that it was unlikely anyone would find it. It had to be far enough back that even if Levi screamed for help, no one would hear him. There would be food and water. The question was, how much food and water? Sims wouldn't have planned on leaving Levi with over a month's supply.

Each step up the road felt like the ticking of an immense clock counting down. How much time was left? Was Levi even now crouched against a locked gate, light leaking around the edges, on the brink of death by thirst or starvation? If he ran out of water, might there be water in the mine itself that he had been drinking to keep himself alive? Ron thought about *Tom Sawyer*, not the hijinks of the little boy, but the awful image of Injun Joe trapped in McDougal's cave. After Ron's dad had read him that part, Ron had nightmares for months about eating bats while trying to carve through a thick wooden door with a broken knife.

Ron quickened his pace, his calves burning, keeping his eyes open for evidence of tunnels not on his map. He'd followed dozens of faint trails to dead end mines in the last ten days, peered down scores of open shafts, rattled the locks on handfuls of metal gates, always looking for a sign, always listening for Levi's voice. He crossed from the valley's shadow into the sunlight, and even this early in the morning the rays heated his shirt. It would be a hot one today.

The road ended at the tumbled remains of a small mill. Busted beams pointed skyward, a skirt of rotten wood at their feet. Ron rested for a moment, his hand against a gray post. Splinters flaked onto his skin. Behind the ruin a narrow path vanished over a ridge. Weeds grew into the twin grooves that were too narrow for an automobile. He imagined steel-rimmed wagon wheels and a cart of ore making its way down the road behind a team of horses. Time seemed irrelevant here. It could be 1880 again, or 2080; the mountains wouldn't know the difference. But he wasn't timeless, and the clock counted; every minute passed was another minute that Levi suffered alone. Could an eight-year-old die of fright? What if he believed his daddy had forgotten him? Ron whimpered at the thought.

His photocopied map called this the Sunderson Mill. Above it were several mines: West Yellow Dog, New Baltimore, and Crossroad. Ron spread the map over his knee. Small Xs indicating digs crowded the gulch. There could be ventilation shafts, drainage tunnels, powder storage crypts, false starts, dead ends and full-bore excavations that needed checking.

It would take all day.


"Come with me, boy," said Charles, his hands shaking. It had taken him several minutes to push open the cabin door. He couldn't shake the impression of the cloud he'd seen around his house in the morning. It seemed to hover still, insubstantial, but present just the same. The sun shone mutedly through it, and the air felt cooler than it did ten feet away.

"It won't work," said the boy. He sat on the edge of his bed, his dark hair disheveled, his gaze steady and challenging.

Charles swallowed hard. "What won't work?"

"What you are planning." The boy came toward him, across the cabin's single room.

Charles backed away into the sunlight, gripping the hammer hanging from his belt. The weight of his satchel tugged at his shoulder. For a second he envisioned beating the boy down where he stood, before he could get away. He forced his fingers from the hammer.

"We are taking a walk."

"I know." The boy strode past him and up the road out of town.

Charles watched him, his breath caught in his throat. Suddenly the air seemed to clear, and the sun pressed against him. Had it always been this way around the boy? Had he been in a daze from the moment the child was born?

It was as if the boy followed a trail traced for him in the dirt. He walked in the road's middle, barely giving way when a wagon came toward him. The horse's nostrils flared at his smell.

Charles caught up to him when they turned onto the Sunderson Mill Road. The mines above it had gone bad the year before, and the mill was closed.

"The mountains hold things, Papa." The boy's hands hung straight at his side, as if he were standing at attention, not hiking a steep road.

He had no words to say to him. Am I the monster? thought Charles. The boy's mother wouldn't want this. Have I done something to deserve a curse? Every step hurt. Part of him wanted to run away. He could do it: leave the boy on the road, catch the new train out of town, and be in Denver before anyone knew. His family lived back east.

Another part denied that anything was wrong. Charles thought, what if I'm insane? My boy is strange, for sure, but he's not evil. What child growing in the mountains with a dead mother and a father who worked the mines wouldn't mature differently?

And a third part wanted to fall on the boy like a bear and rend him, bloody bone from bloody bone.

"Keep going," Charles said when the boy slowed at the mill. The windows were already broken and its door hung askew.

"Don't you love me, Papa?" he said. The boy looked at him sardonically. "A Papa should love his son."

The trail climbed as quickly as stairs for a hundred yards, while the afternoon sun touched the mountaintop before them. Charles choked on the words, "Of course, I love you." And he knew that he did. He loved him even as he wanted to kill him, even as he was afraid. Was this right? He thought of sick children sweating in their fevers, dead children. "They'll burn, Papa," the boy had said.

At the ridge's top, the trail flattened and split. Winding to the right, it led to West Yellow Dog, a fifty-foot drift that started with a yard-wide vein of quartz and wire gold but petered into low-grade ore that wasn't worth the cost of the powder to extract it. The middle trail ended at the New Baltimore, a failed attempt to find West Yellow Dog's wire gold by coming at it laterally. Charles had worked the New Baltimore for six months before the owners shut it down.

He'd never been in the Crossroad on the left trail, but, as the hard rock Cornishman who told him about it said, "The claim was snakebit from the beginning." The rumor was that the first prospector had been drilling into the rock to set a charge, and when he hit the drill for the last time, it disappeared into the rock. There was a tunnel already there. A silly story, but the claim didn't pay out, and there had been accidents.

They took the turn to the left, around a granite wall, out of the sun and into the stone bowl that held the mine. Rock surrounded them on three sides, like a small arena. The sound of Charles' hard-soled boots echoed. At the far side, a metal gate held closed by a clasp lock marked the mine's entrance.

"You're going to be staying here, boy." Charles removed a chisel from his satchel, set its edge against the lock, raised the hammer, then paused. Always he judged before he struck. Was the chisel set correctly? Would the hammer do its job? There could never be a strike without the pause for judgement, where a mistake could be saved. The metal's sharp report reverberated off the rocks. Another blow broke it, then Charles pulled the door open; it screeched against the stiffness in its hinges. He'd never seen a mine entrance like the Crossroad's. The floor looked worn smooth, as if thousands of feet had marched on it through the years. How had the miners done that?

"Don't you love me, Papa?" the boy said again.

Charles didn't look at him. From his satchel he removed a blanket, candles, a small bundle of food and a water bottle. "I'll be back tomorrow."

"You must not be my Papa." He didn't sound insincere this time. "My Papa loves me. He'll find me, my Papa."

"Just get in!"

Charles could barely see the new lock he put on the door through the tears.

Behind the iron gate, he heard the boy move, a large sound, as if what stirred in the tunnel had suddenly grown huge. He fell back. Impossibly, the door stirred in its iron frame, and for a second Charles thought the inch-thick bolts might pull from the rock. He scuttled away. Even at the edge of the granite arena, when Charles looked at the mine entrance, he could hear the boy behind the gate, breathing loud, his heart throbbing. The sky grew dark and the air thick. A noxious cloud seeped around the door's edges, filled the stone chamber, its tendrils crawling on the floor toward Charles. The boy said, his voice full of old mining timbers and cold, wet stone a thousand feet deep, "Papa?"

Charles fled.


West Yellow Dog had been dynamited. All that remained of its entrance was twisted ore cart track. Ron searched the cliff base to both sides. A niche three hundred yards to the right might have been where they stored powder, but it was only ten feet deep and didn't have a door. Below the mine, partially hidden behind scrubby pine growing between the rocks, he found a small tunnel barely tall enough for him to enter on his hands and knees, but twigs and dirt blocked the way a few feet in and it smelled of marmot. Ron sat on his haunches outside the hole and closed his eyes against the sun.

He'd know if Levi had died, wouldn't he? A father and son had a bond, he'd told the detective.

Within his view, visible only because the sun cast long shadows, several foundations rose from the grass in the clearing below the slope. There must have been a small community here, or they might have been part of the mining operation. At the Gilpin County Courthouse, Ron had looked at pictures of the town from the 1880s, and beside them were modern shots taken from the same spot. The buildings changed. Trees changed. But the rocks and mountains stayed the same. He trembled. To the mountain, time didn't exist; all times were interchangable. He glanced at his watch. To a little boy dying in a mine, every second stretched like skin on fire.

He pushed himself upright.

The New Baltimore had a park service gate on it. Ron slowed as he approached. Covered in dust, the remains of a broken lock lay on the ground. He rubbed the scratches in the metal. No rust. Someone had been here this summer.

"Levi!" His voice sounded hollow and out of place.

The gate gave reluctantly, its base dragging over the rock as he pulled it open. Moisture seeped from the walls a few feet in. Resting one hand on the black-slime ceiling just above his head, he shone his flashlight on indistinct footprints on the muddy floor. Back in the depths, a watery *plink-plink-plink* broke the silence. The tunnel split. To the right, a pile of rock and broken timbers blocked the way. To the left, the passage sloped downward for another twenty feet before ending at a pool of water. The footprints led here. Ron played the quivering light across the surface, penetrating to the bottom. Rocks. More timber. Metal so heavily rusted he couldn't tell what its original shape had been. No wrapped bundle. No horror-story patch of white that resolved itself into a face.

He released a pent-up breath. Why had someone broken into the mine? Turning, he studied the walls and ceiling. A slippery, unhealthy looking fungus covered the surfaces, and the stagnant air smelled rotted and mildewed. Near the ceiling to the left of the pool, a patch of rock peered through the growth, as if it had been brushed clean, and above it, a crack wider than his fist swallowed the light. Ron reached in, touched plastic. He found four bags in the crack, about a pound each. A whiff of the first one showed he'd uncovered someone's stash.

Ron left the bags on the floor. Ten minutes wasted.

According to his map, all that remained was the Crossroad. It took a half hour of backtracking across the gulch's east side before he found a faint trail that led to a gap around a rock wall.

He spotted the lock on the door on the other side of the stone arena as soon as he rounded the corner, a brand new, brass padlock, like the row of them on top of Sims' dresser. He ran without thinking about it. Old metal door, not park service. Ron ripped off his backpack, fumbled for the bolt cutter, gripped the handles and squeezed. The lock snapped.

Was now the moment when he would know? Ron had dreamed of finding Levi in a thousand ways. Bad dreams, in some, where Levi was dead. Either dead over a month, or even worse, dead a few days. He'd be starved or dead from thirst or exposure. In some dreams he was alive but sick, damaged from exposure or the time alone. In one dream Levi didn't know him, his mind gone. What could be worse than an eight-year-old driven insane by abuse and fear? In that dream, Ron loved his son back to sanity. No evil could be so bad that love could not change it to something good.

Ron tore the lock from the hasp, jammed his fingertips into the gap between the door and the frame. Pulled.

In the good dreams, Levi waited. "Daddy!" he would cry. He always called Ron "Daddy," like it was a blessing.

The door swung open.


Charles didn't even try to get to sleep. Sitting at the table in his cabin, the tiny slice of moon providing the only light again, he thought about the locked gate and the boy behind it. His intention was to never return.

He thought, what's the greater evil? Every time he closed his eyes, he saw dead children, a fingerprint on their foreheads; he also saw the boy at the Crossroad, staring at a candle, maybe, or sleeping. What kind of dreams would a bringer of death like him have? But Charles was evil too. The boy, no matter what else he was, was his son. A father should take care of his own. One time when Charles was young he locked a storage shed on his father's farm. A week later his father sent him to fetch some tools. The storage shed stank, a solid wall of putridness rolling out when Charles opened the door. A cat had been locked in, its mouth gaping open, dry as dust, the stomach burst. If he had known, wouldn't it have been merciful to have killed the cat a week earlier?

Charles looked through the darkness to his own bed. He couldn't imagine sleeping again. The boy behind the gate moved in his mind. The room was so black, Charles could almost see the boy without closing his eyes. Like the cat, the boy was locked in. But the cat wasn't the devil. No, not by a long shot. Maybe a creature like the boy thrived on the black air behind the gate. Could such a thing be killed by an act as simple as being shut into a mine? What if it could do some magic to save itself?

In a sudden vision, Charles saw himself as an older man walking down a street. A beautiful carriage clattered by, the horses' hooves loud on the bricks. In the vision, Charles glanced up. Sitting in the carriage was his son, grown now, and the look he gave from the carriage was full of hate.

Charles made a fist on the table, alone in his cabin in the midst of the night and moaned. The boy was behind the gate. "I'm cursed," Charles said to the four walls. Already he felt the guilt like a blood-soaked blanket settling over his head, suffocating him.

He's a boy dying slowly, my son, Charles thought. He's a monster who can save himself in some evil way.


Like the New Baltimore, the Crossroad was wet. Footprints showed clearly in the mud. Little prints. A child's shoes.

"Levi!" Ron's eyes strained to see into the mine, pulse throbbing huge in his chest. "Are you there, son?"

He took a few steps down the tunnel. Where was Levi? Ron turned on his flashlight. The powerful beam cut into the air showing the path curving away before him. His feet slipped on the muddy floor as slick as polished marble, and suddenly he felt scared, as scared as he'd ever been in his life. His breath puffed out in a plume before him. Every instinct told him to run. The mine didn't feel right. The air clung to his arms like icy cockleburs, and he had to brace himself with a hand against the wall. Then the floor shook, but it wasn't just the floor; everything jolted or quivered. Every cell in his body flinched. He wasn't sure if he had turned around and was heading out. He thought, the world has shifted.

He stepped forward again. Where am I? Where am I going?

A voice came from the tunnel before him, a little boy's voice.

"Papa?" it called.

Ron rushed forward, his fear forgotten. He would greet him with love like he'd never known.

"Papa?"

His son was coming home.


Charles stood at the Crossroad gate. He'd pulled it open, but he wouldn't step inside. No, he was too frightened for that. He couldn't *see* the boy, or all would be lost. He had one chance to make it right, and only one.

"Boy?" he yelled into the mine.

For a long time there was no sound, then Charles felt a peculiar twitch, like the mountain had shrugged. The air itself contracted, and his ears popped.

He shook his head. Whatever else was going on, he could not be swayed.

"Boy?" he shouted again.

A voice came from far back in the mine. "Daddy?" it cried. "Is that you, Daddy?"

Small feet splashed through the mud, growing louder.

"I knew you'd come, Daddy," the voice exclaimed, very close now.

Charles stood by the door out of sight, his hammer raised high, paused above him. When the boy stepped out, he would bring it down. Oh, yes he would. He would end it here.

And all would be right.

# THE LAST AGE
## SHOULD KNOW YOUR HEART

::::: blink :::::

Marvell checked his clock and power supply. Fourteen thousand years had passed, and the beach-ball sized maintenance machine had six minutes stored before he would have to enter sleep mode again. Other figures flicked through his engineered consciousness: two percent less of the twenty-seven hundred square miles of his photoelectric grid was active than had been there the last wake time, but most of the bad sectors were much farther than six minutes away. They showed as tiny black dots on the power grid's smooth green representation in his display, almost all of them to his west. The sun's energy output had reduced too, by .04 percent. His sensors displayed it as a dull red plain on the other side of the grid, filling half the sky, only a dozen miles above, its wrinkled, gassy surface sliding by at orbital velocity. If nothing else changed, he'd be out for seventeen thousand years, clinging to the sun-encircling grid, gradually storing energy, before waking again. Could he get to the nearest bad sector and at least repair it before shut down?

And where was ThreeAndrea?

At the cost of ten seconds of wakefulness, he powered up the locator. She was on the west edge of her grid, fifteen minutes away, inactive. Somewhat closer than she had been fourteen thousand years ago. What were the odds they would ever be awake at the same time? Sacrificing a few more seconds, he ran a diagnostic on her grid. Nearly the same rate of degradation.

He set course for the nearest bad sector to his east, uncoupled from the system, the copper crimps snapping open in unison, then released the pulse that would send him toward the repair. To con-

serve time, everything on him powered down, except his aware-
ness, but that drew the most energy. He recited poetry during the
drift, from billions of years earlier, his favorite works in a long dead
language from a long dead species, whose connection to the Makers was lost in history. Had they once traded? Had there been interstellar commerce? Were the Makers their descendants who'd moved
from sun to sun, carrying the poetry with them until it ended up
here? There was no way to know. The authors were gone, their star
not even a distant memory. Only the literature lasted, not the lengthy
path it had taken to end up within him.

Marvell's memory banks were extensive, and in the super cold
on the grid's shadow side, he only needed to expend a nanowatt to
plumb his memory's depths. "Had we but world enough, and time,"
he thought, and he let the words cycle over and over. Then he
threaded another line through it, "the grave's a fine and private place,
but none I think do there embrace." Marvell had taken to mixing
and matching his poetry, choosing favorite lines only, since there
was hardly the luxury of the entire poem. Funny, to long for embrac-
ing, he thought.

He tried to remember if he'd dreamed. It seemed unreasonable
that in fourteen thousand years of sleep he hadn't dreamed, but he
couldn't come up with a single image in the silent time while he'd
been shut down. He wouldn't know the time had passed at all except his clock reminded him, and that in the blink the power grid had
gained a few more black spots, but he felt it, hanging on him, like a
heavy ebony blanket, the psychic time of the years passing while he
clung beneath the grid, millions of years old, much closer to the end
of his life than the beginning.

The timer told him he had arrived. Visuals brightened. Above him,
the power grid glided past, a great, opaque sheet between him and
the sun, capturing every stray radiation, converting it to electricity
and storing it in his batteries, but now there was almost nothing to
capture. The sun was only mildly warmer than the space around it.
He slowed himself, unlimbered his arms. As always, links were broken in the fabric above. Time was cruel. The Makers had built the grid
to last forever, and it had certainly outlasted them, but forever is an
unreachable goal. His sensor-laden fingers found the ruptures, wove
them together in automatic competence, measured their capacity.

If he could have shrugged, he would have. All the grid's connections were thinning, breaking down, the essence of their mass

sublimating slowly. He paused while his subtle intelligence did the calculations. Idly, as he waited, he scanned the system. On each corner of his orbiting fiefdom rose the old power transmitters that used to beam the gathered energy to the Makers' planet beyond, but he'd long since lost contact with them. No heat from it. No light. There was no way to sense it, and there hadn't been for millions of years. The towers remained, their mechanisms useless. He recited a bit of verse: "Look on my works, ye mighty, and despair." The calculations finished. "Gather ye rosebuds while ye may," he thought. "Old time is still a-flying." If he was lucky, he might wake up another three or four times. The race was between the sun reducing to so little output that the grid couldn't convert it into electricity, or the grid itself failing utterly.

His arms folded back into his shell. The crimps reanchored. He wondered if ThreeAndrea would see that he'd moved closer to their shared border. Would she do the same calculations and come to the same conclusion. When was the last time he'd talked to her? There wasn't time to access his records. Screens faded to black. Sensors powered down.

Just before his six minutes ended, he said to himself, "That age is best which is the first, when youth and blood are warmer; but being spent, the worse, and worst times still succeed the former."


::::: blink :::::


Seventeen thousand years, almost exactly, and he only had five minutes. More of the grid was down. As it had been for several of the last cycles, it was falling apart faster than he could repair it. His duty was clear. The bulk of bad sectors was to the west. The most efficient plan would be to head for the heaviest concentration and begin repairing there. Already he'd mapped out the best course. He could extend the grid's life by thousands on thousands of years. The sun would go out eventually, but it was dying at a slower rate than the grid, and it was possible that it could flicker into renewed life, that deep inside, where the gravity-tortured physics became unlikely, the chain reactions could push themselves into momentary brightness. Not long-lived, for sure, but the sun could pulse. It had before, and if it did, the power would flow. He'd be able to stay alert indefinitely to completely repair the system.

His job was to outlast the dormant periods.

He scanned for ThreeAndrea. She was on the west edge of her grid, only four minutes away. She must have headed straight toward him during her last active period.

Oh, for the heady days when the sun glowed brightly and energy flowed in abundance! He never slept then, cruising along the grid's protected side, making sure the towers beamed their power to the Maker's planet safely below them. Then, a chain of grids encircled the star like a huge ribbon, and there were thousands of mechanisms like him, sentient, self-aware, independent machines devoted to repairing the inevitable breakdowns. He'd seen pictures of the sun as viewed from the Maker's planet, a beautiful, bright light in the sky with a narrow stripe cut through its middle, the grid's shadow. Now, as far as he could tell, ThreeAndrea and he were the only ones left, two small robots, mending their sections. Then they had power to spare, in constant communication, swapping poems, conversing about their jobs, about their lives. No one lives a limited life, he thought. Our lives are as important as any. He felt a longing to hold onto his, lonely as it was.

But as the sun waned, they went increasingly into sleep mode. He hadn't spoken to her for millions of years (although he'd only been aware of a handful of them), and he realized he might never speak to her again.

Seconds ticked relentlessly, and he didn't move. There were dead patches between ThreeAndrea and him. He could go closer to her, but it wouldn't be efficient. A thought crossed his mind: there are no more Makers. I have no responsibility to them, but the grid called. His programming and habit pulled at him to go west, away from ThreeAndrea and into the heart of the damaged system.

And what would be the use of going her way? She could well move farther from their shared border. He couldn't lock onto her grid any more then she could lock onto his. The connections would be incompatible. To leave his area would be suicide.

A snippet of John Donne surfaced in his memory, "For the first twenty years since yesterday I scarce believed thou couldst be gone away." It was the poem that ended with, "Yet call not this long life; but think that I am, by being dead, immortal. Can ghosts die?" ThreeAndrea liked John Milton, although she dwelt more on the last works of the Makers. The sad dirges to themselves, made as they dug deeper and deeper into their planet, pursuing the heat at the core, breathing air transmuted from minerals and rock, their own atmosphere having long ago frozen and fallen to the surface.

He decided, set a course, unclamped and released a pulse. Duty ruled out. He must repair as much damage as possible.

Then he remembered a bit of Shakespeare, "Let me not to the marriage of true minds admit impediments . . . Love alters not with his brief hours and weeks, but bears it out even to the edge of doom."

Seconds ticked away, much more important to him than distance. The clock ruled what was left of his life. Above him, the blank-slate grid scooted by. Every passing instant was a crisis, a turning point, a crux, a moment lost and a trial of resolution.

Fully formed, the thought leapt before him, I don't need to be duty's fool.

Before he calculated fuel, before he could even determine if what he wanted to do was possible, he unshipped an arm, reached up and grabbed the grid. His metal shell snapped into the black surface. Ripples stretched along the metallic fabric. Connections broke. In a second, more damage was done to the grid than had occurred in the past hundred-thousand years. But his momentum slowed until he stopped, and the grid rebounded, pulling him back. Marvell let go at the end to the bounce, sending himself in the other direction, toward ThreeAndrea asleep on the border.

Only three minutes left. The math was unforgiving. He'd have to stop considerably short of her. By the time he'd recharged himself, she would be long gone. His errand was futile. Still, he plotted the best angle, made a small correction, set his timer and waited. Another poet drifted through his mind, "Now let us sport us while we may, and now, like amorous birds of prey, rather at once our time devour than languish in his slow-chapped power," and if Marvell could have smiled, he would have.

He slowed, clamped. Dug up some Shakespeare to meditate on while he was shut down, if there was a chance for dreams: "In me thou see'st the twilight of such day as after sunset fadeth in the west, which by and by black night doth take away, death's second self that seals up all in rest."

::::: blink :::::

ThreeAndrea hadn't moved. Marvell noted that first. Then, the time, sixty-four thousand years. He'd reduced the grid's capability that much? No. His damage wasn't that big, and the decline in functioning sectors was as predicted. It was the sun, even dimmer now, throwing out less usable radiation, cooling in the universal heat sink. There would be no chance for a saving pulse. The last burst of radiation truly had been its ending gasp, and the decline was comparatively swift and inevitable. Too small to nova, not even enough mass to become a neutron star, it would just continue to fade, like a filament in a light bulb caught in slow motion. Neutrons would break into protons and electrons, and, eventually, those too would go their separate ways, joining the background heat that was all that remained of the universe, but this was unimaginably far into the future, even for an intelligence as old as Marvell's.

Was she dead? Marvell activated his sensors, spending precious seconds of consciousness. She'd done no repairs to her grid as far as he could tell since she'd activated last. More chilling, though—she hadn't budged from where she'd anchored on the closest edge of her grid. He had three minutes to act. Quickly, he unanchored, recalled the course, released a pulse, then turned his sensors off. The numbers said he would reach her with seconds to spare.

Nothing to do in the seconds left but to recite poetry, a little Yeats. At first he considered "Sailing to Byzantium," and then "The Second Coming," but he couldn't imagine a birth in his future, not even the grim one with a rough beast slouching toward Bethlehem to be born. He chose instead some Gerald Manley Hopkins. It called to him pictures of a life he'd only imagined on planetary surfaces he'd never walked on. There were so many terms in it he hadn't experienced, but there was something in the tone:

> Nothing is so beautiful as spring,
> When weeds, in wheels, shoot long and lovely and lush;
> Thrush's eggs look little low heavens, and thrush
> Through the echoing timber does so rinse and wring
> The ear, it strikes like lightnings to hear him sing.

He kicked the sensors back on, slowed himself to a stop, reanchored. Her shell looked whole. The nearly invisible seams where her arms folded into her body appeared clean. No outward damage, but that didn't reflect what might have gone on inside. A critical relay could have broken, or, he thought, she could have ended it herself. They both had the capability. He could shut himself down forever easily enough. Is that what she had done? Why hadn't she moved? How could he communicate with her?

Only seconds remained before he shut down. What could he do? If he could have, he would have wept in frustration. Instead, he extended his arm, his mechanical manipulators, loaded with sensors and so like fingers stretching out to touch her. She was a shade too far. No time to bring it back. One arm out, inches too short, Marvell retreated into sleep mode.

::::: blink :::::

Marvell woke to poetry, and for a moment it puzzled him. It didn't come from within him. He hadn't called it up, but there it was, running through his brain, "When I consider how my light is spent ere half my days in this dark world and wide, and that one talent which is death to hide lodged in me useless, though my soul more bent to serve therewith my maker . . ." He recognized the poet, John Milton.

"ThreeAndrea?" he said. Slowly, far more slowly then he ever remembered, his systems came to life.

"Yes, I'm here."

"How . . . ?" His instruments showed power flowing through his outstretched arm. Finally a visual glowed. ThreeAndrea's hand joined to his, sending electricity into him. His power storage units were empty. "How long has it been? My clock isn't functioning." Several submechanisms weren't responding either. The thruster seemed to be cut off, and although he could sense the arm still stored into his side, it wouldn't respond to a diagnostic.

ThreeAndrea said, "Almost thirty thousand years for me. Somewhat less for you." Her voice was as he remembered it, different from his own, lighter. She spaced her words irregularly. He'd always wondered if it was an error in her programming, or if she did it on purpose to be unique. She continued, "You anchored into an inactive sector, or it broke soon after you arrived. There was no way for you to recharge."

"I thought you were dead. You didn't move."

For seconds she didn't reply. He continued scanning himself. No power. No propulsion. No way to move his arms. He couldn't access his grid to see what new damage there might be.

Then she said, "I was afraid you wouldn't come."

He had no answer for that. "How much time do we have?"

"I haven't been repairing, just storing. Four minutes between the two of us. I can't move you, though. The only way for you to stay active is hooked to me."

"Well, then don't let go." He could feel the power coming from her, and it tingled oddly. His system had to reroute it, and it wasn't exactly the same as he was used to, as if the electricity was flavored by passing through her. It wasn't unpleasant.

"I won't. Have you looked down?"

If he could have shook his head, he would have. He realized that since the Maker's planet had stopped responding, he'd spent every waking period looking up, examining the grid, peering at the diminished sun beyond.

"I don't have the power to," he said.

"Look through mine," she said, and she clicked open relays that allowed him access to her scanner.

The field that was the universe was absolutely blank. An empty distance, devoid of radiation and light; nothing was out there. "Where are the stars?" Marvell said.

"They're gone."

"All of them?"

"All of them."

"Then this is the last?"

"As far as I can tell."

"Walt Whitman would be sad," Marvell said. "He wrote, 'I wandered off by myself, in the mystical moist night-air, and from time to time, looked up in perfect silence at the stars.'"

"He got the silence right," said ThreeAndrea.

Marvell tried to access his clock. It still wasn't working. "How much more time?"

"Not long."

"What's the condition of your grid? Will we wake again?"

Marvell sensed her withdrawing as she consulted her system.

"We might, but it's all grown so old."

He knew she meant the grid, the sun and them. Everything.

"Are you afraid?" Marvell asked. He studied the blankness below them. It was totally featureless, without depth or meaning. All the stars that once shone gone at once, finally. The long play ended.

"Not now. It's just sleep mode," ThreeAndrea said.

"I can feel your hand, you know," Marvell said. His sensors recorded the pressure of her manipulators against his own. Sensitive to the last, his fingers caressed the metal texture, brittle in the deep, deep cold.

"Yes, I hoped you could."


::::: blink :::::

# ORIGIN OF THE SPECIES

Romulus stood under an elm in the moon-washed shadow of the long, green sward between Gray Mountain Golf Course's ninth fairway and the Gray Mountain Country Club, listening to the tinny dance music of Pinehurst High's prom. He pried chunks of bark off the tree absently with his fingernail, but his focus was on the building, pink light leaking from the windows, a hundred shiny windshields catching the moon in the parking lot beyond, and the sad-leafed whisper of the wind. Shadows passed between the light and the windows, couples dancing, heads close together, gliding by during the slow song, and Romulus wondered which one was Fay with her date, what's-his-name, the troll.

He looked through the leaves at the moon, three days short of being full, and he scuffed the ground in disgust. Since September, when Student Senate scheduled the dance, he'd known. All the full moons were marked on his day-planner, mixed in with deadlines for college applications, baccalaureate, Senior Academic Awards night and graduation. There it was, a perfectly circular moon on the Tuesday after prom, and he'd known he would be standing outside, skin a little itchy, jaw aching, watching the dance.

When Romulus was a freshman, Dad told him it was regressive genetics catching up. They'd sat in his bedroom, Romulus' wildlife posters covering the walls, Dad, a little embarrassed, telling him the facts of life.

"You're getting to that age, son." Dad pressed his hands on the tops of his knees and locked his elbows straight, clearly uncomfortable.

"I know, Dad." Romulus scooted farther away on the bed. Dad's weight pressed the mattress down, and no matter where Romulus sat, he felt like he was an inch away from tumbling into him. And

Romulus *did* know. He'd known for years, listening to his parents talking late at night, marking their calendars, Dad slipping out at dusk the nights of a full moon. What kid wouldn't know?

"You're going to start noticing girls more. You're a sensitive boy," Dad said.

Romulus blushed. It was true, he did. They'd walk by him in the halls, their backpacks hanging off one shoulder, intent on conversations with each other, and he'd catch himself staring at the almost invisible hair on a naked wrist, the curve of muscle in a neck. But most of all, it was their smell. For the longest time he hadn't known what it was. Once a month, or so, depending on the girl, he'd catch a stray whiff beneath the shampoo and perfume and hair spray, and his muscles would tense. He hoped to god Dad wasn't going to say anything about that. That would be too much. He'd rather jump out the window than listen to Dad fumble his way through an explanation of the smell.

Instead, Dad launched into an oblique reference to evolution and the origin of the species. "The genes mixed, son. I know what they told you in your science classes about where man came from, but they don't know the half of it, the magical half."

Romulus let out a relieved sigh. Dad wasn't going to talk about girls after all. Instead he talked about elves and harpies, goblins, giants and humans. "The dominant breed won out and all were assimilated. Everyone's human, more or less, but sometimes a regressive gene rises to the surface. Do you know what I'm trying to say?" He put his hand on Romulus's knee. "You're a special kid. There are others like you, some just like you, some from the other races, a little bit of old ancestry, the old mythologies, in everyone, more or less."

"Sure, Dad. Thanks for clearing this all up for me. I've got to do my homework now. Okay?"

"Oh, good." Dad let out a noisy sigh, like he'd just set down a great weight. "So you know why things are the way they are?"

"Yeah, I got it."

Then Dad left. Romulus didn't do his homework, but lay in bed instead, his hands clasped behind his head, staring at the ceiling, thinking about smells.

So he started paying attention to the lunar calendar his freshman year, and as time wore on he grew a few inches, filled out in the chest, found he needed to shave, and the week of the full moon he didn't schedule anything at night. Was Dad right? he wondered. Was *everyone* descended from mythological creatures? Sometimes he wandered the halls during passing period, or he sat in class and tried to figure where the other students came from. Was the cheerleader part elf? Was the junior class president's great, great, great, great (and so on) grandmother a gorgon? She was frightening enough, and there was a snakiness to her hair when she stood in the wind. He sniffed her, but she smelled purely human. He'd never identified anyone's deep ancestry until he smelled the troll in the boy who liked Fay, and that was a pure scary fluke. They'd bumped in the hall. The troll shoved him off, and in the shove Romulus had smelled him. A line of associations clicked—an instinctive recognition—but so strong that for a second the boy's hands were twisted claws, and his incisors hung from his mouth like stout tusks.

Romulus hadn't known whether to run or snarl. And what bad luck! Of all the boys in the school, the troll had to ask Fay to prom.

It wasn't his fault the stupid Student Senate decided this date for the dance. He leaned against the tree. Fay hadn't understood, really, when he told her he couldn't go to the prom. She'd smiled. Was sweet about it. Maybe she even believed him when he stammered his excuses. So she made the date with the troll. Romulus squeezed his eyes shut in frustration. The music changed to a faster beat. Shadows bounced against the window. A couple boys slipped out the doors and walked to their truck, avoiding the security cop in the parking lot. Even from a hundred yards away, Romulus smelled the beer. They only stayed in the truck for a few minutes, then headed back to the dance.

Romulus left the lawn and walked the neighborhoods, choosing streets randomly. He hid from cars—it was long past curfew, and he didn't want to explain to a policeman what he was doing. Sometimes a dog chained in a back yard caught wind of him and howled. He didn't howl back, didn't even growl, but he wished one would break free. They could run the blocks together, or they could stand face to face, teeth showing in the moon. "This is mine," their postures would say. Maybe the dog would leap, go for his throat. Romulus closed his eyes and felt the night air on his cheek, the stoney road beneath his shoes. Or maybe *he* would leap and the dog's throat would be in *his* teeth. He could almost feel the pulse in his mouth.

It seemed for hours that he walked, often with his eyes closed, not paying attention to where he was, trusting his nose to lead him.

When a car turned the corner ahead of him, and he dove into a bush, he was surprised to find he was directly across the street from Fay's house. The car parked. It was the troll's convertible, top down, looking low, black and ominous in the moonlight. Fay and the troll walked to the porch.

"I had a nice time," she said, her hands in his between them.

"Me too." The troll wore a letter jacket over his tux. Even from the bushes across the street, Romulus could see the multiple brass bars glistening in the porch light showing how many times he'd lettered: football, wrestling and track. A thick-necked, thick-wristed, thick-headed wunderkind with perfect balance and the fast twitch muscles of a cheetah. A vague suggestion of Harrison Ford in his chin and smile. A careless black lock of hair that fell across his forehead in an unkempt way that some girls found charming.

Romulus was loath to think Fay could fall for this, but as the two talked, their faces came closer and closer together like an inevitable collision, two lambent planets closing on each other in the night sky, until they were kissing, and Romulus turned away, a bitter tear in each eye.

Later, after Fay went into her house and the troll drove away, Romulus walked back to Gray Mountain Country Club. Other than empty beer cans and broken glass in the parking lot, nothing remained of the prom. He wandered onto the golf course, fell asleep on the third green, and when he woke in the morning, stiff from tiredness and the cold, he saw his own dew-drawn silhouette in the grass.


In the hallways that Monday, Romulus moved listlessly from subject to subject, avoiding Fay until finally he ran into her between Calculus and Mythology, a class they shared.

They talked outside the door. "Did you do your homework?" she asked.

He nodded. They were supposed write a report on a character from Camelot. He'd chosen Uther Pendragon. As always, he found himself staring. Her complexion fascinated him, absolutely exquisite, like polished silk, pale and smooth, dark-blue eyes, a hint of copper in her blonde hair. He thought about a willow wand swaying on a river bank. Looking at her was like listening to water dance over rounded rocks, all foam and bubbles and deep, still pools.

Fay glanced into his eyes, then looked away. "I don't think teachers should be allowed to make assignments on prom weekend."

"You didn't get yours done?" His palms sweated just talking to her.

Fay shook her head.

"You can have mine. I've got an A in there already without it."

Fay smiled. "Really? You'd do that?"

Embarrassed, Romulus put his head down. "It's no big deal."

She put her hand on his arm. "That's the nicest thing I think anyone's ever offered to do for me, but I better face the music on my own." She stood on her tiptoes, kissed him on the cheek, then slipped around the doorway into the room.

Students streamed past him, intent on beating the tardy bell, but Romulus didn't move. Slowly, he brought his hand up to his face and brushed his fingertips where she'd kissed him.

During class, Romulus barely listened. He focused instead on Fay, who sat a row over and two seats in front of him. The troll sat beside her. Halfway through class he passed her a note. She read it quietly, wrote something on it, and passed it back. The troll nodded and put the note in his folder. Mr. Campbell talked at length about the search for the historical King Arthur. In despair, Romulus turned his attention to Campbell. "The real King Arthur, if there was one, may have lived in 5th Century England, a hero because he drove out barbarian invaders. Much of our knowledge of King Arthur came from a historian, Geoffrey of Monmouth, who in the 12th Century set down the reign of British kings. He made most of it up, evidently. But it's through Geoffrey that we first learn of Merlin."

Romulus wrote names and dates disconsolately until Campbell said, "The death of Arthur and disappearance of Merlin are the end of wizardry in the world. Belief in mythological creatures fades with every passing century." He said it within another context, but the words reminded him of something his dad had said about evolution and the magic. Romulus wondered if the biology classes ever touched on this alternate explanation for changes in the species.

Quickly Romulus wrote his thoughts below Campbell's facts: "What if Merlin's disappearance *caused* the downfall of mythological beings?" He thought he'd ask Dad about it later.

Fay concentrated on her own notes. The troll wrote something on a slip of paper, and with a husky whisper, handed it to the boy behind him, a freshman who somehow had been assigned this senior level class—Romulus had stepped between the boy and a pissed off football player earlier in the year, but other than a grateful "thank you," they didn't talk—and he gave the paper to Romulus, muttering, "Pass it on." Behind Romulus sat one of the troll's wrestling buddies. Romulus often found himself a courier for their stream of letters, mostly directions for the weekend's parties. The torn paper sat, message up, on the desk—the troll hadn't bothered to fold it. It read, "I'll nail her tomorrow night." He'd scrawled a lopsided happy face below, its eyes two squashed circles. Romulus' fingers curled up, revolted by the thought of touching it.

Something whacked the back of his head.

"Hand it back, dog breath," hissed the wrestler.

Romulus grabbed the note, twirled in his seat and banged it on the desk. The wrestler leaned away, a startled look in his eyes. He said, "Hey, I was just joking."

After a few seconds, Romulus broke his glare and faced forward, and he heard a sigh of relief behind him.

"Boys?" said Campbell.

"Sorry, sir," said Romulus.

For the rest of the period, the note ran through his brain: "I'll nail her tomorrow." The happy face looked more and more evil in his memory. He opened his text to the illustrations, and wasn't surprised to see a resemblance between the drawing and the book's woodcut of a troll.

After class, in the hallway once again, Romulus pushed his way through the crowd until he caught up with Fay, but once he reached her side, he wasn't sure what to say. The certainty he'd had in class faded. Maybe the troll was talking about someone else. How could he ask her what she was doing tomorrow night? She carried her books against her chest, her chin down, as if she were mulling over something.

"Fay?" he said.

She looked up, smiled at him. "Hi, Romulus. Isn't your next class the other way?"

He blushed; he could feel his face heating, and the heat embarrassed him even more. It was all he could do not to turn away, but he had committed himself now. He had to know.

"I wondered if you wanted to go to the Senior Choral Recital. It's tomorrow at seven." As the words slipped out, he knew he'd never be able to keep the date. At seven the sun was still up, but it was a two hour concert.

Her expression fell. "Oh, I'm sorry. I can't. Not tomorrow. I . . . have other plans."

In the pause he heard the truth. The troll's note *was* about her. And he knew where they'd go too: Chaney Park, a spot on the bluffs overlooking town. It's where the troll always took his dates. He was legendary about it.

Fay smiled again, her face perfect in the bustling hallway. Her eyes glistened. Even as his heart ached, he marveled at her eyes that were brighter than they should be, as if they reflected a crystal light no one else saw. Then he caught a hint of her smell. Like everyone else, she smelled of shampoo and deodorant, but underneath was her own essence, a spring-drenched forest, nothing fleshy at all.

"I'd like a rain check, though," she said. "Ask me again another night."

Romulus blinked in surprise, and she was gone. Just kids bumping against each other, making their way from room to room.

That night the moon rose in Romulus's window, white and fat and unblinking. His lights out, he sat on the edge of his bed, breath short, skin on fire. Inside he was all pressures and cramps, legs trembling. Dad would know what to tell him, but Dad had stolen out the back door when the sun went down. The moon had never seemed so large; it was larger than the window, and the light had never seemed so potent, so penetrating. Romulus scratched at his chest, popping buttons. Where the light touched felt better, not cooled, but caressed in warmth.

Romulus whined, biting in the sound he really wanted to make. He pulled his clothes off. A part of him worried his mother would come to check on him, and what would she think, him standing naked in the pale, moonlit square in his room? She'd caught him in the bathroom the other day, staring in the mirror. She'd said without pausing, "Your father plucks his, you know."

"What?" he'd said.

"Most people have two eyebrows." She leaned past him, buffed a spot on the counter, then left.

Confused, he'd looked at himself again. Although he hadn't been thinking about it at the time, he'd always considered his eyebrows his best mark, in a lupine sort of way, and the shadow between them a distinguishing feature. Dad plucked his?

Of course, he was his father's son—she wouldn't be surprised to see him naked in the moonlight either. Still, he worried she might come in. The other part, though, saw himself leaping through the window. He thought, I must go to the forest. Already the trees quivered, waiting for him. And in the trees they would expect him, the entire panoply: elves, fairies, goblins and giants. The other creatures lost in mythical, evolutionary time.

But there would be trolls there too, and dragons. All the old maps said so: in the unexplored areas, here there be dragons.

From the moon-tinted hills beyond town, a thin howl rose in the light. Very lonely. Very far away.

Romulus tried a howl back, a tentative utterance that couldn't have made it past their front gate.

He did it again, louder. It hurt tearing through his throat that wasn't quite shaped for it, but it felt good too. Once more. A door popped open across the street, and a neighbor stuck his head out. Romulus buried his head in a pillow. No way Dad heard that, he thought, but he didn't try it again; and when the moon rose high enough so the light was not so obvious, he curled on the floor to fall asleep.


The day passed miserably until Mythology, where he hoped he could figure a way to warn Fay, but no matter how he thought to phrase it, his message sounded unbelievable. In the classroom's afternoon mugginess he doodled at the bottom of his notes. Fay split her attention between Campbell, who moved meticulously through the history of the Knights of the Round Table, and the troll, who smiled slyly at her when she turned toward him.

"Many retellings of Arthur's legend say that after the boy king took the throne at fifteen, and under Merlin's tutelage, he rid his country of monsters and giants," said Campbell.

Romulus sketched a sword rising from a lake. If he had Excalibur, he thought, he would rid this classroom of a monster himself.

When the bell rang, Fay continued writing her notes. The troll stood beside her, put his hand on her shoulder, then spoke softly in her ear. Romulus scrunched his toes in his shoes to keep himself from springing from the desk.

*

That evening Romulus finished dinner, told Mom and Dad he needed to take a walk, and went out the back door, but not before he caught a knowing glance between them.

Chaney Park was a six mile hike up a gravel road that rose too steeply the last three miles to bicycle, and Romulus figured he could be where kids parked by 8:30 or so. There was no question about using the car. He shuddered to think of himself behind the wheel, driving a two thousand pound vehicle, and the moon pouring through the windshield like a million biting ants.

The houses on his street were new brick and crisply-painted bi-levels, but a block over was an older neighborhood, where the roofs rose to steep peaks, and every house sported a single attic window, a lone eye watching him trudge toward the edge of town. Behind him the sunset flared orange and yellow, but before him only the bluffs' tops caught the last pale sliver of daylight, and they didn't hold that long. The woods below already swam in shadows. He crossed the railroad tracks; the blacktop changed to dirt, and soon, thin-trunked trees rustling with spring growth lined the path on both sides. He trudged up a long hill. At the crest he looked back, the town spread out behind him, stretched along the river, a tiny fiefdom at this distance. Streetlights could just as well be campfires, the baseball stadium glowing on the other side of town, a castle. He turned and walked into the dale beyond, losing the town and the day's final glow at the same time. A few stars twinkled in the sable blanket.

Romulus took deep breaths. He hadn't walked at night out here before. He felt keen, sharp. Another breath. Oak. Old oak that had started growing before the town existed. There were other smells he recognized too: fox, a shy one who must have crossed this path only seconds before he came into sight; and squirrel, and damp ferns dripping into moldy leaves, some so deep in shadow that winter's frost was only inches below.

In the distance, wheels crunched through gravel, and engine noise rose above the murmuring forest. Romulus loped off the road and into the brush, around a great ball of roots from a fallen tree. He gripped two gnarled, woody wrists and peered out. A moment later a car roared by, radio blaring a steady rap thump. A snatch of laughter and a beer can clattered against a rock. Then dust.

He waited until the air cleared before stepping from behind the tangled dead fall. In the hills above, the car's rowdy passage rose and fell. Hands jammed deep into his pocket, he continued his walk, thoughtful, now that the car had gone. What if Fay wanted to be with the troll? There would be nothing to warn her about. This trek to Chaney Park could be seen as little more than stalking her. There wasn't much he could do anyway. Still, he pushed onward, leaning into the road's steepness, taking each hairpin turn with measured deliberateness. His legs buzzed pleasantly, and he felt as if he could go forever if he had to. With his eyes closed, he imagined trotting along through the forest, tireless, behind deer maybe, waiting for one to drop from exhaustion. He smiled at the image. Several more times he leapt into the covering woods as more cars drove by. He didn't see the troll's car.

Finally the road leveled, but the trees surrounded him thicker than ever, leaning over the road and blocking the stars. It wasn't until he reached a clearing and the forest opened before him that he realized he'd made the top. The moon sat on the horizon, a bloat egg, rich and ivory and huge again, as it had been on Sunday in his room, but now there was no window between him and it.

A full moon in the height of its glory. Romulus had never felt its light so intensely. A breeze swept through the tree tops and the oaks creaked. He looked around for a high place, then saw one, a jumbled pile of boulders that made a miniature mountain to his left. He ran to its base, his wavy, gray shadow flowing over grass and brush and branch. Up he clambered, hands down, like feet, fingernails clicking, leaping from rock to rock until he gained the summit. No forest blocking the moon now. He howled. Not self consciously, but a full-throated paean to the night sky. "Oh," he said afterwards, and he crouched so his hands took part of his weight. Was this the way it was for Dad? thought Romulus, or am I even closer to the past than he is? Could I actually *change*?

He felt the animal shape beneath his human one moving about. Then the sky darkened as a cloud crossed the moon's face. Romulus shook his head to clear it, and he looked about him for the first time. To the east there was no sign of the town, but he knew if he walked a little bit farther along the road, he'd be at Chaney Park, where the bluff offered a view of the entire valley.

A car's headlights cut through the trees below, and in a few seconds, the car itself passed, turned toward the park, and vanished into the forest, its taillights glimmering long after he'd stopped hearing it. The moon was a hand's-width above the horizon. How long had he been on the promontory? Moaning, he ran down the boulders, careless of injury, hit the road at top speed, and raced toward Chaney Park.

Three cars and a van rested on the picnic area's lined asphalt, noses pointed toward town, but none of them were the troll's convertible. Romulus crossed the back of the narrow lot in the tree's shadows. From one car a muffled conversation mixed with the wind. A sticker on the van's bumper proclaimed, "If we're rockin', don't come knockin'."

Past the parking lot the road turned to dirt again to wind up the hill. Every fifty feet or so a private picnic area opened on the left or right, complete with a split-log table and iron charcoal pit. The first one was empty; a rusted pickup occupied the second. Romulus stayed low, just off the path, walking in the soggy remains of last year's leaves, his nose telling him as much as his eyes. The breeze caressed his face. Other cars waited ahead; he could smell them, the still warm engines, their tires, cigarette smoke. Then he caught it, a distinct whiff of the troll. He growled. A girl's quivery voice in a car ten feet away said, "What was that?" Romulus crouched even lower in a run, his hands nearly touching the ground.

Then, ahead, clearly in the forest's silence, he heard Fay. "Don't!" she said. "I don't want . . ."

The road rose. At the crest he saw the final picnic spot in the clearing fifty yards below, the troll's car in the middle, top down, bathed in moonlight. He paused. Where was Fay? He could smell her perfume, and he smelled troll. Romulus spotted them in the back seat, the troll's dark letter jacket blending into the shadow; he was struggling, holding Fay down beneath him. Her hand rose above him, like a drowning person. Cloth ripped.

Romulus charged toward them, his lips pulled away from his teeth in a noiseless snarl, but everything suddenly felt underwater and syrupy. It took an hour for his foot to hit the ground and an hour for the next. Fay's hand froze in the air like a marble statue. Slowly, it seemed, so slowly, he came closer.

The troll laughed, the throbbing sound coming to Romulus almost too low to hear. More cloth ripped. A button, a fine pearl colored disk, flipped lazily into the air. Only ten yards away now, but every step seemed to cover less distance.

Then the air about the convertible changed. Even in his urgency, breath tearing through his throat, his teeth aching to bite something hard, Romulus slowed. The air changed, centering on Fay's hand. A circle of moonlight ten feet around slid toward her. It was as if the light wasn't light at all, but a thin coat of paint, funneling to her hand. For a moment it seemed as if the stars themselves swarmed, each touching her hand until it shone with potency, and her palm turned down. Her elbow crooked as if she were about to embrace the troll. Romulus stopped, nearly touching the car. Now he could see it all. The troll had pushed her back, trapped her legs with his own, pinned her with his weight, one arm stuck behind her, his lips pressed against the side of her face. Her eyes were closed, but not in fear—Romulus had time to study her—she was concentrating. The light flowed down her arm, filled her face. She glowed from within, like a porcelain nightlight. Then all the brightness emptied from her hand in a cascade of sparks, slamming into the back of the troll's head.

He stiffened.

Romulus stepped back, covering his eyes.

When he opened them, he had to blink away a black spot in the spark's shape to see Fay, now sitting up. She'd rolled the troll onto the car's floor, and her feet rested on his back.

"Dang," she said. "Just look at my blouse." She pulled the torn front together, then zipped her jacket.

She turned to Romulus and said in a voice no different than if she'd run into him in the mall, "What brings you to Chaney Park this time of night, Romulus?"

Her face still glowed, and something glimmered in the back of her eyes, very sharp and ancient. She combed her fingers through her hair. Romulus noticed her ears. They were distinctly pointed. He'd not seen that in her before.

"It seemed a good night for a walk," he said lamely. The troll snorted beneath her feet, then settled into a comfortable sounding snore. "What *are* you?" Romulus said.

She stood on the back seat, brushed her hands down her pants in short, brisk strokes.

"Fairy, I think. At least that's what my mother says. And you?" She jumped out of the car to land beside him.

Romulus tried to answer, but all his words had been sucked out of him. He attempted to speak a couple of times, but nothing came out.

Understanding came into her eyes. "It's the moon thing, isn't it?" She looked into the sky. "That's why you couldn't go to prom. Oh, I should have figured it out earlier. But I still don't know why you're here tonight."

Finally Romulus said, "I couldn't sleep." His voice rose at the end, as if it were a question.

Fay glanced at the troll, then back at him. She shook her head. "You're sweet, Romulus." She looked thoughtfully into the car for a moment, then pulled the keys out of the ignition and threw them into the forest. "Would you like to walk me home? I think I've lost my ride."

Romulus nodded dumbly, so happy that if he had a tail to wag, he would wag it a thousand miles an hour.

They started toward town, leaving the sleeping troll and his car behind.

Romulus took a deep, deep breath of night air. He could smell everything, all of it, leaf, branch and tree.

Fay cleared her throat. "You're not going to try to bite me, are you?" She sounded only half-joking.

Romulus let the air out in a relieved rush. "Oh, no! Not you."

"Good," she said. "That would make it tough for us to date." She moved next to him.

They walked down the winding dirt road, hands not touching, but very close, both so full of moonish power they thought they'd burst.

# THE SATURN RING BLUES

O ld Jelly Roll Morton's soulful voice fills the buglighter's cabin.
Nothing more mournful and perfect than a good, solid dose of
the blues while you're waiting at the edge of the ring for the start of
the race. That and the cloud-striped surface of Saturn turning below, the dusky-edged ridge of the rings above, catching a little of
the reflected light, and between them both the sharp-eyed light of
the stars. Lots of sad stringed guitar and bent-note blues harp, and
his whiskey voice down deep. It's a pool hall voice.

I met Elinor in a pool hall. She had an attractive way of blowing
chalk dust off her knuckles that caught my eye. We racked up
games till the bar closed. Only thing I can beat her at. I see the
angles clear. "You got those angle eyes," she said.

It's true. I even like my hull transparent. Most of the equipment's
behind, all that stuff that shapes the forces around the buglighter,
keeping me safe from danger, and, when the need arises, pushing
me where I want to go. So with the hull clear, I'm sitting alone and
pretty in the stars. That's the way I feel, just like those blues songs
tell me: "Lordy, I'm all by myself since my baby done left me."

Lots of buglighters can't do it—perch in the clear like I do—too
much space around them. It's hard on the heart. Elinor said to me,
"Virgil, you're too much of a sit down and look around kind of guy."
She would know, I guess. Of course I wasn't paying attention at the
time; we were playing pool and I said, "Shh. I'm concentrating."

The starter's voice interrupts the music: "Flyers, welcome to
the 17th annual Greater Circumference of Saturn Ring Runners
Challenge, 2,500 Kgram class. Five minutes to race time."

A hundred meters around, dust motes spark off the bubble that
contains me. Zap, zap . . . there go a couple more. That's where we
get the name, buglighter, little bits of ice and rock, zappin' like fire-

crackers in the forces surrounding us. In five minutes the race will start, and I'll adjust the bubble. Instead of flicking that ring sand away, it'll suck it in, transform it in an instant, and shape the pulse into comforting thrust, rolling me around the inside of the ring on fission fire in my perfect sphere of protecting energy, sort of like a transparent cue ball bounding off the bumpers of the ring. From the start, all the way around again, about 578,000 Kmeters, or roughly 15 times the circumference of the Earth.

Over my shoulder, Elinor's buglighter is all aglow. She's a hot one, her. She likes to start these races fast, so she's storing energy in the field. She's always got a plan. Plan ahead, that's her. She didn't see me in her future, I guess. Cut me loose clean. She likes to fly light.

"Gotcha on my backside, Elinor G.," I say on a private channel, figuring that it won't hurt to assay some warmth in her direction.

"Cut the chatter, Delta Mud," she says. That's my ship, not me. Feel that way most the time though, just as low down as can be. So I turn up the music. Little bit of Brownie McGhee and Sonny Terry, "Blues from the Lowlands." I got 'em too. Got 'em bad. Don't know why you're sayin' no to me, Elinor G.

Nothing to do then except study the course ahead, sending out some high-imaging radar. It shows me what to miss—klunking into a chunk of ring matter bigger than a football or so at 50,000 kph would put a dent in my day, and, of course, it'll send that rock flying like a cannonball in the opposite direction—but, it doesn't show me where to go: the rich sand and pebbles I can eat up and convert to thrust. That's the art and joy of ring running: dodging the big ones; following the fuel, shooting fast around the ring without spinning out. My first two chords are clear, but after that, I'll be checking as I go: thousands of kph, glimpsing ahead for widow-makers on the high wire edge of the ring. It's only a kilometer wide, generally, at least only a kilometer of usable rock.

Ring racing is in the chords' progression and rhythm—like the blues—cutting across the arc of the orbit's circle. The way I fly, the shorter the chords, the faster the ship. Look and blast, look and blast. Can't look while you're blasting (too much interference); can't blast without looking (otherwise you'd be sure to fetch up against some pocky chunk of rock, big as a barn and your race would be over forever). It's a funny looking race, if you diagram it. Put two circles on a piece of paper, one inside the other, and the outside one not too much bigger than the inner. That inside circle is Saturn. The outside one is the inner edge of the ring. Now, take a ruler and draw a straight line that connects two points of the outer circle without crossing the inner circle. That's one chord. If you keep drawing chords, you end up with a polygon that goes around the planet. That's the race.

My angle of entry into the rings is shallow, and most of the bigger rocks are deeper in, so I minimize risk while maximizing speed. Elinor, though, she takes these long chords, building up speed on each one; each one dives her deeper into the ring. It's scary genius at work to watch her fly.

So I keep the chords short to play those high speed blues. I take out my c-harp and blow a few chords of my own—still nothing better than a Marine Band harmonica. Well engineered instrument, the harmonica: light, compact, fits in the hand, feels cool on the lips. Good acoustics in a buglighter too. Echoes back in nice and tight, like singing in a shower. I try out a new line for my Elinor Blues. "Elinor, Elinor, you don't be coming round anymore." A common blue's pattern is statement, repeat and a variation. Got the statement and repeat down pat, but don't know a variation yet. I try one out. Five minutes is a long time for a race to start.

"Elinor, Elinor, you don't be coming round anymore.
Elinor, Elinor, you don't be coming round anymore.
Been five long years, baby. Waitin's been such a chore."

Can't think of her as "baby." She's all hard muscle and physic's-brain bright. Give her enough numbers and just enough fuel, and she could with one solid blow, dead-stick the rest of the way a course from the moon, Rhe, to Titan and not miss her orbit slot by a couple of meters. But every guy singing the blues calls his baby, baby.

The signal starts the race. Elinor and a couple others blast on the dot, brightness enveloping their buglighters, glowing like acetylene teardrops. My ship gathers in sand, sucks in a larger pebble or two, most of the mass converted into energy. Screen shows I've got a clear shot deeper into the ring. Greater chance of crashing into something, but the usable detritus is thicker. Let it go all at once. The good, solid thump of the nuclear explosion behind me pushes me into my seat. Thank god for inertia dampers, otherwise I'd be a thin jelly on the back wall of the cabin.

Right off, rocks start clattering against the bubble, lost in bright sparks. I've gained speed, moved up in the orbit, further into the dust.

We run the race on the inner edge of the "B" ring, the bright one you can even see from Earth with a reasonable telescope. The "C" ring below is much thinner. Hard to guarantee you'll find rock to blast with when you need it. The "A" ring is farther out; it's got that cool gap in it where the moon, Pan, orbits.

In my monitor, I see Elinor's ship. She's taken a long chord as her first jump, crossing all that mostly empty space. It's a shorter distance to go around, as I mentioned, but a riskier tactic.

"You like a brief life, Elinor?" I say.

"Brief and bright," she says.

I do some quick calculations and whistle in appreciation. She'll dive into the ring for a couple of hundred Kmeters before she'll have the energy for her next blast. Her radar can't penetrate that deep. Too much intervening sand.

"Going for the record?"

"Already got it," she says.

And she does; won last year, and I pulled up a lame second.

Time for the next blast. Race like this is an art. Sort of a mix between orbital mechanics, demolition derby and pool; the whole thing done with your heart gripped firmly between your teeth so you don't lose it.

"Going slow there, Delta Mud," she says, but I can't answer before I slam through the burn. Bubbles go white and glorious as they store up the energy, then release it all at once. Can't hear it, naturally, though my music gets fuzzy during; way too much radiant activity to avoid that, and the inertia dampers don't completely mask the thrust of it. My seat presses hard into my back. I feel every wrinkle in my shirt.

Monitors are clear. Nothing in my way, so I set up for the next chord.

"Eaten any cold dinners lately?" I say.

"No," she says. "Have you?"

I let that question hang out there a while. It's a friendly response, if I hear it right, and probably because she's got an early lead. Use to be I'd go visit her for dinner pretty regular, and we never did get right to eating it. One thing lead to another, you know, and the dinner would cool off.

So an answer takes a bit of thinking. Is she opening the door here? Are all those cold, cold nights looking out at lonely stars about to come to an end?

I wish I could see her. You know, to watch her face. She's got this way of letting the corners of her mouth twitch up when she's making a joke. It's real subtle. Lots of folk don't notice. And she shakes her head sometimes, like she's getting hair out of her eyes, though her hair is spacer-short.

How's she looking now? What I need is a deep-imaging radar of the heart. Something to peer in there to check on those pocky rocks drifting unseen.

She's about to end a chord, so I check her progress.

Ring racing is the hardest kind there is. *Straight* races . . . well, they're simple. Thrust behind mass, and don't miss. Best technology wins. Pilot might as well stay home (singing the blues). But here—whew! Faster you go, the more dangerous it is. More chances for mistakes. Less time for decisions. All the time risking spinout, missing the ring, flying off with better than escape velocity and no mass anywhere to grab.

She's in the ring now. Gathering energy. Blasting. Her trajectory changes, and she's shooting back out the ring to the relatively clear space beneath.

I've got some time. She'll be checking the path ahead, figuring her next burn.

I make sure the transmitter is off, blow the harmonica some more—make the harp sing:

Elinor, Elinor, saw you walking in the stars.
Elinor, Elinor, saw you walking in the stars.
Venus at your toe tips; your fingers touching Mars.

She said, "I think I can cut four chords off last year."

I shake my head. "You'll be sucking Saturn's atmosphere. Not worth the speed you lose."

She chuckles. "For you, maybe. Have you checked the competition?"

I hadn't bothered. She's the only other ship I care about, but I tapped the display and the others popped onto the grid, way behind.

"Looks like it's just you and me."

"And the record," she adds. "How's it feel to be the second

best flyer in the rings?" She's laughing. Pure speed does that to her.

"When you're beat by the best," I say, "Who cares about the rest?"

"That's sweet, Virgil."

I'm into my next burn. Speed's up, so the bubble fairly crackles, sending dust and tiny rocks in all directions and storing energy. I let it go, and the chair kicks into my back, snapping my head into the support. Inertia dampers are good, but most ships let their thrust out more gradual because they carry mass to convert to energy with them. Buglighters don't carry anything but some maneuvering fuel.

All the rest is gathered in, then, wham, released in a hurry.

A few chords later, speed's way up, and my work's harder. Soon as the interference clears, I check the radar for rocks, plug in the new numbers, and let the computer go to work with trajectories and mid-course corrections. While it crunches numbers, I've got nothing to do but think.

Blues are perfect for space, and I'll bet if B.B. King or Howlin' Wolf or Muddy Waters were alive today, they'd be buglighters. All that other music, well, it has beginnings and ends, but not the blues. You can take any song and run it for hours with variations, letting it build or slide down low. It's back porch music, smokey pool hall music, buglighter music. You can tell when you're in a spacer bar by the music. It's all guitars and bass and c-harp bent all over those blue's notes. Every tune's despairing, but kind of funny too, sort of like cruising in the rings. Part of it's deadly serious, and then you have to laugh. Blues and buglighting and my love for Elinor are just too ironic to keep a straight face.

See, when you're singing the blues, you start off all sad and lonely, but after a while, you're into the music. You forget why you started the song, and you're just doing the song. And buglighting, you forget why you started or where you're going, and you're just flying the chords. There's music in them. Music in the light and the rhythm. Music in the rainbow of colors when the distant sun catches the rings just right. Music in the shadows and darkness behind Saturn. It's the blues, man; everyone knows it's the blues.

We go like this for awhile. I blast three times for every two of Elinor's. It's kind of sobering watching her eat up the distance. She's got so much speed, and it's building. I'm going about as fast as I feel I can go. My burns now just get me into the new chord; they don't add much velocity.

But that's the way it's always been. Old Elinor is always a jump or two ahead of me.

"Doesn't look like you're going to give me a race this year, Virgil."

"It's a long way around," I say.

"I'll have a drink set up for you when you get in," she says.

I'm a ways from my next turn, so I switch to her monitors so I can see what she sees. It's scary. Her angle of attack is high. She can only see a third of the distance into the ring that she penetrates. "Assuming you make it," I say.

Her screen is graying out as she enters the ring. A couple of big rocks glow off her path; they're no danger, but I've never seen stuff that big moving by so fast. She's busy, so I don't say anything and switch back to my own monitor. She fades out as she gets deeper. I won't see her till she exits, and I check my own course again. Looks like clear sailing to me.

"Uh, oh," she says.

I shouldn't be able to hear her yet. I check the screen. She's there, going the wrong direction, outside of the ring. A spinout.

"You all right?" I ask. Silly question, really. If she wasn't, I wouldn't have heard anything at all. She wouldn't be on the monitor.

"Shoot," she says.

I'm running her numbers through the computer. She's got way too much speed, and she's moving away from the ring. My calculations show she can't push herself back to it either.

"What happened?"

"Hit something," she says.

"How's your system?" I check the emergency bands. She's already sent a "come-hither" to the outer stations. I send one too. "Smells bad in here," she says, and she chuckles. "I think I burnt some stuff out. Nothing vital. Heck of a shot. Must have been a good sized chunk."

"Great race while it lasted," I say.

"Yeah," she sounds preoccupied. I roll through my next burn. Our courses are fairly close now, but I'm inside the ring trailing her, and she's outside the ring, rising fast, way faster than me.

"Have you run the intercepts?" she says.

I hadn't, so I plug in the numbers. They don't look good, and I do them again.

I whistle.

"Yeah," she says. "I don't think anyone can come get me in time."

"Your bubble still sound?" I say. My fingers are dancing over the computer keys, inputting data, asking for alternative scenarios. What happens if she uses her maneuvering fuel to slow down? What happens if she tries to push herself back into the ring? None of them look good.

"Yeah." She sounds sad. I'm not sure if it's because her chances are dim or because she's out of the race.

I switch out of our private channel. Titan station is chattering away to miners on Pan to see if they can raise a ship in time, but they aren't geared for quick takeoffs, and the moon is in the worst place right now for them to mount a rescue. They can get to her, but it would be hours too late. If she'd been going a reasonable speed, no problem, but she's got way too much velocity. Without a steady supply of fissionable mass, her buglighter will shut down and she'll freeze solid. Buglighters aren't built for empty space. They're ring-runners.

The other racers are talking too. Somebody says he'll chase her, which is plain stupid because he'd never catch her, and even if he did, what good would it do? He couldn't bring her on board. He couldn't bring mass out to her.

"I'm going to try braking," she says. "It'll slow me up, and maybe someone on the outer rings can catch me."

"No, don't," I say. "Not yet. Save the fuel."

My imaging radar shows me the ring ahead, mostly fuzz since it's pebbles and sand with a few bright spots that represent bigger rocks. I'm looking for the right sized rock on the edge of the ring. Idea's forming. Nothing looks good, though, so I kick through the next burn and start scanning as soon as I'm clear.

"What do you have in mind?" she says.

"Shh. I'm concentrating." I'm thinking about angles, mass, velocity and risk, so I'm not paying much attention to conversation.

Rock can't be too big. It'd kill my ship, and I couldn't give it the speed it'd need to catch her. Can't be too small either. The impact would turn it to dust, and it wouldn't give her enough energy if any of it did reach her buglighter. And the whole idea is a little wacky anyway. The odds of making the shot are incredible. Quite a bit worse than running two bumpers to sink the eight ball in the corner pocket.

On the monitor, a likely candidate pops up. It's on Elinor's edge of the ring. Not too deep. Chances are I can line up on it, not be deflected on the way in, and it won't be deflected on the way out. Hitting right, though, that's the problem. If I miss by even a fraction of an inch, the rock could spew away at a useless angle; Elinor will be in the same fix, and my buglighter will be too busted up for a second shot.

Once the problem's in the computer, it controls my maneuvering jets. I'm running the radar on tight scan now, checking the rock, trying to get more info on it, and the numbers are coming back good.

"What are you doing?" Elinor asks. I know she can see my buglighter on her monitors. She can do the same trick I did earlier and have her monitors display what I'm seeing.

I don't say anything. Not much I can do at this point anyway, but I'm running a second set of calculations, just as an exercise really, since I'm committed to the collision at this point. Thought it would be interesting to do the math though, to see how much energy my bubble will have to take. The figures come back. They're somewhat above what the specs say the ship will handle. Specs are conservative, I hope.

"Veer off," she says. "Virgil, this won't work."

I check my straps and buckles. Inertia damper is going to get a workout here. "Set your bubble up and get your maneuvering jets ready," I say. "Don't know how close I can get this to you. You might have to chase it." I rotate the buglighter so I'll take the force from behind.

Ship's counting down for me: 10 seconds to impact . . . 9 . . . 8 . . . I turn up the music, a little George Thorogood tune, "Bad to the Bone."

5 . . . 4 . . . 3

Sunlight's glistening off the inner edge of the ring flashing past. Gets a man thinking.

When I wake up, it's silent and dark. My neck hurts. Left elbow is locked up. I touch it gingerly. Shirt's torn there, and it's damp. Don't know what might have hit it. But I've got breathing air, and it's not cold. Pebbles are zapping at the bubble boundary, so more's good than bad here. I'll have to thank the designers of the buglighter for the slop built into their tolerance specs.

Computer doesn't answer to voice controls, but when I flip the auxiliaries on, the monitors glow again and start spewing out a list of damages. Radar won't come up, though, and neither will the radio. Some whiffs of fried circuitry float in the air, so I shut down the main routines and go to the backups.

After a few minutes, the radio crackles and I hear Elinor. "Virgil," she says. "Can you hear me, Virgil." She sounds like she's crying. Radar's still blank. Can't tell if I helped her or not.

"I'm here," I say.

Nothing over the radio for a bit. I'm scrambling to get the radar online. Can't tell how fast I'm going or if anything nasty is in front of me.

"You're a hell of a pool player," she says, finally, and I don't hear any crying in her voice now. "I didn't have to use but about half my fuel to intercept the rock."

"Luck," I say.

She snorts. "It was coming pretty darn fast too. But I got enough of it to make a good burn. I'll be back in the ring in plenty of time."

"You're the master in the ring," I say. Radar starts working, and I do a quick scan. Lost lots of velocity. No ship-killers on the screen though. A mini-burn keeps me in the mass field. Don't need a spinout of my own to cause problems.

"Looks like we're both out of the race."

"Could be worse, Elinor." I laugh. My elbow aches, and I unbuckle myself so I can get to the first-aid station.

"I owe you big time," she says.

"You'd have done it for me." The first-aid diagnostic gives me a once over, suggests a pain medication and alerts the Inner A Station that I'm injured.

"Might have tried," she says. "Couldn't have done it."

"Well, I was motivated."

I ease myself back into the chair, swallow the pain meds and set a nice, slow, easy course back to the station, letting the computer do all the work.

"I've been thinking about that," she says. There's a long pause here. "Maybe we should get together and talk about it some. You know, you could drop over for dinner or something."

I smile. It's been a long time coming. Nights have stretched, and I've played a lot of harmonica in the meantime. Around my ship, little blue glitters of rock and ice catch the reflected light off Saturn. I should be home in a few hours. It'll take her considerably longer.

"I'll think about it," I say, and switch my radio off.

Nothing's more quiet than the silence in a buglighter when your heart is in a turmoil and you're not sure if the one you want wants you. I've charted that course before.

The harmonica fits easily into my hand. A tap or two against my leg clears it out, and I try a few notes. They sound good. They always do.

I know how I'll answer. She probably knows it too. But in the meantime, let *her* sing a little of those Saturn Ring Blues.

# HOW MUSIC BEGINS

Hands raised, ready for the downbeat, Cowdrey brought the band to attention. He took a good inhalation for them to see, thinking, "The band that breathes together, plays together." Players watched over their music stands as he tapped out a barely perceptible four beats, then, he dropped into the opening notes of "The King's Feast," a simple piece a 9th grade band might play at the season's first concert, but Elise Morgan, his best student, had composed variations for flutes and clarinets, added an oboe solo, and changed the arrangement for the cornets and trombones, so now new tonal qualities arose. Her neatly handwritten revisions crowded his score, a black and white representation of the opening chords, the musical lines blending effortlessly. Everyone on beat. Everyone on tune. At the state competition, they would sweep the awards, but this wasn't state, and they weren't really a junior high band anymore.

Eyes closed, he counted through the bars. "The King's Feast" recreated a night at Henry VIII's court. Suitably serious. A heavy drum background carrying the load. Not quite a march, but upbeat in a dignified way. Someone in the French horn section sounded a bit pitchy. Was it Thomas? Cowdrey cocked his head to isolate it, but the individual sound faded, lost in the transition to the second movement.

He lived for this moment, when the sections threaded together, when the percussion didn't overwhelm or the brass blow out the woodwinds. He smiled as he directed them through the tricky exit from the solo. His eyes open now, their eyes on him, young faces, raggedy-cut hair, shirts and blouses too small, everyone's pants inches short above their bare feet, he led them to the conclusion, slowing the saxophones down—they wanted to rush to the end—then he brought the flutes up.

Rhythm and harmony tumbled over the pomp and circumstance in Henry's court. The ladies' elegant dress. The courtiers waiting in the wings. The king himself, presiding from the throne, all painted in music. Cowdrey imagined brocade, heavy skirts, royal colors, swirling in the dance.

The last notes trembled, and he held them in hand, not letting them end until his fist's final clasp cut them off. He was the director.

Aching silence. Someone in the drum section coughed. Cowdrey waited for the lights to flicker. They had flickered after the band's first performance here, and they'd flickered again after a near perfect "Prelude and Fugue in B Flat" six months ago. Tonight though, the lights stayed steady. Behind the band, the long curved wall and the window that circled the room holding back the brown smoke on the other side were the only audience. "The King's Feast" concluded the night's performance. Cowdrey signaled the players to their feet. Instruments clanked. Sheet music rustled. He turned from the band to face the other side's enigmatic window and impenetrable haze. Playing here was like playing within a fish bowl, and not just the shape either. He bowed, and the band bowed behind him. Whatever watched, if anything, remained hidden in the roiling cloud.

"Good performance, Cougars. Leave your music on the stands for the section leaders to pick up, then you may go to dinner. Don't forget, breathing practice before breakfast with your ensembles."

Chatting, the kids headed toward the storage lockers to replace their instruments.

A clarinet player waved as she left the room. "Good night, Mr. Cowdrey."

He nodded in her direction.

"'Night, sir," said a percussionist. "See you in the morning. Good performance."

The room cleared until Elise Morgan remained, jotting post-concert notes on her clipboard. Her straight black hair reached the bottom of her ears, and her glasses, missing one ear piece, sat crookedly on her nose. As always, dark smudges sagged under her eyes. She slept little. More often than not, late at night, she'd still be working on the music. "One of the French horns came in late again. I think it's Thomas. He's waiting until the trombones start, and it throws him a half beat off."

"I didn't notice." Cowdrey sat beside her. The light metal chair creaked under his weight. Several chairs had broken in the last few months. Just two spares remained. He wondered what would happen when players had to stand for their performances. "The band sounded smooth tonight. Very confident."

Elise nodded toward the window. "They're tuning the room. Maybe they're getting it ready for Friday's concert."

Cowdrey raised his eyebrows.

Elise pointed to the domed ceiling. "See there and there. New baffles. We've lost the echo-chamber effect you mentioned last week, and check out my flute." She handed it to him. "At first, they just repadded them. Normal maintenance, but they've done other stuff too. It's a better instrument."

He held the flute, then tried a few fingerings. The keys sank smoothly. No stickiness, and the flute weighed heavy.

"Play a note," she said.

He brought the instrument to his lip, but even before he blew, he knew it was extraordinary.

"During the sixth grade, after I won state solos the second time, my parents took me to the New York Philharmonic. I met their first chair, and he let me play his flute. Custom made. Insured for $50,000." She took the instrument back from Cowdrey and rested it on her lap. "It wasn't as good as this one is now. Maybe the Perfectionists are right."

Cowdrey frowned. Misguided students with wacky theories about how they could get home shouldn't be taken seriously.

"How's that?" Cowdrey shook the irritation from his head. He thought he would check the lockers after he finished with Elise. Were the other instruments being upgraded too?

"Maybe what they want is a perfect performance, then they'll let us go. Maybe Friday will be it." She looked up at the nearest window. A brown smokey wave swirled behind it, cutting sight to no more than a yard or so beyond the glass.

Cowdrey felt fatherly. She sounded so wistful when she said, "they'll let us go." He almost reached out to touch her arm, to offer comfort, but he held himself still. No sense in sending mixed signals. "I don't know why we're here. No one knows. They shouldn't get their hopes up. After all, what's a perfect performance?"

"Any sunset is perfect. Any pebble is perfect." She scuffed her bare foot on the immaculate floor. "Weeds are perfect, and so is a parking lot at the mall when the cars are gone and you can ride your bike in all directions without hitting anything." She sighed. "And open meadows where the grass is never cut."

Cowdrey nodded, not sure how to respond. She often reminisced about meadows.

Elise closed her eyes dreamily. "I found a pebble in my band jacket. Sometimes I hold it and think about playgrounds."

"Really?"

She looked up at him, then dug into her pocket. On her open palm, a bit of shiny feldspar the size of a pencil eraser caught the ceiling light. As quick as it came out, it vanished back in her pocket. She made another note on her clipboard. "The Perfectionists are getting pretty fanatical. Others heard Thomas come in late."

"The band will maintain discipline. If anyone has a problem, they'll talk to me. That's why I'm here."

Elise looked uncomfortable. "Are you sure? With Ms. Rhodes gone . . ."

Cowdrey glanced away from her to the empty chairs and music stands. "Ms. Rhodes will be missed, but the band can continue without an assistant director."

"I'm just saying . . . it's a lot for a single adult to handle."

He composed his face to meet her eyes. "The less we think of Ms. Rhodes, the better."

Elise shrugged. "If you want it that way."

"We have the section leaders. They have taken the responsibility." He smiled. "Half the time I think the band doesn't even need me. You all have become such strong musicians."

She wrote a last comment on her clipboard, then slipped it under her arm. "Not strong enough. Nowhere near. Today is Monday. If we don't clean things up by Friday, the Perfectionists could get scary."

"It's late." Without the rest of the band in the room, his voice sounded too loud and harsh. Truly, he could hear a pin drop with these acoustics. "I'll see you tomorrow, Elise."

"Have you thought any more about the wedding?"

"No. We're not discussing it."

Her lips pursed, as if she wanted to say something, but she put her finger to the bridge of her glasses to hold them in place, then stood. "I'll direct breathing practice for the woodwinds in the morning, if you'll take the brass. At least I can help that much."

Cowdrey nodded. In the beginning, after the first week's chaos settled down, Ms. Rhodes had led the woodwinds through their exercises. Rhodes, a somber thirty-year-old who wore padded-shoulder jackets and seldom smiled, would meet Cowdrey outside the practice rooms. He'd hand her the routine he'd written up the night before. She'd study it briefly, then follow the players. In the last few months, she'd spoken about band-related issues, but nothing else. Conversation stopped. He didn't know how to broach another subject. The last time he'd tried, he had said, "How are you holding up?" She'd looked about like a wild bird for a second, as if she heard something frightful, but her face smoothed over and she said, "To improve rhythms, hone intonation, and create dynamic phrasing, we must improve breathing. All music begins with a good breath." Red circled her exhausted eyes.

Lockers lined the hallway outside the performance hall. A cornet rested in its shaped space in the first one. Cowdrey took it out. It, too, had been improved. No longer an inexpensive junior high band instrument, the keys sank with ease; the horn glowed under the hallway's indirect lighting, the metal as warm as flesh beneath his fingers.

He returned the horn to its place before closing the door. Thoughtfully, he walked to the T-intersection. To his left, the student's rooms, their doors shut. To his right, the practice rooms, the cafeteria, and his own room. He trailed his knuckle against the wall, but as he turned to enter he noticed Ms. Rhodes's door across the hall was gone as if it had never existed in the unmarked wall. When did that happen? he thought.

As always, dinner and a water bottle waited in a box on his bed. For weeks after the band had arrived, the students had tried to catch the deliveries, but they never did. If students stayed in the room, the meals wouldn't come, so if they wanted to eat, they had to leave to practice or to perform.

Passable bread. Something that looked like bologna in the middle, but it tasted more like cheese. He washed it down with a couple of swallows. Only the water from the bottles was potable. The stuff from the showers smelled like vinegar and tasted bitter. He wondered about the pets he'd kept as a child, a lizard and two hamsters. Did the food ever taste right to them? Had he ever fed them what they needed or wanted? He rested the sandwich on his lap. Later, he looked down. His fingers had sunk into the bread, and the edges had grown crispy. He glanced at his watch. An hour had passed.

Room check! He walked the long hall past the kids' doors. At first he'd insisted on making sure the right students went to the right rooms, as if they were on an overnight for weekend competition, as if they stayed at a Holiday Inn, but so often he woke kids who had already gone to sleep that now he just listened at each door. Were they quiet or crying? The first week there had been a lot of crying, and they had come close to not making it. Being a band saved them.

That week was his toughest trial. Fright. Fighting. Despair. To end it, he took the only step he knew: he called for a practice, and they became a band again.

Cowdrey trod softly from door to door, pausing, listening, and moving on.

He stopped for an extra long time outside Taylor Beau's room. Was Liz Waters in there with him? Were they in Liz's room? Cowdrey rested his hand on the doorknob. No way they could be serious about a marriage. They were children, junior high students, not adults; under astonishing circumstances, to be sure, but band standards and school regulations glued them together. For all his years as director, Cowdrey lived by one rule: would he be comfortable with the band's activities if parents or school board members watched? This marriage talk did not fit.

No sound beyond the closed door. His hand tightened on the knob; he didn't turn it. Did he want to know?

Next he paused outside Elise's door. She wouldn't be asleep. She'd be looking over the day's notes, rewriting. Cowdrey shivered thinking about her brilliance. What must it have been like for Mozart's father when a three-year-old Amadeus picked out thirds and sixths on the harpsichord, when the father realized the son had surpassed him and would continue to grow beyond his comprehension and hope? But did Mozart eat and breathe music like Elise? Did he ever believe that music would take him home? Cowdrey didn't think so. Maybe at the end of Mozart's life, when the brain fevers wracked him, and he could feel death's hand on his neck. Maybe then he wrote with equal intensity.

Not many teachers ever had the chance to work with an Elise. If they did, they prayed they wouldn't ruin her vision, that they wouldn't poison her ear.

When he reached the hall's end, he turned and repeated the process back to his door. At first, he and Ms. Rhodes had done the room check together, then stood guard in the hall until the children quieted. After a few weeks, they had traded nights. Now, he patrolled alone. Perhaps Elise was right. Maybe it was too much for him to handle.

He sighed. The silent hall stretched before him. He felt his pulse in his arm where he leaned against the wall. Soon, his chin headed for his chest. Cowdrey jerked himself awake, walked the hallway's length two more times before admitting he had to go to bed. In wakefulness' last few seconds, head resting on the pillow, he imagined he heard doors opening, the stealthy pad of bare feet, and the hush of doors gently closing on clandestine liaisons. Could Taylor and Liz be a single case, or had he lost control? A tear crept down his cheek as consciousness flitted away.

In the morning, Elise met him in the hallway. "Here are the variations I told you about for the Beatles medley. Mostly I need the saxophones' sheets, but I also syncopated the drums for 'Eleanor Rigby,' and reworked the trombone bridge into 'Yellow Submarine,' so I'll need their music too."

Cowdrey nodded as he took the scores. "Did you sleep?"

Elise made a checkmark on her clipboard. She moved to her next item. "I thought if we told the sections to treat their breathing exercises this morning like they were all preparing for a solo, we might get better sound from them. Remember, you told us once we should breathe from the diaphragm, and if we missed it, to miss big. I think about that a lot." She smiled, made another check, then frowned. "Also, you need to drop in on Thomas. I heard a rumor." Her pencil scratched paper firmly. "Look, Mr. Cowdrey, the band is on edge. All they think about is music and getting out. To some, Thomas is a handicap. They need something else. A distraction." She made another check on her list, then, without waiting for an answer, snapped the clipboard under her arm, before striding toward the practice rooms, a girl on a mission.

"Good morning to you, too, Elise."

Soon the hallway filled with sleepy kids. Cowdrey greeted them each in turn as they passed. Most smiled. He glanced at their eyes. The red-rimmed ones would be a worry, but they had been fewer and fewer as the weeks since their arrival turned into months. At first there had been nightmares, a reliving of the night they'd been taken. He'd had a few himself: the bus's wheels humming through the night, *Junior High Band Management* open on his lap, and

then the growing brightness out the bus windows, the high screech
that seemed to emanate in the middle of his head before the short
soft shock of waking on the fishbowl auditorium's floor with their
equipment and everything else from the bus scattered about. (No
bus driver, though!) Those dreams had tapered off through the
months. He thought, kids are resilient. If they have a structure, that
is.

Thomas came by last. A short boy who played in the band because his parents told him it would look good on a college applica-
tion, he'd never been an inspired musician, but he was competent
enough. Thomas kept his head down as he passed. "Good morning," he mumbled.

"Can I speak to you a moment?" Cowdrey moved away from
the wall to block his path.

"Sir." The boy didn't meet Cowdrey's gaze, but even his head
held low couldn't hide the bruise that glowered on his cheek.

"How'd that happen?"

Thomas glanced up, frightened for an instant, then his expression went bland and unassuming. "I fell in the shower. Slipped."

The instruments tuning up in the practice rooms filled the silence between them.

Finally, Thomas said, "Look, I want to get away from here as
much as the next person. If playing on pitch, on tune and to the beat
is what it's going to take, then I'll do that."

Cowdrey heard the Perfectionists echo in Thomas's speech.
"There is no such thing as a perfect performance, Thomas." He
thought about Elise's perfect pebble. Perfect because there were
no pebbles here, nor weeds or malls or bicycles. No families. Nothing but each other and that day's playing.

Thomas shrugged. "Yeah, well maybe not, but I can be better.
I don't want it to be my fault the lights don't flicker."

"We don't even know what that means, son. Flickering lights
may not be their applause."

The boy's eyes revealed nothing, and for a moment he didn't
appear seventeen at all. He looked adult and tired and cursed with
a terrible burden.

"Thomas, if someone is threatening you or hurting you, I need
to know about it. That's my job. You don't have to play solo."

Thomas studied the hallway beyond Cowdrey's shoulder. A few
steps past them, the hallway branched to the auditorium with its

enigmatic windows. "My mom told me once that the world is a big place, and I could become anything I wanted to, but it's not. It's no bigger than the people you know and the places you go. It's a small world here, Mr. Cowdrey, and I don't have any place to hide in it, so I'm going to go the practice room to see if I can't get my act together a little better." He pushed past the director.

The director threw himself into the morning's work. Teaching is time management, he thought, and staying on task. He moved from student to student, checking intonation and technique. "It's not all about the notes," he said to a clarinet player. "Once you know the music, it's about feeling the sound from your own instrument and your section. The song becomes more about heart than head." The player nodded and replayed the piece.

For a time, mid-morning, Cowdrey sat in the practice room with the brass section. The leaders paced the group through their pieces, focusing on problems from yesterday's session. Each had Elise Morgan's suggestions to consult. Cowdrey watched Taylor Beau and Liz Waters, the numbers three and four chairs among the cornets. The couple wore matching silver crosses on chains around their necks. He wondered if they had given them to each other. Liz kept her red hair in a pony tail, and when she finished a long run of notes, her skin flushed, chasing her freckles to the surface. Taylor often played with his eyes closed, the music consigned to memory well before the other players. Although he wasn't first chair, the section elected him for solos frequently, which he played with light-hearted enthusiasm. The director thought about Elise's question on the marriage, and he remembered the duet Taylor and Liz worked up for the state competition. They played "Ode to Joy," and when they finished, they hugged. Now that he thought about it, he should have seen the budding relationship in the hug. You can't rehearse so often with the same person that you don't start having feelings about how they play. The breathing. The fingerings. The careful attention to each other's rhythm and tone. Harmonizing. Cowdrey shivered, thinking about music's sensuous nature.

The trombone section leader gave instruction. Cowdrey half listened while thinking about his first year in college, when he'd added the teaching certification program to his music major. Just for something to fall back on, he'd thought at the time. But when graduation came around, he'd found he liked teaching as much as he liked music, so moving into the schools didn't feel like settling for less.

The kids in the room laughed, breaking Cowdrey from his reverie. The section leader was part way through an old band joke that Cowdrey couldn't remember the punchline for. The leader said, "So she dated a tuba player next, and her girlfriend asks how the date went. She says his embouchure was big and sloppy. It was like kissing a jellyfish." Most laughed, even the tuba player. "So, she says she went out with a French horn player next. How'd the date go? asks her friend, and the girl says he barely could kiss at all, his lips were so close together, but she liked the way he held her." A couple kids reacted right away, and ten seconds later, almost all laughed. Some looked embarrassed. "I hope that wasn't inappropriate, Mr. Cowdrey," said the section leader.

Cowdrey smiled. "Maybe you could go through those opening notes again. If you don't come in crisply, the back half flounders." He noticed Taylor and Liz held hands. Thomas, however, wasn't laughing. He clutched his horn close to his chest, his arms crossed over it like a shield. No one seemed to be paying special attention to Thomas. Whoever the Perfectionists were, they hid well. Thomas thought about Elise's suggestion that the band needed a distraction, something else to think about besides a perfect performance. Could that be a way to protect Thomas?

The section leader directed the brass back to the first movement. Pages turned. Instruments came up, and the group launched into the beginning measures. Cowdrey stepped back to watch and listen. They didn't look so young to him anymore. Beneath their long hair or ragged haircuts, their faces had lost the babyish look he associated with fifteen-year-olds. Just two years difference, but he could see they'd changed. Their clothes strained to contain them. Their hands had grown so that no one stretched anymore to reach their instruments' keys. Their breath control had improved since they'd arrived, the improvement that came with maturity. A ninth grader couldn't hold a note like an older musician could. A fifteen-year-old couldn't hit the high parts with the same confidence as these kids could.

How long would they stay here?

Cowdrey walked behind the players. The wall cooled his back when he rested against it. What existed on the other side? Rooms filled with the brown smoke that eddied beyond the windows in the performance hall? He tried to imagine what creatures lurked in the brown smoke. Tentacles? Claws? Amorphous blobs? Or did he lean against a metal shell, inches from interstellar space? Maybe they had arrived on the creatures' home world and an entirely alien landscape waited beyond. Maybe, even, they had never left Earth, a few steps from home, hidden for their captors' amusement (what did they want?).

But the question remained, how long would they stay? What if they would never leave?

Cowdrey frowned. A veteran teacher had told him, "When you teach, your life becomes the kids and the classroom. If there's anything else distracting you, then you're not doing the job." Of course, another teacher, equally experienced, countered, "Teaching is what you do. Life is why you do it."

He left the practice room. Pulsing sound greeted him when he opened the door into the percussionist's area. Their eyes didn't leave their music, and at the place where the bass drums kicked in, with the snares beating out a complicated counter-rhythm, he could feel his heart's pounding change to match it. Watching their hands blur to follow the music, seeing the vibrations from the instruments' side, he noticed for the first time how thick-wristed the drummers had become, like tennis pros who gained an overdeveloped forearm on their racket side, except for them both arms bulged. When Cowdrey had been in college, he went out to dinner with a long-time drummer. On a bet, the fellow had grabbed one table edge with his fingertips, and lifted it, drinks and dinner plates and all by the strength of his hands and wrists. "Years and years working a drum set, and look what it got me, a party trick." The drummer laughed.

Once again, Cowdrey saw that the kids weren't ninth graders any more. When it ended, the section leader turned to him. "I thought these changes in the backbeat Elise wrote were wonky when I saw them on the page, but once we got going on them, wow!" Others in the section nodded.

The morning unfolded. Session after session, the kids' growth struck him. They weren't in any real sense a school band anymore. They had evolved into something that had never existed in humanity before, because where before in human history had these conditions existed?

But it wasn't until he stood outside his room before lunch that he made up his mind. Elise turned the corner with her clipboard in hand, her notes for the day covering the top sheet. Instead of showing them to him, she stopped to look at the blank wall where Miss

Rhodes's door once had been. Clearly she hadn't noticed the disparity in the hallway. Elise touched the wall. For a second, Cowdrey worried she pictured what he had seen when he raised the nerve to go into Rhodes's room uninvited: the sheet twisted into a rope, the cloth cutting into her neck, the pathetic letters home she'd been writing since the first day they'd arrived.

Elise placed her palm flat on the wall where the door used to be. "It's adapt or die all the time, isn't it?"

Her crooked glasses made her look childish, but the top of her head stood almost level with his chin. He remembered when she'd been just a tiny 7th grader who handled her flute with an older musician's authority, but whose feet didn't reach the ground when she sat to play. Cowdrey knew then that Elise had become the band's heart. She drew the thread that kept them together so far, not his efforts, but hers. She held the late-night meetings with the section leaders to go over changes in music. She organized the informal ensembles. She had the energy others could draw on, including himself.

"Yes, it is." He took a deep breath. Cowdrey could feel the shift in his thinking happen. Suddenly, he wasn't a junior high band director. He was an older adult trapped with fifty competent young adults, if he could let them be that. If he could adapt to change. "Let's get them ready for the practice this evening, shall we?"

Elise raised her eyebrows.

That evening, Cowdrey took the podium. Under his hands, he held the music for the practice and his baton. Paper-clipped to the top sheet were his notes for areas to emphasize along with Elise's comments. The group fidgeted and chattered as they always did before practice. Cowdrey liked standing before the full band, when the day's work came together and he could measure the progress, and even though he hated the circumstances, he had to admit he'd never had a better performance facility. The light. The sound. The way the space flowed around them. Only the smokey windows and the hidden audience jarred.

He picked up the baton. They looked at him expectantly. "Breathing first, Cougars. I'll count off the seconds. Inhale." He tapped eight seconds with the baton while they filled their lungs. "Hold." With metronomic regularity he tapped out twenty-four more beats. They exhaled for eight, relaxed for ten, and then repeated twice more. At the end, the percussionists finished their set up and the band waited. Breathing exercises calmed them, put them into the right mind. In his classroom at the junior high, which he could barely picture now, he'd hung a banner at the front: ALL MUSIC BEGINS WITH A GOOD BREATH (AND DIES WITH A LACK THEREOF).

Now they were ready. "An issue has come up that I think needs to be addressed. As most of you know, Taylor Beau and Liz Waters have asked my permission to marry." Whatever whispering that might have been going on when he started the speech lapsed into silence. For an instance, Cowdrey pictured the school board and all the parents sitting in the back. What would they say at this announcement? Would they understand? He brushed aside the image, then plunged ahead. "I have thought about the request for a long time. Considering our situation and Taylor and Liz's character, I think they would make a fine married couple."

Before the last syllable had time to fade, the band erupted into cheers and gleeful laughter. The attention at first focused on Liz and Taylor, who cried and hugged awkwardly from their chairs, their cornets still in hand, but soon Cowdrey saw a good number had surrounded Elise, shaking her hand and clapping her on the back. Cowdrey's jaw dropped. He had, in every sense, been orchestrated. Finally, in the midst, Elise caught his eye and mouthed, "Thank you." He touched his forehead in rueful respect.

Thomas put his French horn on his chair, waiting his chance to congratulate the happy couple. A trombone player stood beside him, and they smiled as they chatted. It seemed as if it had been weeks since Cowdrey could remember Thomas looking relaxed. Cowdrey thought, a good decision and a distraction in one move. He smiled too.

Elise worked her way over to him. "We'll need a wedding march."

"I think Mendelssohn's is in my books. That would be traditional. Besides, it would be appropriate. He was seventeen when he wrote it." Cowdrey reached past her to high five a couple flute players who had joined a conga line.

Elise shook her head. "That's a myth, I think. He wrote it later. Anyway, I have something I've been working on. Something of my own." Her eyes lowered.

"Why am I not surprised?"

It took the band a half hour to settle down. They cut the practice early after just two run throughs of the Beatles medley.

For the first time in two years, Cowdrey didn't walk the halls before going to bed. We are adults here, he thought. The paradigm has shifted. He sighed as he lay down, believing when he went to sleep his dreams would be undisturbed and packed with beautifully played music, but after an hour trying to convince himself he'd changed, he rose, dressed, and walked the hall, listening at each door. Satisfied at last, he went back to his room, and his dreams played undisturbed with flawless performances.

In the morning, he found a note pushed under his door. "A wedding will not get us home. They want a perfect performance! Get us home!" Cowdrey snorted in disgust. Nobody could know what they wanted. They might not want anything. He folded the note in half and put it inside his band management book. Even the Perfectionists couldn't bother him today, and they wouldn't, at least until after the wedding. And who knows, he thought, sometimes the best way to a long term goal is to focus on a short term one.

Elise distributed the new march to the section leaders, who organized a music-transcribing session. For over an hour, the band met in the auditorium to make their copies. "You'd think if aliens could snatch us up to play concerts, they could at least provide a decent photocopier," grumbled the oboist, who had several dozen bars of sixteenths and two key changes to write for herself.

A clarinet player finished, then studied the music. "This is cool. If I knew half as much as Elise does, I'd count myself a genius."

Cowdrey waited for someone to laugh. It wasn't the kind of comment kids made about each other. Someone else said, "Really!"

The rest continued to write. Cowdrey said, loud enough for everyone to hear, "Maybe what they want is a well-played *new* piece. Soon as we finish here, break into your sections and work on this."

For the next three days leading to the Friday concert and wedding, practice went better than Cowdrey could have imagined, and not just on the new piece either. They ascended to new heights during "March of the Irish Dragoons," and they suddenly mastered the eighth-note quintuplets and the bi-tonal passages in "Ascensions" they'd fumbled before. Elise popped up everywhere, tweaking the music, erasing notes and rewriting passages, so every time Cowdrey rehearsed a section she had changed his pages.

On concert day, Cowdrey went to the auditorium early. He'd already realigned the chairs and moved the sections about to get the best sound balance for the new arrangements. The director's platform could accommodate Taylor and Liz when they exchanged vows. He put his hands behind his back and circled the room. Even shoes clicking on the floor sounded beautiful in the auditorium's acoustics. He paused at the window, which cast no reflection. Behind it, the auditorium light penetrated a couple feet into the swirling brown cloud. Cowdrey cupped his hands around his eyes and leaned against the window to peer out. At first he'd been afraid to get against the glass. What if something horrible stepped forward, resolving itself from the smoke? He couldn't imagine an event more startling, but over the years the band had played in this room, no one had ever seen anything. Now the sinuous smoke's motion soothed him, as if he looked into ocean waves. It was meditative.

Elise cleared her throat when she entered. She wore her marching uniform, the most formal outfit anyone in the band had. Soon, the other members filtered in, filled with anticipation, gaily bedecked in their uniforms. A grinning Taylor and bashful Liz came in last, music tucked under their arms.

As he had a thousand times before, the director brought the band to attention, hands raised, ready for the downbeat. He inhaled deeply. A good breath, he thought. Let's all start on a good breath. Soon, they were deep into the Beatles medley. Elise had changed the music so radically the original tune vanished at times, then resurfaced later in unexpected ways. The clarinets swelled with the "Yellow Submarine" bridge as the trombones's improvisational bars ended. Later, out of a melodious but unrecognizable tune, the xylophone led them into "Hey Jude."

They moved through song after song. Never had the band's sound been so tight. Every solo hit right. Even the tricky transitions flew until they reached "The King's Feast," the second to last piece. He wiped sweat from his forehead before leading them into the opening bars, and it wasn't until he neared the end that he realized the French horns had played their part exactly on beat. Thomas had hit his entrance on cue. Cowdrey almost laughed in relief as he brought them to the conclusion. Thomas was safe.

Cowdrey put the baton on the podium and nodded to Elise who had already stored her flute on the stand next to her chair. She came forward solemnly, climbed the platform, then picked up the baton. Shuffling their papers, the band switched to her wedding march music. The baton's tip pointed up. She took her own deep breath.

The march began, a lingering intro that sounded nothing like a march or wedding music, but soon the drums rose from behind—Cowdrey hadn't realized they were playing at all. He'd been paying attention to the odd harmonics in the flute and clarinet section—but there the drums were, dancing rhythms that made him shift his look to them. Then the brass opened, and the tune bounced from side to side, all in a few bars, all too quick before fading for the ceremony. Cowdrey closed his eyes. "What was that?" he thought. He almost asked her to play it again.

He stood to the side on the floor a foot below the director's platform, Taylor and Liz's wedding vows ready to read. On cue, the two held hands and came forward. Music swelled around them as they made their way toward the front. The musicians played with part attention on Elise and part on the young couple.

Cowdrey read a preamble, his heart in his throat, Elise's wedding march still in his ears. Taylor and Liz exchanged vows. They kissed. As they exited, arms around each other, two drummers threw confetti, and the band played the wedding march's coda, seeming to pick up without losing a beat. Nothing Cowdrey had ever heard sounded like this. Clarity of notes. Surprising shifts in scale. A moment where a single cornet carried the music before the band swallowed it whole, repeating the notes but changing them round so what was bright became dark, and the dark exploded like fireworks. The music filled Cowdrey's chest, pressed cold compresses of notes to his fevered head, made him sway in fear that it would end or the band would break, but they didn't. The music ascended and swooped and pressed outward and in. At the end, the sound flooded the room, as if to push the windows open to free the band from captivity and give them the grassy pastures Elise talked about so often, rushing toward the triumphant climax they'd been practicing for the last three days. Cowdrey heard wind caressing the tips of uncut grass. He smelled the meadow awash with summer heat. The music painted Earth and home so fully he nearly wept from it, but then it ended. Elise held them on the last note, her face lit with concentration and triumph. Her fist closed, cutting the band off, leaving the memory of her composition lingering in the air. Cowdrey could still hear it, ringing. The lights began to flicker. They loved it, he thought. He turned to salute Elise, the ringing emanating from the middle of his head. Then, he recognized the sound in the strobe-effect lighting. It built until he thought it would burst him open, and he fell.

A short soft shock of waking.

His cheek rested against cool metal. A weight pressed against his other side. Groggily, Cowdrey sat up. He was in a bus parked in the dark. The student leaning against him groaned, rubbed her eyes, then sat up too. Other bodies stirred in front and behind them. Outside the window, a streetlight showed a long chain link fence and a sign, POLICE EVIDENCE YARD.

"My god," said someone in a voice filled with disbelief. "We're home."

Someone started crying. Their voices mixed. Some whooped and yelled. Some laughed, all at once, voices and sounds mixing.

They poured from the bus into the parking lot, still in uniform, holding on to each other. A boy rattled the gate locked by a large chain and a hefty padlock. A head poked up in the lit window of the building beyond. A few seconds later two policeman carrying flashlights ran out the back door. Cowdrey started counting heads, but someone noticed before he did.

"Where's Elise?"

For a second, the happy noise continued.

"Where's Elise?"

Cowdrey stood on the step into the bus, looking over the crowd. One by one, they stopped talking. They didn't appear so old now, the streetlight casting dark shadows on their faces. He stepped down, walked through them, checking each expression. No crooked glasses. No clipboard tucked under the arm.

Cowdrey pictured her alone in the empty auditorium. Were the lights still flickering? She, the one who wanted to go home the most, stood now, among the silent folding chairs, staring back at the swirling smoke behind windows. What had they wanted from us? What had they wanted?

The band looked at each other, then down at their feet, unable to meet each others' gaze. They looked down, and Cowdrey couldn't breathe.

He moved through the darkness surrounding the band, turning the ones toward him who faced away, searching their faces, but he already had accepted it. He'd lost her. Elise was gone.

As the cops unlocked the gates, shouting their questions, Cowdrey could see the days coming: the interviews, the articles in magazines, the disbelief, the changes in his life. One day, though, after the story had passed, he'd stand in front of another junior high band. He'd raise arms high before the first note, encouraging the players to take that first good breath, but Cowdrey could already feel in his chest the tightness, the constriction, and he knew he'd never be able to make the music good again.

He wouldn't be able to breathe.

# ABOUT THE AUTHOR

James Van Pelt teaches high school and college English in western Colorado. He has been publishing fiction since 1990, with numerous appearances in most of the major science fiction and fantasy magazines, including *Talebones, Realms of Fantasy, Alfred Hitchcock's Mystery Magazine, Analog, Asimov's, Weird Tales, SCIFI.COM,* and many anthologies, including several "year's best" collections. His first collection of stories, *Strangers and Beggars*, was released in 2002, and was recognized as a Best Book for Young Adults by the American Library Association. His second collection, *The Last of the O-Forms and Other Stories*, which includes the Nebula finalist title story, was released in August 2005 and was a finalist for the Colorado Blue Spruce Young Adult Book Award. His novel *Summer of the Apocalypse* was released November, 2006. James blogs at http://jimvanpelt.livejournal.com

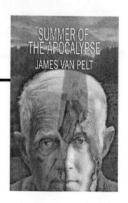

LaVergne, TN USA
16 November 2009
164255LV00002B/2/P